Also by Basil Sands

65 Below
Karls's Last Flight
Faithful Warrior
Midnight Sun

Ice Hammer series
Invasion
Insurgent

ICE HAMMER

INVINCIBLE

BOOK THREE

ICE HAMMER
INVINCIBLE

BOOK THREE

BASIL
SANDS

PERMUTED
PRESS

A PERMUTED PRESS BOOK
ISBN: 978-1-68261-700-7
ISBN (eBook): 978-1-68261-900-1

Invincible:
Ice Hammer Book 3
© 2019 by Basil Sands
All Rights Reserved

Cover art by Christian Bentulan

PERMUTED
PRESS

Permuted Press, LLC
New York • Nashville
permutedpress.com

Published in the United States of America

CHAPTER 1

Brad

A blinding white light exploded across his senses, so bright it seemed to have a physical texture that burned trenches across the inside of his eyeballs. The wall of sound struck a second later like a hammer blow from the blacksmith of the gods. Brad Stone found himself falling hard, he and the other men in the room blown off their feet. Shards of window glass sprayed their faces and their hands flung up protectively against hundreds of flying razor blades.

Brad struggled back to the window, carefully raised his head to look outside, and stared down at the mess his men had created on the street below. Vehicles smoldered in front of the high-rise hotel. Limbs, heads, and torsos lay scattered across the pavement amidst pieces of vehicles and weapons. Flames licked up from the underside of the overturned Suburban, its glossy black paint shimmered in the fiery reflection.

A hand appeared from inside the vehicle. A person, struggling their way out. Head and shoulders raised from the open window, a woman. She pushed herself up until she was halfway out of the vehicle. Tears of blood streamed across her cheeks.

She pulled her hair out of her eyes and, staring up, looked in Brad's direction.

Youngmi.

His wife.

His heart trembled in his chest, her face, the impossible existence of that lovely visage, filling him with horror.

He had seen his wife's dead body, two years earlier, only days after the war had started. He'd been certain it was her. Her new Mercedes SUV with the custom license plates had been shot up. Inside, she was wearing her favorite T-shirt, and she was definitely dead. Her face had been blown apart, opened up and peeled back, like a rose blossom from the gardens of Hell.

Youngmi stared at him, her face a rictus of shock and recognition mingled with terror. Flames reached the fuel tank, erupting in a roaring blaze. The fire stretched its greedy fingers around the edge of the armored SUV and tugged at her clothes.

She did not scream, not at first. Her mouth hung agape as she realized her own husband had killed her.

The flames erupted with new energy, enveloping her body. Her clothing lit, turning her into a human torch. Her face contorted in agony and the scream finally came.

"BRAAAAAAD!"

Her voice echoed his name across the city, bouncing off the walls of the surrounding buildings, boring into his ears. It careened off the inside of his skull, forcing him toward madness.

A smaller scream joined the cacophony in his head. His eyes grew wide as Youngmi's charred, skeletal hand reached inside the SUV and pulled out a small bundle. She heaved it out and away from the inferno. It arched skyward, flames trailing like a comet's tail.

The bundle crashed into the room Brad was watching from, landing with a thud and rolling several feet. Its wrapping, a soft blanket, came undone and Brad's newborn daughter lay before him, naked but for the filth that covered her legs. Her tiny screams grew in intensity and volume until everything else was drowned out, driving into his eardrums like ice picks.

Brad suddenly jolted upright into the early morning sunlight.

Sammi, his much younger second wife, stood at the small changing table in a corner of the room, cleaning Victoria's bottom and singing gently to the tiny girl. She glanced over at her husband where he sat on the edge of the bed. The visions in his head subsided, sight gradually returning to the warmly lit room, a peaceful place. Her eyes stayed on him as he consciously put away the horrors of where his mind had just been.

He squeezed his eyes shut and opened them wide several times, then refocused on Sammi. She was real. He was in his house in the town of Chiknik on the south side of the Talkeetna Mountains in Alaska.

"The dream again?" she asked.

"Yeah," Brad muttered as he rubbed the heels of his palms into his eyes, trying to wipe the memory of the nightmare from his mind.

He had not told Sammi about what happened in Anchorage at the end of last winter. He could not tell her. Months earlier, he'd led a team of Rangers into the city to assassinate General Zhang and his mistress, a local collaborator Kharzai had nicknamed "The Dragon Lady." The moment he'd ordered his man to fire an armor-piercing rocket into the general's vehicle, his mistress's face appeared in the open passenger-side window. It was Youngmi, Brad's wife of over twenty-seven years, a woman who'd been Sammi's mentor for nearly a decade, a woman whose mangled body he'd found in her destroyed car only days after the war had started.

As the armor-piercing LAW rocket impacted the general's vehicle, Brad's world took an instant, sickening jolt to a new and horrid reality.

He had not told Sammi what he had seen. Brad's brain tried to tell him over and over that it was not Youngmi, that it was just someone very similar.

He kept trying to convince himself.

It didn't work.

The connection made by nearly three decades of marriage, twenty-seven years of waking up every morning to see her face, was unmistakable. He was not sure anymore whose body it had been in Youngmi's car. But he was absolutely certain, down to a spiritual level, that his wife had been in the general's car. And that she had been laughing the moment the rocket slammed into the armored SUV with an explosion strong enough to flip the four-ton behemoth into the air.

The message they'd received from their intel source inside the Chinese HQ verified that the general had survived with moderate injuries, yet made no mention of the woman in the car with him.

Brad was guilty of murdering his own wife.

CHAPTER 2

Major Chi

Major Guo Hung Chi leaned back in the black mesh office chair, pressed his fingers into his eyelids, and pushed back from the desk to stretch his legs. As commander of the Information Technology Batallion for the Alaska Command, he was in charge of the teams of computer hardware and network technicians and Information Security Officers that ensured access to data and information related to the People's Liberation Army Alaska Command only ended up in the hands of those with the proper clearance and a need to have that data. Everything from payroll sheets to inventory lists to unit rosters and top-secret military intelligence flowed through his computer network. The file structure on the encrypted servers was highly organized and access to specific data was tightly controlled. Due to the fact that he needed access to every type of data, Chi's security clearance was the absolute highest level, higher even than the intelligence chief, Colonel Ping.

He stretched his back, eliciting a series of pops along his spine, then continued the series of therapeutic manipulations radiating from his core out to his hips and shoulders and following through his limbs until he had activated every muscle and joint out to the tips of his fingers and toes, and the top of his skull. The three times a day routine had come from his mother who had been a yoga instructor in the small town he'd grown up in. She led a class of what seemed to him to be mostly grand-motherly women doing healthy stretches and very mild aerobic exercise. While it all seemed like unappealing old-lady stuff to him as a twelve-year-old boy, grown up Major Chi realized there was a lot more to stretching and yoga than just touching your toes and popping your back.

Feeling his spine straighten and slip into alignment, he leaned forward in his chair, reached to the edge of his desk and pulled himself back to an erect position in front of the dual twenty-seven-inch monitors that displayed the documents and camera feeds he always kept alive on his desktop. He peered at a particular digital document that had come through with the highest level of security. The subject line of the encrypted email read COMMANDING GENERAL - EYES ONLY. It read:

The request for mass buildup of the Palmer Base has been approved by the High Command. The Palmer location is to be con-verted to a full divisional base, commanding forward operating bases to the north and east, along the highway routes and for preparing and staging offensives against remote insurgent bases.

Chi, whose given name, Guo Hung, meant Fortress of Courage, kept a keen eye on every bit of information that passed his desk. He mentally cataloged what was more likely to be of potential use to enemies of the PLA (People's Liberation Army) in order to keep it out of their hands. After, that is, he made a copy of it to send to the specific anti-PLA resistance groups that he'd verified had no leaks that could be traced back to him.

Major Guo Hung Chi had been an officer in the Chinese PLA for ten years. He was also known by a codename to his handlers in the American CIA, for whom he'd been working for twelve years. The spooks called him Smaug, the smoking dragon.

California-born Chi, née Michael Everett Kang Jr., was the son of second-generation Korean-American parents. He excelled in languages and lettered in theater in high school. His father was a U.S. Marine who had retired from service as a MARSOC (Marine Special Operations Command) Master-Gunnery Sergeant. Michael grew up at various military and state department installations around the world, particularly in Asia. Both of his parents were polyglots. His mother held a PhD in linguistics from UCLA. She spoke more than a dozen languages, most with nearly native fluency, and often worked as a translator wherever they were living at the time. She taught her son those same languages until he was natively fluent in five and proficient in half a dozen more, as well as dozens of dialects within languages.

Noticed by and recruited to the CIA as a teenager, his northeast Asian features and native fluency in two dialects of Mandarin and several dialects of both North and South Korean sealed where he would serve. At nineteen, they created a back story and got him into the PLA Officer's Academy. He became Guong Ho Chi, an orphaned country boy from a region near the North Korean border where birth and education records were slim to none. He passed the entrance exam with a high enough score to earn a place as a cadet, but not so high as to seem suspicious for a self-educated country boy.

Martin Jr. not only shared his mother's affinity for language, he also shared his father's addiction to adrenaline-laced action. The young man combined their contributions with his own talents as a stage actor and made his new self seem completely real to anyone who questioned him.

To that end, ten years as a career IT officer, a very observant career IT officer, had netted a lot of vital information for his home country. Sadly, two years earlier, he had not been in the right circles to know enough specifics of the invasion to pass to his handlers before PLA and Russian Forces showed up on

America's front step, kicking in doors and smashing all in their paths. Once his unit had settled into the assignment of controlling the Alaska-Yukon region of conquest, Major Chi worked his way invisibly into the resistance infrastructure and opened multiple channels to send vital information to those who made his PLA peers lives miserable.

The discovery that one of his mother's dearest friends, Youngmi Stone, had been forced to become General Zhang's mistress had opened a whole new and unexpected channel directly from the general's desk. As hard intelligence goes, the information she provided was fairly thin, primarily clarifying data he'd already collected himself. But her loyalty had been tested and she'd passed the exam. Her being appointed by the general to be director of the food distribution program gave him the perfect way to get information out with less risk to himself and others in the resistance network.

And then came the day when he managed to snatch a copy of the general's classified schedule, which included his projected trips into Anchorage proper for either work or personal reasons. That schedule included a high-priced dinner with senior officers at the Crow's Nest, the fanciest restaurant in the city. What Chi hadn't learned in time, was that the officer's dinner was postponed due to sudden operational changes, but Zhang had simply changed the reservation from twelve people to two. The general took Youngmi out for what would be a nice dinner for just them, looking out at the spectacular view of Anchorage and the surrounding mountains and ocean from the twenty-second floor of the Hotel Captain Cook while enjoying fine French cuisine.

Zhang and Youngmi never made it to that dinner. The information he'd passed on to Ice Hammer's organization had caused the resistance fighters to target Zhang for assassination. Much to Chi's chagrin, Zhang survived with relatively minor injuries. Youngmi, though, had been banged up pretty bad. She had to be put into an induced coma for most of a month after the attack to save her from irreversible brain damage. She recovered and seemed mostly normal now, but he was not sure how to proceed. She would probably realize that he was the one who had set her up, that she herself had actually passed the data card that had the schedule to the resistance. She would also discover it had been her husband who had given the order to kill her.

Chi thought desperately to come up with a plan to avoid his intel network imploding from these events. If she was no longer in the chain, it would be very difficult to reroute the process. And, he had to consider what to do in the event she turned against her husband and the resistance altogether.

There must be a way to both keep the information flowing and keep Youngmi active in the chain. I cannot have her turn against the resistance because of these events. I cannot afford for her to turn against her own husband.

He scrolled through a series of heavily encrypted notes he kept in a folder on his computer desktop until he found what he was looking for, an observation he'd made almost a year earlier, an interaction he'd overheard. Colonel Ping of the intelligence command had been flirting with Youngmi, trying to win her over from Zhang. She easily, and quite succinctly, rebuffed his advances by saying that if he wanted personal tutoring from her, he would need to request it through General Zhang. Ping had been furious but hid it well enough that only someone who'd been watching him for years would have seen it. Chi had been watching him for years. He had long ago noticed Ping's jealousy of Zhang's happy marriage to his first wife, and had suspicions that Ping had something to do with her death. Based on observations of the colonel's reactions and attitudes at the time, Chi was certain her cancer was somehow influenced or even caused by something Ping had done. He suspected she had slowly been poisoned, but of course could prove nothing.

Judging by Ping's apparently similar jealousy of the general's relationship with Youngmi, he feared for the safety of his mother's old friend. That said, Ping's actions could also provide the wedge he needed to keep Youngmi from fully accepting the kindness of the Chinese Army.

CHAPTER 3

Youngmi

Youngmi slid her hand into the bright beam that slanted into the room, floating dust motes rendering it like a Hubble telescope image of millions of tiny galaxies spinning in the greater universe. Pleasure warmed her as the heat soaked into her skin from the powerful arctic summer sunlight that streamed through the window of the apartment she shared with General Zhang, located in the headquarters building on what used to be the U.S.A's Joint Base Elmendorf-Richardson, locally referred to as JBER, pronounced 'JAY-bear.'

Previously known as two separate bases, Elmendorf Air Force Base and U.S. Army Fort Richardson, the two had been converted to a single base in 2010, after a series of planned base closures struck across the nation in the post-9/11 years. Chinese Forces Alaska, General Zhang Ko Bai now commanded the massive base renamed Arctic and Northern Command Fortress of The Chinese People's Liberation Army.

She glanced out the window. Across the parade ground, nearly two hundred meters distant, a tall pole held a large red flag that fluttered lazily in a light breeze, occasionally opening far enough to reveal the one large and four small yellow stars in its corner.

Beneath it, on two parallel poles, were similar flags, although both were only two-thirds red, one with a blue bar and the other with a green bar across the bottom denoting People's Air Force and People's Army. The two military flags held the same large yellow star in the top left corner, but instead of four smaller stars around it, the symbols for the numbers eight and one appeared next to the large star, remembering the founding of the People's Liberation armed forces on August 1, 1927.

They were the flags of the conquerors.

The flags of the enemy.

The flags of the man who had sat by her hospital bed as she recovered from a rocket attack that had put her in a month-long coma and badly damaged her hearing.

The intelligence office report stated that according to traffic intercepts, a resistance fighter was captured, moving after curfew the night of the attack which had been ordered by the resistance leader called Ice Hammer. The prisoner had confessed under interrogation that Ice Hammer had been there in person, directly commanding the attack.

Ice Hammer. The rebel leader who'd earned his name by dispatching two Chinese soldiers with a mountain climbing tool. That action had been caught on video by drones monitoring the battlefield. Super high-resolution images put his face, twisted into an unrecognizable snarl, in 4K Ultra High Definition. His eyes burned with the singular desire to kill his enemies as he slammed the serrated edge of the tool deep into first one enemy, then a second. He moved as if he had practiced for that day all his life, the motion mere reaction and muscle memory. It was inspiring.

The file was leaked to the public, somehow going viral in spite of the heavily restricted communications. A deed of horrifying violence enshrined the man as the symbol of the resistance. Ice Hammer's image led the fight against the invader. A face that she had looked into every morning for twenty-seven years. Brad Stone, her husband. The face that had ordered her death, and that could easily be connected back to her. As much as he had broken her heart, she would not let herself be used as a tool to capture the man she would always love.

The general's daughter, Mai, a lieutenant in the intelligence unit, considered Youngmi to be something like a beloved aunt, an accepted step-mother even. In the course of her job, Mai discovered Youngmi's true identity and connection to the rebel leader and had modified records in the state and municipality databases to remove any digital connections between his life and hers. Her actions left that end of the trail clear.

While the digital trail was intentionally clean, Youngmi could not fathom how any of her and Brad's many friends and acquaintances had not reported their relationship to the police. Not only would it be highly rewarding to turn in such a significant spy, it would be a terrible blow to General Zhang himself to have it revealed that his supposed mistress was the actual wife of the resistance leader. It would also be a great victory for that resistance if the highest traitor in the land, said general's mistress, were to be brought down in a very public manner.

Youngmi expected that hammer to fall every morning, wondering each dawn if that day would be her last. But the accusations never came. She had been recognized in public many times, but so far none turned her in. Either those that knew her thought she was an agent on the inside, or they were all more terrified of the general's wrath. Of course, there was one other option. It could also be that anyone who knew both her and Brad by sight was dead already.

Until just several months ago, Youngmi knew only that Brad was the leader of the Chiknik militia, one of the largest and best-organized fighting groups in Alaska with a refugee community in the thousands and a well-organized army estimated to have between five and fifteen thousand, highly trained soldiers based in the hills about a hundred miles northeast of Palmer. She'd had no significant detail as to what he was doing in his personal life until a few weeks before the attack on her and General Zhang.

Mai had come to their suite and given Youngmi new information that had been learned about Ice Hammer. Pictorial evidence had been found on the body of a resistance fighter killed in a failed ambush. Brad's face stood out among the others in the center of the photo. He was surrounded by about a dozen others, mostly medical types with stethoscopes around their necks, a couple wearing scrubs. Her husband had lost a lot of weight, probably a hundred pounds or more, since the last time she'd seen him. He looked almost as fit as when they'd first met when he was a 160-pound, twenty-year-old corporal in the Marines. His current body looked strong, but the youth of decades past was long gone. Lines in his face combined with graying temples to highlight the shadows of nearly fifty years of a hard arctic life, emphasized by the horrors of the last two under the thumb of ruthless invaders. In the picture Brad was smiling, a truly happy smile in spite of the wear on his features. He had one arm around the shoulders of an attractive woman in her thirties, his other hand rested on her very round belly. The way he held her, and the way she smiled as if in response to his touch, made the relationship obvious.

"I am so sorry, Ayi," Mai's voice sounded in her memory. The young woman's tone sounded almost as if she were apologizing for Brad. "From what you have told me about your husband, I do not believe he would be unfaithful to you. He has to believe you are dead."

Such a declaration didn't make the discovery any easier. Not only had he remarried barely a year after her supposed death, but his new wife was a woman she and Brad had known since she'd been a young teenager in their church. He was more than fifteen years her senior. Sammi Park had been a student in his church youth group, and later was a teacher and served as assistant director of their Sunday school department. Sammi Park had been one of Youngmi's favorites; she'd considered her to be like a younger sister.

Once Youngmi was able to digest the images in that photo, she realized for the first time since the war started that her husband, her protector and defender, would never follow through on his promise to find and rescue her if anything happened.

Anything like a war.

Brad was not coming to find for her. All those promises turned out to be nothing but empty words when the real thing crashed down on them. Her husband had made the easier, more attractive choice. Rather than search for her, he replaced her with a younger woman.

Youngmi's heart ached still deeper with the knowledge that her husband, the man who'd sworn to protect her and their boys, had personally tried to kill her. After believing her dead for nearly two years, had he discovered she'd become the enemy general's companion? Did he think she would willingly live in this situation, forced to give comfort to the enemy?

She let out a sigh. The blame battle suddenly hissed out, quenched by the knowledge that there was no sanity, no logic in war. Youngmi forced the pain back, surrendering to the fact that there was only the moment, only now.

As if God had swiped his hand across her heart, the pain no longer raged in her chest. The heat dissipated as she decided she would not live in misery, in perpetual mourning for the return of a life that could never be brought back. The door to her past slowly closed. New reality implanted itself, taking firm hold.

Life moved in cycles, she had once read in a blog by a philosopher she liked to study. *Today you may be happy in this current reality, but tomorrow's reality may render those things in which you find happiness nothing but a faded memory. When that time comes, you must find a new center, a new place from which same happiness can continue to grow in its morphed state. Something new, something better.*

The door to the apartment opened. She turned toward the sound. General Zhang walked in dressed in his light green, short-sleeved summer uniform shirt. He slipped out of his shoes just as the door clicked shut, lining them up squarely inside the entry area. The pair of gold embroidered stars underscored by a partial laurel wreath shone on each of his dark green shoulder boards. They sparkled when he stepped into the sunlight, sending a scattered rainbow of colored reflections glittering across the wall, then ceiling as he crossed the room toward her. His smile elicited a laser-like spark as the same sunlight danced off his unnaturally white teeth.

Youngmi had often wondered as she got to know him how he kept those teeth so bright, especially considering the copious amounts of coffee and nightly glass or two of wine. Over the past two years, she had gradually realized that the only answer had to be that it was genetic. Everything about the man shone at an equally 'bright' level.

In his mid-fifties, Zhang moved with the elegant fluidity of a man half his age. She couldn't help but think that if Zhang had grown up in America, he probably could've been a famous model or a heartthrob movie star. His appearance was always impeccable, his body clean and fit. His face shone with a confident strength that emitted an aura of natural predatory violence, tempered by a barely concealed hint of compassion and tenderness deeper inside. He emanated a signal that said he knew what he loved, and he would utterly destroy anything that threatened his loved ones.

Part of the image he exuded, the military officer, was fairly simple to cultivate and maintain, not unlike any of the other officers in his command. He had a staff of stewards to press his uniforms, polish his boots, and messmen to ensure he was well fed. But not all men of equal rank stood out so impeccably as did General Ko Bai Zhang. The difference was that he recognized early on in his career the need for personal self-discipline and for working both his appearance and his personal interactions as none other than his own responsibility. In other words, the stars on his shoulders did not speak for him; Zhang Ko Bai's personality spoke for himself, and his soldiers listened.

Youngmi had never seen him unshaved, or his hair a mess. He never had pillow wrinkles on his face, or bad breath when she saw him at the breakfast table at six o'clock every morning. He was always fresh and immaculate before he came out of his room.

After waking from the coma, Youngmi had learned that General Zhang had been at her bedside at the hospital every off-duty hour that he could spare, sometimes even sleeping on the uncomfortable cloth-covered rubber chair in the corner of her room. The memory of those actions in particular caused him to glow even brighter in her eyes.

"Good evening, Youngmi," he said, smile stretching wider as he approached her. "You look absolutely radiant."

She blushed, rising to her feet and walking his way. They met in the middle of the room.

"Thank you, my general," she replied, hands clasped in front of her, bowing her head demurely. "And you look particularly handsome yourself, especially after such a long day at work."

"It was a long, boring day," he said as he set his briefcase and a red binder on the dining room table, "going over lists of promotions, unit transfers, and things that generally mean lots of paperwork."

"Well, now you are home," she said, taking his hand in hers, "and you can relax."

She squeezed his fingers softly, gave a slight tug, and led him to the brown leather sofa in the living room. She pulled him down beside her. They sat facing the pair of large windows framing the slowly greening Chugach Mountains that surrounded the military base. In the distance, a large gray concrete sign stood out in black iron letters stating CHINESE PEOPLE'S ARMY OF THE ARCTIC, ALASKA COMMAND.

Out of view to the west, the opposite side of the building in which they were housed, stood the city of Anchorage. Smoke no longer rose from that horizon, except for the occasional resistance bomb attack. Life had returned to a new type of mostly normal as far as she could tell from her times behind the food distribution tables.

He put his arm around her shoulder. She leaned into his chest, wrapping her arm across his middle, hand resting on his abdomen.

This was a fairly new wrinkle in their relationship. For over two years, theirs had been a completely non-physical arrangement. He gave her room and board in exchange for a platonic friendship that revolved around talking, laughing, and smiling with each other over private meals and occasional dinner dates or events they would attend. After learning of her husband's remarriage, followed by the assassination attempt that included her, Youngmi decided that she had no more ties to Brad. There was no waiting for him to come to her. She was free to make a new life too.

"Did you have a good day?" Zhang's deep voice rumbled from his chest, a warm feeling rising in her chest. Safety. Peace. Strength.

"I did," she replied. It had been a fun day. She had taught English to the female officers and NCOs, always a pleasant time for her. The women of that class treated her as the matron of the division and had taken turns caring for her during and after her hospital stay. "The women's classes are usually very enjoyable. It is good to be back at it now."

"Good, good," he said. "How are the headaches?"

"Very mild today, barely noticeable."

'The headaches' had been intense for several weeks after waking up from the attack. The doctors said she'd had a major concussion, seriously knocking her brain around inside her skull. They'd put her in an induced coma to keep the life-threatening swelling to a minimum, giving her body time to heal and hopefully avoid major brain damage.

The headaches persisted, lately receding a bit more into the background. This was one of the first days she found the sunlight tolerable for anything more than a few minutes.

He put his large hand on her temple, wrapping his fingers around to her forehead. Heat radiated from his skin, flushing out the remnants of pain almost immediately, his body force, his Qi, infusing her like a magical spell. She listened to his heart beat through his chest, felt the matching pulse in his hand. An even rhythm underscored by his steady, calm breaths. His other arm clasped her hand on his abdomen. Youngmi felt safe in this man's arms, wrapped in a warm cocoon.

A small red-breasted robin alighted on the window sill, chirping its pretty call. Looking in at them, it broke into song, high-pitched notes rising and falling in a long, complicated praise of summer joy.

"Robin red-breast is serenading you."

Youngmi could hear the smile in his voice as Zhang spoke. They listened to the songbird, watching as it expanded its tiny chest to project its performance.

"It's like a Disney movie," Youngmi said, "the unconditional joy of nature."

"The little bird knows nothing of what we humans inflict on one another," Zhang said. "I hope he never knows, too. Because without his song, there would be no hope for us."

Youngmi gently caressed the back of his hand with her thumb as she watched the robin sing. This man, her enemy, her general, her protector, her comfort. Her anchor to this world. She wished she could see her sons again, wished she could be with her husband again, but now, in Zhang's arms, feeling his warmth and life and love, she knew that this was where she needed to be.

CHAPTER 4

Scouts

Ian glanced back down the trail at the group of a couple dozen plus men, women, teenage boys and girls. Ranging in age from twelve to about fifty, at first glance, they gave the impression they were the decimated remains of a village of refugees. On closer inspection, these haggard refugees, most of them at least, did not retain the look of the surrendering type. This was not a panicked run-for-your-life march. This group of refugees were in more of a tactical retreat to regroup and find reinforcements and return to kicking ass.

The remnants of Boy Scout Troop 104, an amalgam of several troops although the majority were from the namesake troop, made the trip back across the wilderness over the same ground through which they had originally traveled more than two years earlier. This was their third move, after both previous encampments had been destroyed by the Russian army. The journey had been a lot longer the first time as the tender young boys and handful of adult men adapted to make a full-time living off the land, a skill long lost, even among Boy Scouts, in most of the modern world. Of course, then they were neither known nor wanted by their enemies and had time to settle and begin the training they would need to survive.

Ian recalled the terror everyone felt as they witnessed American fighter jets get shot down right over their heads at the Gorsuch Boy Scout reservation during their summer camp. They were just a bunch of boys, young adult staffers, and middle-age scoutmasters running for their lives. The memory of being chased down by helicopters that mercilessly machine-gunned them as they tried to run across Knik glacier brought a lump to his throat. Even after having killed so many men with his own hands, the raw fear of that afternoon, of running into what seemed like certain death with legs that had to be forced to keep moving like in a nightmare during that first direct contact. That was what Mike called it: contact. Like what he'd learned in the classes for the electronics merit badge, two power sources touching each other, if they are matched, they make a circuit and power flows. But if they are not, explosions happen, and damage ensues. They lost nearly a third of their number on the glacier.

Commander Mike, retired Special Forces master sergeant who assumed leadership of the scouts and men, got the survivors across the ice and into the forest. Over the next two years, he taught them many things, ranging from living completely off the land foraging and hunting animals for food and clothes, to learning how to navigate and track prey, and to kill without mercy in order to survive.

Of the original sixty-plus men and boys from a mixture of troops that had left from Camp Gorsuch Boy Scout Reservation two years earlier, only twenty remained in the group. Nearly half of those who had survived the glacier turned back on that first trek. They'd been unwilling to commit to following Mike and his military partner Tommie, a contract mercenary who worked with him training Alaska National Guard soldiers in unconventional, AKA guerilla, warfare. Those men and boys found Mike's overt religious tones and apparent comfort with Old Testament-style violence an incompatible match with their modern secular urban sensitivities. They had gone back west toward Palmer and Anchorage in hopes of reuniting with their families. Ian had no idea if they'd made it back, and if so, what their fate had been.

The face of one of those boys drifted across his mind. Aaron was the only member of the original Boy Scout Troop 104 to turn back. He'd been a whiny boy the same age as Ian, who had grated on the others' nerves with constant complaining and physical weakness. After a couple weeks in the bush, he'd started to shape up, but when the opportunity to turn back came, he decided to go with the other dads and boys. Ian often wondered what had happened to them. He hoped they at least made it to their families if they had survived.

Along with the remnants of Troop 104 were a dozen survivors among the women and girls that had joined them early last winter, including Linda, the defacto leader of the women, and Katarina, who had grown very close to his brother Ben. Tommie the mercenary was now in command. Along with him, Scoutmasters Steve and Ron, and Walt the hostler, keeper of the reindeer and sleds, were the only male adults to survive the Russian attack on their last camp by Klutina Lake. Commander Mike had been among the dead, as had Ian's best friend Charlie.

He shot a quick look back toward his brother and Katarina several paces behind him as they hiked through the forest toward Chiknik. They had been told a large settlement of refugees was there, run by a famous militia leader known as the Ice Hammer.

The troop skirted the blackened remnants of a small forest fire from a year earlier, most likely a product of lightning, nature's way of cleaning up the clutter in the wild. Hundreds of acres of burned spruce, birch, and alder stood like a zombie forest, small patches of wildflowers struggling to return life and color to the bleak scene.

★　　★　　★

"How much farther do you think it is?" Katarina asked as she reached down and plucked up a 'giant puffball' mushroom the size of her hand. She quickly kicked dirt and leaves into the hole so the mycelium would be able to grow more of the fungus for the next person, or animal, to walk by.

"Not much," Ben replied.

They'd been paralleling the highway for the last two days, keeping a couple miles south of it until they were at a place where they could cross over with the least chance of being detected. She pulled out her small pocket knife and trimmed the base of the mushroom, cutting off the soil-encrusted parts and gently scraping more dirt off the stem and top with her fingers.

"Once we cross, then what?"

"Then we go to Chiknik."

"And how far is that?"

She sliced the mushroom in half lengthwise, inspected the pristine white flesh for bugs or worms, nodded in satisfaction, then passed one piece to Ben.

"Depending on where we cross, and not being found by the bad guys, probably two or three more days of hard marching."

"Once we get to Chiknik, what are we going to do there?" Katarina took a bite of her half of the puffball, the firm flesh squeaking like Styrofoam as she chewed.

"Join them if we can." Ben took a bite, his squeaks keeping time with hers.

She swallowed and asked, "And if we can't?"

"Then we make a new place like before," he said. A tiny piece of mushroom shot from his still-full mouth on the last word. He caught it in mid-air, put it back in his mouth, then stuffed the rest of the mushroom in.

"Where would this new place be?"

He gave her a sideways glance, then swallowed enough to talk again without spraying her with mushroom chunks.

"You sure ask a lot of questions."

"Well, this is a pretty boring walk and it's not like I can turn on the TV or re-read one of the four books we still have," she quipped.

He finished the last of his mushroom and wiped his hand on his pant leg.

"I thought you grew up without TV and stuff."

"I'm not Amish," she said.

"Yeah, Old Believer," he said, "the old-school Russian church that has issues with each other's fingers."

He made a clumsy motion of crossing himself to illustrate he remembered the description of her people she'd given when they'd first started getting to know each other. The Russian Old Believers and Russian Orthodox Church had split from each other in the seventeenth century, the 1600s. The rift was apparently mostly over the way they held their fingers when they crossed themselves. That and other changes brought on by Patriarch Nikon led to a persecution that caused tens of thousands of Old Believers to scatter to the corners of the world. Before the war, more than twenty-five-hundred of them lived in Alaska, in ethnically Russian villages mostly on the Kenai Peninsula. Ben had often seen members of their community in Anchorage, shopping at Costco or the Fred Meyers grocery chain. Their clothing was always a colorful, traditional style, with men and boys wearing sparkling silk shirts and handwoven belts, and women and girls wearing colorful embroidered ankle-length dresses, their heads covered with equally colorful scarves. Lots of satin, silk, and bright colors. Since he'd met her, Katarina had only worn jeans and T-shirts under her parka. A totally modern version of her seventeenth-century conservative ancestors.

"We had both television and internet," Katarina said. "We didn't always have time to use either, because living on a farm is that way, but it was there."

"Oh yeah," Ben said, eyes scanning the woods on his side of the column. They'd not seen another soul in the time they had left their camp. He wondered if the Russians had dismissed them as a threat after decimating their camp, but wasn't counting on it. "What was your favorite TV show?"

"There were two," she replied, her own eyes scanning the other direction. "American Ninja Warrior and the 2004 remake of Battlestar Galactica."

"Really? I pictured you as more of a Downton Abbey/Food Network kinda girl."

It was her turn to give a sideways look.

"Are you serious? Downton Abbey was my mother's favorite. Too stuffy and dark for me. And while I do love cooking and eating, I do not enjoy watching other people cook stuff when there is no way I can get ingredients for it up here in Alaska."

"Okay, but Battlestar Galactica?"

"Oh yeah, I loved that show," she said. "I was only in first grade when it started, but when it came on Netflix, my dad and older brothers and I watched several episodes every weekend until we watched the whole series, twice. Then I binge-watched the whole thing again, plus the Caprica spin-off like three more times on my own."

"Really?" he asked again.

"You need to enlarge your vocabulary, Mr. Stone."

"Oh, how's this," he replied, then said, "No way!"

"Way!" Katarina said in a sing-song Valley Girl tone.

"I say that because my dad and brothers and I did the same thing, except I only watched the whole series once. My older brother Jay and our dad watched it all religiously when it was live on television. Then about the same time you were watching it on

Netflix for the first time, we all watched it together. Even Mom got into it. Dad and Ian watched it at least two more times all the way through."

"You didn't watch it more times though?"

"Nah," Ben said, "I can't watch a movie more than one time. If I see it more than once, I get super bored since I already know what is going to happen. Although I will admit that Galactica was a really smart show. I started expecting archeologists to find evidence of ancient human aliens or Cylons in the news any day when I was in middle school."

"Ha," she barked, "that's funny."

"Well," Ben mumbled, suddenly self-conscious, "I was a rather impressionable twelve-year-old kid."

"No, I mean it like 'that's a funny coincidence' kind of funny," Katarina said with a chuckle. "My older brother always wanted to be a science fiction/fantasy writer. His freshman year of college, he took some kind of fantasy writing class and actually drafted a whole story about someone in the near future finding a Colonial Raptor and a couple Vipers as well as some Cylon fighters buried in Antarctic ice. In his story, the discovery sets off a race to get the tech for space travel and sets off a new world war."

"Wow, that's very cool."

"It kind of sucked, actually," Katarina said with a slight smirk.

"That's harsh," said Ben.

"Harsh, but true," she replied. "The concept was admittedly pretty awesome, and the story started out okay, but all he really had was the concept of a story; there was no actual meat on the bones. Maybe he could be an okay screenwriter, but novelist? No, not at this point anyway."

"Hrm, meat on the bones," Ben said. "So you're saying that you prefer cookbooks?"

"Uh…no. I just like my stories to have more than spaceships and aliens blowing stuff up while being chased by scantily clad girls begging to commit pornographic acts on a nineteen-year-old boy that barely even shaves yet."

Ben rubbed his chin, smooth and still nearly hairless a week after his last shave.

"Anyway," Katarina glanced his way, a blush lighting up her cheeks, "like I said, the idea was good and maybe once he has more life experience, he could make an actual, even believable, story out of it."

"I'd read it," Ben said.

"At any rate, you still haven't answered my question," she said, reorienting the subject.

"There was a question? What question?"

"Where would this new place be?"

"You should Google the answers to your questions," he said.

"Nah, I like the sound of your voice when you try to talk like you know stuff."

"Try?" Ben gave her another sideways glance, one eyebrow at full tilt this time. "Do you doubt my astonishing mind?"

She gave him a quick punch on the shoulder. "I have to keep you on your toes."

Out of the corner of his eye, he saw Tommie's fist go up, the signal to halt. All the chatter stopped. The members of Troop 104 lowered themselves into a defensive perimeter, weapons pointed out, reindeer sleds in the center. Team leaders Ben and Todd moved up to see what was going on.

"We're here," said the Irish mercenary. "This is where we'll cross."

More than crossing the Tazlina River one person, or animal, at a time via a heavy rope they'd stretched across its icy torrent, this would be their most exposed movement. The Glenn Highway stretched from Anchorage in the southwest to Glennallen in the east and was the major thoroughfare used by both the Russian and Chinese forces traveling from Anchorage and the Matanuska

Susitna Valley to points in the east, including Valdez and the missile defense base at the former Fort Greely in Delta Junction.

To prevent accidents with moose and bears, animals large enough to totally destroy a normal automobile if struck at any speed, as well as to disallow easy ambushes by groups like theirs, the foliage alongside the highway had been trimmed back a hundred feet on either side of the highway wherever possible. With this being the most remote, and hopefully least watched, crossing, there was little choice. As in all things though, there were no real guarantees.

"We have to get everything across as quickly as possible," Tommie said. "That means we're going to have to help the reindeer get the sleds over the slope leading up to the road."

The sleds had been terrific transportation during the winter, gliding over the snow and ice and super smooth ski-like runners designed by Walt, the eldest of their group. The ski runners were not nearly as smooth in summer though. To make them work, Walt had specially fitted wheels to the sleds that had been taken from several broken down four-wheelers they'd found at an abandoned mechanic's shop in a burned-out village. Once the wheels had been added, the sleds suddenly became all-terrain vehicles. An excellent mode of gear transport. On raiding missions, the sleds meant they could take more loot faster. Today, it meant they could keep a lot of their existing loot, items such as food, ammunition, and winter clothing, through the spring thaw and summer as they made the month-long trek over two hundred mountainous miles.

As they drew nearer the highway, the sound of a distant helicopter chattered in the sky. Judging from the direction, it was a Russian patrol most likely looking for them. They kept everything in the trees just out of view of passers-by, or passers-over, in case the helicopter came any nearer.

Tommie pointed to Ben. "Take your team across first. Move fast. Up, over, and into the trees. Once you've got security set up, give us a signal and I will send Todd's team over with one of the sleds, the others following in five-minute intervals once we get the all-clear signal from your side of the road."

Ben nodded at their new commander, then motioned for this team to form around him. He repeated Tommie's orders to them and they started across moments later while the rest of the scouts waited, concealed inside the tree line. Ben gave a five count, then the team rushed in a single-file line out of the trees, five running steps between each team member, across the clearing and up the embankment. They sprinted across the road, then into the woods a hundred feet beyond. The dozen men and women of the first platoon scrambled over ahead of him. As the last of his squad passed the middle of the road, Ben cinched his rucksack tight, the weight riding high on his upper back, pressing into his shoulders. He took off at a sprint. The hundred feet of open ground between the woods and the highway had been mown, trees and all, into something that looked like mulch in a giant's garden.

He wished he had tightened his boot laces as the fist-sized pieces of wood threatened to sprain his ankles with every step. When he finally crunched up the gravel roadside and onto the pavement, he realized he really needed new summer shoes. While branches and other objects had yet to pierce the soles of his hiking boots, the blazing hot pavement quickly burned into the soles of his feet through the leather. Heat rose from the asphalt like fire through the bottom of a frying pan. As soon as he stepped off the road surface and back onto the rocky embankment, the temperature dropped from hellish to just plain hot. He kept going until he was in the woods.

No incidents. No enemies. All seemed as it should be. He verified his people were in place and gave the signal for Todd to come across.

The next team rose from their positions and moved into place to start the crossing. This group was much slower as they had a reindeer cart and two extra animals. Ron and Walt came with them to manage the reindeer.

They started from the trees like Ben's team had. A third of the boys charged across while the others supplemented security.

The first modified sled came out of the trees, Walt jogging along, leading the pair of reindeer by their bridles at a trot. The cart bounced over the shredded tree stumps that carpeted the ground. The reindeer stumbled a couple of times but never lost their footing.

The animals, averaging five hundred pounds and able to pull twice their own weight on a sled, struggled a bit getting up and over the road with the heavy load, but quickly got it under control and less than a minute after setting out were again under cover. Walt ran back to let the others know what to look out for with the next sled. He then went with that next sled to the far side.

The third sled was ready and Todd took that one as soon as the others were back under cover. He got it up to the road, taking Walt's advice to find a smoother path than the first one that had been taken. The reindeer quickly got to the road and surefootedly climbed the rocky base. As the rear wheels of the converted sled rolled over the lip of the berm, part of the asphalt crumbled away at the edge, creating a pothole that trapped one of the wheels. The reindeer lurched to a halt, straining against the harness.

Todd ran to the back of the cart to aid the beasts by pushing it up from the rear. Just before he got in position, a loud snap drew his eyes back to the front. The harness, made from hand-woven rope and leather straps, partially dangled from one of the reindeer, a piece of wooden yoke swinging like a pendulum from its shoulder.

Walt scurried up the road to check the animals and help get them across. Two other boys ran up from behind to join Todd pushing the cart up onto the pavement. They got it up on the flat surface, relieving tension on the lines as Walt inspected the tackle.

"Damn," said the older man, "snapped that yoke right apart." He inspected it a little closer. "Todd, there's a bundle of five-fifty cord and a roll of black duct tape in the kit box on the sled. Could you bring that up here?"

Todd reached into the metal ammo container attached near the handrail and pulled out the hundred-foot bundle of military-grade parachute cord, tossing it to Walt.

"You two," Walt motioned to the other two boys, "post security on either side of us while we fix this thing."

The boys each knelt on either side of the sled, rifles up, eyes out for trouble.

Within a couple minutes, the old hostler had the harness patched.

"This should get us out of the road," he said. "I can fix it more permanently once we're under cover but let's—"

Walt's words vanished in the summer air. Everything from his chest up vanished in a pink mist. Todd felt something hot, wet, and heavy slap him on the cheek. In confused shock, he wiped his face, coming away with a golf-ball-sized chunk of flesh covered in gray hair.

The crack of the shot came a second later.

The boy guarding the sled on Todd's side split into two pieces. His legs and everything below the ribcage stayed in place, kneeling on the pavement. His body from the ribs up spun skyward, arms flailing, weapon spinning away.

Todd grabbed the reindeer by the harness and yanked them forward, off the road, toward the far woods. He made it halfway across the expanse when the reindeer nearest him exploded in a shower of gore.

Todd quickly snatched his tomahawk and hacked the lines Walt had just repaired to free the surviving reindeer.

"Ian!" Ben's voice boomed from the trees. "Get that sniper!"

Ian was positioned on a rise overlooking the road above the tree line. He'd not seen the first shot, but the flash of the second pulled his eye to the west. Judging by the damage on the road, the enemy shooter was using a weapon just like the pre-owned Russian 12.7mm ASVK anti-personnel/anti-armor rifle Ian had pressed into the pocket of his shoulder. Similar to a U.S. .50 caliber Barrett rifle, the ASVK was a mangler of flesh. A destroyer of souls.

He scanned the position through the day/night-range finding scope, yet couldn't find his mark immediately. The shot that killed the reindeer gave him the clear mark he needed to hone in on. Ian sucked in a breath, let half out, then squeezed the trigger. An explosion of red and a flying arm, shoulder still connected, was the response from the sniper's hideout, over eight hundred meters distant.

Movement from the area suggested he fire another round that way. He did. A moment later, he watched a dazed Russian soldier drag himself out of the position. His ghillie suit, torn across his backside and barely connected with a few strands of mesh material, made him look like some kind of otherworldly monster. The pitiful creature clawed across the ground like an animal, his mouth stretching with agonized screams, the sound of his terror dying in the air between them.

It was like looking at a live version on The Scream by Edvard Munch he'd had to study in the eighth grade. He hated that painting, it was the stuff of nightmares. And now he had a three-dimensional live action version of it seared into his brain.

None of the others could see what he could at this moment. He alone had this view.

Through the high-powered scope, Ian saw the man's right leg was gone from just below the hip, the top six inches of femur wiggling uselessly like a shiny piece of white chalk as the hip socket scrambled frantically to make the missing leg gain purchase on the ground.

A stream of blood jetted from the remains of the femoral artery with every heartbeat as the man struggled to find his way home before bleeding out.

Home, his final one, turned out to be a lichen-covered rock jutting from the hillside near his hide. The last streams of his blood coursed over the rock, quickly drying into a black sheen that covered his resting place.

Ian alone would bear the image of that scene in his mind, but for him it would be no nightmare. It was merely a tally mark, counting two more ticks off the trail to finding to his mother.

"Why did they wait 'til the last cart?" Ben asked Tommie. "Why not hit early to stop us from crossing?"

"They might have only just been setting up, or maybe were looking the wrong direction at first," the Irishman replied. "We'll never know, 'cause your brother did a pretty bang-up job of putting them down."

Walt and Devon, the boy scout who had died, were buried at the edge of a flower-filled meadow a short distance into the woods. Devon had been a fifteen-year-old from Idaho the day the war started. He joined Troop 104 during the escape, refusing to stay behind with his home troop after the first attack at Camp Gorsuch. The boys did not know that the rest of his troop and all the other scouts and leaders that had stayed behind at the campground had been massacred after Troop 104 had escaped.

"Over the past two years," Steve said as they gathered around the graves, "Devon was an excellent fighter and faithful member of the group, always willing to help and train others."

He paused for a moment to let the boys consider the memory, before continuing, "Walt's work with the reindeer and building the sleds has been indispensable. I really don't know what we're going to do without him."

The old hostler had been tutoring several of the boys and some of the girls in how to handle the reindeer, Katarina among them. But none were nearly as adept as he at the art. The boys called him "the reindeer whisperer."

"Let us pray," Steve said, removing his head gear and bowing his head, the others following suit. "Father God, we pray you receive these souls into your eternal rest and that they find no more strife, but only peace under the shelter of your protective arms. Bless us as we continue along the way, that we may carry on both in deed and in words and to honor those who died in defense of our homes."

He and many of the others crossed themselves in the Catholic manner, while the rest muttered personal prayers or stared silently into the dirt.

"Our numbers keep dropping," whispered Ian. "If we don't get to Chiknik soon, there won't be any of us left to join Ice Hammer."

CHAPTER 5

Brad

"Wasilla, eh?" Brad leaned forward in the chair behind his desk. The desk was new, replacing the folding table he'd been using for the past year. This one had been made out of a birch burl. A burl is a type of deformation on trees, the tree version of a wart, that grew out of the main stem. Burls were typically harder than the rest of the tree, their grain being different, even turning in on itself. In the case of his desk, this one had been cut, worked, and polished into a very comfortable surface that was also beautiful to look at. If sold on the market before the war, a piece of furniture as large and well-crafted as this one would have cost as much as ten-thousand dollars. This one was presented to Brad as a gift from the people of Chiknik after the birth of his daughter.

"You're telling me the other militias want to coordinate for operations?" Brad's eyebrows creased in doubt at what he'd just been told.

"Their leaders were impressed with what you did in Anchorage," Kharzai said. He cleared his throat, realizing too late that Brad wanted to forget that whole mess. "They want to coordinate better with our Rangers in and around Wasilla and Palmer."

"Why now?" asked John Charles. "They haven't wanted to work together much in the past."

While Brad was the leader of the people of Chiknik as a whole, John Charles was the commander of the military forces of Chiknik, including the village guard, the Patrol Force, and the Rangers. Each group's duties extending from the village in an ever widening circle, with the Rangers going the furthest. They patrolled from ten miles out of the village to as far as their feet and the fight could carry them. The Rangers were the razor edge of the resistance, the lethaly sharp edge around the point of the spear Brad was jabbing into the eye of the invaders.

"Things are getting bigger than the local groups can handle," said Kharzai. "The number of Chinese troops in the valley has more than doubled since our raid on their FOB"—Forward Operating Base—"in Palmer last year. That raid of ours turned out only to be a minor speed bump for ol' Zhang's mission planners because that base is now more than half completed, and growing more well defended every day."

Brad twisted his neck, eliciting a series of little pops that sounded like someone squeezing a strip of bubble wrap.

"Are they looking to attack the Palmer FOB?" he said, referring to the forward operating base housed at what had been the former Matanuska Susitna Borough government headquarters.

"They want to explore the feasibility of such an attack, I think," replied Kharzai.

"We could get a few of the officers over there to parley with them," John said.

Kharzai raised a finger and shook his head, his huge mane of curly hair quivering like a mass of black Jell-O. "There's a catch."

"Oh?"

"They will only agree to meet with Brad and either the Swede or myself. No emissaries."

"Sorry," said John, "that sounds like a plain and simple trap to me."

"It's not," Gunnar spoke up. "Fuzzball and me have both met most of these guys on several occasions. They are sincere. They trust Kharzai or me only to bring the real Ice Hammer. That said, you'd have a half-company of Rangers with you for security. Fifty good fighters watching your back. Most of the individual groups in the valley can't muster that many men on their own."

"A couple of the groups in the Palmer-Wasilla region can get almost a hundred total men, but they're not warriors, and few are properly trained," Kharzai picked up from the giant Swede. "They need organization. Some of the leaders over there picture themselves as 'warlords'," he used air-quotes, "but they are little more than petty tyrants, unable to organize anything on a large scale. Since the Chinese wrapped up operations on the Kenai Peninsula and have full control of the major sea lanes, they have a lot more forces available to deploy here. Most of the resistance groups realize they don't have what it takes to keep fighting for long now that the enemy is getting more firmly established with a large, permanent presence."

Gunnar took another turn speaking, as they tag teamed the presentation. "There is talk that Zhang is putting a satellite HQ into the Mat-Su Borough building to be closer to the action. The Palmer FOB will soon be a full-on military base with three battalions of regular infantry including artillery, as well as Zhang Junior's shock troops."

"That's about two thousand well-trained, well-equipped, rested-up soldiers and a special operations company of a couple hundred right on our doorstep," Kharzai said.

"I thought Zhang Junior swore he'd never come back here," John said, referring to the confrontation the previous winter where Kharzai and Gunnar and a platoon of Rangers ambushed

Major Po Zhang's special forces patrol, killing more than half of them and forcing Zhang to make the promise not to return.

"Yeah, well," Kharzai said, "given that he was speaking to save him and his men's lives, he gave that promise with good intentions at the time. Even if he was sincere, though, he has no say in his own future. He is a man of his word, his word being anything that comes from his superiors. Wherever he is told to go, his own desires fly out the window and he just obeys like any good soldier in the People's Army."

"And plus, he did have a kind of fingers-crossed-behind-his-back tone in his voice when he said it," added Gunnar. "So I didn't believe him either."

"When are they wanting to meet," asked Brad, "these resistance leaders?"

Kharzai walked over to a large three-month calendar hung on the wall at one side of the office. Items such as nice printed calendars ceased to be available to folks like those who lived in Chiknik once the war began. The one on Brad's office wall was hand-drawn by a draftsman who set up shop making a variety of such things the old-fashioned way. From maps to signs to public notices, his business was in full swing.

Circling a range of days with his finger, Kharzai said, "Next week or the following are what they were shooting for. Just a short planning meeting with the top brass of each organization big enough to have top brass. If we took off in the next day or two, we could be at the meeting point by Monday next week, with enough time to scout for any traps."

Brad ran through possible scenarios in his mind. None of what his imagination presented him had anywhere near the level of success he hoped for. Not for a major operation against the People's Republic's finest.

"How do you guys see this playing out?" he asked.

John took a sip of water from a bottle, swallowed with a short sigh, then said, "If you meet up with them and it turns out to be a trap or ambush, you can always hightail back here the long way. If it's not a trap, and all is legit, who is going to take on primary leadership responsibility for the operation? We can't have a dozen company-sized or smaller independent elements running around with their own ideas of how to win a battle, let alone a war. And, related to that, we also can't have such groups backing each other up in combat if they're not trained the same way, and don't fully understand the expectations being put on them. How many of these groups of guerilla fighters are actual military veterans, especially their leaders?"

"Nearly all of them are veterans, boss," said Gunnar. "Don't forget that before the war, twenty percent of the adult population here in Alaska were veterans or active-duty soldiers."

"Yeah, but two-thirds of them were staff and rear echelon types," John said. "In the Army's case, we know they all got at least some basic rifle training and some personal combatives classes. Few Air Force vets have ever had a day of combat training."

"Don't forget the Marines," Gunnar said. "They're never allowed to quit, right? Just like Brad here."

"Half the veterans are also gonna be middle-aged to elderly. Well past their prime," Brad said. "Like me."

"This is a war on their own land," Kharzai said. "And while only a handful are combat trained, and even fewer are combat veterans, most are hunters and outdoorsmen who do know how to shoot and move. It won't take much to get these guys rocking like Delta Force dudes in no time."

"Okay," John said, "I'm rather doubtful of the Delta comparison, but I will concede they can be trained. Hell, a bunch of illiterate Afghan goat herders kept major world powers at bay for thousands of years, from Alexander the Great to the good old U.S. of A. What I am asking, though, is this: Are those groups capable of augmenting our size and skill set to the point of ensuring success in an attack on the big bad wolf? Or will they be a detriment, getting in our way, and likely getting themselves killed in the process?"

Kharzai raised a hand like an overeager fifth grader. "Ooh! Ooh! Pick me!"

Brad closed his eyes and let out a short sigh. "Speak."

"Yes!" Kharzai shouted. "And no!"

"Huh?"

"Yes, they can augment us with minimal training," the hairy man went on. "And no, they won't get in anyone's way."

"You that sure about these guys?"

Kharzai leaned in, eyes widening to the size of golf balls, his nose almost touching Brad's. "Trust me. Me and the Swede have thoroughly vetted most of these guys, and we're cool...dude."

"Weirdo." Brad sat back in his chair. "Alright, we'll go."

He glanced over to the wall calendar, then continued, "We will leave day after tomorrow. Gunnar, you pick the Rangers that should be on this team, but you'll stay back with John to run things. Keep security tight while we're out. John," he motioned to the general, who had replaced the silver star made for him by the silversmith with a more subdued one of stitched black thread, "you make sure the council doesn't run wild. Fuzzball," he pointed at Kharzai, "go pack and tell Jung I promise not to let you get killed."

"You can do that?"

"Let me restate that," Brad said. "I promise not to kill you."

"It will soothe her gentle heart," said Kharzai. The very thought of his girlfriend Jung, a fifty-two-year-old tomboy who'd owned several mechanic shops before the war, put a sparkle in his eye. "She's so tender and gentle for me when she thinks you may have tried to hurt her fuzzy-wumpkins. She doesn't even use the whip these days...sadly."

John and Gunnar shot a look at each other.

"Uh, boss?" said the big Swede. "Permission to go outside and puke?"

"Granted," said John with a wave of his hand. "Save a spot for me."

CHAPTER 6

Sammi

rad stepped into his house a short distance from the headquarters office. A delicious aroma wrapped around his head, his senses sending his salivary glands into overload.

"Hi, honey," Sammi called from the kitchen at the sound of his boots stepping onto the hardwood floor of the arctic entryway. The bench inside the entrance creaked as he sat to remove his boots. While it was nearly summer, springtime in Alaska meant that there was still plenty of mud around. Therefore, shoes in the house were a definite no-go. "Did you have a good day at the office?"

Sammi poked her head around the corner of the kitchen and looked into the foyer. Their house was a simple box structure, 24x24 feet with an open floorplan. Built several years prior to the war, it was heated by water pipes embedded in the concrete floor, the liquid brought to near boiling by an outdoor woodstove, the kind that was popular throughout rural Alaska since the early 90s, and circulated through the house, making a very comfortable place in the dreadful cold of winter. Brad stepped into the arctic entry, a four by four-foot area jutting from the edge of the insulated concrete floor of the main house. In the space between the inner and outer doors he sat on the bench and removed his boots. The space between the two doors allowed the house to keep the warm air inside without losing it to the outside every time someone came or went. Past the interior door a large open space contained the living room/dining area. The kitchen was behind a wall at the back of the room. A small bathroom took up the other corner. The house was topped with a barn style, gambrel roof that added a whole floor of usable space without having to build full walls in addition to a standard pitched roof. The second story contained one large and two small bedrooms. A large wood stove stood in the center of the living area provided additional heat as needed. As the May temperatures had finally decided to stay above 60 degrees, neither the inside nor the outside stove was lit.

While the town of Chiknik did have electricity available due to the power plant that ran the mine, the council had decided to only allow minimal use of power, as there were very few spare parts for the generators two years into the war. During the winter, power was turned on for two hours every morning from seven to nine and three hours every night, from five to eight. This allowed for electric cooking, hot water tanks to heat up for bathing, refrigerators and freezers to chill, recharging battery powered lamps, and so on. All houses, cabins, and dugouts were heated with either wood or coal stoves, some with the same large outdoor wood/coal boilers behind the house. No one in town went cold in the long days of winter. From May through mid-September, the power was cut down to one hour in the morning and one in the evening, as there was no need for electric lights in the twenty-four-hour sun.

Brad stepped across the length of their living space in his stocking feet and planted a kiss on his young wife's lips. She wrapped her arms around him and squeezed. There was a lot less of him than when they'd reunited at the U-Pick farm in the days

44

after the invasion. As long as she had known him, almost twenty years, he'd always tended toward the heavy side body wise. He was strong and very fit when he was in his thirties, and she still in high school, but he was never thin in her memory, not even close, built more like the squat brick shape of a powerlifter than the V-shape of a bodybuilder. From the time the war started to now, he'd probably lost over seventy pounds, now topping out at about one-eighty according to their bathroom scale. These days, he was not so much the strong, yet cuddly teddy bear type of man, but more lean and muscular with broad shoulders and thick bones, probably much what he had looked like when he'd met his first wife, Youngmi, while in the Marines almost thirty years earlier.

"You're home early," Sammi said.

Victoria let out a squawk of greeting from the bassinet nearby. Brad released Sammi and crossed the room to where their daughter lay, arms and legs pinwheeling as she tried to climb the air toward her daddy. Gurgling delight, her face lit up with a smile that glowed like the sun for him. He picked up his daughter, joy filling him as he gazed into the tiny human's eyes, a tiny human that he and Sammi had made together.

Sammi had taken a two-month maternity leave from her job as vice principal and first-grade teacher of the Chiknik school. That covered her through summer vacation as well. Not that that meant she was getting 'paid time off' from the school, as they did not receive salaries. It just meant she didn't have to worry about work for a few months while she and baby recovered.

She stirred a pot from which tendrils of savory steam curled lazily toward the low ceiling, meaty, and thick with vegetables. The scent of fresh barley bread drifted from the small wood burning cast-iron oven in the kitchen. Barley was one of two grain crops that thrived in the local soil.

Decades earlier, Brad's grandfather had taken a sample of his own barley to the 1962 World Expo in Seattle where it had been tested by a group of NASA scientists searching for the best food products to be used by the space program. His sample was declared to be among the highest quality barley they'd ever seen. Other than barley, oats were the only other grain hardy enough for the ground and climate. Sadly, selling the Alaska grain to mass markets in the rest of the country was simply not profitable due to the expensive cost of shipping, so it never became a business reality.

"That smells absolutely delicious," Brad said.

"Rabbit, turnip, and potato," Sammi said, "with wild onion, devil's club buds, and chickweed. And a splash of that cranberry wine you made."

"You broke that out already?" Brad asked. "That was for next Christmas!"

"Actually, this one broke itself out," Sammi said. "It popped its own cork. I think you bottled this batch too soon."

"Oh crap," Brad said, "popping my cork too soon is not good." He wrapped his arms around her waist. "Best that I should wait and pop that cork when you are ready, yes?"

"You are a dirty old man," Sammi growled back at him.

"Is that a bad thing?" he replied.

"Only if you don't like your dinner burned," she said.

"Whoa!" He backed up. "No burnee dinnee!"

She quickly slid the pot of stew from the hot burner to the cool countertop. Brad grabbed two birch bowls from the cabinet and two spoons. While many houses did have commercially made dishes and flatware from before the war, not all did. With the constant influx of people swelling the population of Chiknik, there was a constant need for more of such things. The local tradesmen had a booming craft, most of it paid for by way of the old-fashioned barter system. A wooden bowl, sturdy and heavy, would cost a day's ration of meat or fifteen potatoes, whereas a bowl made of fired Alaskan clay with its unique swirls of white and rusty brown, while prettier, was also easier to make, and much more easily broken, therefore was a little less expensive. Brad liked the feel of the wooden bowls, thick and sturdy. They had been a wedding gift the previous year when he and Sammi had married.

The stew was thick and delicious, bursts of multi-hued flavor filling his senses. He didn't know how she did it, but with minimal ingredients, Sammi made some of the most amazing food he had ever tasted. Her mother had had the same skill, he recalled, being the best cook at the church he'd worked at for over twenty years. Anytime Mrs. Park was cooking for an event, he made sure to be there as no one could match her talent, a talent she had diligently passed on to her daughter.

Brad tore a thick chunk of barley bread off the loaf, sopped up some of the broth in his bowl, then bit off the tender morsel.

"This is incredible, honey," Brad said, lifting another soaked bit of bread to his mouth. After spending weeks eating meager field rations while on the mission to Anchorage, having food with flavor was nearly sensory overload. "I wish I could pack this stuff up and seal it long enough to last for the next mission."

Sammi's spoon stopped halfway to her mouth. "What next mission?"

Brad swallowed the next bite before replying as nonchalantly as possible, "We've got a meeting with the other militias in the valley. I have to leave the morning after tomorrow to make it happen."

"So soon?" Her voice had a stressed edge to it. She tried hard not to allow too much edge into it, so that Victoria would not pick up on mommy's tension. "You just got back from the last mission."

"I know," Brad reached across the table and took her hand in his, "but this is a major development. The first time these groups have wanted to meet in person to plan a big project. If I don't work with them, we will have a huge Chinese base right on our doorstep that could spell the end of Chiknik."

"Why can't Kharzai or Gunnar, or even John take care of it?"

"Because these group leaders have specifically said they will only work with us if they are certain I am the one leading it."

"But I need you here!" Her voice was suddenly very angry. "I am tired of sharing you with the entire population of Chiknik! You are my husband! You are her father!" She pointed to Victoria's bassinet. "She needs you. I need you to be home!"

"I..." Brad started, but stopped at the furious look on Sammi's face. For such a delicate-seeming woman, porcelain white skin and gentle demeanor, when she got mad she turned into an entirely different person. Face mottled with red spots, rage filled her eyes in a way that he had never known she could express until after they'd married. "I have an entire city to run, baby, an army."

"You have a family as well," she growled. Victoria let out a terrified whimper then started to cry. "You have us!"

"If I do not keep this city together, I will have none of that. I have no choice Sammi," he pleaded. "I have to do this. You knew that when you married me."

"I did not know that you would be more dedicated to people you don't even know than you would be to your wife and daughter," she said. "Maybe Youngmi got the better deal."

Brad sat back, stunned. Words could not form in his head. How could she have said that? How could she, his dead wife's favorite assistant, think that? Before he could form any words, Sammi rose from her chair, lifted Victoria from her crib, and stomped upstairs.

"You can pop your own cork tonight."

CHAPTER 7

Gunnar

"You know, we've been together a little more than a year now," Kharzai said to Gunnar as he ran a cloth over the barrel of the rifle he'd just finished cleaning.

"Does that make us a couple?" The big man grunted, flicking a bit of dirt out of the ejection port on his own weapon. He wasn't going on the mission with Kharzai and Brad, but still religiously cleaned his weapon every day whether it had been fired or not. "Are you about to propose to me?"

"You'd have to fight Jung if you're trying to win my heart." Kharzai smiled at the image of the fierce, yet loving woman he had been with since the beginning of the war.

"Oh, hell no." Gunnar put his hands up. "You are not worth the risk; she'd eat my soul."

"Good," Kharzai said as he stowed the cloth into the cleaning kit. "Speaking of souls, I have a question to ask."

"Ask away."

"Like I said, we've been together for a little more than a year now."

"Right."

"And in that year, we've done, what, half a dozen long-range patrols?"

"Yup."

"And been in a couple dozen combat actions."

Gunnar raised an eyebrow. "Is there actually a question in this question?"

"Here it is." Kharzai took a deep breath, blew it out, his eyes stretching wide as if the coming query may not be welcome, then blurted it out in a fast string of words. "Every time we take off on a mission or are about to make contact with an enemy, you reach up with your right hand and rub something under your shirt. What are you rubbing?"

Gunnar's eyebrow was still raised, the other eyebrow joining the expression by crunching downward. The big Swede drew in his own deep breath, studied Kharzai's face, now stretched into a wide-eyed quizzical look. He let the breath out, reached up with his hands, and pulled a necklace chain out from the collar of his shirt. On the chain dangled a one-inch long pendant that looked like a miniature boat anchor with swirls and whirls decorating the whole device.

"It's Mjölnir," he said, holding it out for Kharzai to look at. "Thor's Hammer, from old Viking mythology."

"I know what Mjölnir is, but why do you wear it? I thought you said you were Lutheran."

"I am Lutheran, but I am also descended from Vikings. My family actually has a genealogy of our ancestors that shows we are pure Viking blood."

"I didn't realize Vikings kept genealogies. Thought they were mostly illiterate."

"They were, but when Christianity came, so did writing." Gunnar stowed his own cleaning kit and leaned his rifle against the fallen tree he was sitting on. "When my ancestors became

Christian in the thirteenth century, they learned to read and write and they wrote down the oral traditions of our family line."

"Usually, cultures that have a significant change in philosophy tend to start rewriting their own family histories without including their more dubious forebears."

"Yeah, well, the list shows names of relatives about one hundred years prior to their conversion. But at the point in the 1200s when they changed religions, there is a line that states, 'All these our forefathers were born in sin and unrepentant of their bloodsheds and destructions, pray their souls may be redeemed from the flames,' then lists names like Olaf Redbeard, and Hrothgar the Spike, and so on."

"Interesting," Kharzai said. "So why do you rub your little Mjolnir before a fight?" He wasn't going to let his friend escape the answer.

"Good luck ritual, I guess." Gunnar put the silver pendant back inside his shirt. "I also say the Lord's Prayer under my breath."

"So, if you get whacked, should I make sure you're holding an axe or something before you expire?"

"Only way to make it into Valhalla is to die with your weapon in your hand."

"I'll keep that in mind."

CHAPTER 8

Youngmi

With her duties overseeing the food distribution network throughout the city of Anchorage, Youngmi was no longer expected to teach daily English classes to the headquarters and command staff, although she did voluntarily continue to host a class for the female officers every Thursday evening. It was regularly attended by a dozen or so young women and while they did study English, it was much more of a casual setting than a typical class, allowing the women to enjoy polite conversation while Youngmi helped them improve their pronunciation and grammar.

"Ms. Ma," one of them called, "you told us before that you moved to America when you were a young woman, only a high school student still."

Youngmi glanced at the speaker. It was recently promoted Captain Hong, commander of the Communications and Digital Technology company in the headquarters battalion. She was chief of the telecom and computer technicians and network administrators. She was the kind of extremely intelligent woman who had a mind like a whip and a figure that drew men's eyes across rooms. No woman in her right mind would allow Cpt.

Fan Hua Hong to be alone in a room with a man they had any claim on. Her name alone insinuated she was not safe for men to be around, as Fan Hua meant Lethal Flower. Someone in her family saw her potential it seemed. Lucky for Youngmi, Fan Hua wasn't interested in widowed, fifty-four-year-old generals, so in her book, she was a nice young woman.

"Yes, Miss Hong," Youngmi replied. In this particular class, ranks were not used in order to accustom them to non-military patterns of English speech. "I was sixteen when I moved here."

"You came here at an age very close to some of our soldiers that are here," Fan Hua said. "Did you study English when you were in school in Korea?"

"No," Youngmi said, thinking back to her teenage years living with her father in their town not far from the North Korean border. "I did not study English in school, at least not anything beyond what was required in high school."

"I am twenty-eight, and have studied English since I was fourteen. And yet my accent is so thick, I am afraid to speak to an American."

Youngmi nodded. "I did not study it, but there was an American military base near my house where I grew up. While I never understood what they were saying, I did grow up listening to the rhythm and cadence of the language."

"What is ridemencainz?" Mai asked, misunderstanding the new term.

"It is not one word," Youngmi replied, unable to stop a smile that tightened her lips at the misunderstanding. "I was referring to rhythm, like the beat of the drum, 'budum bum bum'," she mimicked beating a drum with her hands, "and cadence, like how you march. Once you learn the rhythm and cadence of a language, it is much easier to speak it."

"But English is so very unmusical sounding," Fan Hua said. "It is like they are chopping off all their words."

"To me," said Lee Ming Ling, a very tall and solidly built, 180 centimeters (nearly six feet) tall, lieutenant from Mai's unit, "American English sounds like snakes hissing."

"Like snakes?" said Na Fenfang. "That is not nice! I think English sounds very romantic."

Ming Ling rolled her eyes and shook her head. "You think anything said by any man with muscles and money sounds romantic, Fenfang."

"I do not!"

"Yes, you do!" All three of the other women said in unison.

Fenfang blushed. "Well, not all men! Besides, I think English is a strong sounding language, very macho."

"You better be careful or someone might say you're too interested in American men," Mai said.

"That may be, but I can't help it if I find their voices attractive," Fenfang went on. "Mrs. Ma knows what I mean. She was married to an American for a long time. Didn't you love the sound of your husband's voice, Mrs. Ma?"

A brief awkward silence fell on the room. All of these women knew the circumstances of how Youngmi came to be a resident among them. How she'd been taken prisoner by force, and lived as a virtual prisoner in the headquarters. Most of them assumed she'd actively been General Zhang's bed mate since shortly after being taken. Only Mai knew that not to be true, or at least Youngmi thought Mai believed that.

Youngmi took a breath and let it out, then gave an understanding smile. She'd accepted her plight, and the new way of life it had foisted upon her.

"Yes, Fenfang," she replied. "When I was married to my husband before the war, I loved to hear his voice. He had a very deep, resonant voice, and used to sing me to sleep when we were young. I would put my head on his chest and feel the bass in his voice vibrate. As we got older, his voice got even more gentle, and at the same time, stronger. His very sound made me feel peaceful, safe, and protected. I loved his voice very much."

A couple of the girls caught their breath at the romantic imagery. Mai blushed at her Ayi describing her husband so lovingly.

"That is such a beautiful image," Fan Hua said with a sigh.

"Yes, well," Youngmi's voice had an edge to it that cracked the momentary reverie, "he is dead now. It is a fond memory I cannot forget, but not something I can continue to hope for."

"General Zhang has a very nice voice like that, too," Fenfang said, cutting off a beat too late, as if realizing she'd unexpectedly said it out loud.

Youngmi let out a snicker that turned into a smile then a gentle laugh.

"Yes, honest and innocent, Na Fenfang," she said, leaning forward and patting the young woman's knee. "Yes, he does. He has a very lovely voice."

The rest of the women joined with nervous laughter of their own.

"I don't think I'd use innocent and Fenfang in the same sentence, Ms. Ma," Fan Hua muttered.

The whole group burst into real laughter, Fenfang included.

CHAPTER 9

Brad

The hike across the Matanuska valley toward Hatcher Pass was brutally hot. As often happens in early summer in the sub-Arctic, the twenty-four-hour sun was unrelenting, pounding down harsh and dry 90-degree temperatures that baked the men as they marched cross country with enough gear for a month-long, round-trip trek. Brad remembered many years of coaching little league teams that his sons were on, as the heat baked their bodies and turned dirt on the diamond into a fine powder that kicked up at the slightest breeze, coating them in layers of fine sticky dust. Kids in cleats running down the baseline made billowing clouds that looked like Roadrunner escaping from Wile E. Coyote. By the end of a game, everyone on the team would be covered in yellowish dust from head to toe. It also found its way into their eyes and lungs, and earned a lot of money for companies making allergy medicine. In addition to the dry, dusty air, the seasonal heat also meant a nasty hatching of mosquitoes in deeper parts of the forest where the warmth hit, but the direct sun did not. In the shade of the thick spruce mosquitoes could erupt in dense clouds of bloodsuckers that brought a constant buzzing in the ears and merciless bites even through jeans and shirts. It was enough to drive one mad.

The patrol was left with two basic choices, as far as the journey itself was concerned. Walk in the open, directly in the blazing sun where the tiny beasties were not too keen to get baked alive, but where a passing helicopter, drone, or satellite could easily detect them. Or stick to the cover of the trees and the slightly cooler shade they offered, and get eaten alive by the tiny bloodsuckers.

In the end, they stuck mostly to the trees, covering themselves in whatever DEET they had available, as well as rubbing pineapple weed over their skin as an added deterrent to the miniature vampires.

"I think mosquitoes are an invention of Satan," Martin Staley said, "or at least if God created them, Satan must have somehow twisted their little souls into some type of evil demon spawn bent on eradicating humankind by driving us all crazy."

His brother Philip tugged at the mosquito net that hung over his face, clearing enough of the insects that he could see the trail ahead for a few moments. The nets, a fine mesh of green fabric that draped over the head and neck, didn't protect the whole body, but at least kept the eyes and nose a little safer from bites and swelling.

"I agree," said the elder brother. "They are definitely evil creatures. I can't think of a single redeeming quality of the little buggers."

"Actually," said Kharzai, "those evil little bloodsuckers do have a couple good things going for them."

"Really?" Brad said. "Enlighten us before we start an all-out species war."

"Well," Kharzai took on the air of a television commercial college professor type, "mosquito larvae happen to be the main food staple of numerous fish, such as many of those you guys like to catch and eat in our streams. Trout, grayling, and so on thrive on them. So without mosquitoes, there's no grilled fish for dinner."

"Okay, that's one fact, what else?" Martin adjusted his rifle in his arms to scratch at a bite on the back of his hand.

"And just before the war, there was a lot of research going into mosquito saliva for medical purposes."

"What are you talking about?" Philip said. "What in the world is mosquito spit good for?"

"Heart disease," Kharzai replied. "Their spittle, as it turns out, contains some pretty high-quality anticoagulants which thin the blood enough for it not to clot while they suck it down their cute little tiny mouth straws. Turns out it might be very helpful toward curing a fair amount of heart and vascular issues."

"Provided the research survives the war," said Brad.

"Yeah," Kharzai scratched at a bite on his otherwise smooth face, "there is that kind of over-arching issue of the war."

"How does your face feel?" Martin asked Kharzai.

"Weird," the Persian replied, as he rubbed his bare cheeks. "I haven't shaved in more than a decade, and the last time was because I was running for my life. I've only shaved twice in my entire existence. I had more beard than this when I was in kindergarten."

He had shaved off his beard, one of the prides of his appearance, for the team's sake. The Chinese had come up with a fairly simple plan to discourage rebels outside their control areas from coming into the towns they ruled. They had made beards illegal. Since men from the bush, and those in the local militias were mostly bush types, tended to wear long, thick beards, criminalizing them helped to identify strangers rather quickly when they came into town for the first time. As a precaution, Brad had ordered everyone to be, and stay, clean shaven while on missions so they didn't set off alarms as soon as they came near a settlement.

"What did Jung say?" Brad asked.

"She said my face looked as smooth as a baby's bottom." Kharzai scratched again. "Then joked about putting a diaper over my mouth to shut me up."

The Ranger walking point, the position ahead of the rest of the patrol that scouted the route before them, suddenly froze. He raised his fist, signaling the group to halt. They lowered silently into the brush, the first platoon leader moving to the head of the patrol to learn why they stopped.

"What's up, ranger?" he said.

"I smell a human camp, sir," the soldier replied. "Faint smoke, body odor, fish drying."

The lieutenant sampled the air, detected a barely identifiable odor of forest. Nothing out of the ordinary.

"You must have a nose like a dog, Colbert," he replied. "I can't smell a thing."

"That direction, sir," Colbert said, pointing ahead and to the left. "Maybe a few hundred yards."

Kharzai and Brad made their way forward. The lieutenant met them halfway.

"Colbert says he smells a camp a little ways up ahead." He pointed in the general direction. "Should we go around it or make contact?"

"Smells a camp?" Brad said, unsure how to take that.

"His nose has been pretty reliable in the past. He once saved us from an ambush when he smelled a Chinese soldier's flatulence, could tell the difference between theirs and ours apparently. Turned out he was right."

"Think this might be some of our guys?" Brad asked Kharzai.

"It's not where we planned to meet," replied the Persian. "But they might be on their way to the place."

"Maybe we should recon the camp," said the lieutenant. "I can send a squad to check out their site and find out what they're up to."

"Do it," Brad said. "We'll hang back until they return with news."

The edge of the encampment was, as Colbert had stated, about three hundred yards from where he'd detected them. It was a semi-permanent camp that included what appeared to be a long deep dugout with a log roof that was covered with the remains of a blue polyethylene tarp and topped over with sod. The weather being clear and sunny, the inhabitants were milling around outside the shelter, more than a dozen people visible altogether, four men, three women, and five children. The rangers found no guards set around the camp, although there was a fairly worn trail leading off into the woods that looked like people regularly used it. As Colbert had said, there were a couple of fires smoldering. Poles with what looked like trout laid open and hung to dry stretched over the coals, thin tendrils of smoke lazily swirling around the meat as they rose skyward. People stood or sat at various tasks around the camp, looking like everyone had something important to do. Two of the seemingly older children worked with one of the adults preparing some kind of food. The other three kids played together near a couple female adults.

This went on for more than an hour with little change as the Rangers silently observed the site's residents. Satisfied that these people were not a threat to them, they backed off and returned to the rest of the unit.

"Looks like a couple of families that spent the winter over there," said Colbert. "We saw no guards or lookouts, but they might have a few people out on a hunt or patrol or something.

There was an obvious trail that gets a lot of use going in and out of the camp."

"Mostly," said the lieutenant, "they look like refugees just trying to survive. Reasonably healthy as far as we could tell, didn't see anyone sickly looking. That said, we heard some voices from the shelter, but didn't see inside, so we can't know if they were sick or not."

"Let's keep quiet and go around them for now," Brad said. "No need to give away our presence to anyone we don't need to get in touch with yet. We can swing by on the way back and maybe make contact then if they're still here."

CHAPTER 10

Scouts

"You can stop right there," a voice called out from ahead of them.

Todd, son of Mike, the late leader of Troop 104, did just that, jutting his fist into the air to signal the rest of the group to freeze. It had been his turn leading the march in the point position as they approached the last few miles to Chiknik. The rest of the group took up a defensive posture.

"We've been watching you all morning," said the voice. "You guys are pretty sneaky for such a big group."

Ben, second in the pack, searched the forest in the direction of the voice, but couldn't see a thing.

"We're trying to find Chiknik," Todd called out.

"You're there," replied the voice. "At least you're near there, and on the right trail. Question is, do we want you to find us?"

Tommie came up beside Ben.

"Who are you?" the voice called out. "Where are you from?"

Tommie rose to his feet, hands up, slung weapon hanging across his chest.

"We're the remains of Boy Scout Troop 104 from Anchorage."

"But your accent tells me you are not Alaskan."

"Irish," Tommie said. "Tommie Dolan is my name. I have a couple of the surviving scoutmasters with us, as well as the scouts and some women and girls we rescued from the Russians last winter."

"Where are you coming from?"

"We had a camp south of Klutina Lake, but the Russians found us. We're roughly half of the number we had a couple months ago."

There was a long silence. Then the voice said, "Have your whole group put their weapons on the ground and stand up. One of our guys is going to come over and scan you for tracking devices."

"You stand up and show yourself," Tommie replied, "and we will comply."

A figure rose from the thick underbrush about twenty yards ahead of them. He was covered by a ghillie suit made to look like a mound of grass and alder branches.

"I'm Terry Berryhill, captain of Alpha Company, Chiknik Rangers," the man said. "My technical sergeant is going to come over and run a scanner over each of you and your gear before we can let you enter Chiknik proper. We've discovered a lot of tracking devices in equipment we took from the bad guys."

A soldier approached Tommie and Ben. His weapon was up, his expression serious. He took a device from his pocket that looked like a largish GPS that had been seriously modified and clicked it on, the device giving a short buzz as it booted up. He ran the device over Tommie's body, gear, and weapon, then did the same to Ben and Todd.

"Your name wouldn't happen to be Franklin, would it?" the Irishman asked.

The soldier froze, took a step back, fingers tightening around the handgrip of his rifle. He said nothing, staring up at Tommie with an expression that demanded an explanation.

"Mojo Johnson came into our camp a few months back," Tommie said. "He had a device exactly like that that he said a super smart guy in Chiknik, named Franklin, gave him. Said his wife knew you from Fairbanks."

"Yeah?" The soldier kept a hard stare on them. "What was his wife's name?"

"I don't know," Tommie said, "he didn't tell us her name. But he did say she and their daughter have been missing since the beginning of the war."

"Interesting," said the soldier. "Stay here. We've got a dozen sharpshooters with a bead on you and your group. Anyone acts crazy, you all get capped. Got it?"

Tommie nodded his acceptance of the order and stayed put as Franklin, or whoever he was, went over everyone in the group, as well as the sleighs and gear on them, having the scouts remove every item from the sleds to be individually scanned. After half an hour, he came back up the line, passed Tommie and Ben, and went back to his leader.

"I'm not Franklin," said the soldier. "But he is the one who made the device." He turned to his officer. "They're clean. And they seem to know Mojo."

"I also know Seirim Al Gul!" Tommie called out. "Or at least am acquainted with him."

"Who?" asked the captain.

"Crazy guy, skinny, huge hair and beard," Tommie said. "I believe you might know him as Kharzai."

John and Gunnar sat across the table from Tommie and Steve. The four men sized each other up like two pairs of mountain lions trying to decide whether to challenge each other to mortal combat.

"You know Mojo and Kharzai?" John asked. "How?"

"Kharzai I've known about since, oh," Tommie paused, counting the years in his head, "a decade or more before this war started. I was a military contractor in Africa and the Middle East. He was pretty well known in certain circles in the special ops community, although most folks in that part of the world thought he was on the terrorist side. It wasn't until much later that most of us learned he was actually a CIA deep cover operator."

"And Mojo?"

"Him we just met early last winter when he was passing through on his way back up to Fairbanks," Tommie said. "He said he saw our boys perform an ambush on the Glenn Highway while on a patrol with your men."

Gunnar stared at him the whole time. Tommie was not a small man, scarred knuckles and wiry muscles evidence of a lifetime of physical violence. Gunnar dwarfed the Irishman by six inches and probably fifty pounds, his movements fluid and precise for such a large man. The two would make a fairly equal match in a cage fight.

"I saw you, too," Gunnar said. "This was the man that was supervising the ambush where we saw that kid with the little hatchet kill the survivors."

"Ah, yes," Tommie said, "that would be Ian, leader of the murder squad."

"You taught these kids to be that violent?" Gunnar asked, a rising anger in his voice. In his military and law enforcement careers, he had witnessed the effects of children raised with the concept of extreme violence being the norm. Often, abusive parents led their children into lives that emulate the beatings they received as children, sometimes turning those whose souls have been completely broken into criminals and the occasional serial killer. But the level of systematic surgical savagery he'd seen this boy named Ian engage in, he'd only seen repeated by children whose entire life had been a bath of brutal ferocity. Child soldiers in Africa and Central America. Young recruits into MS-13, Yakuza, and other murderous gangs. He'd seen a lot. But kids like this Ian, who seemed to enjoy what he was doing, were at a different, even psychopathic level.

"Oh no," Tommie shook his head and wagged a finger, "no one taught that kid; he is a natural. At thirteen, he shot two caribou, in three seconds. He'd stalked them until he was only fifty feet away and killed both with a .22 caliber bullet through their right eye, straight into the brain. 'So I don't put a hole in the hides I need,' he said. He actually made the tomahawk he uses with the help of our smith. He's also an incredible scout sniper. He's got some magical power, wouldn't you agree, Steve?"

"He's something, that's for sure," Steve said.

"And what about you, Steve?" John asked. "You don't look the mercenary type."

"Retired Navy F-14 pilot. Until this war, the only kind of killing I ever came close to was in exercises from a couple miles in the sky."

"How'd you two get to be with these boys?" John's expression grew slightly less suspicious.

"I was their scoutmaster," said Steve. "At least, I was scoutmaster of the original Troop 104. A number of other scouts joined us when we boogied out of Camp Gorsuch on the first day of the war. That's the Boy Scout Camp in Chugiak."

"I'm very familiar with it," John said. "I was a scout as well, in the early nineties. Spent several summers at Gorsuch."

"So, if we let you and your group stay," Gunnar said, "what can you offer us in return?"

"We've got twenty boys who have been fighting a running guerilla war for more than a year, raiding and plundering the enemy every chance they got," Tommie said in reply. "A couple months ago, they and a number of the ladies with us successfully defended our village against an attack by a Russian infantry company led by a squad of Spetznaz soldiers."

John nodded slowly in response, weighing the men up.

"The only reason we won that particular fight is that Lady Fate intervened. Ian's brother Ben shot a guy with a laser designator, and their own missile wiped most of them out. Then Ian and his squad ran onto the field like berserkers and dispatched the survivors, took all the guns and ammo they could carry, and we, as a group, escaped and evaded for two months through the wilds to find you."

"How did you know where we were?" asked Gunnar.

"Mojo Johnson told us," Tommie said. "Like I said, he visited us early last winter, after seeing you folks. We also got more details from a friend of our former leader Mike, God rest his soul. That man being Alex Tatum, kind of runs as a spy/saboteur among the Russian forces. He knows a little bit about everything going on."

"We know him," said John. "He helped me and Gunnar locate a fugitive in Glennallen a few years ago."

"Good man," Tommie said. "Among the truest men I know."

"He is," said John. "What's your story?" he asked the Irishman.

"Former Irish protestant as a teen," Tommie replied, "turned SAS later, then became a contractor with one of the major private military firms. Freelancer after that. How about yourselves?"

"Gunnar and I were also freelance contractors," John said. "But here in the States, we were tracking fugitives for law enforcement and the U.S. Marshals. We were National Guardsmen as well, deployed to both Iraq and Afghanistan multiple times."

"So, are one of you the one they call Ice Hammer?" Steve asked.

"No," John replied, "neither of us is Ice Hammer. He's out on a mission right now, left this morning. He and Kharzai should be back in a couple weeks."

"So, is there a place for us in your little army here?" Tommie said.

"We have three layers of defenses here. The Village Guard, the Tactical Patrol Force, (TPF), and the Rangers. The first one is comprised of every male from fifteen to seventy who is not a member of the other two, and any female volunteer. TPF are likewise volunteers aged fifteen to fifty who are a little more into the military bit. They're given regular Army-style training and patrol up to ten miles out. The Rangers are exactly what you are probably picturing, modeled directly from U.S. Army Ranger training, of which we have both been instructors in the past. Like the old one, our Rangers are volunteers, men and women over age sixteen who are required to undergo selection testing prior to acceptance. After the initial seven day 'Indoc' phase—short for 'Indoctrination'—they are placed in a company and receive the rest of their training in unit and via live patrols. Somewhat similar to how Marine Force Recon trained their new guys. Of course, we don't have airborne or scuba phases, but they get some pretty serious infantry experience. Once deemed active by their NCOs, the Rangers go out as far as Anchorage getting intel and smashing things. From what Gunnar and Kharzai said about that attack they witnessed, your boys are pretty skilled, so any of them who want to and can hack it are welcome to try out."

CHAPTER 11

Brad

A short series of clicks on the radio indicated they had arrived at the location they were to meet. They were four days earlier than scheduled, intentionally. Brad wanted to watch all of the other groups come in, to get a measure of them and see how they would act. Getting there before anyone else, it'd be a lot easier to detect a rat before it bit them and vanish into the mountains before they could be betrayed. The Rangers formed a perimeter, half facing inward, the rest outward, behind them. They quickly and almost silently dug fighting holes, covering the positions with branches, moss, dead leaves, and other foliage. Blending with nature, they disappeared from view, an invisible, yet very alert camp. They settled into a silent routine, lying in wait for whoever may come their way.

The next morning, just such a whoever did come their way. A group of men in various types of military garb stalked into the area, many wearing ghillie suits that rendered them as sasquatch-sized walking bushes. They approached from the same direction as Brad and his men did as if they'd tracked his team. The newcomers were quiet, cautious. They moved almost silently across the ground.

Professionals.

Serious professionals.

Twenty men in all, they moved double abreast, five yards between them side to side and front to back. The first several ranks moved past the Ranger's positions like ghosts, then the movement slowed. The sound of a woodpecker froze them in place, gun muzzles up and out. The rapid-fire chirp of an offended squirrel laid them flat on their bellies or kneeling beside trees, the group facing 360 degrees. The last pair of militiamen stopped directly between two of Brad's men's positions at their in-facing line. They silently knelt, less than ten feet from either fighting hole, and with the same level of stealth Brad's men had employed, dug their holes. If he were not watching the work these new soldiers were doing with his own eyes, he would not have believed anyone could dig into hard forest vegetation and soil with so little sound. Just as the Rangers had, the new men camouflaged their positions with sticks, vines, and foliage to make their hides invisible to any other passersby.

Sergeant Phil Staley was a lifelong Alaskan bushman. He'd grown up on a homestead in Palmer where four generations of his family lived since the early 1920s and worked in his father's mechanic shop. One of the original members of Brad's group of refugees who'd survived the invasion and the attack on the wilderness retreat they'd wintered in, he had killed one of their own group who had snapped and attempted to rape the young woman to whom Phil was now married. He had served with the Rangers in countless violent operations way behind enemy lines in the year plus since they had settled into Chiknik. Phil, and his younger brother Martin, were what could only be described as 'warriors' in the most traditional sense. They had first killed men in battle as teenage boys during the invasion and in those early days had distinguished themselves as men to be reckoned with. Now at the ripe old ages of nineteen and twenty-two, neither had been able to keep count of the Chinese soldiers they'd sent home in black bags.

Phil Staley was an experienced man of war who realized his own mortality. He knew the exhilaration of the kill. He also knew when to be afraid. Phil nearly pissed himself when he heard footsteps draw near and saw a dark shape approach from the corner of his vision.

He had camouflaged the fighting hole well, giving plenty of cover that turned it into what looked like a mound of grasses intertwined with the branches of a dead fallen tree. There was enough room for him and his teammate to stretch out without fear of pushing the camouflage off kilter. They had even dug individual pee-holes on each side of the space so they could relieve themselves without leaving their hide, and without getting it all over their clothes. Even with all the precautions, one of the new militia soldiers walked to the mound and lifted an armload of leaves and some sticks directly over Phil Staley's back. He felt the cool woodland air seep through the thin layer of leaves that had fallen through the stick mesh above him. He worked the moves through his mind, planning his actions if he was discovered and it came to a fight. Phil tightened his hold on the pistol grip of his Chinese QBZ-03 rifle, a weapon he'd taken from a dead enemy soldier. His heart pounded in his chest, ramping his senses up several notches, vision clarifying, focus intense. 'Fight or die' was rapidly growing into the only option.

Then the man silently turned and walked away.

Phil forced his heart to slow. He breathed slowly into the dirt, forcing all of his effort to not let out an audible sigh of relief. The others eventually settled into their position, facing the opposite direction as Phil and his man.

This was going to be a long couple of days.

CHAPTER 12

Youngmi

The late sky was still fully lit by the arctic sun. Youngmi could not fall asleep. She lay awake until well past midnight, glancing at the illuminated hands on the small bedside clock every few minutes. After hours of struggling, and failing, to fall asleep, she rose and walked into the living room. The midnight sun shone through the living room windows, illuminating the space with a surreal flat light that seemed to render real life into a two-dimensional painting, letting the imagination create what it wanted to see, but not promising to show that imagined reality.

Youngmi stood in the middle of the room, staring out at the empty parade field, trying to recall a perfect life with her husband, Brad. Instead, half-dreamed images flooded her mind of Brad trying to kill her, to wipe the earth of her memory. Images of him willing her out of existence so he could marry a younger, prettier woman. Her conscious thoughts told her this was a ridiculous line of reasoning, but every other part of her mind told her it was logical, obvious. Brad would be much happier with a young, beautiful wife than he could have been with a fifty-year-old Youngmi. Why not take advantage of such an opportunity?

Then her thoughts returned to her own situation. Here she was, alone, yet not alone. Abandoned, yet loved by a man who, while her enemy in every sense of the word, had showed her unconditional affection. Zhang had sacrificed the comforts due a general just to watch over her as she lay in the hospital. Perhaps there was more to come in her life than she'd thus far accepted. Perhaps Zhang was the man she was to be with for the remainder of her time here on this earth.

Youngmi took two steps towards Zhang's room, freezing in the middle of the living area, arms crossing her chest as she talked herself into what she was about to do.

I am not surrendering to the enemy. I am only realizing I am in love again.

She forced herself forward, toward Zhang's door. Youngmi put her hand on the knob, her heart pounding in her chest. Energy pulsed within her chest with such power that though she would be burned to cinders if whatever magic was in play grew out of control. She twisted the knob very, very slowly, pushing the door open as the bolt slid out of the jamb. Her heart leaped from her chest to her throat at the soft creak of a hinge as it opened into his room. She made her way toward General Zhang sleeping quietly in his bed, lying on his side, very alone. She slid into the blankets behind him and wrapped her arm around his belly, and held on for dear life. Within moments, she succumbed to his warmth, and fell into a deep, deep sleep.

The blatant arctic sun bore through the partially open curtain like a laser beam, waking any and everything in its path as it forced the day onto the inhabitants of the northland. Youngmi opened her eyes, at first not remembering where she had wandered in her late-night delirium. She felt warm, protected. Wrapped in strong arms. Suddenly, it all came back to her. She was in Zhang's bed. She opened her eyes, to find the general staring at her.

"Good morning, beautiful woman," he said in a deep voice. "I hope this is not just a dream."

Youngmi tried to gather her thoughts. What had she been thinking? Why had she made such a huge mistake?

"Good morning, lovely Youngmi," Zhang said again. "I am both surprised and exquisitely pleased to see you here."

"I am sorry, my general...I..."

"There is nothing to be sorry for, Youngmi," he cut her off. "I am the one who should be apologizing for not having invited you to my room before."

"I hope I am not an embarrassment to you in front of your servants," Youngmi said.

"They are sworn to secrecy," Zhang said. "And those among them that will talk have already been saying for months that we are bedmates. No sense in officially turning them into liars."

He pulled her close, into his embrace, and kissed her softly on the forehead, then again on the lips. And they made love. A sweet, blissful escape to a place of ecstasy that had for too long been a foreign land to both of them.

CHAPTER 13

Rangers

When Steve communicated the options to the members of Troop 104, most of them, including Steve and the remaining adult leaders with the exception of Tommie, declined the Rangers. They had no desire to actively seek out the enemy on their own territory anymore. The boys and men had spent more than two years in regular assaults on Russian convoys to steal supplies and weapons. They had lived in constant fear of being attacked at their home base or worse, being captured and facing horrendous tortures at the hands of Colonel Grall and his minions. Now, for the first time since it all began, they could lay in a bed and sleep, full-on deep body and mind REM sleep, without fear of the enemy sneaking into the camp to kill them. They were allowed a week of pure rest and relaxation, with no village duties or expectations, unwinding from the world they'd endured for so long.

Almost everyone in Chiknik had had terrible experiences, some very similar to those of the scouts, but here within the walls of the city, there was safety, security. At least safe and secure relative to the outside world where the enemy reigned. Post-traumatic stress was an everyday issue for a large part, maybe even most, of the residents of Chiknik. Their entire world had burned and the majority of the residents that made up the community had barely escaped with their lives. The structure and orderliness of the community provided a way to cope. A meaningful job providing for those around them. To be with friends working toward growing a thriving town. Hopefully to not have to kill other humans in order to survive day to day. Most of the young men and women were happy to be members of the Village Guard or the TPF. They would do almost any kind of other work long as they did not have to constantly be looking over their shoulders or enduring nightmares of trudging through fields of blood.

For others among them though, combat had become a defining way of life. Taking lives, a source of spiritual energy. A reason to live. Killing the enemy was the purpose for their very existence. Life simply boiled down to doing away with everyone who had hurt their families and created their misery. They could think of no other point to survival than destroying those who had invaded the Greatland and wrecked the idyllic lifestyle of Alaska.

Ben, Ian, Todd, and a handful of the boys from the kill squad, as well as Katarina and one of the other older girls, opted to volunteer for the Rangers. The selection process for the Rangers was a brutal fourteen-day test of physical fitness and stamina, as well as intelligence and military mindset. It started with a version of something like the infamously well-known U.S. Navy SEAL's 'Hell Week.' The Ranger's slightly less well-known weeding-out process was dubbed 'Indoctrination Week.' Similar to SEAL training, a brass bell had been hung in front of the barracks, the bell having been found in the house of a retired fisherman who donated it to the cause. The purpose of the bell was to allow a way out for those who realized they were in over their heads before they committed to months of severe training. Any volunteer who came to the understanding that this was not the path they wished to take only had to walk up and ring it once, and they would immediately be removed from the program, no questions asked, no reasons needed, and no judgment given.

After their two-week rest and recuperation period, the candidates started training. With his lifelong experience, Tommie was brought right in as part of the leadership cadre. The first morning of Indoc began with a 'Black Hat,' an instructor identified by a black Army uniform hat, charging into their rooms at the way too early hour of oh-four-thirty and informing them in a growling voice that spoke barely above a whisper that they had sixty seconds to get into formation in front of the barracks.

"Full ACU uniform, boots, and canteen for a pleasant ten-mile run," the black hat said, "to earn your breakfast."

There was no shouting. There were no abusive attitudes like the stereotypical drill sergeants and drill instructors of boot camp in the Army and Marines. He spoke in nothing more than harshly whispered orders that the hearer had to consciously choose to follow or could easily ignore. Any deep sleepers, anyone who did not instantly wake on the whispered commands, would be quickly cut from the program. On that first morning, none missed the wake-up call. They rose and quickly dressed in the hazy mental fog of early morning, gathering out front in a sharp formation, three rows of twelve candidates, standing at attention awaiting the next orders. A total of thirty-one men and five women stood in the flat early-morning sun.

The sergeant came out in ACUs and combat boots, walking with a naturally confident stride that said he knew his place in the scheme of things and while he did not want to force anyone to join his team, he would have no mercy on any man or woman who failed to meet his standards. He stopped directly in front of the ranks of candidates and said in a calm, no stress voice, "We will run for a bit now. Follow me, in columns of two."

The sergeant turned, then without another word, took off at a fast jog. The candidates followed keeping pace as he led them around the perimeter of the camp. No cadence songs, no speeches, just the sound of their boots hitting the dirt road.

Ninety minutes and ten miles later, the Ranger candidates jogged back into town, near the barracks. The group was not as tightly formed as when they had left, some farther back than others, some struggling to stay on their feet by their own power. Ian led the pack with Tommie, Todd not far behind, Ben opting to stay beside Katarina in the next cluster, even though he looked barely winded. They arrived back at the barracks parade field, some panting hard from the exertion, some pressing fingers into their aching sides, others puking out what little contents they had in their guts, dry heaves nearly breaking a couple of them in half.

The scouts of Troop 104 made a good show of the first test. Not a single member had dropped or reacted more negatively than heavy breathing to the run, all having become accustomed to long runs and marches on the way to and from ambushes and raids. To a man, and woman, Troop 104 looked like they had merely endured a good hard jog through a park, as opposed to nine minutes per mile for ten miles straight. As the whole group pulled in, out of thirty-six volunteers, five, three men and two women, decided that the Rangers was not their cup of tea, rang the bell, and left the group for positions in the TPF.

The rest ran into the barracks, washed and changed their clothes, then sprinted to the communal dining hall before seven o'clock for a fifteen-minute breakfast. Once served, they scarfed down their food: oatmeal, eggs, and a sausage made from chicken and wild sage. After exactly fifteen minutes, they formed up outside and hurried over to the classroom building where they received four hours of lectures on military tactics, infantry skills, and map reading. The classroom training was followed by an hour of intense physical training, called 'PT' for short. Push-ups, pull-ups, sit-ups, interspersed with rapid-fire question-and-answer sessions over the topics they'd learned that morning. This was followed by a fifteen-minute lunch, and a two-hour session on the shooting range. A pattern similar to this was held every day for the entire seven-day period. The morning wake up time, and length of allowed sleep, grew both earlier and shorter each day until they were working on two hours of sleep a day for the last three days. The runs and PT sessions also grew in length and intensity each day until every candidate was working under complete exhaustion all day, every day.

By the end of the first week, the platoon of candidates had dropped from thirty-six to twenty-four. Those who rang the bell returning to the TPF until they could, if they wanted, try again in six months. When the platoon finished Indoc at the end of two weeks, only eighteen remained, a fifty-percent attrition rate.

The Indoc phase, as it was designed, was not so much an actual training period as it was a weeding-out period. While there was real training involved, the primary goal of Indoc was to verify that the candidates were both physically and mentally fit for the lifestyle demanded by membership in an elite military unit. It was a time to show that they knew basic military and woodsman arts, had the physical and mental endurance to keep up with an intense mission schedule, and had the capacity and determination to commit to violence of action when needed. They were observed for natural ability in tracking, stalking, and shooting, as well as psychological traits like calmness under pressure, the ability to make smart decisions when exhausted, and the will to commit to deadly violence when needed, without hesitation, while not condoning or accepting murder and general violence. They had to be hard and strong killers, but never psychopaths or sociopaths, traits not held among the common population. Every one of the members of Troop 104 who started the Indoc, eight in all, completed the selection and were accepted into the Rangers.

The following two weeks were spent being further evaluated as to any specific skills each person had. They sharpened their shooting and hand-to-hand combat skills, as well as orienteering, the ability to find one's way in the wilderness with or without a map and compass. Every candidate who finished was awarded an embroidered Ranger shoulder tab for their uniform shirt, similar to the ones the U.S. Army issued its Rangers, but with the words CHIKNIK RANGERS in black thread on an olive drab background. By the end of Indoc and training, the Stone brothers and their friends had impressed the leaders enough that they were immediately assigned to an active combat company. The group from 104 had been fully vetted and accepted.

CHAPTER 14

Youngmi

The convoy slowly pulled into the parking lot of the hotel, guards dismounting and adding themselves to the already tightly secure area. The general's VIP guests could now head to their rooms and prepare for dinner. The drive from Anchorage to Seward had taken more than twice as long to cover the 140 miles from the headquarters building on the former Fort Richardson than it would have before the war, about two hours during peace time, four hours and twenty minutes today.

The thirty-mile-per-hour average pace was due in part to concern over possible IEDs, Improvised Explosive Devices, hidden on the narrower sections of the highway, but in larger part to the desire of the VIP passengers to see wildlife along the highway. A pair of airborne drones flew ahead of them scanning the ground for potential traps and ambushes.

Seward is one of the most important commercial fishing ports in Alaska, bringing in nearly fourteen thousand tons of seafood annually before the war. Now, going into the third year of conflict, production was almost back to those normal levels. Regardless who is in charge, everybody has to eat. And most of the world loves seafood.

Renowned for some of the best salmon, halibut, rockfish, and even octopus in the world, the fishing tourism industry had mostly recovered shortly after open hostilities ended in the Kenai. Charter boats were running bounteous fishing trips out into the waters of Prince William Sound and the Gulf of Alaska just like before the war. At six o'clock every weekday morning, scores of customers waited on the city docks for their charter captain to pick them up and take them out for a full day of deep-sea fishing and whale watching. The main difference between before then and now was that back in the day, a majority of their customers were middle-age bucket listers and rich foreigners from all over the world, while the present customer base consisted mostly of military officers and rich foreigners who were members of the Communist Party of China and her allies.

"It was delightful listening to your stories, Comrade Li." Youngmi smiled brightly at him as the vehicle came to a halt. "You have such a wonderful family."

She gently patted the hand of the sixty-eight-year-old member of the Politburo, China's ruling committee. Li, vice-chairman of the military spending committee, had the appearance of a kindly grandfather and had spent a significant part of the trip telling them stories about his children and grandchildren.

"It is delightful to have such a lovely person to share them with," Li replied with a broad smile that deepened the lines on his face in a way that made Youngmi imagine a Hahoetal, a kind of traditional Korean theater mask with a comically exaggerated smiling face. She'd bought such a mask at Hahoe Folk Village on a high school field trip the year before she moved to America. That mask always gave her a feeling of good memories. It was still hanging on a wall in her house the day she'd abandoned it, and her life had so irrevocably changed.

The passenger door opened and General Zhang rose from the vehicle. The man who'd sat across from Zhang, General Fang

Ho Shin, the four-star in charge of Western Canada and Alaska commands of the People's Liberation Army, Zhang's direct commander, waved a hand for her to go next.

"After you, Ms. Ma," he said in a deep voice.

She gave a demure smile, slid across the bench careful to keep her skirt in place and rose, accepting Zhang's outstretched hand as she exited the vehicle. General Fang exited next. Rising to his full height, he matched Zhang's six-foot-tall frame, the pair dwarfing most of the other men around them. Unlike Zhang, who had a professorial, fatherly look about him much of the time, General Fang looked like the aging former athlete he was, a professional soccer player who had competed internationally before and during his army career. Tall, lean, and muscular, he had never lost that athlete's competitive edge. Despite being one year younger, he had earned his fourth star in the same year Zhang earned his second. Part jock, part academic champion, Fang was a powerful leader, with a vibrant personality who had risen to rank incredibly fast.

Comrade Li exited the opposite side door as did the fifth and final passenger was also a senior member of the politburo. Comrade Guo had a mousy sort of face and build that made Youngmi imagine Hitler's SS leader Heinrich Himmler. Guo did not look like a fun date at a party.

As the others got out of the vehicle, Youngmi scanned down the length of the row of vehicles. General Zhang's son, Po, a major in command of the special security team, commanded the hand-picked soldiers who moved into positions that provided a ring of security around the vaunted guests. Even with all the people and the massive military apparatus humming all around them, the natural beauty of the mountain and ocean vista from the steps of the hotel near the city harbor was breathtaking.

The waters of Resurrection Bay rolled slowly on the incoming tide, waves swishing gently against massive stones at the nearby shore. A family of otters floating on the swells nestled close, baby on the mother's belly, enjoying the sunny day. Tall mountain fjords surrounded the town, mile-thick glaciers glistening white against a perfect blue sky. Seward was indeed a beautiful city, even when the weather turned foul, which it often could. The city averaged about 72 inches of rain each year.

The forecast for the next three days though, was mostly sun, with no rain in sight. Perfect weather for the once-in-a-lifetime fishing charter they would be going on in the morning.

Then she noticed Colonel Ping step out of a TIGR several vehicles back, and the beauty of the scene dimmed around her. Since he had attempted to rape her in the headquarters building, she had tried her best to avoid him. The times they had run into each other, he had acted as if he did not suspect she knew it was him. She'd not seen him when he'd come up from behind and knocked her to her knees on the floor in the ladies' room, then attempted to raise her skirt and violate her. Po had heard her cries and rushed in. Ping ran as soon as the door started to open and jumped out a window, escaping. She had not seen his face, but she knew without a doubt it was him. His smell was burned into her memory, a sour sweat that reeked of rage and fear that permeated his presence no matter how much he bathed. It was as if his body was being dissolved in acid from the inside, the noxious fumes seeping through his pores.

Youngmi and Po had agreed not to tell anyone about what had happened, Po insisting that he would take care of the man. She did not know how he would do it, but the way the words came out, she had no doubt in his promise.

The party did not have to wait for check-in and were immediately escorted to their rooms, luggage already having arrived ahead of them. Zhang and Youngmi went into their top-floor suite, tipped the porter, and closed the door.

"Look at that view," Zhang said as he slid open the glass door that led to the narrow balcony. "This is simply breathtaking."

She stepped out beside him, leaning slightly into his arm. "Oh! Youngmi, look!"

He pointed to the sky, toward a massive bald eagle gliding in to take a rest on the top of the tallest spruce tree in the area. The eagle flapped its wings several times as it settled into position, its talons somehow grasping the very tip of the tree where it perched, muscular breast thrust out, wings folded. The majestic creature stood over a meter-tall, gazing out like a monarch surveying the realm. Its wings and body were dark, nearly black. Head with a snow-white mane of feathers, a wickedly sharp-looking yellow beak, and bright yellow eyes.

The bird snapped its head toward them, its unblinking stare boring directly into their own awestruck faces. Those eyes, electric, laser-like, seemed almost surreal, rendering the bird like some kind of mythical creature. It rustled its feathers, wings pumping slightly, stare never breaking from them. The air stood still.

Neither of them moved, not even daring to breathe lest the spell be broken. The eagle suddenly snapped its eyes away, locking onto something in the water beyond the rocky beach. It rose to its full height, gradually stretched its tremendous, nearly three-meter wingspan, loosed a powerful thrust of those wings, and dropped out of the tree. The raptor formed into a focused dive, body rigid as it became a blur, flashing across several hundred meters of water. It abruptly braked its wings, backpedaling, head stretching forward as it snatched at the water with its talons, powerful pinions rotating forward, pumping mechanically until the bird's feet rose from the water, a salmon nearly as large as itself wriggling in agony its grip.

The eagle skimmed only a meter above the water until it reached the beach and landed on the rocks with its catch. It jabbed the razor tip of its beak into the body of the fish several times, until it fell mostly still, talons pinning it to the ground. The fish succumbed to its wounds, suffocating in the air. Its tail fluttered lightly as its life force ebbed. The eagle ripped a strip of flesh from the salmon's hide and gracefully rose back into the air, flapping its wings with a satisfied ease as it ascended higher, returning to the nearby trees. It flew past the tall spruce from which it had launched its assault and continued to a large, deciduous tree, stark and leafless. Its upper branches split away from the main shaft, parallel to the ground and diverging from each other before twisting 90 degrees to stretch back skyward like fingers grasping at heaven. In the palm of the hand stood a twisted mass of sticks and moss. Two tufts of gray stretched up from the mass, oddly shaped large heads rose, gawky necks struggling to hold up the burden. The eagle descended, alighting on the edge of the nest. It set the strip of meat at its feet then proceeded to rip it into smaller pieces. It picked up the pieces and tenderly put them into its chicks' mouths.

Having fed the young ones, the eagle rose back to its full height, fluttered its wings a few times, then sealed them back against its body. It glanced first at the sea then at the mountain behind it, then slowly rotated its gaze until once again it rested on them. It stared for several seconds, turned back toward the sea, and let out a shriek. The cry echoed across the water, gradually fading.

They stood in silence, neither willing to let it be over. Zhang was the first to release his breath, a gentle hiss rushing between his lips. Youngmi, only now realizing she too had been holding her breath, exhaled long and slow. Her body hummed inside, a physical rush.

"That was," Zhang started, "the most," he paused again, eyes scanning the space around him, as if searching for the word, "incredible, thing I have ever seen."

He inhaled sharply and let it out with a whoosh.

"Absolutely incredible."

"It was," she said. "In almost thirty years up here, I have never seen that."

"It has to be a good omen."

"Yes," Youngmi said, wrapping her arms around his middle. "I'd say this means that we're going to have an amazing day of fishing tomorrow."

"Well, let us dress for dinner and tell the others of this most auspicious event," Zhang said, a twinkle in his eye.

Youngmi had been to Seward many times with her husband Brad, but they had never eaten at the Aurora Fjord restaurant. It was located eighteen hundred feet up the face of a mountain behind the hotel, reachable only by cable car gondolas. Zhang, General Fang, Comrade Li, and Comrade Guo, with their immediate staff and bodyguards, stood collectively silent as they stared out at the scenery. Other than Zhang, his son Po, and Youngmi herself, this was a first-time experience of Alaska for everyone else in the gondola. The vehicle slowed, swaying slightly as it came to a gentle stop. The door hissed open and the awed occupants stepped out onto the landing platform.

Inside, they had an even better view than on the ride up. The restaurant jutted from the face of the mountain in a half circle with a full view of everything from the mountains to the northeast to the vast emptiness of the northern edge of the Gulf of Alaska in the southwest. Twice awarded 'The World's 50 Best Restaurants' and several James Beard awards, as well as three Michelin stars, it was the kind of restaurant whose pre-war clientele jetted across the globe just to spend three to four hours consuming fifteen to twenty-four courses while listening to speeches by cash-bloated oil magnates and penny-stock billionaires. Open to the public only when there were no reserved parties, once or twice a week at most, it was the kind of restaurant, so uncommon for Alaska as to be unique, where dinner for two costs upward of a thousand dollars, and usually had to be pre-paid months in advance just to secure the reservation.

A few months before the war, Youngmi had done some web-design work for the owners of the Aurora Fjord, advertising certain features for a select clientele. One of the most amazing things about the restaurant she remembered reading, was that the three-hundred-foot-long window contained no seams of any kind and was built to withstand a direct hit by a five-hundred-kilogram explosive projectile. That very specific selling point, and the fact that the website itself was accessible by invitation only, gave her the sense that the target audience included world leaders and perhaps even some real-life Bond villains.

For those reasons, she had never seen it from the inside. General Zhang's staff had the entire facility booked for the next several days. A party of fifty diners, every evening for three days. In pre-war days, the dinner tab for this weekend would have been about equal to the annual income from her business. Under Chinese rule, the price for such luxury was undoubtedly higher. She wondered how this squared up with communist philosophy in the eyes of comrades Li and Guo. This restaurant was definitely a bourgeoisie venture in that regard.

"This is a truly stunning view," General Fang said. "Probably the best I have seen in this entire continent, and I have been to most of it by now."

Everyone took their seats. The handful of senior colonels and the various staff members invited to the dinner were seated in appropriate groupings near the head table. Youngmi personally ensured that Ping would not be sitting anywhere near where she would be. He was assigned a seat as far to the edge and facing away from Youngmi as possible in hopes of keeping his leering eyes focused on the ocean and his own tablemates.

The two generals joined Li and Guo along with Youngmi and a trio of very attractive young female officers from head-quarters, to ensure she was not the only woman at the dinner. Youngmi had been asked to hand pick the women, who were to be captains at least, and women she knew to be conversationally adept and exceptionally bright and confident. The three women she picked had to meet some specific criteria based upon profiles of each of the three special guests.

Captain Hong Fan Hua was the twenty-eight-year-old chief of the IT department for the headquarters. She had been Mai's roommate since they occupied the headquarters building. Fan Hua was physically attractive in what the internet previously referred to as 'sexy-nerd' girl style. While most definitely strik-ing to the eyes of any man of most any ethnic background, the primary quality for which she was selected to be General Fang's companion for this evening's dinner was his love of all things related to strategy, particularly games. In the two-plus years Youngmi had known her, Fan Hua had created a small and lucra-tive business making puzzle and game apps for mobile phones in her spare time, puzzles that were slowly becoming the go-to place for hardcore math nerds and gamers. She was also known to be extremely good at mahjongg, holding international standing as a competitive player.

Sitting beside the grandfatherly Comrade Li was Major Ming Pei-Pei. Thirty-one-year-old Pei-Pei was the Senior Records Management Officer for General Zhang's command. She held a master's degree in library sciences from Shanghai Jiao Tong University, ranked as the top school in all of China. Those few who attended Shanghai Jiao Tong University nearly always ended up with senior level party or government positions. Her military job held no command authority, only supervising a staff of one lower ranking officer and ten enlisted clerks, but it performed a bureaucratic position that ensured nearly all papers and documentation were managed in an orderly filing system both digitally and in physical copy. This also meant she had one of the highest security clearances and that she knew when and when not to speak on sensitive material. She also had a sharp wit and was very popular for telling stories of ancient Chinese historical lore among her friends. Pei-Pei maintained a blog online dedicated to the subject of the historical use of tea in China, a surprisingly interesting subject when she got her spin on it.

Narrow face, thin lips, and barely a visible line on his pale face, Comrade Guo was joined by Captain Han Mi Ching, General Zhang's personal secretary's assistant. Very small and petite, twenty-nine-year-old Mi Ching was excellent at intelligent discourse, was especially well versed in communist philosophy, and had a degree in public speaking and modern Chinese political rhetoric. On top of those admirable traits was the fact that she was a near clone of the famous Chinese movie star Zhang Ziyi, considered one of the most beautiful Chinese actresses of the twenty-first century.

None of the women were expected to provide anything of a sexual nature to the senior members and General Fang. Their presence at the meal was for purely conversational and companionable purposes.

The party ordered drinks and were almost immediately brought the first of what turned out to be a twenty-course tasting menu of local delicacies, as well as inspirations based upon each of the senior guests' 'likes profile.' Youngmi had eaten some very fine meals in her life and eaten in restaurants one or two pegs below the Aurora Fjord, but she had never seen this many incredibly tasty bites of food cross before her. Seafood, the local wild game, the abundant vegetables, both sea- and land-based, and the unbelievably satisfying desserts, all were perfectly paired with wine or a spirit that accentuated the flavors in each dish.

As the last of deserts were removed, a final tray of traditional Chinese green tea was brought out. The waiter set the cups before each of the dignitaries and their companions, as his assistant set a tray on a stand next to the table. With a pair of ornamental tongs, he reached into a small open bowl and pinched out an amount of tea leaves, gently dropping them into the open top of a fine China teapot. Pei-Pei reached over and picked up a few individual tea leaves from the bowl in her fingers. She held the delicate dried green leaves, curled into a spiral by the special drying procedure, and told its story.

"This tea is now called Bi Luo tea, because many many years ago it used to be processed at a nunnery at Bi Luo near Dongting mountain region near Lake Tai, Jiangsu. The name was given by Emperor Kang Xi, fourth emperor of the Qing Dynasty. It is said that there was a very delicious tea grown near the peak of Bi Luo Mountain, where local villagers often picked the fresh tea leaves and roasted them. They called their tea Xia Sha Ren Xiang, which literally means 'scary fragrance.' It got this name because once a young woman had run out of room in her harvesting basket and stuffed a large amount of the tea between her breasts. Activated by her body heat, the tea leaves let off a very strong odor that surprised her. Once, during his incognito travel to the south, Emperor Kang Xi was offered the Xia Sha Ren Xiang tea. After drinking the tea, the emperor was impressed by the special fragrance and taste. It may be prudent to note here that it was no longer processed between the breasts of young women of the area," she said, being rewarded with a laugh from all around the table, even Guo.

"He thought its name too common to match its high quality," Pei-Pei continued, "so the emperor renamed it "Bi Luo Chun" (literally 'jade green spiral spring'). According to an ancient legend the emperor had learned as a young man, a kind and pretty girl named Bi Luo fell in love with a young fisherman named Ah Xiang. Unfortunately, an evil dragon wanted the girl as its concubine. To save her, Ah Xiang went to fight the dragon. By the end of the battle, Ah Xiang became unconscious from excessive bleeding. Frantic, Bi Luo climbed up the mountain to find some herbal medicine. She saw a cluster of tea bushes and picked the leaves to boil them. After drinking the soup, Ah Xiang recovered. Unfortunately, Bi Luo died from extreme exhaustion. Ah Xiang cremated his true love and put her ashes under the tea bush she had used to save his life. Surprisingly, thereafter, the tea bushes in that area all thrived. The emperor therefore named the high-quality tea Bi Luo Chun to honor the girl."

"That is a fascinating story," said Comrade Li. "I love hearing such history, and you are wonderful storyteller, Pei-Pei. When my grandchildren are old enough for college, I hope they will have teachers like you to teach them our rich history."

"Oh!" Fang pointed out the window to the south, excitement in his eyes.

The others at the table follow his gaze to see a pod of whales breaching the water's surface, distant swells one after another, spouting jets of white spray upward in a random sequence, like a steam-powered calliope. Massive flat tails rose and slapped the water as they dove below the surface, reemerging moments later in a powerful hypnotic rhythm of motion that went on for a great distance before the whales followed the leader deep below the surface, not rising again within sight.

"That!" Fang shouted. "This!" He waved his arms. "These are some of the reasons I am glad *we* got this part of the beautiful state of Alaska and not those damned Russians!"

"General Fang," Guo said, "surely you do not disparage our allies."

"Disparage them?" Fang raised a challenging eyebrow. "Hell yes, I disparage them. Their General Brozhnenko took me for one-million-yuan last week at mahjongg during the Central Command Generals Conference. Between him and General Johnson, I was robbed!"

Youngmi had heard about this American general. Alfred Ryngold Johnson, Lieutenant General, formerly of the U.S. Army and lately of the People's Army, had been the deepest of deep sleeper cell members. As the three-star general serving in the position of the Director of the Joint Staff, JS, he was in a position directly under the Chairman of the Joint Chiefs of Staff, JCS, the committee of generals that controlled the entire U.S. military. In that capacity, he had access to more sensitive information than any deep-cover spy any enemy had ever planted before. He had even more and stronger information than the intelligence agent from the National Security Agency, the infamous NSA, who several years before the war had divulged a large trough of classified documents to those same enemies that now stood on our doorstep. Johnson outdid that agent by the fact that he had not only raw data from intelligence sources, the position of Director of the Joint Staff gave him nearly unfettered access to any and all classified information, and regularly put him in the personal presence of the president and highest-ranking senators and congressmen.

He not only had data but was able to manipulate how the nation's leadership reacted to events. Johnson had dirt that could stir up enough drama that could bring down the most powerful men in the U.S. Born and raised in a family of devoted closet communist agents, he was able to set in motion things that helped bring victory to the invading armies. Through politically motivated social experimentation, lowering of physical requirements, poorly managed expenditures—including steering purchases directly to Chinese manufactured components that contained backdoor hardware to give the People's Army a way to bring down our technology in a blink of an eye—Lieutenant General Alfred Ryngold Johnson played a very major role in ensuring the United States would not be ready when his comrades came to call.

Youngmi knew these things because it had been the talk of the table at a special dinner with the command staff and a small cadre of generals who'd come for an inspection the year before. They had talked about the man as if he were a hero, which to them, of course he was. Johnson's lifelong duplicity had made their jobs as invaders a whole lot easier, which meant a whole lot of them were alive that would not have been had a significant part of their enemy's military not been blindsided by one of their own commanders. Johnson was a kind of deity among them by the way they talked. She, of course, did not share their warm fuzzies.

"They had to have been cheating," Fang continued. "Americans and Russians should never be able to beat a Chinese man at mahjongg." He leaned over and gave a polite bow to Youngmi. "Present company excepted, my lady, I am sure you would best any of us at mahjongg if we dared play you."

"Would you believe me, General," Youngmi replied, "if I told you that my uncle, in South Korea in the 1980s, owned several mahjongg gaming establishments near Seoul?"

"Really?" Fang's eyebrow went up. "So, you must be very good at the game yourself then?"

"I practically lived in one of his shops for several years," Youngmi said. "I can hold my own pretty well, but I would never wish to play someone like you."

"Oh really?" Fang seemed truly intrigued. "Are you saying you are too good for me?"

"Oh no, quite the opposite actually. I would be no match for someone like you as I have not played in years. But," Youngmi pointed toward Fan Hua on his right, "that young lady next to you happens to be an internationally ranked competitor in mahjong."

Fang's eyes stretched wide as he slowly took in the attractive young woman to his left. "I have been chatting with you for more than two hours and you failed to mention this to me, Fan Hua?"

"I did not think it prudent to discuss such things with a man of your high standing, sir," Fan Hua said, her voice a small, humble sound, like a subservient young girl.

"Well, would you be willing to accept my challenge to a match," Fang said, "just for fun of course? No money."

"I am flattered, sir, and yes, I am very willing to accept such a challenge," Fan Hua said. "But, I am afraid to say that I must require one qualification before I commit."

"Require of a four-star general?" Zhang said, eyebrows arched high. "You are a very confident young officer now, aren't you, Captain?"

"It is alright, General Zhang," Fang said, waving a hand in dismissal. He gave a twisted smile and playful look at Fan Hua. "I am fully and truly intrigued now. Just what would this requirement be?"

The captain leaned close to him, put her hand on his knee, and said in a sultry voice that was anything but subservient young girl, "That there will be no bad feelings when the general is trounced by a girl."

"Ladies and gentlemen," Fang announced to the room, "I do believe the gauntlet has been thrown. This should prove quite interesting."

Due to the early-morning fishing trip—they had to meet the boats at the dock at six AM—the dinner party had officially broken up by eight. Before it was over, Fang and Fan Hua had managed to play one game of mahjongg on a set of tiles that one of the general's staff had produced. The man apparently brought one everywhere he went just in case. She had beat him soundly after a hard-fought match. After that one game, Zhang and Youngmi retired back to their room on the first tram back to the hotel.

Zhang climbed into bed, brushing his hand against the base of the touch-sensitive bedside lamp to turn it off. He pulled the fresh-smelling linen sheet and down-filled duvet up to his chest as he lay back into the pillow. Youngmi rolled into his shoulder, pulling his arm around her and nestling into his chest. The scent that came from his body was intoxicating, a combination of just-showered freshness, new sweat, and something else. A light musky odor that made her feel safe, at peace, secure. She wondered if that last bit was the actual aroma of testosterone. Brad had had a similar smell when clean. Both of them were strong. Both masculine, but not overpowering. The scent of the only two men she'd ever loved was, in her mind, the scent of manliness.

They lay silently for a long time, neither sleeping. She gently stroked his belly with her fingertips. He stroked her shoulder. Both staring into the darkness, deep thoughts swirling at the surface of the minds.

At length, Zhang sucked in a long, lung-filling breath, held it for a count of five, then let it out equally slowly.

"I cannot stop thinking about that eagle this afternoon," he said, voice vibrating in his chest, the rumble calming and peace giving. Youngmi wrapped her arms tightly around him, drawing closer.

"It was beautiful," she murmured.

"I cannot help but think it is an omen," he continued. "A very good omen."

Youngmi took a deep breath of her own. The meaning of their shared vision from earlier—a vision was the only thing her mind could reconcile it to be—indeed held meaning in her mind too.

"What kind of omen do you think it portends?" she asked.

"It is obvious, isn't it?"

"What is obvious to your military mind," she said, "may not be so much to my web-designer mind."

"Maybe so," he said. He lay quietly for a moment, allowing several breaths to flow in and out before speaking again.

"In my mind, my military mind as you put it, I see it this way. The eagle represents me, the chicks my army and the people of this land I have been placed in authority over. The salmon represents the resistance. We were being shown that we will be victorious in ending this bloodshed and caring for the soldiers and people of the land in peace."

"Oh," she said. "I thought it only meant we'd have a good fishing trip tomorrow."

He let out a laugh. "Really? That was a pretty impressive display for whatever god-like entities there may be out there just to bless an overpriced fishing charter."

"It could be," she said, her voice spreading in an audible smile. "But I agree with you. It was far too impressive to be something that simple."

None of the other guests at dinner reported seeing having seen anything like what they had seen. They all shared having seen fish jumping or eagles flying, but not one of their stories told of what she and Zhang had shared. It was as if the whole thing had indeed been a vision sent from God. A vision with a much deeper reason than mere entertainment.

"Yes, far too impressive." He stroked her shoulder gently. "The fact that no one else reported having seen it during dinner leads me to believe that if there is a message to be had from it, it is for us alone to see."

Youngmi blinked in surprise, her eyelashes fluttering against his chest.

"What?" he responded to the tickle of tiny hairs against his chest.

"That is exactly, literally exactly, what I was just thinking about the others."

"Even more auspicious," Zhang replied with a short laugh. "The true meaning of this vision is verified even more! You are such a good person to have around, my very own good luck charm."

"Is that all I am to you?" Youngmi said. "A lucky charm?"

"Oh no," Zhang said, rolling onto his side to face her, "that is only the tiniest facet of you. You are like a diamond, that every time I look at you, I see some new reflection of the light that is around you. I could never limit you to a single description of any kind."

She smiled and let herself be wrapped in his arms. The heat from his body filled her with warmth. Within a few minutes, his breathing slowed to the unmistakable rhythm of sleep. She stayed there, eyes open in the darkness.

The eagle vision definitely had a meaning; she could not escape the truth of its meaning. She was shocked at how different Zhang had seen things but understood that such was the way men thought in her experience. Always wanting to win, at all costs. Not seeing the destruction they leave in their wake. What they leave for the women and children, their widows and orphans, to clean up and bring back to normal.

Youngmi was saved at the start of the war, and plunged into her new, unwanted life, given access that no other non-Chinese person had in this entire theater of the war. She was to use her special situation to feed and care for her people, her Alaskan people. She was to be strong, but the lives of so many others depended on her to do the right thing. The vision was her call from God to do everything in her power to take care of the people whose lives she'd been entrusted with.

CHAPTER 15

Youngmi

Youngmi rose early, opening the door at just after four a.m. to receive the room service breakfast she had ordered for herself and the general. As the small cart was wheeled in the sound of a door opening a few rooms down the hall caught her attention. She glanced that way and saw Fan Hua emerge from General Fang's room. The young captain pulled her shoes on then leaned in toward the door. Her face obscured by the entryway, the sound of a tender kiss and whispered giggles made its way down the hall to Youngmi's ears nonetheless. Backing into her room to tip the room service attendant before Fan Hua re-emerged, Youngmi wondered if she had made a big mistake pairing the attractive computer nerd with the powerful, and unmarried, general.

As the attendant wheeled his now empty cart out the door, Youngmi caught the sound of hurried footsteps as the mahjongg champion walked swiftly down the hall to the elevators. She closed the room door, locking the chain and deadbolt, and returned to the small table where their morning feast had been set out. A large carafe of black coffee stood on the table between their place settings, sparkling white ceramic mugs with the logo of the People's Army Alaska Command emblazoned on them on either side of it.

Zhang stepped out of the bathroom, body steaming from the hot shower he'd just taken. White clouds billowed behind him as he strode to the table wearing a hotel bathrobe made of luxuriously thick cotton. He crossed the room and sat in the chair opposite Youngmi as she poured coffee for them both, light roast, black, no sugar. The way they both liked it. Brad had always liked his coffee made with those awful burnt to cinders French roast beans. It smelled like a campfire every morning when he made his coffee. She preferred hers from much more gently roasted beans, where it looked more like strong tea than motor oil. They had needed to have two separate coffee makers on the counter in order to share morning coffee together before he left for the office, and she started schooling the boys and working on her own web-design business.

Zhang reached around behind himself and pulled on the chain that opened the Venetian blinds covering the sliding glass doors onto the balcony from which they'd watched the eagle the day before. The late summer sun was already lighting the morning sky, although it had not yet broken the horizon to the east. He glanced up to the tree that looked like a hand reaching heavenward but saw no sign of life around the eagle's nest yet.

The sound of metal utensils clinking against fine china brought his attention back to the table. Youngmi had ladled a large portion of steaming hot grits onto his plate. She set two dollops of freshly churned butter on top and placed a pair of softboiled eggs into the center of the grits. Several slices of bacon lay across a small plate beside the main course.

"You knew to order my favorite," Zhang said, taking her hand and kissing the back of her fingers. "Did I ever tell you about the first time I ate this type of food for breakfast?"

"No, you didn't," Youngmi said.

"I was temporarily assigned to The Presidio military language school in Monterey, California as part of my doctoral thesis in the nineties when I was a senior captain. I was part of an exchange duty with the American army, where they sent several officers to train with ours for a few months or a year, and we would send several here for the same period."

"What year were you there?" she asked.

"1991," he said.

"Wow," she said, eyes wide. "We may have seen each other then."

"Really?"

"Yes, my…" Youngmi stopped, suddenly unsure of how to say what she'd started, "…um…my husband, was a student there for a few months in '91. We lived in a short-term apartment just off post for most of that summer."

"Very interesting," Zhang said. "Which language was he studying?"

"I don't recall exactly, he wasn't allowed to say at the time," she said, feeling strange to be so easily talking of her husband's life with her lover. "I think it was some sort of Eastern European language for a deployment his unit took a few months after we returned to Pendleton. He was injured before they deployed and I never learned where they'd been sent."

"Pendleton," Zhang said, an admiring frown stretching his mouth briefly. "Your husband was a Marine then?"

"Yes, he was, a Force Recon Marine, actually," she said, a bit of pride rising in her chest at the thought of her once young husband.

"Impressive," he said. "You pick tough men."

"Or they pick me." She smiled. It bothered her that she didn't feel guilty talking about Brad with this man. She decided to change the subject back to where he'd been going. "You were saying about how you first tried grits."

"Oh yes," he exclaimed, swallowing a mouthful of coffee. "While there, I became friends with an American captain named Marvin Butts. You would not believe the amount of jokes that man had to endure his entire life." Zhang smiled as he scooped a spoonful of grits and egg-yolk into his mouth and swallowed, eyes rolling up, lids fluttering in pleasure at the sensation.

"Marvin was from Alabama," he continued, "and insisted that I try both this soft-boiled eggs and grits dish and his personal favorite, fried chicken and waffles. I could never get my taste buds around covering delicious fried chicken with sickeningly sweet syrup. But this," he scooped another mouthful, this time adding a bite of crispy bacon to the mix, and spoke around the food, "this dish stuck with me. I have loved grits ever since that trip."

"Did you keep in touch with your friend Captain Butts?" Youngmi asked.

"We did for many years," Zhang said. "He actually visited me in China twice. Once, a couple years after our time at school, and again when he was stationed in Afghanistan during the American war there."

"Do you think he is still serving the American army now?"

"No," Zhang said. "Sadly, he was killed by a Taliban bomb a few weeks after we last met."

"That is very sad," she said.

"It is, but it is also the nature of our chosen careers as soldiers." Zhang swallowed a large mouthful of coffee and let out a satisfied breath. "But that is too depressing a path to go down today. For today, we shall conquer the Great Emperor Halibut of the Sea!"

He raised his fork like a weapon, jabbing it victoriously skyward.

The group arrived at the city docks at just before six in the morning, congregating around two moderately large charter boats, the *Eye of Odin* and the *Ice Dog*, kitted up with deep-sea fishing gear and American crews, attended by a handful of Chinese minders. Zhang and Youngmi joined the important guests on the *Eye of Odin* with a small number of staff and four of the colonels, including Ping. The bulk of the staffers, those who had been granted permission to go fishing, were on the *Ice Dog*. Two small naval harbor patrol boats, armed with a pair of .50 caliber machine guns, anti-ship and anti-missile rockets, as well as sophisticated anti-submarine measures, and a squad of a dozen heavily armed marines each accompanied the pleasure craft.

It took nearly two hours for the boats to reach the fishing grounds. Some spent their time watching the scenery go by, the occasional wildlife coming into view in the distance. Others snoozed, trying to gain back some of the sleep they had missed while continuing the after party at the restaurant. Fang dozed lightly, leaning against a window. Fan Hua sat beside him, losing a battle against sleep that had her slowly leaning into the general's shoulder as she succumbed.

The sleepiness dissipated instantly when the boat came to a stop and the anchor was dropped.

"Here we are, folks," the captain said through a translator, his weathered features shaped into a polite facsimile of a happy entrepreneurial boat captain that likely hid a deep desire to throw every Chinese soldier on the boat into the ocean. "My crew and I will load bait on your hooks and show you how to set the rigs to catch halibut. That is what we are fishing for at this spot, halibut. Our sonar shows that there is a good-sized group of them about four hundred feet below us. Be advised that pulling up a halibut of any size all the way from the bottom is strenuous work. If it is a big fish, it will be a whole lot of strenuous work. The average size of the halibut is about thirty pounds or around thirteen kilograms, making it the biggest flatfish in the world. That said, there have been some halibut caught here that weighed over five hundred pounds and eight feet long."

The captain let the impression of what that size meant settle in for a moment before continuing. He knew he'd hit his mark when some of them started talking and pointing to the space available on the deck between them all. They were realizing that a fish that size would fill a large part of space they were standing in.

"That's right," the captain went on. "As you are imagining, a fish that size would be very dangerous to have flopping around on deck; therefore, any fish over one hundred pounds need to be shot before we can bring it on board. Due to security precautions, my crew will not be allowed to do that, as we have no firearms. Therefore, one or more of your security personnel on board will need to be ready in the event we need him."

Major Po nodded his assent and gave a quick look at a couple of his soldiers who nodded back in acknowledgment.

"When a fish is on your line, it feels like someone is trying to yank the pole from you. When you feel this, start reeling it up and call out saying 'fish on.' You need to get the fish up to the surface of the water, but one of the crew will help bring the fish into the boat."

The action started moments after the first lines dropped to the bottom of the water, five-pound lead weights carrying hand-sized hooks with half a herring run through as bait.

"Fish on!" cried Comrade Li as his pole dipped, its tip nearly touching the water as he pulled back with all his might.

"Steady! Steady, comrade," said the crewman in accented Chinese. Anyone in any business these days had to learn at least some Chinese. But in a business like this, where Chinese officers were the only ones that could afford such a luxury as a fishing charter, the only crews that would have any kind of success had to be able to communicate with their customers quickly and succinctly both for their best chance of success with the fish and for their safety.

"Do not lean so far over the railing comrade, Li," he said. "You do not want to fall over into this freezing water."

"I may not look like it, young man," Li said between long pulls on his fishing rod, slowly bringing the beast to the surface, "but I grew up on the sea. My father owned a fleet of fishing vessels in the East China Sea." Another pause to pull the fish another ten feet, then he spoke as he reeled in more line. "I was on boats much smaller than this in the open ocean. I do indeed know that the ocean is a very unforgiving place."

"Yes, comrade," said the crewman, "but the East China Sea is far south from the waters of the Gulf of Alaska." He pointed to the distance where a large white object glistened in the sun. "That berg over there is the size of a twenty-story building, the vast majority of it being under the water. Bergs like that are all over up here, like ice cubes in the drink of the gods. This water stays only a few degrees above freezing and could mean death from hypothermia in minutes for someone who went overboard, even if they were rescued."

He paused as Li struggled. The elder's grip slipped on the reel, releasing a long run of line before he could click the lock back down.

"Got it, sir?"

"Yes, yes," Li replied with a laugh. "That's what I get for bragging about my fishing skills."

"Well, sir, like I said," the crewman returned to his previous topic, "you don't want to fall into this water. More often than not, the icy water causes its human victims to seize up from the cold and they sink like rocks below the surface before they can be hauled out. I've seen it happen three times while doing this for a living. Sometimes the bodies wash up ashore near enough to Seward that someone will find them and they can be recovered and given a proper burial. A lot of times though, they're never seen again, having become part of the food chain."

The crewman realized he'd crossed a line when he saw the look of alarm Comrade Li and the soldier both gave him.

"Not on this boat," he quickly added. "No one has ever fallen off this boat. And those other times were over a period of twenty years too."

"Glad to hear no one has fallen from here," Li said, "but I will be very careful."

The elderly politician kept his full attention on the task of bringing up the fish, grunting with exertion as he slowly reeled in the creature. The closer it came to the surface, the more it fought, its weight bending his pole nearly in half. The crewman and one of the security soldiers stood on either side of him. The young soldier's eyes were wide with anticipation.

"Don't help me unless I fall overboard," he called out. "I'm going to beat this monster!"

"Go, Comrade Li!" Youngmi cried out from close by, cheering him on. "You can do it!"

The boat rose on a high swell, sending a tickle through her belly that increased in intensity as it dropped back into a trough between what the captain had called two- to three-foot waves. It felt more and more like a roller coaster to Youngmi. While the day had turned out to be beautifully sunny, the area where Prince William Sound meets the Gulf of Alaska is always choppy. This day's seas were somewhat calmer than the past few weeks had been according to the first mate of the vessel as he baited hooks for some of the others.

She took a few tentative steps closer to Comrade Li, hoping to watch him pull in his fish. The boat rolled back the other direction and she grabbed the rail to keep from sliding back the way she'd come. The wave passing under them, the boat rolled the other way, sending her up against the portside railing, another body slid into position right behind her, a hand brushing against her rear end. She thought nothing of it, as the pitching motion would make it hard for anyone to keep from touching another person.

Then she caught the smell of the man behind her. Sour, decaying. The odor of spite and hatred. She glanced back. Ping smiled apologetically.

"I am sorry, Ms. Ma," he said. "I am not a sailor. Hard to keep my legs under me as this ship tosses us around."

She gave him a look that let him know she did not believe it was an accident. A loud shout followed by whoops and yells erupted as Li's fish peeked above the water and its true size was finally revealed. The crewman leaned over the railing holding a large metal hook on a pole that he slid into the fish's gills and heaved up hand over hand. Seeing the strain on his face one of the other crewmen joined him. Half out of the water, the giant fish thrashed its body, whacking its tail against the hull of the boat, sending a shockwave through the feet of everyone on board.

"Shoot it!" the lead man shouted to the soldier. "Shoot it before it pulls us over."

The soldier pulled out his sidearm, aimed at a point behind the weird-looking eyes, eyes that were both on the same side of the fish's head, and pulled the trigger. The fish instantly fell limp. The crewmen held the beast as another man dragged a line from an overhead boom arm mounted over the cabin. They hooked the fish into the line, walked it to the stern of the boat, and winched it aboard, letting it hang over the back deck as the captain read off the weight from a panel on his console.

"298 pounds!" his voice exclaimed. "Ladies and gentlemen, Comrade Li's fish is an actual record for the *Eye of Odin*."

The boat rolled again as the passengers all cheered for Li. The old man proudly posed for a picture beside his fish, holding on to a post so as not to fall into it as they rolled back again.

Youngmi felt another touch against her body that seemed more than accidental, the unmistakable shape of a hand slid across her lower back dipping to again brush against her bottom. Turning, she found Ping nearby behind her, looking the other way.

Like some naughty schoolboy, she thought. *I am going to tell the general. I will not stand for his rudeness anymore.*

Ping quickly moved off, joining the others in grabbing their own poles to get in on the action. For the next several hours, cries of 'fish on' rang out both from the deck of the *Eye of Odin* and across the water from the *Ice Dog*. No one else managed to bring up anything even remotely close to the behemoth Li had dragged up from the ocean depths. The next largest was only sixty-five pounds taken by Colonel Gao, commander of the infantry brigade soon to be sent to take over the Palmer FOB. Most of the halibut taken were, as the captain had stated they would be, in the neighborhood of thirty pounds give or take.

When the per person limit of two halibut was taken, the crew switched them over to the tackle and bait for salmon and rockfish, which were pulled in with a similar abundance. Most everyone had a pole in hand at any given time, even Youngmi, Fan Hua, and the other two women on board. Comrade Guo even cracked an uncharacteristic smile as he was photographed with a large yellow rockfish hanging from each hand, Mi Ching kneeling in front of him with a large silver salmon in her hands.

Ping did not come into physical contact with Youngmi again for the remainder of the trip, but several times she caught him watching her from across the boat. His leering stare eliciting a queasiness in her gut that left her feeling like she needed a bath in bleach to clean off an imagined slime that grew from his gaze. She actively made it a point to avoid looking in any direction he might be.

As the poles and tackle were being stowed away, the passengers made their way back into the large cabin for the long ride home. Youngmi wanted to get into her seat where General Zhang would join her, hoping he would come quickly to act as a barrier between her and Ping so she would not even have to look at his face. She took her seat and glanced back through the door to see Zhang standing on the rear deck laughing with Colonel Gao and General Fang, Fan Hua standing beside the latter, as if the last twenty-four hours had seen her become his personal consort.

Ping's face suddenly came into view, making his way toward the cabin. Eyes on her, he made a beeline straight for where she sat. Just as he was about to enter the space, a tall, dark figure appeared between them. Major Zhang Po's black uniform rendering him as a muscular shadow, he cut off Ping's view of her.

"Get out of my way, Major," Ping snapped. "I want to sit down."

A couple of others passed from behind her and went out the same door Po had blocked the colonel at. Youngmi whispered a quick thank you to Po and slipped out of her seat. She hustled further up toward the bow and walked out a different door onto a side deck. She took a set of stairs up to the second-level observation deck, then over and back down, returning to the main deck several yards behind Ping. She looked back toward the cabin. Ping stood inside, an angry look of frustration obvious on his face.

Po stood a few feet away from the door he had blocked. They made eye contact for a brief moment. He gave a barely discernable nod in her direction then turned and started speaking to one of his sergeants that stood nearby. Ping made no more attempts at contact for the remainder of the trip back to Seward.

CHAPTER 16

Brad

On the scheduled day, forty-eight hours after their arrival, Brad's team watched as several groups filed in. Most were cautious, hanging back in the trees as they arrived, watching and observing before stepping into the meeting area. A few others strode directly in, confident in the idea that there was no danger, no potential setup. As they came in throughout the morning, some of them greeted the others with friendly gestures, handshakes, smiles, even a few man-hugs. Some of the others, not so much, holding themselves back.

The groups mostly ranged in size from five to ten men, several female soldiers with them as well. It became quickly apparent, as Brad observed their interactions, that some of the officers considered themselves to be superior to the other leaders. Over the following twenty-four hours, several more small groups showed up, coming from different trails, some walking right over the positions from which Brad's men and the other professionals were silently observing the meeting area.

Late that afternoon, the angry squirrel chirped again and the group of professionals that had camped beside his own men rose from their hides like demons crawling out of the abyss, dark shapes that looked more goblin than human. They crossed most of the distance to the camp hunched in a shooter's crouch, weapons up, stalking slowly toward the main group. No one among the waiting seemed to notice them moving on the camp. As they emerged from the trees into the clearing, they shed the hoods of their ghillie suits, heads suddenly becoming visible. Gasps of surprise were matched by some reaching for their weapons. The leader of the professionals stopped and raised his hand, making a sideways waving gesture. His men dropped their weapons to low guard, pointing the barrels to the ground at an angle from which they could swiftly be raised again, trigger fingers out of and across the trigger guard, at the ready, a twitch away from the kill position.

"We're here for the meeting," called out the leader. His voice was strong, commanding, not forceful, but full of a clear and natural violence. "From the Trapper Creek area."

Some of the others relaxed a bit as they were able to focus on the bearded faces of the men that approached. These men with their illegal facial hair were definitely not Chinese. Those who had also dealt with the Russian soldiers to the east, men who could easily blend in with most Alaskan soldiers, were less ready to put down their weapons.

The leader of the professionals raised both hands and dropped the green wool blanket that had been covering his shoulders, revealing a dull black leather biker jacket. He looked about the same age as Brad but exuded a much more sinister toughness by several degrees. The left breast pocket of his jacket held a patch, a black triangle with white letters spelling '1%er' on it. On the right, he wore a blue hexagonal shield with five stars encircling a skull on a red diamond. The emblem of the U.S. Marine Raiders that had been resurrected in the later years of the wars in Iraq and Afghanistan. Brad's grandfather had been an original Marine Raider in World War Two, under Lieutenant Colonel Evans

Carlson, fighting his way north through the Pacific campaign with one of the most violent units in American military history. His granddad had been a serious bad-ass, and his Raider stories had been part of the reason Brad himself had joined the Marines and become his era's Raider equivalent as a Force Recon Marine. The Raiders had been disbanded toward the end of WWII, as many Marine leaders felt that having a unit that was considered "the elite of the elite" was redundant. The Raider designation had been taken away until more than sixty years later, when it was resurrected by the great-grandsons of the original Raiders in 2006 as MARSOC, Marine Special Operations Command, which was created to provide a maritime special forces unit with duties somewhere between those of the Navy SEALS and Army Green Berets. Their primary missions were piracy interdiction and shock and awe operations within one hundred miles of the coast. As he watched the leader of the professionals, Brad remembered his own special operations deployment aboard the USS *Peleliu* (LHA 5), an amphibious assault ship that during his tour was diverted to the evacuation of American citizens from the Philippines during the eruption of Mount Pinatubo. His recon team was assigned to form port security against possible terrorist attacks during the American evacuation. Lucky for him, none of the terrorist organizations had time to try to kill Americans while the island was blowing up. Some of his teammates though, especially those who were still in when the Corps switched them back to the Raider name, got to see a whole lot more action than he'd had to reckon with. This leader of the professionals may have been a new Recon Marine around the time Brad himself was, he may even have been there in the Philippines operation, probably retiring not long after the rebirth of the Raiders only a few years ago.

By seven o'clock on the scheduled day, the total sum of the gathered soldiers was just over a hundred, about twice Brad's own group. He was surprised that these groups, being from two of the larger cities in the state of Alaska, were so much smaller than his own, which was just refugees from all over the area. Some of the groups wore relatively matching uniforms, while many wore a mish-mash of hunter's garb of jeans or Carhartts and whatever camouflaged shirts they had. The weapons they carried varied even more wildly, from new Chinese-issue QBZ-95s, to Russian AK-12 rifles, to hunting rifles and U.S. Army M-4 carbines. Some carried forty or fifty-year-old AK-47s and even a few WWII-era SKS-style rifles, one of the most common hunting rifles in the bush, reminding Brad of Alaska's Russian heritage. There was even an almost new-looking World War II-era Lee-Enfield No. 4 Mk. I sniper rifle, a weapon made famous by Canadian sniper Harold Marshal. The scope on the .303 caliber rifle was of much more modern make. As Brad observed, it was obvious that while some, like the owner of the Lee-Enfield, knew how to carry, and properly use, their weapons, some of the others did not seem so well accustomed and trained on theirs.

"So, what do you think?" one of the soldiers, who was apparently from Palmer, asked. He looked like an eager young man. The assumption that he was from Palmer was based on the patch on the shoulder of his ACU, Army Combat Uniform, jacket. It featured a charging moose, symbol of the high school sports program for the city of six thousand people. Judging by his demeanor, his whole pre-war military experience was probably high school junior ROTC. "Will Ice Hammer actually show up?"

"They said he would," replied another man, older, steaks of gray in his beard, "but we'll soon see if this is real or just another hoax."

"Another hoax?" said the young man. "You mean there were other times it wasn't him?"

"There have been a number of people pop up claiming to be him, but they all either proved to be liars or were killed trying be like him," the old man replied. "But the stories keep showing up with his name attached, like the attack on the Chinese commandant, Zhang, a couple months ago."

Another man added his observation, "And the crazy man with the beard and his giant Viking friend have been in contact with us several times. Ice Hammer is real, I am sure."

"But is that who is meeting us?"

"If the hairy man says he's coming, I believe him."

"I will believe it when I see it," said a middle-aged man with a black embroidered colonel's insignia patch on his collar. "I spent thirty years in the Alaska Air Guard, and never heard of anyone with the call sign Ice Hammer. If this guy is the real thing, we should be able to size him up pretty fast. It is pretty easy to tell if a man is a real killer or not."

"Oh," said the leader of the professionals. "You know many killers, do you, Colonel?"

"I have been a military man my entire adult life, since I was seventeen," came the reply. "You don't need to question my judgment on such things."

"Really," the biker said. His men, similarly violent-looking, sat behind him eating their evening meals. "You must be a real badass then, Colonel. That must be why your boys look so hard, I'm guessing."

"We fight with our wits." The colonel puffed his chest up, looking down his angular nose at the rough-looking man, as if that answered the challenge.

"Yeah, well, your wits don't seem to have stopped the Chinese from tramping over the valley at will."

"While you and your...men..." he said the word as if it pained him to recognize them as actual humans, "ramble about the woods murdering whoever you come across, we have to live inside the occupied zones, with our families and children, and do our missions without being discovered."

"That's fine," said the biker leader, "just don't confuse what you are with actual professional killers. Such thinking might get you into positions you can't get yourselves out of. How do you know he hasn't been here watching this place since long before you got here?"

Listening to exchange, Brad got the distinct impression the colonel's career had been dedicated more to paper-work accuracy than to engaging men in combat of any type. The man was dressed to impress, but that was about the only impression he made. The biker, on the other hand, was indeed a real killer. Not a man to be messed with.

At eight o'clock that night, Brad signaled his men to move out of their hides.

"You ready for the big lights," he whispered to Kharzai.

"I love this part of the show," replied the hairy man in an almost giddy voice.

As the other militia groups were sitting down to dinner around their campfires, he and his men rose from positions all around the meeting area; a couple of them had actually made their way to within the cluster of tents and fires. As they rose from the ground, men backpedaled in terror away from the shapes materializing among them like forest spirits. He could almost hear their hearts stutter with the shock.

"What the f…." the expletive died on the soldier's lips as he jumped to his feet in fright, scrambling for his weapon.

"Good evening, folks," Brad said as he strolled quietly into their midst. "I understand some of you weren't sure I'd be here." He looked directly at the Air Force colonel. The man visibly shrank in front of him, then tried to recover his dignity. "Well, here we are…and yes, I am the one called Ice Hammer. I am the leader of the City of Chiknik and commander of the Chiknik Rangers."

"I am Colonel Wonderbrandt," he said offering his hand to shake. "Commander of the First Palmer Militia."

Brad looked at his proffered hand and repeated back to him the line he had used earlier.

"It is pretty easy to tell if a man is a real killer or not."

His stare bore into the man's eyes.

"You..." the colonel started. "I...."

"We've been here for four days, watching the area before you and your boys arrived."

"You were here for that long and didn't show yourself?" Wonderbrandt seemed irritated more than shocked now. "Were you spying on us? You didn't trust us?"

"Yeah," Brad replied, "I didn't trust you. I also didn't and don't trust most of the other groups here, especially after you all walked right past me and fifty of my men and his twenty men," he pointed at the professional, "and set up camp without even noticing we were within a few yards, even inside your camp."

His expression deepened to a glare.

"Colonel, if you expect to mount an attack against the Chinese main force, you and your men are in dire need of more training and less bullshit bluster."

Brad looked at the biker and immediately held out his hand to the man.

"You knew we were out there?"

"Yeah," the leader of the professionals replied. "We noticed several of your positions as we came in. You didn't smell like soy sauce or vodka so we figured you weren't Chinese or Russian and would reveal yourselves when the time was right."

"Brad Stone." They shook in greeting.

"Ken Caulkins," the biker said.

"Marine Raiders?" Brad asked, nodding at the patch. "Recon, I assume."

"Second Force from '91 to '96," he replied. "First from then to 2006. MARSOC after that 'til I retired as a lieutenant-colonel in '09."

"A lieutenant-colonel?" Brad said, one eyebrow raised. "You outrank me for sure. I was with first force, '88 to '91, but alas was med-boarded out when I was only a lowly corporal."

"Brad, you most definitely outrank me," Caukins said. "I lead a gang of thugs killing any Chinese soldiers who step into my AO *(area of operations)*. You, on the other hand, run an entire city and a professional army. One that was good enough to remain invisible in plain sight while all these nitwits wandered right over your hides."

"He's the Ice Hammer, did we mention that?" Kharzai interjected. "The real one, not the Walmart knock-off brand. He'll be signing autographs after the hors d'oeurves."

"Enough," Brad said, giving the hairy one a sideways look.

"He hates it when I do that," said Kharzai with a wink and smile.

Brad turned and put his hand out to Wonderbrandt, finally accepting the greeting.

"Colonel, I know we all have different approaches to what we are doing," he said as his hand was taken, "but this mission we are meeting about, is not one about protecting your families or being cautious with our lives. This is all about killing and destruction. I hope you and your men understand that."

Wonderbrandt took a breath and steeled his posture between the two hard, cold warriors.

"I just want to get rid of the enemy," he finally said. "Same as you do."

"Then let's plan this out."

As he said those last words, one of the men who was with Caukins came into clear view. Brad paused for a second, recognition flashing across his mind. The other stepped closer, also studying Brad.

"You used to be the IT manager at the VA, weren't you?" the man said as he approached.

"Yeah," said Brad. "I saw you there a lot. Never got your name though."

Brad clearly remembered the first time he'd seen the man at the Veteran's Affairs Hospital. At the time, nearly fifteen years earlier, Brad was still a senior technician, not yet promoted to manager. He'd been working on a printer in the vocational rehabilitation office when the recently retired veteran came to the counter and enquired as to what kind of re-training benefits he might be able to get. The clerk behind the counter, a cranky old guy named John Lime, was a retired Vietnam-era Air Force loadmaster in his sixties. Lime asked the veteran what he did in the military before retiring.

"What I did in the military doesn't cross over into the civilian world," he replied.

"Oh, you'd be surprised," John Lime said. "The vast majority of military jobs cross over very easily into the civilian world. Just a matter of getting the right sheepskins to prove you know what you're talking about."

"Mine doesn't," the man said.

"Okay, well," the clerk said, "we'll need to know to help get you on the right track."

The man stared at him for a moment, his face paling by a shade.

"I killed people."

"Excuse me?"

"I killed people. Professionally. For over twenty-four years."

"I see," John said with a look that said he didn't totally believe the man. A lot of posers crossed his desk every week, people claiming to have been something they were not; Special Forces, CIA, black ops ninjas, usually they had been desk clerks or administrative staff of some sort. "Let's have your social security number so I can pull up your record and verify your eligibility."

The man gave his social then waited as John pulled up the record. Several minutes went by before the older man responded. He cleared his throat and said, with a little less volume, "Uh, you retired as a sergeant-major in the Special Forces after your final assignment?"

"Special Forces was all of my assignments. Fifth, tenth, and third special forces groups. In that order. I was deployed in combat areas in Europe, the Middle East, Asia, and Africa for sixteen out of twenty-four years in the Army. My primary jobs during that time were sniper, sniper instructor, and CQB (Close Quarters Battle) instructor. My MOS (Military Occupational Specialty) was weapons sergeant."

"So you basically..."

"I killed people for a living, and trained others how to do that job in half a dozen different allied countries," said the man. "I used to like killing people. Specific kinds of people, of course— child traffickers, drug lords, terrorists, but it got boring. I don't enjoy the killing anymore and would like to do something different. Pastry chef maybe. Or aerobics instructor."

Brad let out a snigger at the suggestions. He made eye contact with the man and saw that he was serious. Over the ensuing years, he saw the guy at the VA every couple of months. They'd say hello, but little else. The retired Green Beret eventually did get a degree in culinary arts, specializing in baking and opened his own pastry shop in Wasilla, the town made famous by former politician turned conservative media star Sarah Palin. The radio advertisement for his bakery touted "Come try the Killer Crullers at Murphy's Bakery. They're to die for!"

"Pat Murphy." He shook Brad's proffered hand. "Pastry chef."

"Good to meet you on a more personal level at last."

"Likewise, IT guy."

"Wait a minute," Colonel Wonderbrandt burst into the conversation. "The infamous Ice Hammer, was only a corporal, and has been an IT guy since then? How exactly does that qualify you to lead an entire army?"

"Because," said Caukins, "he kicked ass, and got caught on drone video doing so. And has continued to do so for the past couple of years. Plus, he runs the largest militia in Alaska."

Wonderbrandt looked as if he were about to say something in response when Murphy added, "When was the last time you blew up General's Zhang's personal vehicle in an ambush, Colonel?"

"From one officer to another, let me say that it is not the rank that counts, Colonel," said Caukins. "It is the drive, the desire, and the balls to murder the enemy relentlessly within and without his own territory, and with passion. I, for one, am putting my men under the Ice Hammer."

CHAPTER 17

Youngmi

"This has been a very memorable trip, Comrade Generals," said Guo as the servers of the Aurora Fjord removed the dessert dishes and refilled cups of tea. "The very fact that we could even endeavor such a trip as today demonstrates to me that you, without a doubt, have this region firmly under control. You have done a tremendous job here, Comrades. The people are indebted to you."

"All of the credit for the tactical success here in Alaska is due solely to General Zhang, Comrades," said General Fang. "He had full authority on the ground here. His plan to placate and subjugate the Kenai Peninsula was excellent work. He saved a tremendous number of lives on both sides achieving peace by letting the local population continue their lives as always but under more efficient Chinese rule. Would you believe that many of those who once fought against us are now party members?"

"Judging by those we have met here in Seward," Guo said, nodding slowly, "both in the hotel and on the boat, they do all seem to have accepted their destinies as it were. You have it well under control here, much more so than many other parts of the revolutionary struggle in America."

"Thank you. We have worked very hard toward that end, Comrades," Zhang said. "Tomorrow, we will take the train ride through the mountains back to Anchorage. The following day we will take a trip to our northernmost outpost. We will be traveling with a heavy security presence due to the fact that there have been ambushes along that route by the well-organized resistance leader known by the code name Ice Hammer. Once you see the lengths we are taking to ensure safety from such bandits along the major highway corridors, you will see that we are still very much on combat footing here."

"I understand your concern, General Zhang," Comrade Li joined the conversation, "but you really do have it well in hand here compared to some areas of the country. In the areas of some of the cities that were originally attacked with nuclear weapons, the local population is nearly suicidal in their fighting zeal. We are told it is because they have been affected by radiation that has turned them into irrational beasts."

"In other areas, those Muslim terrorists that joined with us when it suited them have now turned against us," said Guo. "They used our weapons and ammunition, spoke on radios we supplied, and used satellite GPS's we provided to defeat their enemies, then they turn around and break their word and use our own equipment against us."

"I had heard of them turning like that," Fang said. "To be honest with you, I never did trust them to keep their word. In my experience, they never do."

Youngmi tried unsuccessfully to stave off a yawn, turning her head and covering her mouth as it stretched involuntarily. As the yawn released its grip on her, her eyes reopened. She noticed Po near the tramway exit speaking with a captain who had just come in with a new squad of security forces. She turned back to the table and caught the eye of Fan Hua who looked as tired as she felt. Youngmi signaled with a raised brow over droopy eyelids that it was time to leave before they all fell asleep. They verified the same inclination with the other two women, and Youngmi cleared her throat to speak.

"Gentlemen, it has been a wonderful day," she said, "but I am afraid we ladies are going to ask to retire to our rooms early while you all talk the business of war."

The men rose from their chairs as the women prepared to leave. Youngmi noticed the studied absence of any kind of eye contact between Fang and Fan Hua. She also noticed them withdraw hands from one another as they stood.

"Perhaps we should accompany you all back down in the tram," Li said.

"Please no, enjoy each other's company here," Youngmi said, motioning toward the exit to the tramway where Po and a squad of his men were being relieved by another squad. "Major Zhang and his men will be able to protect us from the terrorists on the way down."

Li smiled. "Indeed, he will."

The women bowed, crossed the room, and stepped onto the tram. The ride down was quiet and uneventful. Other than the attempts by several of the soldiers to steal glimpses of three lovely young women at her sides, that is. Surely, they would not be looking at *her* like that; she was old enough to be the mother of everyone in the tram.

They stepped out of the tram and into the rear lobby of the hotel. The muffled sound of music pulsed through the thick walls that separated the lobby from the nightclub built inside a man-made cave at the back of the hotel. With no rooms to disturb above them or to either side, the party went until the wee hours of the morning with impunity.

The women barely stifled giggles at the posturing and openly flirtatious looks the soldiers dared. They obviously did not know that the three young women with her were all officers. Their sergeant shouted an order and they snapped to attention and focused on him, forming up in neat columns, weapons across their chests. The soldiers turned and followed Major Po at a quick pace across the lobby, past the elevators and out the main doors, into the dusky evening.

Youngmi accompanied the others up to their rooms, one floor below those of the politicians, generals, and colonels. They said good night, and she continued up one more level, exiting the elevator and turning down the hall toward her room. Youngmi noticed that the pair of guards that usually stood outside the elevators were not there.

Maybe it has something do with whatever had Po and his men running outside like that.

The other elevator pinged behind her as she turned the corner to head two doors down to her room. As she got to her door and put the key card in the slot, the elevator door slid open. She did not hear anyone get out. Youngmi glanced that direction, saw no one, and pushed her door open. Someone had probably pressed the wrong floor. She held the door open, cursing herself for not leaving a light on in the room when she and General Zhang had left after changing for dinner. Fumbling for the switch in the dark, she finally found it and stepped into the room, releasing the door.

CHAPTER 18

Ping

The noise in the night club was becoming unbearable. He'd had several drinks, but instead of feeling relaxed he was even more tense. General Zhang and his big shot friends had not invited the colonels to join them for dinner this evening, opting instead to keep the nice restaurant all to themselves and those whores Youngmi had culled from the officer ranks. He had even heard that Captain Hong Fan Hua had been seen coming out of General Fang's room in the very early hours of the morning. Reasons like this are exactly why he did not support women in important roles in the military. To have a slut like Hong Fan Hua in command of an entire company of soldiers with a job as important as managing the computer network was a disgrace.

He very much preferred the old Japanese Imperial Army's approach to roles of women in the military. He believed that every company of soldiers should have a squad of comfort women following with them to provide for all the men's baser needs. Clean clothes, good food, and sexual release. Those were the only things women should have any part of in this army. If he had it his way, that is how it would be.

He threw back the rest of his third or fourth double gin martini, he'd lost count, put down the glass, and pressed a finger and thumb into his temples. His head throbbed to the beat of the music. He needed to get out into the brighter lights of the hotel and find some air fresher than the alcohol steambath inside the nightclub. He made his way to the exit, stumbling slightly as he reached the steps that led up to the door.

Ping pushed the crashbar on the darkened glass door and stepped out of the all-encompassing rumble of noise into the rear lobby of the hotel. He felt weak in the knees all of a sudden as the pounding music that had been holding him up vanished behind the very well-insulated walls. He righted himself against the wall, refocusing his eyes in the bright light of the hotel proper.

In the near distance stood the target of a lot of his ire. Just on the other side of a bank of elevators by the open door of a tram, Youngmi and her hand-picked whores were flirting with Major Zhang and a squad of his men. He watched as the soldiers jogged off, leaving the women with nothing to show for their slutty behavior.

The four women got into an elevator. Ping made as if to rush to get in with them, but the ability to move with any kind of speed escaped him. The floor tipped slightly, sending him crashing into the wall after only a few steps. He briefly wondered if it were an earthquake.

"Don't drink during an earthquake," he muttered. "Advice to remember."

He steadied himself on his feet just as the ding of the closing elevator door rang out.

"Damn!"

He walked carefully to the bank of elevators, deftly evading a large potted tree that seemed to loom out of nowhere. Once at his destination, he pressed the button. It took a very long time for an elevator to arrive. When the door finally swished open, more than a dozen young people poured out, most not in uniform. Ping managed to stand straight and scowl as they passed, several reflexively saluting as they saw him. They carried on and he stepped into the elevator car. The door slid shut.

Ping pressed the button for his floor. Moments later, the elevator decelerated. He heard the beep of the adjacent car's door open. A few seconds later, his own door opened. He carefully glanced around the corner to make sure no sentries were on duty.

He looked left.

There was no one.

He looked right, and his heart stopped.

Youngmi.

Ping knew that walk. He could identify her by the way she maneuvered that perfect figure, hips swaying invitingly as she strolled away, form-fitting blue silk dress accentuating her feminine shape.

She arrived at her room door and turned her head to glance his way. He ducked back into the elevator. Her door lock clicked and she pushed it open.

Have to move fast to get what is yours.

With a suddenly sober mind, he rushed out of the elevator and moved with what felt like amazing dexterity. Perhaps he'd not been as drunk as he thought. As he approached, he saw that the door was still open, the interior of the room dark. A lamp suddenly flicked on, spraying a fan of light across the carpet in the hallway. The hinges on the door creaked slightly as the self-closing springs pulled it shut.

Almost.

Ping shoved it open too hard, banging loudly against the wall. Youngmi let out a scream of surprise, tipping off balance as she cringed, turning toward the sound. Her already terror-widened eyes stretched even further as she saw his face.

"You bitch!"

Ping tried to slap her but she spun away too quickly. He did manage to grasp a handful of hair. He yanked, eliciting another scream as the door slammed shut behind him.

"You're finally going to be mine, you filthy Korean whore."

CHAPTER 19

Po

Major Zhang Po gritted his teeth in anger as the lieutenant tried to explain why he'd been called down. He put his hand up, effectively shutting the young officer up.

"They are boys, Lieutenant," Po said. "These are not a threat."

"But, sir, they snuck up to the vehicles in the shadows and appeared to be attempting sabotage."

Po looked at the pitiful gang of rebels, four boys all about nine or ten years old and a fifth child who, judging by the missing front teeth, was about five or six.

"Are you terrorists?" Po asked in English.

"No, sir," they all replied over each other.

"We just wanted to look at your cars," said one who seemed to be the leader. "We think your army cars are cool!"

"Especially the TIGRs with the bomb guns on top," blurted another, pointing at one of the TIGRs where it sat with a sentry manning a fully automatic grenade launcher. "That's my favorite."

Po looked at them with a cold glare, slowly running his eyes from one to the next. Each of the four older boys melted under his intense stare. The fifth, smaller than the others, with an unruly head of curly red-brown hair, stared right back at him. Not defiant, but also not afraid.

"Are you their little brother?" he asked.

"No," the curly-haired child said.

"Why are you here with them then?"

"I'm his sister," came the reply, a finger pointing to one of the boys. "I am not a boy, I am a girl."

"I see," said Po. "Please forgive my mistake."

"And those other three are not my brothers, just my brother's stupid friends," said the little girl. "Can we go now? My butt hurts from sitting on these rocks."

"Why are you children out so late at night?" Po asked in a gentle, fatherly voice. "It is very late for children to be out."

"Our parents are here, inside," said one of the boys. "They work in the bar and are working a party thing. Not a fun-for-kids party with cake and stuff but a boring grown-up party where everybody drinks beer and talks too much."

"Did your parents give you permission to be out of your house this late?"

"We can be out as late as we want," the girl said. "We don't have a bedtime."

"Maybe not," said Po in a contemplative voice. He pursed his lips as if in thought then added, "But there is a curfew at eight o'clock. Do you know what a curfew is?"

"Yes," said one of the other boys, his eyes filled with terror. "That's when we all have to be inside unless we have special passes to be outside, and those are only given to grown-ups, never kids. That's what I told them but they said it was okay because our parents work here."

"Shut up, Henry," one of the boys hissed.

"That is correct…Henry," Po said. "And do you boys know what happens to people who are out after curfew without a special pass?"

They all stared at him, faces draining of blood, mouths dropping open as they began to understand just how much trouble they were in.

"They get beat up and arrested?" said the little girl, a mischievous grin on her face.

Po's voice turned from fatherly teacher to icy monster.

"They are shot."

He turned to the lieutenant and continued in English in the same terrifying tone, "If these children are not inside their homes and up in their rooms in less than fifteen minutes, I want you to set loose the dogs to capture them, and then send the eagle drones to snatch them with their talons and bring them back here. Tie them to those trees over there and shoot them in the knees. Then put honey on their heads so that the ravens will come peck their eyes out. If they are still alive in the morning, shoot them in the face. Do you understand me, Lieutenant?"

There was a short pause. Based on Youngmi's reports from when she ended her regular English classes with the junior officers, Po knew that this particular lieutenant had understood only half, maybe less, of what he had said. But he apparently got the idea as he snapped to attention.

"Yes, sir!" the lieutenant replied in heavily accented English. He turned his eyes down to glare at the children. "Ravens eat boy eyes!"

"No," the little girl shouted, her voice coming like a tiny roar. She stomped to her feet and jabbed a finger at the lieutenant, her eyes squinting in a pint-sized threat. "You will not do that to my brother!"

"Oh," said Po, leaning down to look her in the eyes on her own level. "I will. I am Major Zhang Po of the special service unit. I always do what I say I will do. And do you know what else I will do?"

"What?" she growled, refusing to back down. "You don't scare me."

Po really liked this little girl. She was like a little white female version of himself at that age. The four boys looked convinced that this Chinese officer was not exaggerating their fates.

"Lieutenant," he said, keeping his eyes locked on hers.

"Yes, Major?"

"If they are not in their houses in," he raised his watch up for her to see, "thirteen minutes, do what I said to the boys. And put this girl with the slaves we are taking back."

"Yes, sir!"

"She will be my slave worker," Po said.

"No!" the girl said, a tear forming in the corner of her eye. "You can't do that! I'll tell my daddy!"

"And shoot her father in the arms," Po added, "so he can never hug her again."

"NO!" The little girl's resolve started to crumble.

"And break her mother's fingers, so she can never brush her hair, or touch her face again."

"Yes, sir!"

"...no..." the little girl let out a sob. "Leave Mommy and Daddy alone. It's my fault, I'll go home. I promise."

"We promise," chorused the boys. One had wet himself.

"You have eleven minutes left," Po said in a sinister whisper. "I would run if I were you."

The boys leapt to their feet, three sprinting away; the fourth grabbed his sister's arm and dragged her back. She kept her tear-rimmed eyes locked on Po's as if burning the image of his face into her memory. He imagined standing in his father's office years from this day, stars on his own shoulders, she returning one day to assassinate him. He really liked the little girl.

It was nearly eleven o'clock and the sun had only just vanished behind the mountains, bathing the town and the sea in darkness. Moonlight reflected a blue-white glow from the glaciers across the bay as the children disappeared around a corner, their footsteps fading rapidly. Po turned to the lieutenant, the younger man smiling as he watched the children vanish into the darkness. His smile quickly evaporated when he saw his commander's expression.

"Lieutenant, I am going to go to my room," Po said, his lips tight, eyes burning a barely controlled rage. "If I am roused by another emergency, you had better be certain it is not a bunch of children."

The lieutenant snapped a crisp salute and Po stalked away. He went inside and rode the elevator up to the floor where the mid-ranked officers had been billeted, just below the politicians, generals, and colonels. He heard the muffled sound of female laughter float through a door part way down the hall as he entered his own private room. The 'companions' Youngmi had brought for the guests. Surveillance video had seen Captain Hong enter General Fang's room late the previous evening and not leave until early morning, just before people were coming out of their rooms for the fishing charter.

In spite of the twenty-five or more years in age difference, he thought as he pulled off his pistol belt and his jacket and draped them neatly over the back of a chair, *they seemed at a glance to be a couple made for each other*. Fang was a handsome middle-aged sports star turned four-star-general. Hong was an extremely intelligent and stunningly gorgeous captain—more than just a 'good catch,' she was the kind of woman that could give Fang a run for his money, possibly even long term.

People did not think he saw things like that. The soldiers under him only ever saw him as a hard, unfeeling leader. The officers above him saw him as a tool of war, a machine that was very good at accomplishing was it was designed for. That was as it should be. But what truly made him good at his job in the special service unit was that he could read people. And using the knowledge of how to read others, he was able to render himself unreadable.

He wondered, with such a talent, if he would ever be able to convince a woman to trust that he was not simply using her. If he could reach a point in his life where he would be able to open his own soul enough to allow himself to be read by someone else. He would like to have a wife one day, if the army allowed it. He was thirty years old, six years older than his father, General Zhang, was when he married his mother. They were married for nearly thirty years before the cancer took her. He had always seen his father as a hard man, a warrior. Although he seldom caught a glimpse of the tenderness his father showed his mother in private, he had no doubt they loved each other deeply.

Po wanted to have something like that one day. He had only been with a woman once in his life, during college. A one-night stand with a girl who had been arranged for him by his friends. Afraid of the mockery they'd make of him if he failed to follow through, and he had to admit he was truly curious of what it would be like, he did what came naturally. The experience left him feeling exposed, humiliated, and dirty. Such relationships were not what he needed or wanted. He wanted to meet a woman he could trust. He wanted to meet a woman that could be for him like his mother was for his father.

God he missed his mother. He…

A muffled scream followed by a loud bang yanked him into a heightened state. A second scream triangulated the location of the noise in his head. His father's room. Ms. Ma was in danger.

Po snatched his pistol belt up and wrapped it around his waist as he sprinted out of the room. Three running strides and he threw open the door to the stairwell and leaped up the concrete steps four at a time, rounding the switch-back landing and up the final steps to the next floor. He poked his head out the door, pistol at the ready position, and scanned left, then right, then left again, in the direction of the scream and the sound of a struggle. He sprinted to the room. The door was locked shut. As commander of the security unit, he had a master swipe card that could open every room in case of emergency. He pulled it out of his pocket and slipped it into the slot. The small light flashed green and he shoved the door open.

Ping was standing inside, his hand gripped around Youngmi's wrist. The air reeked of hard liquor, enough to make Po's eyes sting.

"Hey!"

Ping spung around, yanking Youngmi sideways in his grip.

"Get out of here, soldier!" Ping slurred at him. "Leave us alone."

Po clenched his fingers around the grip and held his pistol up, considering whether he should just shoot the bastard colonel and be done with it. In the second before he pulled the last millimeters of his trigger he was blinded by a flash of light. There was a loud crack and Ping dropped to the floor as if someone had just turned off a switch, blood dribbling from the side of his head and down his cheek.

"Are you alright, Ms. Ma?" he asked Youngmi.

"Yes," she said, a dresser-top lamp in her hand, power cord twisted across the carpet, prongs bent from being yanked out of the wall socket. "That is twice you have saved me from him."

Po looked at her for a moment, shoved his pistol back into its holster, grabbed Colonel Ping by the back of his collar, and dragged him out into the hallway. Ping's own room was several doors down. Apparently, no one else on the floor had returned to their rooms yet. The hallway was empty and silent. Po dragged him to the door of his room, dropping him with a wet-sounding thud, his face mashed into onto the hallway's carpeted floor. Ping immediately started snoring. Po slid his card in and opened the door, propping it with a foot as he rolled the colonel onto his back, put his arms under the other's armpits, and lifted him to his feet. He backed into the room, the colonel's heels scraping against the carpeted floor.

Once inside, Po turned, shuffling around in the foyer until the unconscious colonel was facing into the room. He shifted so that his hands were under the man's arms, then shoved him forward. Ping hinged over, body almost rigid, and face planted into the floor with a sharp crack. Blood spattered sideways from his shattered nose, the snoring becoming wet and sloppy sounding. Po backed out and let the door bang shut behind him.

Youngmi stood in the entry to her own room. He went to her, wiping his hands on his pants.

"May I wash off his stink in your room?" he asked.

"Of course," she said, stepping back to let him in.

He went into the bathroom and washed his hands under the warm water, lathering up well to get the pungent stench of alcoholic body odor off his skin and forearms. If he'd worn his jacket instead of just the black undershirt when he'd handled the bastard, he would consider burning it rather than trying to have it cleaned.

"Is he going to be okay?" Youngmi asked.

"Yes," he said, "unless he drowns in his own vomit later tonight."

"Let's hope," she said. "Do you think he will remember what happened?"

"Probably not," he said as he dried his hands on a clean towel. "Although if he does, what is he going to say? That his nose was broken in a fall after he got smashed in the head with a lamp while trying to rape his general's woman?"

Youngmi gave him a look.

"What?" he said as he stepped out of the bathroom into the foyer.

"You called me his woman," she said, "as opposed to his mistress. Sounds like a promotion."

He gave her a look, thinking his words over before speaking a response.

"You," he said, taking a deep breath, "are not his mistress. He is not married. You and he are both widowed. Therefore, it is not adultery."

"I do not know where my husband is," Youngmi said.

"It is easy to assume he is dead," Po said. "Or we would have found him, I am sure."

"Perhaps," she agreed.

"Just do not hurt my father," Po said. "Do not hurt my sister."

"What about you, Po?"

"A stone cannot be hurt."

CHAPTER 20

Ian

Two days after the end of training, the new Rangers found themselves leaving on their first mission, a twenty-person platoon on a ten-day, intel-gathering patrol. They would observe the highway forty miles east of Chiknik, watching for and cataloging all Russian and Chinese traffic passing across the highway in the area near Chiknik. They were delivered to a site ten miles from the proposed OP, Observation Post, in a pair of SUSVEEs, lightly armored tracked vehicles, that could carry up to 12 Rangers and their equipment per vehicle. After hiding the vehicles in a heavily forested area, they humped the last ten miles under cover of the trees, then up and around the face of a small mountain until they found themselves looking down on the highway. For the former members of 104, there was something very familiar about the view.

"This is where that sniper hit us when we crossed the highway," Ian said, pointing toward the spot they had crossed a month earlier. "I'm going to see if I can find their position."

"Ask Sergeant Taylor first," Ben replied. "Don't run off without letting him know."

Ian quietly made his way toward the sergeant.

"Sergeant Taylor," he called out in a low voice, pronouncing the rank like a seasoned soldier of the old U.S. Army, 'Sarn't.'

"Yeah?"

"About a month ago, me and the scout troop crossed this road right down there." Ian pointed to the spot where they'd crossed, dark bloodstains still visible, burned into the asphalt by the arctic midnight sun. "We came under sniper fire from a position just a little bit north of here. They killed a few good men, including our caribou whisperer." He referred to Walt, the hostler who had trained their small herd of caribou to haul carts and payloads for them. "I wasted two of them from down there, just around the hill, maybe two hundred yards. I'd like to go check out that position and see if the bodies and weapons are still there; might score us a nice Dragunov or something."

"Go for it," Taylor replied, "but take a couple guys to watch your back."

"Thanks," Ian said.

He moved out, tapping his brother and Katarina. "Come with me. We're gonna find that sniper position."

They crept around the side of the mountain toward where he remembered having fired. Just about exactly where he had thought it would be, they found the decomposed bodies of the men he'd shot. Rather, they found the remaining pieces of man-flesh. Not much was left intact after a body was hit by 12.7 millimeter rounds, even if the hit was in the extremities. The remnants were dried and desiccated from a month of twenty-four-hour sunshine. A complete arm lay ten feet from a corpse missing the right half of the upper chest, its legs looking as though they'd been partially eaten by a large predator. Probably a wolf, Ian surmised by the shape of some of the bites, long and narrow like a dog's muzzle instead of wider and less deep like a bear. Another corpse, missing everything above the breast, lay a few yards away. At its feet was a surprisingly clean looking OSV-

96 sniper rifle, chambered in 12.7x108 millimeter, a round as big as a man's index finger. Similar to a U.S. .50 caliber, it was a bullet that could explode a human body into a puff of pink mist from two-thousand meters, as Ian had seen it used both against his teammates and against his enemies. The boy's own similar weapon had taken out both shooter and spotter. Big caliber didn't matter as much as a talented shooter.

"The size of the man in the fight," he muttered to himself, paraphrasing a saying his father used to repeat to them, "matters less than the size of the fight in the man."

He picked up the weapon and six fully loaded five-round magazines in pouches on the headless shooter's hip. After more than a month in the elements, there was a surprisingly small amount of rust on the rifle, but that could be easily cleaned, and with a bit of oil, the weapon would easily be back to good fighting shape. They also found a very nice night-vision-capable, range-finding, spotting scope on a tripod. The scope was pristine, having fallen at the base of a tree that seemed to have protected it from the rain and weather. There was no fog in the lens, and the battery for the range-finding laser was still mostly charged; apparently, the spotter had turned it off just before Ian had blown him apart. Nearby, Ben found a handheld device that looked like a GPS.

"Either they didn't put their last coordinates in to their HQ before they died," Ben said, "or the Russian army doesn't bother to recover its dead."

"Probably both," Katarina said. "They're real bastards, those Commie...um...bastards."

Ben let out a chuckle as she fumbled the phrase.

"Let's go," Ian said. "We should take the scope and Dragunov, as well as their rifles, ammo, and sidearms. I've got the spotting scope."

The trio slinked back around the mountain, returning to the main body of the group. They reported their findings to the sergeant, offering the gift of the sniper rifle and scope, as well as two folding stock AK-12s and a pair of good quality Kalashnikov PL-15 9mm pistols. All of them would need to be cleaned well before being used, but thanks to a mostly dry summer, they were in very good shape.

"The stuff's yours," Taylor said. "You killed them, you get to keep their booty. Like in the old-fashioned Viking days."

"Thanks," Ian said with not a breath of protest. He moved out with his newfound toys and took up a position on the observation line with his squad. He already had a Dragunov of his own but kept the spotting scope for himself, leaving the big rifle and the rest for Ben to distribute to the others as he saw fit.

He wiped the scope down, tested the knobs, and applied a little oil to help free up a number of spruce needles that were jammed in between the housing. Once satisfied it was working, he set up the tripod and started glassing the valley below and the ribbon of highway that ran through it.

The days in position were for the most part very boring. By the morning of the last day, they had counted six moose, twenty-four caribou, a hundred or more hares, a pack of wolves, and two bald eagles, but not a single human outside their own group.

"There must be something going on," Ben said. "I have never seen there be absolutely no traffic for this long on the Glenn."

"Maybe there's a truce or something?" Katarina suggested.

"Or a ceasefire," Todd said. "Maybe the war is over."

"Not likely," Ian said. He studied the spot they had crossed with their reindeer-drawn sleds earlier that summer. Brown stains still marked the pavement where Walt the Caribou Whisperer had been blown in half, along with two of the boys and one of the reindeer.

Something glittered on the horizon. Ian raised the scope, adjusting the mesh covering that extended beyond the front-facing lens to block reflections of sunlight that could reveal his position, much like what had enabled him to kill the previous owners of this very expensive equipment. More than thirty miles distant, he could make out a column of vehicles coming their way.

"Contact," Ian said.

The sound of vehicles rumbled on the horizon. A couple minutes later, a Russian military convoy appeared. Twenty vehicles, TIGRs, TYPHOONS, a heavily armored mine-resistant troop transport, and even a couple of tanks outfitted with wheels, four to a side, providing security for three tractor-trailer vehicles carrying some unknown cargo to the west.

Ian desperately wanted to blast the engine blocks out of the vehicles and descend upon the convoy to take whatever prizes he could find. This was a recon-only mission. Watch and observe; do not contact the enemy. This was not something he was accustomed to, but he could see the logic in it. He would obey. He was now under the orders of other men and accepted that he could not simply kill at his whim. That last gave him comfort. He was no longer the judge of men's lives. Others would give the orders and he could pass the guilt to them.

The convoy passed. They waited two hours, then made their way back to the SUSVEEs they had hidden in the forest, taking their information and new weapons back to Chiknik.

CHAPTER 21

Brad

Brad and the others made their way back on a trail near the one they had come in on. The large group of campers they'd bypassed on the way to the meeting was still in the same area, but the group appeared to have grown by several people. Three more men and four more women, young looking and armed with rifles of various makes, had joined them, most likely having returned to the camp from a hunt. The known total of the group so far stood at eighteen. Several of the other adults were also armed or had a weapon nearby. In addition to the long dugout structure the patrol had initially seen, there was an outdoor cooking and eating area. Several hares and a number of grouse hung from poles held up by tripods made of long, thin poles near the fire pit, smoke wafting over them that would preserve the meat to last in storage for months on end in the natural refrigeration of the arctic. Herbs of some sort hung to dry on a string tied between two nearby trees, likewise to provide food and flavor for the winter months. At a distance from the eating and living area stood a covered latrine made of branches and a brown tarp.

Brad's men drew near enough to hear the people talking to each other.

"I think someone has been nearby," said one of the young men in the camp. He was of average height and quite thin, the thinness not unexpected for people who survived a winter in the forest. In spite of the often-harsh conditions, he looked marathon runner fit as opposed to starved. "About a hundred meters just north of us. I thought it was a moose trail or something when I first saw it, but then I noticed a couple bootprints on the trail, a week old, a little more maybe."

"You think it is the Chinese?" asked another man, older, taller, with graying hair and a beak nose.

"I don't think so," said the young man. "The bootprints were different from each other. The Chinese all wear the same kind of military-issued boot, don't they? Besides, one of the prints had part of the Vibram logo and 'Size 10' in it. Chinese soldiers wouldn't be wearing stuff with English words on it, I think. And I am pretty sure they don't use our foot size system."

"Where is it?" asked a nearby child with an unexpectedly deep voice. Brad looked closer and realized it was not a child who had spoken, but a grown man who happened to be a dwarf. He was maybe four and a half feet tall, his torso somewhat small compared to his disproportionately large head and muscular arms that hung almost to his knees. His hands were large with sausage like fingers, calloused both on the palms and the back of the knuckles, the hands of someone who did hard manual labor his entire life. His legs were short and thick, giving him a perceptible waddle when he walked. He moved with confidence. When he turned to talk to someone else, Brad saw that he wore a 1911-style .45 caliber pistol on his hip and a serious expression on his face.

Brad and Kharzai exchanged a glance, then gave each other a quiet nod.

"Hello in the camp," Brad called out.

Several of the inhabitants reflexively let out startled screams. The dwarf instantly had his weapon up in a well-trained maneuver, a couple of the younger people nearby following suit.

"We're friendly," Brad called out. "I'm going to stand up, unarmed. Don't shoot me."

"Come on up then," the short man said. "Keep your hands where I can see them."

The men and women with rifles formed a ring facing out in all directions. The others urged the children into the nearest shelter or the dugout. Brad slowly rose to his feet, a move made easier these days by the fact that the deprivations of the war had allowed him to lose, and keep off, more than eighty pounds over the past two years, relieving his knees from all the mass he'd accumulated as an IT manager who sat at a desk the majority of every day before the war. He held his hands up at shoulder level, palms facing the people in the camp, his rifle and sidearm on the ground at his feet.

"I am Brad, leader of the city of Chiknik," he said. "There are fifty armed soldiers around your camp, highly trained Rangers. We passed by here just over a week ago, like that young man was saying, about a hundred yards north of here on our way to meet with some other resistance fighters. We're heading back home but wanted to ask if you'd like to come with us."

The group looked back at them for a long while. Brad let the silence stretch, keeping his arms up for nearly a minute. The short man stared into Brad's eyes the whole time, weapon at the ready but pointed at the ground two-thirds of the way between them.

"I don't believe you've got fifty people out there," he said at length. "We'd have heard something."

Brad let out a short whistle and half the team rose to their feet, weapons in their hands, muzzles pointed to the ground.

"That's half," Brad said. "The others are pulling security a little farther out, including snipers and machine guns."

The people of the camp instantly deflated at the show of force.

"We're really not here to hurt you, or take advantage of you," Brad spoke as he slowly strode nearer. He lowered his hands, keeping his palms open and facing them in a placating gesture. "Just offering a better chance to survive in mostly modern conditions, if you want it."

"Chiknik, you say?" said the short man. "So that'd make you the Ice Hammer?"

"Yup," replied Kharzai. "Brad here is THE Ice Hammer. And, if I might add, I'm the one who discovered him." He walked briskly toward the short man, switched his rifle to his left hand, and extended his right in an offer to shake. "I'm Kharzai, Ice Hammer's booking agent, if you're up for a great bit of entertainment and maybe some karaoke and chocolate éclairs, Brad is your man! His éclairs are simply to *die* for!"

"Uh…" Brad interjected.

"Who…what in the world are you talking about?" said the short man. The others near him had confused looks too.

"Alright, Kharzai," Brad said.

"Sorry, boss," Kharzai said, still holding his hand out to shake. "I just get excited when we meet new people, you know."

The short man didn't take his finger off the trigger of his weapon, which had been pointed at the crazy man's belly for a tense moment. Then he glanced around and saw just how many guns were surrounding him, the faces of their owners were not smiling. He lowered his gun.

"Well, I guess if you guys wanted to harm us, you'd have already done so," he said, decocking his pistol and sliding it back into the holster on his hip. He finally accepted Kharzai's hand. "Come in and let's talk."

Brad came forward, one of the Rangers collecting his weapons from where he'd left them on the ground.

★   ★   ★

The Ranger captain posted a guard with half his men while the other half ate their rations and rested. Brad and Kharzai sat on sawn log benches around a fire pit with the apparent leaders of the camp.

"I'm Matthew, Matthew Corwin," said the short man, brow deeply furrowed. He had the look of a man buried in the tense exhaustion of living with nothing but uncertainties for tomorrow. "Before the war, I farmed a hundred acres near Willow and ran a bed and breakfast with my wife. Now I live here with my friends, trying to survive."

"And my name is Karl Stepovich," the beak-nosed man said with a nod. "I was a snow machine and ATV mechanic at the Polaris dealership in Wasilla for more than twenty years."

Kharzai nodded, mentally starting an inventory of talents that could place them in the community.

"Your camp looks pretty well-established," Brad said. "How long have you folks been here?"

"Last summer, Chinese patrols burned several properties and executed a bunch of people in our area in retaliation for a resistance ambush," said Matthew. "I was at the back of my hay field, almost a mile away. My wife and two of our neighbors were lined up and shot at the end of my driveway. After that, we gathered anyone willing to come and set up camp here in early August, dug in, and made a winter home," Matthew said. "Five of our original group didn't survive the cold."

"What did you eat?" Kharzai asked.

"We got lucky last fall and got a couple moose and a bear," Matthew said. "We jerkied the meat and raided an abandoned farm where the previous year's potatoes and cabbages and other vegetables had come back wild. There's also a couple good fishing holes with trout and salmon a short distance from here, as long as you can get them out before the ice sets in."

"Had a dozen chickens too," said Karl, "but come the big freeze in January, they all died from the cold. No more eggs but we had chicken soup for a few weeks."

"We barely made it, though. By the end, it was starvation rations."

"We have a city of about four thousand right now," Kharzai said. "School, farms, doctors, and an army to protect it all. You are welcome to join us."

Matthew looked back at the dugout, then exchanged looks with Karl.

"If we stay here another winter," Karl said, nodding slowly, "I don't think many will survive. I think they'll all agree. Safety in numbers."

"Alright," said Matthew, "let me go talk to the others."

He rose from the bench and went into the dugout. A few minutes later, he came out with several people following, including four children. They approached the newcomers apprehensively, wariness in their eyes.

"They agree," said Matthew. "We will come with you. But first, have a feast with us."

Martin Staley and a couple of other Rangers offered to supplement the feast with more meat and went on a short hunt, setting a handful of snares along the trail as they went out. Within less than two hours, the three of them returned, each carrying a brace of hares, a cluster of grouse hanging from their belts. Another hour after that and the meal was all coming to a nicely roasted doneness. The Rangers added some variety to their meals, sharing packs of MREs with the new people.

As they ate, Phil Staley shared a story.

"Our great-grandpa hunted this same area back since the '30s," Phil said after swallowing a mouthful of roasted meat. "He said back then, there was a guy that lived in the woods a few miles out of Palmer, somewhere not too far from here, I think. He was this Polish guy with a name that was all c's, and x's, and y's. No one could pronounce his real name so they all just called him Polish Joe. He said that Polish Joe always wanted a horse or a mule to help with his gold stake, but couldn't afford one. He made enough money on gold from his claim to have bought both a horse and a mule if he'd wanted, but Polish Joe had an addiction to a particular girl named Sally Mae who worked at the saloon that doubled as the local cathouse. He spent all his money on whiskey and Sally Mae every time he came to town, which had grown from once a month to once a week and sometimes more."

Phil nibbled on the small bit of meat left on the thigh bone of a grouse, the morsel about the size of a small chicken wing. Brad smiled as he recalled Phil and his brother filling many winter nights with stories such as this during the first year of the war. They'd been living in a mansion in the middle of nowhere, a remote private arctic resort for billionaires, he and his original band of a handful of refugees had stumbled upon while on the run. It was an idyllic existence while it lasted. One that could have gone on for years, maybe even outlasted the war. But a vengeful thug whose men had been beaten by Brad's team brought the might of the Chinese army down on them.

The escape had been harrowing at best, but here he was, a year and a half later, bringing a group that numbered about the same as his original members in to his own fold. While the Chinese army was not bearing down on them as it was for him back then, he was right now rescuing these people in much the same way that John had rescued him and Sammi and all the others that had been with him.

"Is this a porn story?" Kharzai said, "I am not allowed to hear porn stories. Jung doesn't want me coming home with any crazy ideas."

"Um...no," Phil said. "This is not a porn story. Anyhow, Polish Joe wanted to impress Sally Mae, in a very non-pornographic way that is. During a weekend-long stint with her, he kept trying to convince her to give up her sinful ways, leave the cathouse behind, marry him, and move into his cabin with him. Well, Sally Mae didn't want to give up her livelihood for a bet on a man whose gold claim could run out at any time.

"She said to him, 'Joe, you can't even afford a horse and carriage to take me out to your cabin. You expect me to walk all that way on my delicate feet?' Now, Polish Joe realized she had a point, a good one at that. He knew just how delicate her feet were for a fact, as Joe was so much in love with this woman of perdition that he was the only client in the house ever to pay a girl to let him give her a foot massage. That's how in love with her he was, willing to forego the traditional, um...line of services offered for purchase...in order to show her his true feelings."

"Nice non-pornographic way to say it," Kharzai said. "Carry on, young man."

"Polish Joe smiled real big and said, 'So if I get a horse and carriage and come here to pick you up, Sally Mae, and if I give you a big gold ring, will you marry me then?' To which she replies that yes, if he ever showed up with a horse and carriage and a big gold ring, she would marry him."

"Uh-oh," said Brad, looking around at the others, all staring at Phil in rapt attention, the magical power of story having drawn them in. "Sounds like Polish Joe is about to have a bad day."

"Well, having spent a whole month's worth of earnings on that weekend-long stint with Sally Mae, he had nothing to buy a horse or carriage with. He tried to get a loan from the local banker, but alas, with many of the gold claims drying up and miners moving out, no one was willing to take a risk on him."

"Not even for love?" said one of the Rangers.

"Nope," said Phil, "not even for love."

150

"This obviously is not the Princess Bride," Kharzai said.

"Not unless Princess Buttercup came from a whorehouse."

"There are children present!" Kharzai hissed dramatically.

"Finish the story!" shouted Doc Darryl, competitive power-lifter and doctor of chiropractic turned Ranger medic.

"Of course," replied Phil. "So, dejected, Polish Joe trudges back to his cabin. As he comes up on his tiny little abode in the woods, he notices a good-sized bull moose munching on a thicket of willow at the edge of his cleared land. Its antlers were spread a little over five feet wide on a massive head that stuck out from an even more massive neck. Even with its size, Polish Joe could tell it was still pretty young, not more than a year or so away from its momma. He calls out and the moose gives him a quick look over, then returns to munching the leaves. An idea strikes Joe's mind in a way that ideas are wont to do, especially if you are someone like Polish Joe, who according to great-grandpa used to come up with new schemes so fast that many thought he was the inspiration for Wile E. Coyote. Most of his schemes were just as ill-fated as ol' Wile E. as well. Polish Joe looked at that moose, saw how it was surprisingly similar in shape and build to a horse, albeit larger, and with a notably less intelligent look in its eyes."

Children and adults alike stared at Phil as he wove the tale, mouths open in anticipatory smiles. It made Brad imagine scenes like this stretching back to the dawn of mankind. Stories around a fire, a foundational part of humanity. He wondered how their own exploits would one day be told around campfires.

"Over the course of the next couple months, Polish Joe set about trapping the bull moose in his yard, feeding it regularly until it was comfortable eating right out of his bare hand. That moose eventually let Joe put a harness on it, and he named the gentle giant Gunnar, after the Swedish Viking that invaded his native country and spread his seed among the prettiest women in the land."

The other Rangers around the fire chuckled at the use of their senior-enlisted commander's name in the increasingly bawdy story.

"Was Gunnar a farmer?" asked one of the children.

"Um, yes, honey," one of the mother's tactfully said. "He was a farmer...of sorts."

"Did they have tractors back then?" another child asked.

"No, Caleb, they did not have tractors back then," replied one of the men, then grinned and added suggestively, "although they did have plows."

"The kind that has two balls and you pull it?" the child said.

The adults burst into laughter. The children joined in, older children grinning and whispering in each other's ears as they got it, the younger ones with confused looks on their faces.

"That's *bulls*, honey," the mother corrected. "*Bulls* pull an old-fashioned plow."

It took most of a minute for the uproar to subside, folks catching their breath and motioning for the story to continue.

"I guess I kinda forgot just how PG-13 this story was," Phil said, then proceeded. "With a little more training, the big ol' beastie even took to bridle and bit. In time, Polish Joe and Gunnar built a relationship of trust, the moose even allowing Polish Joe to hitch him up to a decent little two-wheeled buckboard wagon, although one of the wheels was more of a roundish oval than a full circle, and the other, while almost perfectly round on the inside of the wheel, had a slightly flat section on outside of one such that when it rolled it went kind of 'swish-clack, swish-clack.'"

The audience was fully engaged, wide eyed and grinning as the story went on.

"Polish Joe had built a frame over wagon that he covered with a pair of stitched-together bear hides. It was the only bear skin covered wagon ever made, and it was made out of the hides of two of the meanest grizzlies that ever did live."

"How did mister Polish Joe get the hides off the grizzly bears if they were so mean?" another child asked.

"Well, now, that is a whole other story that we'll have to do later, as it takes a long time to tell on its own," Phil said, patting the boy on the shoulder. "Now, Sally Mae had started to think that her rebuff had driven away her best regular customer. She worried that she had maybe been too harsh on the sweet man and hoped he'd not done something drastic. Then, on one fine summer day, after nearly three months away, Polish Joe comes riding into town in his hand-made, moose-drawn carriage, the massive bearskin over the frame as it went 'swish-clack, swish-clack' over the hard-packed dirt road.

"Sally Mae stood there dumbstruck as the carriage came to a stop, the mostly round wheels wobbled more noticeably as it slowed. Gunnar stared about at his surroundings, utter confusion in his eyes. 'He actually did it,' muttered one of the other women standing next to her. 'Are you going to marry him then?' another girl asked. 'Well, I guess I kind of have to now,' Sally Mae said. 'Yeah, but that's not a real horse,' the other girl said. 'Yeah,' said a third, 'that's a trained moose.'

"Sally Mae agreed that it was not a real horse, but said, 'I am thinking this is even better though. It must be a lot harder to train a dumb moose to pull a carriage than it is to train a smart horse.'

Phil took a drink from his canteen, swished it around his mouth, then swallowed, slow and deliberate, letting his audience form the scene in their minds before continuing.

"Polish Joe pulls up in front of the saloon, right up to where Sally Mae and the other girls are standing. The carriage stopped with loud clack as it settled on its flat side, skewing at a slight angle that made Polish Joe have to twist his neck a little more than was comfortable to look directly at the love of his life. He wished he'd taught the moose how to reverse, but hadn't really thought of it before. 'Sally Mae,' he said, twisted around to halfway behind himself, 'I know it ain't a real horse, but who else has ever trained a moose to be a horse to impress the love of his heart so she will be his wife.'

"Before Sally Mae could get a word out, three things happened that would leave an impression on the people of old Palmer for generations. First, Polish Joe's neck started to get sore all twisted like that and he decided to stand up and turn toward her. Just as he was rising from the seat of his homemade carriage, Gunnar let rip with a stream of moose nuggets that the beast must've been holding under pressure for a long time. Those little pecan-shaped treasures shot straight sideways and right into the front of the carriage, all over Joe's mostly polished boots. Then the sheriff started their way, an angry look on his face. 'Polish Joe!' he cries out, 'It's against the law to domesticate moose. They can't be tamed. Get that thing out of here before it does something crazy!' and then the third thing happens, something Joe had never even thought about living in his quiet cabin in the woods. The owner of the hotel across from the saloon comes out of his building and steps into his little old black Ford Model A, presses the starter button, and BANG!

"The moose had remained fairly calm up to that point. When that engine backfired, the beast instantly jumped out of its skin and back in. It burst into a run that broke the yoke holding it to the carriage. Polish Joe slipped in the moose poo at his feet, sliming his clean getting-married clothes with the brown mess. His entire back side now lubricated with fresh yuck, he slid right off the bucking contraption and into the dirt street. Meanwhile, Gunnar the moose charges off, the carriage twisting on the remaining bits of leather harness still attached to it. He ran south, bits of shattered carriage scattering in the dirt street. The moose, seeing oncoming traffic in the shape of another automobile, pulls a sudden U-turn and charges right back at Polish Joe, who runs with all his might away from his once-faithful friend Gunnar who had apparently lost his tiny little moose mind. Gunnar chased him straight into the saloon, smashing tables, and terrifying diners in its rampage until its antlers got stuck in one of the gas chandeliers that lit the place up. As Gunnar the moose tried to break free from its new bonds, the velvet on its antlers caught fire, making it panic even more until it broke the chandelier free, sending burning jets of gas across the ceiling and setting the place ablaze.

"In the end, the saloon burned to the ground, and Gunnar the moose was shot by the sheriff, his meat shared out to most all of the damaged parties. Polish Joe was arrested and jailed for causing a disturbance to the peace. He was set free with no charges the next morning before a trial was even scheduled. Apparently, Sally Mae knew something about the judge that the judge didn't want his wife knowing. The saloon owner tried to force Polish Joe to pay for the burned-down saloon, but when the charred remains of the building were cleared away, the greedy old man's lockbox was discovered, broken open by the heat. Inside was charred evidence that he had been cheating on the local miners, stealing part of their gold, including that of the mayor and the sheriff. Joe didn't have to pay back a dime, and the saloon keeper/pimp went away never to be seen again."

"Yeah, but what about Sally Mae?" someone called out.

"Would you believe, that woman was so impressed with the lengths that Polish Joe had gone to that she ended up quitting the cathouse, which was easy since it had burned down anyway, and married him. They converted the old cabin and property into a small trading post that in time grew into what eventually became Menche's Roadhouse, Menche being Sally Mae's maiden name. In the 1950s, they had become quite well off by selling a large part of their land to the state to reroute a section of the Glenn Highway. By the time they died in the 1990s, themselves nearly one hundred years old, they were two of the richest millionaires in the state. Sally Mae had convinced Polish Joe to invest in some of the state's first modern shopping malls and created a real estate empire that was making bank right up to the start of the war."

"Now that seems like a truly Alaskan tale," said Kharzai. "A prostitute and gold-miner ending up as highly respected millionaire real-estate moguls."

"It'd be more believable if they became politicians instead," Matthew muttered as a comic aside.

Laughter and conversation filled the next hour as they ate and got to know each other. After satisfying themselves, the residents of the camp rose to prepare for the journey and pack what belongings they had.

"Brad, your men can stay with us tonight," Matthew said, "and we can move out in the morning if that works."

"That works fine," said Brad. "Welcome to the family."

CHAPTER 22

Kharzai

One of the women at the fire rose to refill her cup with water, taking the empty cup of the young man beside her as well. She returned a moment later, leaning to return the now filled cup to the man. As he took it, she glanced across the fire, her eyes connecting with Kharzai's. They were large and green, almond-shaped, betraying a Central Asian heritage. She smiled at him, a sparkle glinting against perfectly white teeth.

Pakistan maybe. Very pretty.

Her jacket slid open, revealing a saffron-colored silk scarf, surprisingly bright against the backdrop of the forest. A jolt of lightning hit his mind and the sound of conversation ceased. The people around him vanished and for a moment, nothing more than a handful of heartbeats, all he could see, all that existed were the flames and memory of his greatest hell. Long before this war. Long before Brad and Jung and Chiknik. A memory he kept locked away, suddenly exploding in full view as if it were happening again.

Southwestern Punjab, Pakistan
Eight years earlier

"Ali aga, how long will the meeting be today?" Kharzai fidgeted as he spoke, looking out the window at the dusty landscape that passed them by.

Ali turned in the front passenger seat and glared at Kharzai over the top edge of his mirrored sunglasses.

"Al Gul, your wedding plans will be as scheduled." Ali used the cover name Kharzai was known by among the Taliban and allied organizations. "The old man made that very clear."

"How did you know that's what I was thinking?"

"Because that girl is the only thing you have been talking about for a week."

"I've talked about more than Leila this week."

"No." Ali shook his head. "No, you have not."

"I did too." Kharzai looked indignant. "I told you we needed to resupply the ammo cache at Bahawalpur."

"That was business. I mean, other than business, you have not brought up any other subject but this girl you want so bad. If you were so horny, you should have just gotten a prostitute. Hell, get a young boy to take around as your pupil…at least you won't have to worry about making more kids that way."

"You Arabs are sick."

"Arabs? You Persians have no room to speak. What's his name…" Ali tapped his temple to draw up the memory. "Iraj Mirza, the poet. Diddling boys was all he wrote about."

"Apparently, I do not read the same poets as you," Kharzai said. "That stuff never happened in my family. Our fathers made us iron chastity belts with razor blades around our bungholes."

158

"What?"

"Yeah, they had a hole for us to let out waste, but blades around the rim of the hole to protect us from any wrong-way traffic. It was hell on the furniture, but any man who thought he could enter me or my cousin's back door would've enjoyed a second circumcision."

Ali chuckled. "You are a strange man, Seirim Al Gul. Very strange indeed."

"All right, time to get serious," barked the driver. Kharzai's face reflected back at him in the rearview mirror. The driver's eyes were shielded by silver aviator sunglasses as well. "We are here."

The column of vehicles pulled into a cluster of single-story mud-brick houses and animal pens that played at being a village. Children scuttled between the houses in some sort of game, and a herd of goats looked up at the vehicles with the blank stare of bestial curiosity. Before the vehicles came to a complete stop, a cluster of laughing boys surrounded them, chattering all at once like a gang of monkeys, wide expressions of innocent joy on their faces, ignorant of the cold violence embodied in these men to whom they clamored for attention. Ali and the others pushed the boys out of the way, projecting a cruel terrorist persona. Some of the boys cowered and shrank back. Others ignored the mean men and homed in directly on Kharzai.

In spite of his reputation as a cold-blooded killer—Seirim Al Gul literally means hairy demon—Kharzai loved and was loved by children. He trotted into the mob of boys and with the toe of his shoe, snatched a soccer ball from one of them, starting an instant game of keep away. Boys chased him, tripping over each other, laughing at Kharzai's silly faces as they tried in vain to get the ball back.

Leila came out of a nearby house and stood at the edge of the play area. The loose end of a clean white dupatta draped around her shoulders and head fluttered in the warm breeze. The sunlight set her unblemished face aglow like a goddess. Like a manga artist's dream of beauty, large almond eyes peered at him from beneath the fringe of her dupatta, pools of deep brown that drew him in. Her bright orange loose-fitting shalwar kameez made him think of sunrise and fresh fruit. The baggy Pakistani clothing was not nearly as formless as the infamous burka, and while being modest by western standards, it allowed her femininity to remain apparent as she moved. Around her neck hung a thin gold chain with a heart-shaped pendant Kharzai had made from a twisted braid of gold wire. His mouth stretched with a huge smile and he winked at her, flashing bright white teeth through his thick black beard. She giggled in response.

"Al Gul," one of the men from the convoy called from the door of a house.

He kicked the ball over the heads of the boys, sending them on a chase as it bounced into a goat pen. A few of them followed behind Kharzai like a gaggle of goslings as he jogged toward the house. The man at the door snarled at the boys, stopping them short in fear.

"Go play," Kharzai said with a swoosh of his hand as he entered the house. They ran off. He glanced over to Leila as she walked into one of the other houses. A jolt of nerves wriggled through his belly as the door closed behind him. He mused how funny it was that al Gwahari's daughter could make him feel so giddy, especially in light of the fact that he was going to kill the man within the week. Then a different thought hit him.

I am about to kill my fiancée's father. What if she doesn't like me after?

But then he remembered that, although she could never say it aloud to anyone but him, whom she, like the others, only knew as Seirim Al Gul, she hated her father and everything he stood for. He was a companion of men like Osama bin Ladin and Iman al Zawahiri, mass murderers who controlled the population with terror. On the day he proposed to her, Leila confided to Kharzai that she hated the jihad. She hated the war and the fighting and the killing and wanted to run away from everything. She wanted to move to Australia or the United States and make a new life where she could be free from the fear that always surrounded her home.

When he asked how she could trust him with such words when he was a fighter like her father's men, she told him that he was different. He was not just another crazy jihadist. Something set him apart, but she could not put her finger on it. They would marry, then disappear and live happily ever after.

Kharzai entered the house and was led to the room where al Gwahari sat on a carpet, his war chiefs in a circle around a small table.

"Al Gul," his voice a gravelly rumble. "My son-in-law, please sit. Join us for tea."

Kharzai sat on the floor across from the older man. Al Gwahari did not look the part of a terrorist warlord. He lacked the evil sneer of bin Ladin and the dull-eyed mask of al Zawahiri. His grandfatherly appearance had worked in his favor to acquire alliances, but those who crossed him soon learned that it was a ruse. The kind-looking old man had no qualms in ordering, and overseeing, the wholesale massacre of villages that refused his demands. He had personally executed two Pakistani Intelligence, ISI, agents and Kharzai's CIA previous contact—luckily, the latter died without revealing Kharzai's duplicity. Al Gwahari still trusted him, as far as he knew.

"Thank you, sir. I am flattered you would invite me in." Kharzai bowed his head, his gaze focused on the floor in a gesture of humility.

"No, it is I who am flattered that a famous warrior of the prophet like you would marry my daughter."

"I look forward to being your son-in-law."

"The ceremony begins tomorrow, and the rest of the guests will be here by morning," al Gwahari said. "The next four days and nights will be for celebration, but now there is work to be done."

"Then I will not waste your time, sir."

Ali motioned to Kharzai. "Al Gul, bring in the case of surveillance information we left in the car. After that, you may go to the mosque and begin your purification while we discuss the mission schedule."

"Thank you, Ali aga."

Kharzai stepped out the door and back into the bright sunlight. The boys had given up on their soccer game and sat on the shaded side of the house playing with marbles in the dirt. Leila approached holding a tray of cups and a pot of steaming tea. Her head bowed in modesty, she turned her eyes up to him and smiled when he looked back at her, adding an exaggerated swish to her hips as she drew near.

"Three more days, my love. Only three days and we will be one," he said.

She twisted her face into a pout.

"I don't know, I think I might change my mind."

Kharzai raised an eyebrow and forced his face into a serious expression. "If you change your mind now, I'll strap on a martyr's vest and throw myself into a train."

"Then I will have to marry you. You're too cute to blow yourself up!"

They laughed. He held the door open and she walked into the house. Their eyes locked as she passed, like magnets unable to resist each other. The door closed behind her, breaking the bond. He walked to the car, practically floating above the ground, opened the trunk, and retrieved a suitcase of files and photos. Most of the images were already in the hands of the CIA and ISI, and counter-ops were already working on defensive measures.

As he lifted the heavy case, his cell phone bleeped with an incoming text message. Kharzai set the case on the lip of the open trunk and pulled the phone from his trouser pocket. He thumbed the text message button and read the words on the screen.

Impact imminent… DUCK!

A bright hiss screeched in the distance, growing louder fast. His heart leaped into his throat and he started for the house. He opened his mouth, shouting for the boys to run, but the words were shredded in midair, his breath torn from his lungs as the house erupted with an earth-shattering roar. The force of the explosion threw him back and over the car, and he landed in the dirt with a brain-rattling impact. He willed his stalled lungs to expand, to suck in air. Slowly, he rose to his hands and knees, pushed until he was on his feet, and tentatively stepped forward. Kept moving.

Where the house had stood was a heap of shattered bricks and splintered wood. Clouds of dust slowly settled over the rubble. Terrified villagers peeked from inside their homes, looking first at the destruction then up to the sky, lips moving with prayers beseeching Allah that no more bombs would be on the way.

Kharzai stumbled into the ruin like a man in a dream, a nightmare, searching for a way to get out of it, to rewind the events of the past few minutes. He scanned the area around the collapsed structure. He called her name, praying that she had stepped out the back door, or by some miracle had been protected.

He froze, voice caught in his throat, eyes locked on a flash of bright orange. It practically glowed, sharply contrasted against the shattered brick and charred wood. He moved toward it, saw her stockinged foot twisted beneath a large mass of crumbled stone. He started to reach down, to dig her out. A glimmer of gold sparkled two meters away to his left—her necklace. He stepped toward it, a trembling hand reaching to pick it up. His eyes clouded with tears. He wiped them away with his other hand. As he pulled the chain, a stone rolled aside. Thick strands of long brown hair wavered in a breeze that kicked up low to the ground. He glanced back at her foot and instantly realized that Leila's hair and necklace were entirely too far from her feet. He gasped as if he'd punched in the gut, struggled to force himself to a place of detached calm. He pulled a folding knife from his pocket and cut the hair as close to the source as he could, refusing the urge to dig her out, not wanting to see her face, moments before full of life and beauty, now mangled in death. He had the memory of the living woman he loved; that was the image he wanted to keep. He tied the lock of hair into a knot around the gold chain and pushed them into his pocket.

Six days later, Kharzai walked into a Lahore coffee house, the acrid smell of tobacco smoke and strong coffee stinging his nostrils as he crossed the mostly empty room to a table in the far corner. A deeply tanned Caucasian man looked up from the table and acknowledged Kharzai's approach. He started to rise, but Kharzai's expression advised him to stay seated.

"You were supposed to wait for my signal, Michael," Kharzai growled.

"We had the house on satellite," Michael said, leaning casually back in his chair, positioning his hand near the butt of a nine-millimeter pistol in a shoulder rig under his sport jacket. "Command knew we would only have one chance to get the whole leadership."

Kharzai struck out like cobra, snatching the pistol from him with one hand while wrenching him out of the chair with the other, jamming a knee into Michael's groin before he was fully on his feet. The agent let out a sickened grunt, doubled over and wretched, vomiting the chai tea he'd been drinking all over his shoes.

He sucked in a breath, sputtered, "We gave you a warning message."

"You killed a bunch of kids!"

Kharzai yanked him upright, leaning in, keeping him off balance. Kharzai clenched his fist, cocking his arm back. The CIA man's face twisted in expectation of the blow.

"They were playing marbles!"

Instead of hitting him, he dropped Michael back into the chair. He landed off balance, man and chair crashing to the filthy floor.

"Blame the Taliban, not me," Michael shouted as he struggled back to his feet, unable to stand fully erect, one hand protectively clasping his groin. "They're the ones who hide among civilians!"

"You could have waited until my signal."

The man tried to stand taller, attempting to assert his perceived authority. "Al Gwahari would have slipped away again. It was worth—"

Kharzai rammed his fist straight into Michael's nose. Blood sprayed across the man's shirt and he stumbled backward, knocking the table over and falling back to the floor. The man rose to his knees and touched his face. He winced and looked down in horror as blood continued to pulse from his nose and spread over his hands.

"Jesus," he whimpered. "You broke my nose!"

"You killed my wife," Kharzai growled. He picked a napkin up from the table and wiped Michael's blood from his knuckles. "Tell your boss that I'm out. I quit."

"You can't quit," Michael squawked, his voice liquid, nasal. Blood spattered from his lips with the words. "You're all we've got."

Kharzai stared down at him, quivering with barely controlled rage.

"Then it looks like you've got nothing," his voice was deep, bestial, violence not only implied but promised. "Tell them that I am dead. And tell them that if anyone comes to find me, they will be dead too."

★ ★ ★

"Hey, man." Brad's hand was on his arm. "You alright?"

Kharzai blinked his eyes, the people around the fire suddenly taking form again, the Turkish girl smiling at him, an odd expression on her face, as if she'd just seen him make a silly face she didn't like.

"Kharzai." Brad shook his arm.

He glanced at Brad, shook his head vigorously several times, and blinked several more.

"Yeah. Yeah," Kharzai said, giving his head a quick shake. "I'm fine."

"You sure?" Brad asked. "Because for a second there, your eyes got really weird and you looked like you'd seen a ghost."

"Sorry," Kharzai said. "It's nothing. Just a little unexpected déjà vu."

"What'd you think you saw?"

Kharzai looked at him, then looked at the fire. He stared for a long moment, took a deep breath, then looked back at Brad.

"Did I ever tell you about Leila?"

CHAPTER 23

Youngmi

"Youngmi Hwaejangnim," called the too-easily-recognizable voice from behind her, addressing her with a Korean title similar to CEO, a term the Communists despised as part of the capitalist religion, as opposed to the more commonly used Chinese word 'Tongzhi' which translated as 'comrade' in English. While the title was correct—she was the director of the Food Distribution Department—his tone was noticeably less than honorific. There was no mistaking the ingratiating, slithery tones of Colonel Ping trying to sound like he didn't despise the recipient of his attentions.

His words were rendered almost comical by the still stuffy headed sound of his voice, his nose still healing from being flattened in Seward a month earlier when he'd 'tripped over a loose spot in the carpet and fallen.' He'd only recently been able to remove the wads of gauze packed into his nostrils by the surgeon who'd straightened his nose back out. The man seemed to have no memory of his drunken attempt to rape her for a second time. She was certain this was the case because he did not even feign trying to hide guilt like the previous time. He did not avoiding her gaze or move away when she was near. He was guilt-free, because he was memory-free.

"You have been doing such a great job with feeding all these pitiful civilians." No matter what he tried to say to Youngmi, his words almost always came out with the weight of an insult. He continued in heavily accented English, "You must be very well loved by the masses of poor people that come for food."

He came up from behind the distribution table she was manning. Youngmi smiled at the family she was handing a parcel to, shook both the mother's and the father's hands, and gave the small girl and her older brother a candy, watching as they walked away. She moved back, directing another worker to take her spot and attend to the next family. Youngmi turned toward Colonel Ping and his entourage of assistants and bodyguards.

"Colonel," she said, ignoring his stuffy-headed slight, a tight, acquiescent smile playing across her face. She would not allow his poisonous name to cross her lips. "What a surprise to see you here. I was not expecting you. If you'd let me know you were coming, I would have ensured there was a place at the tables for you to meet the people personally."

His lips instantly curled into a sneer, rage seething in his features. It felt good to see him crash against the edge of control. Ever since his attempt at raping her the first time, he had dropped most pretext of politeness outside of General Zhang's presence. She, since the second attack, had taken up the tactic of antagonizing the oppressor, bullying the bully.

"That would not be necessary, Hwaejangnim," he snarled, then he returned to Mandarin. The vitriol in his voice was unmistakable. "I have no desire to…interrupt your aid to these conquered peoples." He emphasized conquered.

"Then why did you come, Colonel?" Youngmi looked at him with a well-practiced innocent expression only women seemed capable of mastering as a group on the scale of the entire human race. She had switched to a now nearly flawless Mandarin, instantly throwing him off guard.

"I am here to observe the 'groveling masses' for the presence of insurgents, and terrorists," he replied to her in Mandarin as well but used the English phrase, as if he wanted the civilians to hear and understand, although his thick accent left the word unintelligible to his intended audience. He continued in unadulterated graduate school-level Mandarin. "Unlike yourself, my mission is not to feed the families of the enemy, but it is to find their rebellious members and eradicate them."

He paused, then added with an almost generous air, "For the safety of the masses."

"Well, Colonel Ping," Youngmi said, unflustered by his attempts at linguistic superiority in Chinese, "you will find that the valiant soldiers of the People's Army and their fellow civilian party members are doing a very fine job of keeping such rabble away. We have had no attacks in over six months, and program participation is up nearly twenty percent. The people trust that General Zhang's government will treat them fairly, as all true Communists should."

Ping's expression turned sour; he'd obviously expected to come in under control, and to stay there, only to quickly find himself over his head, intellectually and linguistically, even within his own native language, moments into the encounter.

"If the colonel wishes," Youngmi continued, "I can supply you with reports and solid data supporting these facts."

"Such a report would be very helpful," Ping replied, a forced politeness in his voice. "Keeping track of the enemy is a communal endeavor, yes?"

"Yes, Colonel," Youngmi said, with a slight bow. Her posture, her voice, she would never show surrender to this man. She would never show fear.

"I will be here frequently in the coming weeks, Youngmi Hwaejangnim," he said, drawing out the title. "We have reports that enemy agents may be using the food distribution to pass on stolen and illegal information. They are twisting your very kind gesture to the defeated people to their own nefarious purpose. It is of utmost importance that we capture the criminals and insurgents, wherever they may be."

"But of course, Colonel Ping," she said. Her heart pounded against her ribs at that revelation. She forced a mask of peace to cover her face, wondering if he were here to arrest her for her own participation in the resistance until recently.

"They will be caught," Ping said with a smug expression, his wavering self-confidence rising on another crest.

He made no move, gave no orders for his men to take her. He puffed up his chest at her lack of reply, apparently thinking he'd gotten the upper hand. She let it go.

"You must keep us safe, Colonel."

CHAPTER 24

Chiknik

"This is Franklin," Gunnar said. "Our resident techno-geek."

"Nerd, please," said the relatively short, dark-skinned black man, thin but fit with broad shoulders and a well-groomed afro. Without looking up from the magnifying lens through which he was studying an electronic circuit board, he continued, "Geeks are the guys who pulled the heads off live chickens. Nerds only pull the heads off digital chickens."

"Okay then," the big Swede replied. "Gentlemen, let me introduce you to, Franklin the Super Nerd. He just got back from a foray into civilization for pieces for his Lego collection."

"You are just jealous that it was the Danes that invented Legos, and Swedes only have salmon and pickled herring," Franklin said.

"You're mistaking us with Norway," Gunnar said. "We have Nokia, Ericsson, IKEA, SAAB, and Volvo."

"Whatever."

The man rose from his stool, arching his back then bent almost double, touching his toes. His spine replied with a sequence of pops that was audible to all in the room. He straightened up and stretched his hand toward Tommie and Steve in greeting. "As much as I would love to, I wasn't shopping for Legos. I went into town to get electronic parts that I needed for our anti-aircraft array. Where are you folks from?"

"Anchorage originally. We were camped out south of Klutina Lake this past winter," Steve said. "And did you say anti-aircraft array?"

"I did," Franklin replied with a nod.

"I didn't see any anti-craft systems deployed around here in the month we've been on site."

"It is pretty well concealed a good distance out of town," Franklin said.

"Are you the one that made the RFID scanner?" Tommie asked.

Franklin screwed up his eyebrows in a look of surprise. "How'd you know about that?"

"Fella named Mojo showed us one that was given to him."

"Wow," Franklin pursed his lips and rocked his head in a slow nod, "small world. You guys were running missions on the Glenn Highway a while back, right?"

"All last winter we were pretty active," Tommie said. "Continued up to when our camp was discovered."

"How'd they find you?" Gunnar asked.

"There was a guy one of our patrols had rescued and brought in to camp. He'd said he'd escaped Valdez and had been roaming alone in the woods for a few months. One of the girls in our group recognized him as a pedophile who'd molested her just before the war started," Tommie said. "The girl freaked when she saw him and he made a runner into the snow. We think he got captured by the Russians."

"What was his name?" Gunnar asked.

"He told us it was Roger Anderson," replied Steve. "But the girl said it was Merrill Treadmore."

Gunnar and Franklin gave each other a dark look.

"Merrill Treadmore was banished from here for murdering a teenage boy," Franklin said.

"And for orchestrating the deaths of a number of our citizens for political gain," Gunnar added. "We couldn't prove the charges firmly enough for execution, but the council was convinced he'd at least had a major hand in it all. We banished him last September."

"That's about the timeframe we found him," said Tommie, "just before the first snow."

"The bastard apparently survived," Gunnar grunted.

"If he's the one who gave the Russians our location," said Steve, "hopefully he expired during the interrogation."

"That's all water under the bridge," Tommie said. "What's this stuff you're working on, Franklin? Building a motion-sensor grid?"

"Uh," Franklin seemed shocked that the Irish mercenary knew what he was looking at, "yes, actually. How did you know that?"

"I may seem like just another hairy-armed knuckle-dragger," Tommie replied, "but as it happens, I also have a degree in electrical engineering. And I have installed motion-sensor grids in combat zones behind enemy lines on many occasions."

"I see," Franklin said. "Well, then you'll probably recognize some of this stuff then as it is recovered military gear. But I have modified and enhanced most of it with various parts I've either scrounged or made. Better sensors, battery life, solar cells. And a really awesome feature I call the *frequency encryptor*."

The three men exchanged impressed looks. Gunnar turned to Franklin and said, "Unlike Tommie, I am not a hairy-armed knuckle-dragger with an electrical engineering degree. I am just a plain, old, regular hairy-armed knuckle-dragger. What is a *frequency enscriptor*?"

"*Encryptor*. And it is exactly what it sounds like," Franklin said. "Rather than merely using frequency hopping to break up a 256-bit encrypted packet into jagged pieces—technology that has been around long enough that someone has definitely hacked every possible combination, and can be quickly be replicated by the Chinese within hours of the first signal bleep then easily be decrypted using a receiver that has the same algorithm—my setup does a four-fold encryption. Like the old stuff, first it encrypts the data to be sent, then it schedules to change the frequency every one-tenth of a second. This is old fashioned stuff so far. After that, it multiplies the 256-bit AES code by the sum of a randomly selected sentence from my favorite book ever—'The Destroyer Volume Three: The Chinese Puzzle'—best book ever by the way. Anyway, the sentence is converted to binary and then we add up all the ones and multiply by the original code. It then encrypts that file again with a program I've written that is kind of proprietary to this system, mainly because I really don't understand how it works, except that it does. Anyway, that encrypts the entire frequency as it jumps into the next one, then it uses the end receiver's personal identity verification they have assigned from Chiknik operations to decrypt the whole thing."

Steve raised a questioning eyebrow. "How is it even possible to encrypt a radio frequency?"

"Okay, so, it's not actually *encrypting* the frequency, per se, I just call it that because what it creates is a signal that the other electrons have no idea how to deal with and so just ignore. These bad boys also create a multi-band roaming frequency jammer, so even if the enemy did start to detect a pattern, the jammer would scramble the signals such that they'd never get more than about one-tenth of any message and the chances of decrypting that data would be like, tens of gazillions to one. Our files can get back and forth to whoever or whatever we want to communicate with near invisibility."

"Near invisibility?" Tommie asked.

"Yeah, well," Franklin said, "you can't be ready for what you don't know exists; that is why I almost never answer in absolutes. I am all about random luck."

Steve scratched the top of his head, then glanced from Tommie to Gunnar and back to Franklin. "I have only the most basic understanding of what you just said, as in, *'Wow, that sounds really smart.'*"

"I have learned to just smile and nod," said Gunnar.

"So," said Tommie, "what you have is basically a multi-tiered encryption algorithm that turns every packet into a part of a Babushka doll, but each layer is actually a completely different design representing a different species with a completely different logic table."

"Uh…" Franklin smiled. He wasn't used to normal people understanding his work, let alone a hairy-armed knuckle-dragger. "Yeah, pretty much. Huh…that's a really cool analogy actually. Can I steal that?"

"It's yours."

"Where did you learn this stuff?" asked Steve.

"In the Navy," said Franklin.

"I was an officer in the Navy for more than twenty years, and never learned anything like that."

"Yeah," Franklin blushed slightly, "they don't usually trust officers with stuff like this."

CHAPTER 25

Ian

"We go in, load up, and we get out," Tommie said as they stood over the sand table mock-up of a Russian supply dump. "Recon said there is a half-strength company, about fifty soldiers, guarding it. Key items we need to snatch are mortar tubes and whatever ammo they've got for them."

General John Charles looked around at the group of Rangers, many of them veterans he had trained himself in the early days of the war. Intermingled with them were several of the scouts who had qualified to join them. Both Ben and Ian Stone were included in that group, as well as Tommie, now the eldest Ranger, surpassing Kharzai by two years.

"The recon team found a couple of these posted at the Eureka Roadhouse and at a couple other places they spied on." He held up a paper with Cyrillic and English writing describing three photographs.

"Is that a reward poster?" someone asked.

"Yup," said John. He handed it over to the nearest Ranger, letting it work gradually around the group, eliciting whistles and a number of looks toward their newest members, Tommie and the Stone brothers. "It says 'Most Wanted by Russian Forces Alaska' there at the top, and the rest of the page is in both English and Russian. You can read the dollar amounts beneath each picture."

When the paper made it around to Ben, his eyes went wide, a stunned look on his face as he handed it to his younger brother. Ian's expression hardened into a stone like mask. The pictures were shots of them and Tommie, not quite high definition but clear enough to be easily recognizable by an observant person. Before the war, Russia had been famous for dashcam videos posted all over the internet. These three shots looked like had been snipped out of just such a video. They were arranged two across the top, and one slightly larger at the bottom. Tommie's and Ben's images were labeled as 'Enemy Leader' and 'Enemy Officer' respectively and listed a reward of fifty thousand dollars, dead or alive for each of them. Beneath Ian's picture was the title 'Dracovacz.' Unlike the others, there were two reward amounts listed under his name.

DEAD - $75,000

ALIVE- $100,000

Report all sightings, or other information, to Colonel Grall, Commander, Spetsnaz GRU

"What is Dracovacz?" Ben asked.

"Dracovacz, The Dragon's Harvester," said Tommie. "Its a mythical Eastern European forest goblin that collects the souls of sinful men and children who died unbaptized. The latter to be given a chance to choose baptism, the others," he paused and drew in a deep breath, "to be slowly consumed for a thousand years by dragons."

Ian handed the paper to the Ranger next to him. The young man glanced at it, then immediately looked back to Ian, then back to the page. Mouth agape, he passed the picture to the next man.

"Dracovacz is usually depicted as a tall hairy wild-man with a battle axe or a scythe for harvesting the souls," Tommie continued. "In Scotland and the UK they have a similar creature called a Redcap, who eats the babies too."

"Dude," whispered the Ranger next to Ian, "that is seriously badass."

Ian gave him a look that said he did not want to talk about it.

"Now," Tommie said, a grin on his face, "how does a nice kid like you end up with double the bounty on your head than an old soldier like me and a rather cool nickname like that?"

"Must be my pretty face," Ian grunted back at him.

"According to our contact, a fellow called 'The Sourdough,'" John said, "this Colonel Grall is a Spetznaz officer."

While the term 'Sourdough' could be used to refer to almost everyone in the present group, it was commonly used in the arctic to describe non-native elders who had lived in rural Alaska or Canada's Yukon Territory. The nickname originally referred to the yeasty sourdough starter those prospectors, trappers, and traders used in order to make bread, some strains being kept alive for generations such that a person could eat bread made from the same lump of sourdough their great-great-grandparents had made bread from. This instance, though, referred specifically to the code name of Alex Tatum, hunter, trapper, wilderness philosopher, former assistant director of the NSA, and national security advisor to several presidents, who'd retired back to his Alaska bush childhood home after thirty years of government service.

"Apparently, this Grall personally tortured Merrill Treadmore to get the location of your merry little band of Boy Scouts. I am told that the wonderful Mr. Treadmore is no longer among the living. I, for one, will not weep for that loss," John said. "I wish that meant Grall was not a bad guy, but it seems he is indeed a very, very bad man. Regarding the present mission, keep in mind that this is an acquisition raid, not an ambush or hit. We want no gun play unless absolutely necessary."

"Translation," Tommie said, "if and only if the fecal matter hits the oscillating atmospheric impeller, we are to fight our arses out of that place as fast as humanly possible, then escape and evade."

"You're taking two of the Urals to load up the booty and two of the TIGRs to run security," John said, referring to the large six-wheeled medium cargo trucks and the Russian equivalent of light-armored Humvees.

"The Sourdough provided us with all the correct paperwork that should get you through the fence and up to the bunker. Load up as fast as you can and get out of there with as little attention as possible."

"Only Russian speakers will be in the cab of each vehicle and sitting at the ends of the truck beds where they are most likely to come in contact with the local soldiers," said Tommie. "If you don't speak fluent Russian, do not attempt to communicate or respond to anything."

Sunlight glinted off the windshields of their vehicles, blinding the drivers as they approached the road block protecting the small supply dump. The site was laid out like a temporary fire base, an almost medieval-looking fortress of earthen embankments topped by concertina wire and mounted with machine guns and sharpshooters. The only way in was through a hastily built log and razor wire gate guarded by a TIGR with a turret-mounted 12.7-millimeter machine gun focused at the column of vehicles. The Ranger's column was led by their own similarly armed TIGR followed by two six-wheeled Urals. A second TIGR, fully automatic belt-fed 40-millimeter grenade launcher pulled security to the rear. Weapons swiveled their direction from several positions along the barricaded perimeter, eyes focused on the newcomers with a calmness bred of boredom.

The Rangers spared no detail in their preparation. From the vehicles and weapons, to their uniforms, there was nothing that made them stand out as anything other than more Russian soldiers doing their job. Aibek Kaspersky, the driver of the first TIGR, had been a teenage refugee who had escaped from the Soviet Republic of Kyrgyzstan shortly before the fall of the Soviet Empire in 1991 and spent twenty years in the U.S. Army as an intelligence operative against running human intelligence missions against his old Russian overlords for his new country. Now in his late forties, with the cold demeanor of a man who'd seen too much violence, Kaspersky wore the rank of a Russian Master Sergeant, called Starshina, and looked every bit the crusty old NCO who knew nothing but war. His face was that of a man who realized he was getting too old for this game, that he was one of the walking dead whose time could be up soon. It also held onto the distinct look of one who was not yet ready to surrender to the boatman without a fight.

"What are you doing here?" shouted the guard at the gate, a junior sergeant, equivalent to a corporal in the U.S. military, younger-looking than Kaspersky's own youngest son.

"Command ordered us to come take some of the mortars and ammo for an assault force that needs them immediately," Kaspersky said in a perfect Kyrgyz accent, as if he'd never left.

"You got orders?"

"Yeah, I got orders." Kaspersky held out a clipboard with a paper that contained written data as well an RFID, Radio Frequency Identification, chip that contained digitally signed authentication codes for the orders to remove the gear.

The guard scanned the page and chip with a digital reader and verified the orders were authentic. He glanced at the young Lieutenant in the seat beside Kaspersky, then back to the older man.

The junior sergeant gave a wary nod and handed the clipboard back. "I know you've got your orders but damn, Starshina, I'd hate to be you when Colonel Grall finds you snatched his equipment."

"I don't give a shit. I just do my goddamned job," Kaspersky said, setting the document on the console between the front seats. "And *I* am not snatching his equipment, *General Galerkin* is. Now if you will kindly open this gate so I can get that job done, it would be very appreciated."

The young man backed off, signaling two other soldiers who lifted the log and wire barrier and dragged it aside for the small convoy to pass through, closing it behind them as the trailing TIGR passed the wire. Guns remained facing outside the wire, no longer pointing directly at them. The hairs on the necks of the men in the truck beds stayed rigid as the vehicles backed into the space in front of the entrance to the bunker containing the booty they'd come for.

The Rangers jumped down from the backs of the Urals, AK-12 rifles hanging on tactical slings connected to their body armor, uniforms perfectly accurate. Three real Russian soldiers came out of the bunker, a log-walled structure surrounded by stacks of sandbags and covered with a massive green tarp. One of them wore the insignia of a political commissar, a resurrected position in the New Russian Federation which was modeled identically after the Soviet version of the job that enforced 'right thinking' and 'public morale.' The position of commissar held no authority to make military decisions, but the holder of that rank could still get a man in a lot of trouble if he gave an unfavorable report. The Russian-speaking Rangers surreptitiously kept themselves between these soldiers and the rest of their own men.

"Who are you?" demanded the commissar. His voice was a high-pitched, almost serpentine sound, his tone as imperious as his title.

"I'm the goddamned tooth fairy," said Kaspersky. "Who the hell are you?"

The man's face reddened, rage instantly simmering in his eyes. "I am Senior Commissar Radin of the Vladislovska Division. And again, I ask, who are you?"

"I apologize for the insult Commissar Radin." He snapped a neat salute, although his eyes retained the sarcasm. "The sun is at your back and your rank is in a shadow. I am Starshina Kaspersky of the First Special Operations Group. I did not realize this piss-small outpost warranted such an esteemed political officer as yourself."

Radin eyed him closely then blurted out, "Let me see your orders, Starshina."

He handed the clipboard to Radin. The commissar studied the pages for a long time, glancing back up at him and the men and vehicles around him. He handed the clipboard back, eyebrow raised as he read the signature at the bottom.

"Get to work then," he said. "General Galerkin is not a man to keep waiting."

"No, he is never pleased with waiting," replied Kaspersky. The man turned away, surveyed the others briefly, then strode off toward a cluster of sandbagged structures that looked like a hastily built office. Galerkin, whose signature and digital encryption validated the orders, was commander of all special operations forces in the northern region. He was known to frequently order quickly planned assaults, diverting gear from regular forces much to the consternation of other unit commanders.

Kaspersky waved his hand and the men went straight to work loading cases of new mortar tubes and ammunition from a pile. Gunnar, wearing the rank of a senior sergeant, directed one team, Kaspersky the other, filling the backs of the two trucks. Within ten minutes, they'd loaded a pallet of rifle ammunition, several cases of rocket-propelled grenades, a dozen 2B25 silent mortar kits, and several hundred mortar rounds. The 2B25 was exactly what they came for, a small lightweight 82mm mortar tube easily carried by one soldier. The ammunition was designed such that when fired, the gases are captured inside the long tail of the projectile itself, driving the round by way of a piston slammed back against the mortar tube, producing neither fire nor smoke as opposed to standard mortars. The sound of a shot from the 2B25 runs about 135 decibels, the same as a loud hand clap, while a standard mortar blasts the air with nearly 180 decibels of body-shattering noise. A shot from the 2B25 would be undetectable from a hundred yards away when sitting inside a running vehicle, making it a perfect ambush or hit-and-run weapon.

It took moments for the Rangers to finish loading the weapons and ammunition. Just as the last crates were being hauled from the storage bunker, Commissar Radin returned.

"You." He pointed to the soldier nearest him, Ivan Czyrgiczlicz. "What is your unit?"

"Uh, sir...I..." Ivan stumbled over the words as he recalled the unit they were told to reply with in answer. "I am from the sixth and was assigned to this unit as a driver just a few days ago."

The Romanian archery expert's Russian was good, but clearly accented by his ancestry.

"Your accent is very strong. Where are you from?"

"I grew up in Romania, but my family moved to Russia when I was a young man."

"You need to work on that accent, you sound like a kolkhoznik." Commissar Radin said, referring to the Russian equivalent of a country bumpkin. "If you sound more Russian, you will have much more success in your career."

Ivan nodded slowly, as if taking in the political officer's words of wisdom. Radin slowly walked past the vehicles, eyeing each of the men studiously as they finished their tasks. He continued toward the bunker, glanced through the opening, then entered.

Ian was the last man still inside the bunker, placing the last explosive charge on a crate of hand grenades. He'd set the charges to start going off in thirty minutes or to be detonated by a remote if needed sooner. Radin glanced at him. Ian's tomahawk handle jutted slightly beneath his tunic, the axehead imprint barely visible against the cloth.

"That is not a regulation piece of equipment, soldier." Radin pointed to the weapon. "For cutting down trees, I assume?"

Ian, not able to understand the man's words, rose to his full height, glanced at the man, then slid the explosive charge out of view behind his back, blade arm toward the commissar.

"Don't you know how to talk?" Radin persisted. "What is that weapon on your hip, soldier?"

Ian tensed, edging further into a shadow behind the pallet of rifle ammunition.

Radin followed him.

"What is that in your hand, private?" he demanded. The commissar lurched forward, reaching out to grab Ian's arm.

Ian swiped his hand away. Radin's face contorted, a purple rage lighting his features, he balled bony fists, tightening until the knuckles white.

"How dare you touch an officer in such a manner," Radin growled.

The man postured to deliver a slap to Ian's face. Ian turned toward his attacker's direction, features becoming fully lit by the direct sun. Before he could deliver the blow, Radin's eyes widened in sudden recognition. "You're the one on the poster, Dracovacz."

He withdrew his hand and fumbled for the pistol on his belt, drawing in a breath to cry out. Before he could shout an alarm, Ian's left hand shot out, a ten-inch stiletto knife extended from his fist. The razor-sharp double-sided blade drove up under the man's jaw, crunched through his sinus cavity, and stopped with a solid jolt as the tip of the blade met the top of Radin's skull from the inside. Ian gave the knife a sharp left to right twist, scrambling the political commissar's frontal lobe. He kicked the man in the chest, letting gravity free the knife, the blade scraping against the man's teeth on the way out. The bully crumpled without a sound. Ian dragged him into deeper shadows between piles of AK-12 ammo. He wiped his hands on the man's clothes and hurried back to Tommie beside the trucks, clipboard in hand, four stars of a captain on his shoulder board.

"We have to go now," Ian whispered urgently. "I had to kill the commissar guy. I think he recognized me from the posters."

Tommie grunted and spat on the ground, then cleared his throat with three more grunts. The prearranged signal that they had to leave immediately. The Rangers finished loading whatever last item they had in their hands, mounting into the vehicles as they secured their loads. As the last few men climbed into the truck beds, the engines roared back to life. Metal tailgates were pulled and latched into place. Ian stood at the open back of the last Ural, rifle slung across his chest, safety off, left arm wrapped around the steel post that held the canvas cover over the back.

A cry exploded from the bunker, clearly audible over the rumble of the engines and tires crunching on gravel as they rolled toward the gate. A figure ran out of the shadowy entrance into the light, frantically pointing at the convoy making their way out of the base.

"We're made!" Tommie shouted into the radio. "Ram the gate! Ram the gate!"

Ian let off a three-round burst from his AK-12, dropping the screaming man in his place.

Explosions erupted as the lead TIGR's 40mm grenade launcher opened up with four successive high-explosive rounds shredding the gate, and the men manning it. The shocked Russians spun toward the noise, confusion freezing them in their tracks as they tried to figure out what was going on. As the lead

185

TIGR started into the open gate of the compound, two other soldiers from the bunker raised their weapons and opened up. The gunner on the rear TIGR returned fire, dropping them in their tracks. Then the whole world erupted in the chaotic roar of battle once again. The Ranger next to him, a man named Tony, yanked the pin from a grenade and hurled it out the back of the truck toward a mass of soldiers coming from the side, weapons up, muzzles sparkling with shots fired in their direction. The grenade exploded in the air at head level a few feet in front of them, shredding half a dozen men with white-hot shrapnel. They dropped like puppets whose strings had been cut. A dozen more were behind them, though, starting to get organized. Bullets snapped past the Ranger's heads, pinging off, and sometimes through, the light armor of the truck bed. A trio of men came around the corner of a structure, one of them carrying an RPG, the rocket launcher raised to his shoulder, hand outstretched, finger wrapped around the trigger. Ian watched as flame burst from the rocket launcher, the explosive projectile making a bee-line for his truck. He could actually see the rocket coming right at him, make out its shape, the displacement of air as hot gasses left a trail of wavy light behind it. Time shifted, stretching and slowing as the rocket inched its way toward him but, like in a dream, he could not move out of its path. He emptied his magazine into the team of men who had fired the rocket, spouts of blood geysering from their bodies as the stream of rounds hit them. The rocket streaked past him close enough that its exhaust burned his skin. It slammed into a heavy wooden post ten feet away as the truck sped through. The explosion sent a cloud of dust and shrapnel into the air, hissing past his ears like a cluster of flaming hornets. He felt several tugs at his uniform as shards of white-hot shrapnel passed through his clothes and ripped into Tony, pulping his face in an instant, the man toppling into the truck bed, his body wedged between the sidewall and the cargo.

The truck bounced heavily, lurching back into line as the driver corrected from being tossed about. Another boom and the truck bounced heavily. Ian felt himself rise into the air, feet leaving the metal floor of the truck bed, his body sailing up and over the tailgate. He slammed into the dirt, narrowly missing the rear-guard TIGR's body crushing tires.

He rolled to a stop, the scent of peaty earth and diesel fuel filling his senses for several moments. He pushed himself up to his hands and knees, tried to look up, then overcome by dizziness collapsed, face down in the dirt. Darkness took him.

The convoy streaked out onto the road, dust rising from their tires. The gunner of the last vehicle swayed violently in his turret, a burst of machine gun rounds spraying wildly over the heads of their opponents as the driver swung wide, over-correcting from the impact of the explosion.

The soldiers in the camp finally organized enough to pull vehicles together for a chase. Gunnar glanced at the side mirror on the truck he was in and saw them getting their stuff together. He picked up the remote detonator from the console between the seats, flicked the arming switch, and pressed the button. A loud boom sounded from inside the compound, followed half a second later by another, much larger, explosion. The concussion rattled the bones of anyone within a mile radius with a blast that sounded like the earth had been ripped open. A giant fireball ascended skyward, forming a dark mushroom cloud that flashed red and yellow, accentuated by more explosions as the pallets of ammunition inside the bunker cooked off.

Without enough survivors on the base to both save it and give chase, the pursuers never materialized. The Rangers continued down the highway for several miles as fast as they could go. They eventually pulled off the main road and followed a logging road deep into the densely forested mountains north of the small town of Glacier View. The town itself only had about 250 residents before the war, most of them, those who'd chosen not to join Brad's people at Chiknik, had been relocated to 'safe zones' near population centers. Those 'safe zones' being little more than concentration camps. The surrounding area was filled with a spider web of hunting and logging roads that meandered through the countryside. The Rangers were very familiar with this area, many having hunted there with their fathers since childhood. The convoy made their way to a thick copse of trees at the periphery of a long-abandoned logging site. They parked the vehicles under cover, killing the engines on the vehicles after pressing against a cliff wall sheltered by overhanging spruce and willow. They added camouflage webbing and tarps to break up the shapes so as not to be caught out in the open by a pilot or drone.

Moments later, the sound of a pair of double-rotor HA-52 Havoc attack helicopters bounced off the rocky mountainside around them with an echo that reverberated against every solid surface, making it impossible to tell where they were coming from. The helicopters seemed to hover for several minutes, their sound not changing. A Ranger dropped to a knee, Stinger anti-aircraft missile on his shoulder, scanning for the helicopters. After ten tense minutes of listening, the echo of the gunships faded in the arctic summer light.

Gunnar let out a breath. "Alright, let's get the wounded assessed and get ready to move again."

The plan was to take the Russian vehicles through back trails that wound through the mountains, allowing them to return to Chiknik with only a few short races on the main Glenn Highway out of the hundred-mile run. If all worked well, they would be home with their captured prizes in two or three days.

Ben walked through the men in the trucks with the medics. He had picked up a lot of field medicine while with Troop 104 that was well beyond the basic first-aid taught to Boy Scouts. Over the past two years, as Troop 104, the boys had been trained to nearly the level of paramedics. They were more than willing to assist the team medics. Two Rangers had been killed, their bodies laid out beside the ammunition in one of the trucks. There were several wounded, one bad enough that he would likely die before they made it back to the hospital in Chiknik.

"Where's my brother?" Ben called out.

"He was in the second truck with Tony when the RPG hit," one said.

Ben called out for Tony.

"He's dead," replied one of the medics.

Ben looked that way, to see a virtually faceless man lying flat on his back behind the URAL. Ivan, who had been on the 12.7mm gun in the rear TIGR. jogged over.

"Your brother fell out after that RPG. He was alive," he said. "I didn't see him until we passed too far from the gate, but the blast knocked him out of the truck. I saw him on the ground when the dust cleared, but we were too far away to do anything. The Russians were grabbing him when the depot went up."

Tommie gave Gunnar a look.

"You and your men don't have to come," he told the big Swede, "but I cannot leave Ian behind. That kid has saved our asses too many times."

"Let's take half the team in the TIGRs and go get him," Gunnar said. "The rest will start back with the trucks."

CHAPTER 26

Ian

Colonel Cristobol Grall was ten miles from the ammunition and supply dump when the fireball rose into the sky filling the large windows of the Eureka Roadhouse, his temporary command center, with panoramic views of the pillar of smoke. The glare in his eyes could not be mistaken for anything but rage. A radio crackled on a table at one side of the room.

"Da," answered the corporal manning it. The room fell silent as they listened to the survivors at the camp relay back what had happened. A constant string of explosions and small-arms fire punctuated the desperate tones in the speaker's voice. More than half the men manning the small post had been killed in the fight and ensuing explosion, over sixty dead, and another two-dozen injured beyond the ability to fight.

"We have also captured a prisoner," said the distant voice. "He matches the description of the wanted rebel known as Dracovacz and even has a tomahawk hanging from his belt that looks like the one described in the warrants."

"Dispatch a pair of HA-52s to find and destroy the thieves," Grall ordered his executive officer. To the radio operator, he said, "Have them deliver the prisoner to me here. Make sure the bastard is alive and healthy; do not harm him. I have special plans of my own."

The Eureka Roadhouse had been a popular hangout for hunters, bikers, and snow-machiners, or as they're referred to in the Lower-48, snowmobilers. With its four-thousand-foot runway, aircraft of all sizes could make a pit-stop or an emergency landing at any time. Eureka had been in constant operation for nearly a hundred years. They were quite famous for their world-class snow-machining, hunting, scenic views, and homemade pie, but especially for their locally roasted twenty-five-cent coffee in the era of five-dollar coffee at the fancy shops and coffee carts in Anchorage and Fairbanks. Hosting everything from biker rallies to snow-machine races to rock concerts, hunting derbies, and private airplane shows over the years, Eureka Roadhouse had a storied history.

The high alpine, nearly treeless tundra also offered a very convenient location for a FOB for the invading forces. Since the invasion, it had been turned into a small forward operating base with a company-sized unit plus an additional half-company hundred-man quick reaction force, QRF, to support forward firebases, such as the one for which the ammo dump was prepping supplies for. The rebel attack had been done and over so swiftly that the QRF was only able to aid the injured and bolster security, rather than confronting the insurgent force.

Twenty minutes after the radio call, a vehicle rolled to a stop at the edge of the open parking area. Grall stepped out of the lodge into the bright, hot sunlight. The main building of the roadhouse complex contained a large dining room that now served as the mess facility for the soldiers stationed there. The area between that building and the runway was dotted with several smaller out-buildings, including what had been the private residence of the owners. Those owners had been sent to a 'safe zone' and the base commander and his staff took over their house.

A small building that acted as sleeping rooms for the roadhouse staff had become officer and senior NCO quarters. The small number of staff who were not related to the owners were allowed to stay but were required to sleep in the storage room in the back of the kitchen. Outside, the remaining spaces were filled with rows of heavy arctic-weight canvas tents, their wall flaps rolled up to let the heat vent from inside so as not to turn the sleeping quarters into ten-man ovens in the constant summer sun. Green mesh screens remained secured to keep the mosquitoes at bay as much as possible.

Two fierce-looking guards, blue and white striped undershirts marking them as paratroopers, stepped out of the vehicle and approached the main building dragging a lone figure between them. They came to a stop, the man staggering as they jerked him upright.

Their captive was a tall young man, with almost features that could have been native, or Asian. He was athletically thin at the waist but had a thick neck and well-muscled shoulders. As Grall approached, one of the guards raised a truncheon and slapped the prisoner across the back of his thighs with a painful sounding 'thwack.' The blow forced the man to his knees, a grunt escaped his throat, bruised face twisting in a pained grimace. The man's arms were bound behind him, hands crossed over back to back, pinkies and thumbs tightly zip tied together. Grall looked down at him, an ugly sneer distorting his red face, lips turned up in a demonic-looking facsimile of a smile.

His hand flashed up. A crack sounded, Ian's head snapped sideways, the riding crop tearing a bloody gash across his otherwise smooth cheek, his knees buckled. Before he could . Grall grabbed him by the throat and jerked him upright, forcing him to lean back just enough to keep him off balance, his muscles stressed trying not to fall over. Grall leaned in to look closer at his prisoner, eyes inches from the young man's increasingly purple face.

"You are just a boy," Grall hissed in English, a sickening smile contorted his face. The pungent odor of alcohol puffed on his breath, forming a cloud around Ian's head. "But since you kill like a rabid animal, you will pay the price of a rabid animal."

The colonel let go of him, letting him drop back to the ground as he gasped for air. Grall flicked a finger toward his vehicle. The guards grabbed Ian's collars and dragged him across the gravel parking area toward the waiting convoy. He struggled as they forcefully raised him to his feet. The larger of the two soldiers punched him in the solar plexus, instantly crumpling the young man, his face again going red then purple as he forced his lungs to suck in air. They heaved him bodily into the back of a modified four-door GAZ TIGR command vehicle, its backseat space having considerably more leg room that a normal TIGR. Ian's lungs finally expanded as he slammed into the seat frame and steel door on the far side of the passenger compartment. Missing the actual seat itself, he ended up tangled in the footwell. He started to right himself, but froze as Colonel Grall entered the vehicle and took the other seat, Ian's tomahawk in his hand.

"You really should get into your seat and buckle up," Grall said, "for your own safety." The colonel leaned over and yanked Ian halfway up as if to assist him climbing into the seat properly. At the same time, he locked the boy's feet under the frame with his own boot, twisting his legs as he pulled. Ian's knee gave an audible pop at the pressure. He screwed up his face in pain but refused to cry out. "Oh, so sorry, mighty Dracovacz, Harvester of Souls," the colonel mocked. "Please don't put your blade into my skull. I was only thinking of your comfort and safety!"

Grall barked a harsh laugh, noxious clouds of alcohol vapor billowing on his breath, then dropped Ian back to the floor, sneering at the boy.

"Move!"

Moments later, the TIGR moved with the other vehicles of the convoy. Grall stared ahead as they got underway, keeping Ian's feet locked at an uncomfortable angle under the seat frame with his boot. Grall admired Ian's tomahawk in silence as the line of vehicles slowly ambled eastward on the Glenn Highway toward the main Russian base at Glennallen. The pressure of the zip ties on Ian's thumbs and little fingers had gone from highly unpleasant, to definitely painful pins and needles as the blood supply to his digits diminished. He started to wonder if he would lose those appendages before this was over.

"So, young sir Dracovacz," Grall finally said, his accent giving him a decidedly sinister aura to complement the evil blackness in his eyes. "I think you may be wondering to yourself right now, 'why does this mad man use two zip ties for one prisoner by tying his thumbs and little fingers like this instead of just using one zip tie around the prisoner's wrist?'"

Grall's expression went from evil sneer, to malicious grin, to malevolent grimace all in a blink, like he was possessed by a demon.

"Is that not what you are thinking?"

Ian continued to stare, unexpressive.

"I see. You are shy." Grall pulled a flask out of his trouser pocket and slugged a mouthful of its contents. He hissed out a vodka scented breath that caused Ian's eyes to sting. "I will answer that question you are too shy to ask then."

He moved his boot forward, releasing the pressure on Ian's own feet for only a second before he slammed his boot back with as much force as he could create in the confined space. Ian squeezed his eyes shut, jamming his lips tight, teeth grinding against the pain of Grall's attempt to dislocate his knees as he levered them against the steel seat frame.

"I do it," Grall snarled between gritted teeth, "because a mighty warrior like yourself is more likely to accept the consequences of tearing off his own fingers one by one in order to escape the disgrace of capture, than he is able to accept losing both hands as a whole."

Grall raised his eyebrows as if he were awaiting acknowledgment that his student understood the lecture he'd just received.

"You see," he went on, "men like you continue thinking, 'I only need one finger to pull a trigger, I can sacrifice the other nine as long as I have one left to kill a Russian.' Is that not what you think, boy?"

Ian stared back, expressionless. That was exactly his thought. He would resist until there was nothing left to fight with. He would kill every Russian and Chinese he had to in order to make his way back to his mother. He jerked back to avoid Grall's riding crop as it slashed carelessly past his face. Something sharp pierced the back of his hand as he leaned against the door. He pressed his fingertips onto the edge and found a centimeter-long twist of ripped metal, a recent bit of damage judging from the razor-sharp edge. Ian twisted his wrists and began to slowly saw the plastic tie that bound his pinky fingers.

"Why are you here?" Ian managed to blurt out.

"Excuse me?" Grall drunkenly smirked his direction, caught off guard by the question.

"Why are you in my country?" Ian asked back.

"Why are we in your country?" Grall laughed out loud, as if that were the funniest joke ever. He leaned back, raised his leg as if to slap his knee in his mirth, then stomped down on Ian's foot, sending a jolt of pain that made him twist his body in agony. The zip tie on his pinky gave way, and as he sat back up, he was able to reposition his thumbs against the same sharp edge.

"Ah, but you are young and idealistic, aren't you, Dracovacz." Grall laughed again. His words came out in a mocking slur. Grall's face suddenly morphed from one of hysterical laughter to a mask of red-faced hatred. "You have no idea—"

An explosion boomed near the front of the column. Black smoke rose into the sky from the distance. Another explosion damaged the front tire of the vehicle directly in front of them causing it to skew sideways and crumple to the pavement.

"Go around it!" Grall shouted to his driver. The rush of adrenaline instantly sobered the Colonel up. The radioman in the front passenger seat repeated his orders. "Keep the convoy moving!"

The convoy started again, making their way around a recon vehicle that was being shoved to the side of the road by the following unit. Gunfire erupted all around them. The soldiers started to open fire from the turrets of the tactical-armored TIGRs. The ambushers put a halt to that with a hail of rocket-propelled grenades one of which exploded against the hood of a truck full of men, spinning it with such force that bodies spun out of it into the air, propelled by a few tons of centrifugal energy.

Grall's driver yanked the wheel to the left, throwing the vehicle far out over the shoulder, avoiding the ball of fire erupting in front of him. The concussion from the exploding truck nudged them hard, sending them over the embankment, the body of a soldier thrown from the unarmored truck bed thumped against Grall's door, his face slamming the passenger-side window and sliding off, leaving a trail of blood and other fluids.

The driver fought to regain control but the TIGR floundered in a patch of loose gravel, sending them down the steep road embankment. He recovered as they reached the bottom and were back on nearly level ground twenty feet below the highway between a twenty-foot-high wall of fist-sized stones and a dark forest. He gunned it with hopes of getting around the ambush, back on to the highway and escaping with his commander and the prisoner. The vehicle bounced as if a giant had stomped the ground next to it, all four wheels leaving the ground as the air convulsed with the force of a huge explosion on the road above. The vehicle rocked sideways, stones and debris clattering against the side like rapid gunfire. Suddenly, a massive shadow loomed over them. The earth rumbled as a tractor and trailer loaded with two out-of-service TIGRs rolled over the embankment toward them.

The plastic tie on Ian's thumbs finally broke through, the sharp metal piece slicing into the meat of his hand. His head smacking the door frame as the vehicle lurched again, sending a brilliant burst of white stars flashing in his head. The massive trailer with its sixteen-ton payload of up-armored TIGRs crashed into them like a giant baseball bat, sending the vehicle airborne toward the forest where it came to a thunderous stop against a very large spruce tree. The driver's side front door burst inward, shattering the soldier's arm with an audible crack. The radioman slammed against the corner of his set so hard his skull shattered, the plastic earpiece embedded inside the hole where his ear had been moments earlier, dead eyes staring at driver in surprise.

Grall slammed against his seatbelt, a strangled grunt half escaped his lips as the shoulder strap caught against his throat, visibly crushing his Adam's apple. Struggling to breathe, his eyes rolled back and he seemed to lose consciousness. He slumped in his seat, a string of bloody saliva ran from his mouth, drizzling his shirt as he tried to hold his head steady. It was his turn for his face to turn purple.

Ian lunged at him and snatched back his tomahawk. He tried to grab Grall's pistol from his thigh holster. The weapon was wedged against the mangled door, the seat frame, and Grall's own body. He gave up on the gun and dropped back against the door behind him, groping for the handle to open it.

The driver bolted awake and glanced into the mirror. Seeing Ian free from his bonds and trying to get out, he drew his own weapon and turned to shoot the prisoner. He twisted, screaming against the pain of his shattered left arm as he tried to get his pistol over the seat and aimed at the boy. Ian's hand flashed up, the spiked end of his tomahawk puncturing the side of the soldier's skull puncturing at an angle just below the temple and continuing through, the point a bloody spike that jutted from the top of the man's head. The pistol fell from his hand into Ian's lap then clattered to the floor.

Ian tried to retract his tomahawk. The blade was stuck fast, wedged into the skull bones of the driver, and he couldn't get the leverage he needed to pull it free. He reached behind him and found the door latch, snapped it open, and immediately collapsed out onto his back, scraping his flesh on jagged gravel and rough tree roots. He snatched the pistol from where it fell at his feet. The battle still raged on the road above, gunfire and explosions rippling the air. He reached into the cab of the TIGR, twisted the dead man's head around, grasped the handle of his tomahawk, and yanked the homemade weapon from the skull with the all-too-familiar grating sound of bone on steel, a gush of blood following in a thick bright red ooze. His eyes landed on an AK-12 next to the radio man's corpse, he reached for the rifle then changed his mind when he noticed the barrel was visibly bent. Instead he reached across the driver's body and snatched the two spare pistol magazines from a pouch on the man's belt, then ran into the woods, in the direction of the ambushers, stripping off the Russian uniform shirt he'd been disguised with for the initial raid. It'd do him no good to escape from Grall only to be shot by his own men.

Four men crouched behind a fallen tree poured machine gun fire into the column of vehicles on the road.

"Chiknik Rangers," he called out.

They looked his way, weapons ready, but recognized him immediately. Twenty yards further, he made eye contact with Tommie, the latter sounding the retreat signal. The rest of the group quickly broke contact and rushed into the woods, disappearing as fast as they'd come in.

★　　★　　★

Ben dropped to the ground, sitting next to Ian where he leaned on a rock outcropping. He tapped him on the shoulder with a brown plastic bag, offering the packet of Russian MRE potatoes and beef to his little brother. Ian tore the package open and spooned a mouthful, grimacing at the flavorless glue-like substance.

"Here." Ben handed him a miniature glass bottle of tabasco, the kind from an American MRE packet. Ian often wondered how it was his brother somehow always had one of the little spice shots on hand, "Put this on it to flavor that bland crap."

"I think that this may be the reason they invaded," Ian said, his Adam's apple jumping as his throat labored to force down the chewy paste. "They are just in search of flavor and texture."

"Glad we got you back, little brother." Ben patted him on the knee. "That was pretty scary."

He swallowed another spoonful of the now spicy grey mash, still bland but with a vinegar and chili pepper aftertaste, and washed it down with some water. "How did you know which vehicle I was in?"

"Well, to be honest. We didn't," Ben said. "We kinda guessed."

Ian gave him an incredulous look. "You mean, you started blowing cars up *hoping* I was not in one of the ones that you destroyed?"

"Basically, yeah," Ben acknowledged. "Like I said, it was pretty scary."

CHAPTER 27

Sammi

"Hey baby, I'm back! I've got great news!" Brad's voice echoed in the small house.

Four weeks after he left on yet another mission, he walked back into the house as if he was never gone. Sammi was not going to run to the door and hugging him like this was some kind of *Hallmark Moment*, not this time. She had been working on the next school year's curriculum while trying to soothe a three-month-old baby who hadn't stopped crying for what felt like days. She did try to call out a response from the loft bedroom upstairs but had no energy left, not even enough to form a single word. Victoria snored softly next to her, the silence after his announcement rolling like an ocean over her, pulling her into a blissfully dark abyss of exhausted sleep.

"Sammi?"

She heard what sounded like her husband's feet coming up the steps to the second floor. The design of the house left the main room below open to the second story. Radiant heat pipes in the cement floor worked together with the iron woodstove outside to spread heat to the whole house, including the two bedrooms upstairs. In the summer heat, the stove was left unlit, leaving the floor cool under their feet. The bedroom door creaked open, light from the upper windows streaming across the open space, illuminating the bed. Sammi cracked her eyes open just enough to see Brad's shadow standing in the doorway, backlit by the bright subarctic summer sun.

"Honey?" he whispered the word. "You asleep?"

Sammi tried to respond but it felt like her words were absorbed by a dream, failing to drift his direction. Her mouth unable to form the shape of sounds, weary muscles refusing even a twitch at the voice she loved so much. The sound of the voice that belonged to the man who had abandoned her twice when she needed him most. In the last months of her pregnancy, he had taken off to Anchorage to assassinate the Chinese general, a mission that failed to do more than put the general's mistress in the hospital. And then, when she was utterly exhausted and needed his help with their daughter, he leaves for another month on some secret rendezvous with other resistance fighter groups. Her body had no energy to move, but her mind could not stop racing.

If he loved me like he says, why does he keep leaving me?

He stood over her, looking down with a loving expression at her and their child. He stared, contented. Then his expression hardened, the smile going flat, eyes filled with some odd combination of fear, love, and hatred.

Is he angry at me? Why is he angry at me?

He sucked in a breath, wiped his hand across his face, then leaned down and gently kissed mother and child on their heads, three times each as he always did. He had explained the ritual shortly after they'd married the previous summer.

"Once to thank God for giving me you. Twice to thank you for loving me. A third for the future, whatever it may bring."

She liked it, whatever the meaning. He rose, turned slowly, and left the room. Sammi drifted into a deep, dreamless sleep.

CHAPTER 28

Brad

He stepped into the house and called out.

"Sammi?"

No answer. The house was dead silent.

"Sammi?" he called again.

His voice echoed against the high ceiling and upper spaces. Still no response. He slipped off his boots and padded up the stairs to the second-floor loft bedroom. The door was partially open. He pushed it gently with the tips of his fingers. Sunlight streamed from the second-floor windows, bathing the bed in bars of light, showing him a most beautiful sight. His beautiful young wife and their daughter, lying side by side on the bed, pale cherubic faces in states of totally peaceful relaxation. His heart thumped a couple odd beats at the sight of the two women he loved more than anything in the world. He blocked the direct sunlight that shone on their faces with his body, not wanting to wake them. Enjoying the moment of peace.

Then his mind exploded with the memory of Youngmi's face in the passenger seat of General Zhang's SUV, stretched in terror as the explosion tossed the vehicle on its side, flames licking up and around. The image switched with a mental pop and click like an old-time slide-projector. In its place was Youngmi's new Mercedes with the custom license plates, and her body slumped in the front seat, blood staining her favorite T-shirt, blotting out half of the once sparkly sequins, her face an unrecognizable pulp, blown out by the bullets that had punctured the luxury SUV at dozens of points.

Which one is real? Which one is my wife?

He had been asking that question for months now. He had seen his wife dead in the opening days of the war. Then two years later, he saw her very much alive, and the apparent mistress of his enemy. He blinked back tears of frustration.

One or the other is real. If she is dead, I will see her in Heaven one day. If she is Zhang's mistress, then she might as well be dead to me.

He wiped his hand across his face, trying to shove the past behind him. He wondered where his sons were. He'd heard rumors about what happened to slope workers like his oldest, Jay, a twenty-seven-year-old chef who ran the dining hall at the North Slope's largest airport. Those who renounced their U.S. citizenship and swore an oath to Russia were allowed to live as slaves in a virtual gulag on the icy Arctic coast. Those who refused were beaten, then forced to work at half rations until they collapsed and died, any who dared speak out in opposition were summarily executed. He had no idea which of those camps Jay fell in to. His son had a strong will to live, but also was not one to back down from bullies.

He had seen Ben and Ian from a distance during the initial days of the war. Brad and Kharzai, having met only days earlier, attacked a company of Chinese helicopter troopers coming after the scouts. Through a combination skill, and a seriously lucky shot, the pair of them downed one helicopter full of commandoes and killed the remainder of the surviving enemy on the ground in a gunfight that turned hand-to-hand in the most intense violence he'd ever experienced. In the end, the two of them had killed sixty men in a matter of minutes, allowing the boys the time they needed to have a chance to escape and survive. The troop had not all made it though. The second helicopter had killed a dozen or more, some with gunfire, but most when it crashed into the edge of the glacier they were crossing. Brad could still see their crushed bodies floating away in the frigid river that surged from beneath the eons thick ice. He and Kharzai and raced further down river to find their way across. They did not see any of the bodies sa they went, the clothing of the dead having most likely filled with glacial silt that dragged them to the bottom, buried beneath the river until some future ice age recedes to reveal them again.

He was certain his younger two sons were not among the vanished dead. Something inside him knew that they were alive and free somewhere to the east. He'd taught them woodcraft and survival skills from before they could walk, both as a Boy Scout dad and on family hunting and camping expeditions. From the time they were five years old and big enough to hold the little Henry .22 caliber lever-action rifle, they had learned to shoot and dress game ranging from snowshoe hare or grouse, to animals as large as moose and bear. He hoped that along with those physical skills he had managed to pass on to them a will, a desire, to survive whatever it takes.

He took a deep, cleansing breath, held if for a second, and let it out. Then leaned down and gently kissed Sammi on the head, three tender brushes with his lips, a ritual he always followed. Once to the thank God for his wife, a second time to thank her for her returned love, and third for the future, whatever it may bring. He repeated the ritual with baby Victoria, took a step back, then slowly turned and walked out of the room.

CHAPTER 29

Jung & Kharzai

"Just one time?" Kharzai said, his voice begging.

"No," Jung said. "I do not do that sort of thing."

"You can try," Kharzai said, adjusting his position on the bed so her head was farther up on his lap. "Just one time is all I ask, and if you don't like it, I will never ask again."

She pushed away, backing out of his loose grip.

"I said I don't do that sort of thing," Jung repeated, a stern look on her face as she stared directly into his eyes.

Kharzai let out a frustrated sigh and dropped back against the bedstead, a resigned look on his face.

"Not ever?"

"Never!"

"Okay, who should I ask to do it for me then?"

"There is a whole town of nice young women out there who would be more than willing to take care of you with all the enthusiasm you want, just not me, not that way at least."

"You've seriously never done it before," Kharzai asked, sounded genuinely confused, "like with other partners?"

"No, not for anyone, ever," Jung replied. "Not even my ex-husband. I will watch, but I will not participate."

He let out a long sigh.

"Alrighty then, fine. I'll see if Erica, the baker's daughter will do it. She seems pretty open to things, a bit adventurous even."

"That's fine with me," Jung said. "She's young and energetic, very pretty. She is actually a good match for you, I mean like coloring wise. Her hair and skin would offset yours pretty nicely. You'd look good together."

"She is incredibly fit too," Kharzai said. "I saw that earlier in the year at the end of winter party. She just kept going and going. And she has a nice throat, and good breath control."

"Yes, she really was quite lovely," Jung said. "Outdoing everyone."

"Best talent show ever," he said. "But that was a solo song and dance act. Can she sing and dance a duet, do you think? Especially in harmony?"

"She has a really good mid-range voice and a superb ear for music," Jung said. "If you can get her to do your little piece together, who knows, you might just win the show this time."

"Are you sure you don't want to sing with me?"

"No!" Jung grasped at the thick matte of hair on his chest and pulled herself up until she was face to face with him, eliciting a painful grimace that screwed up his eyes. A grunt escaped his throat through twisted lips. Jung stared squarely into his eyes, her nose touching his. "I said I do not sing on stage with anything less than a fifty-person choir to hide my voice in. And I NEVER dance on stage."

Kharzai looked dejected.

"But!" she said, "there are some things that I do like to do only as a duet."

"Oh my." Kharzai's eyes went wide.

She planted a kiss on his mouth and pulled the blanket up over their bodies.

"This performance," she growled in his ear, her hot breath sending shivers down his spine, "is for a private audience only."

CHAPTER 30

Brad

The stack of papers on his desk looked overwhelming. Lists of projects, harvest numbers, supplies brought in by patrols, items lost or destroyed in contact with the enemy.

How could a town this small generate this much paperwork?

Recon team reports were what he primarily wanted to find in the stacks, but only a couple had been filed while he was out. Other teams more recently returned to the town from their forays into enemy territory had not had time to write their reports yet. Nestled in among the sheets of rough homemade paper was a leather binder that contained a number of criminal cases being tried by the council judges, a team of three men and three women chosen by the community to adjudicate disputes and preside over the trial of actual criminals. The reports ranged from a teenage boy who stole a pie from an open window to an accusation of rape of a child. The former would be given a slap on the wrist and additional community service chores; the latter, if found guilty, would face public execution.

Brad looked up as his recently assigned clerk stepped into the office.

"Mornin', boss," said the clerk. "You ready to sign these?"

"Morning, Sam," Brad replied. "Sign what?"

Sam the clerk's full legal name was Samwise Gamgee Underhill. That was the man's real, legal name. Underhill was his actual family name. That said, Frodo's famous stalwart sidekick from the *Lord of The Rings* trilogy was his parent's favorite character of the books and the 1978 animated movie. When he was in elementary school, most of the kids thought it pretty cool. But when the movie series came out at the turn of the century, the then thirteen-year-old Samwise quickly learned to keep his full name a secret if he wanted to avoid the inevitable mockery and bullying kids heaped on anything different. Now, nearing early middle-age and disabled from wounds incurred in the Army in Afghanistan, combined with much more serious wounds from his time with the Chiknik Rangers, Sam found himself serving the role of supporting character in real life.

"These are the awards you are presenting at the special formation today." He handed Brad a stack of certificates, about sixty of them. "Put your Brad Hancock on the line at the bottom of each."

They were nice-looking computer printouts, full color, and on surprisingly good paper stock with what looked like actual gold threads woven into the pages. The paper itself had been handmade by the village print shop. The writing and scrollwork, elegant, hand-drawn calligraphy. Brad wondered how much of this kind of quality stuff they'd be able to do for future events. They had a few computers and laser printers that still worked, as well as a large professional grade color copier/printer that had probably cost the mining copy twenty-five thousand dollars or more new, but now was worth more than a Gutenberg original would have been. All of the electronic items were sparingly used as it was nearly impossible to get parts or new toner and ink; therefore, most documents, posters, and other items were hand-drawn with ink made from berries, dried leaves, or soot.

Items requiring mass dissemination were manually copied with an old-fashioned pre-electric hand cranked printing press. They even had a couple of the kind of ditto machines Brad remembered from his high school days back in the early '80s. The certificates he was signing were very fancy compared to those old homework assignment sheets with the watered down purple ink. These were the work of skilled craftsmen who'd reverted to the old ways as a matter of course.

The event these certificates been created for was the first award ceremony since he'd taken over executive operation of Chiknik just a little more than a year earlier. While his position was as much to be a figure head as an actual working leader, kind of like being the King of England but without the personal fortune as Kharzai had once put it, he was a figure head that still had very real responsibilities, like being the face of the resistance. The Chiknik Council ran the village just fine, and could do so without him or any of his meager skills. What they could not do was lead warriors into battle. They had been unable to take the fight back to the enemy. John and Gunnar were both excellent soldiers, and excellent leaders of warriors, but neither had the stomach for any kind of diplomacy or people skills. They easily formed a band of war fighters, but they had not been able to encourage normal civilians, people who weeks earlier had been students and grocers and physical therapists and landscapers. Brad, as it turned out, had both the training and natural talents of a warrior and the innate ability to draw people to himself and motivate them. Whoever in the world would have said before the war that Brad Stone, an IT manager for a government agency and long time Sunday School director, was the kind of guy who could actually be the political leader of thousands of people, would have been considered seriously demented.

It had been weird being thrust into a position that literally saw him go overnight from leading a group of just over a dozen stragglers who'd 'roughed it' at a luxury resort for billionaires in the Alaskan wilderness to managing a city of thousands of people, a city that continued to grow over the following months to more than four and a half thousand. And yet, here he stood, in just that position.

Going into the third year of the war, new arrivals had declined significantly both in frequency and in group size. Groups like Matthew's band were very few indeed. This was good for the fact that the area could not naturally sustain many more. On the other hand, it also meant that there were simply not enough people left who could escape and survive this long.

He had only been back from the mission to meet the other militia leaders for two days when the latest long-range patrol came back from what had been planned as a quick raid but had morphed into an all-out battle and the loss of four Rangers dead, with many more injured.

"The troops will be ready in formation in about thirty minutes," Sam said as Brad started signing the stack of awards. He grabbed half a dozen pages and fanned the certificates to expose just the signature lines, signed them quickly, placed them upside down in another pile, then repeated the procedure, keeping the signed copies in the same order as originally handed to him. "Gunnar and General John will address the formation with a short speech, news updates, and unit assignments for upcoming projects. Then you'll come out kind of like doing a military review, with John presenting the troops."

"A review of the troops?" Brad said. "Whose idea was this? I am not some stinking king or something."

"No, but while you were out, we all agreed that the review and the ceremony would be good visual symbolism to the population that we're organized and doing well," Sam replied.

"Who is this 'we' who agreed to this?"

"All the members of the council, as well as John, Gunnar, and myself, and Sammi too."

"My wife agreed to this?" Brad was actually kind of shocked; she'd barely spoken a word to him since he had returned.

Kharzai popped into the office without knocking. "Hey, Brad, everybody is getting lined up out here. Is there some kind of show going on? If so, I hope it's a musical, I absolutely love musicals! Oh, hi Samwise, how's things in Hobbiton? Have you got your talent show act together yet?"

"Fine, blue boy, I see Jung let you out of your bottle again," Sam replied to the hairy one's *Lord of the Rings* jibe as he always did, referring to him as the Genie from *Aladdin*.

"She likes to take advantage of me special powers, yes," the hairy Persian replied in a cheap knockoff of the Lucky Charms Leprechaun.

"You look silly without a beard," said Sam.

"And you will be cursed forever for even noticing the lack of my beard. When it grows back, it will kick your butt in a game of chess."

"We'll see about that," Samwise replied. "You haven't beat me yet, beard or no."

"Yes, Kharzai," Brad said as he signed the last certificate in the stack and placed it with the others. He'd not even read any of the names or citations of what they had done; he'd have to do that as he passed them out. "There is a show, but, to my knowledge, there will be no singing. It's an awards ceremony for the militia members."

"The award recipients will be arranged in a single group standing out from the others," Sam handed Brad a wireless microphone receiver and continued as if he'd not been interrupted. "Four columns, three rows deep and fifteen bodies wide, arranged by seniority of length of service, longest-serving vets first, newest members at the end. The certificates are ordered starting from your left and moving right at the first row, then right to left for the second, and so on. Got it, sir?"

"Yes, yes, I got it," said Brad, rising from his chair and handing the signed certificates to Sam. "Let's raise the curtain and get this show on the road."

CHAPTER 31

Ben

They had gathered in a large central courtyard, the space reminding him of the village green at the scout's first encampment, near Tazlina Lake. They had built that entire place, dubbed Scout Town, by hand with raw materials from the forest. Dugout cabins, half underground with round sod roofs and wood-burning fireplaces made from stone and baked clay that kept them warm even when temperatures dropped below -40 degrees. That village had been obliterated by Russian missiles after a two-man special forces team spying on them had not radioed in their evening report. That report had been missed because the pair had been killed by Ben and his team of scouts.

This field had the same sort of look to it, but not the same kind of feeling. This was someone else's place, built by other hands. He still wasn't quite sure what to make of living with this many people. It felt like he was walking around in a giant bullseye and that they would one day wake up to a rain of bombs. Now that he was in the Rangers, he was relieved that he may not have to stay in the town very long, or very often. They spent the vast majority of their time living in the field on their own, just the way he'd begun to prefer.

He stood next to his brother in the last line at the rear of the group of soldiers that had been separated from the main body. The formation stood in front and to the side of the others. The whole assembled group looked like it numbered in the hundreds, if not a thousand or more. It seemed as if he'd never seen that many people in one place at one time even before the war. Only a few of the faces in his section, faces of both men and women, were recognizable. Being so new to the group, he still had a lot of people yet to meet.

He wasn't sure why they had been separated from the others, and why he was among these that had been in the Rangers for a lot longer. Someone had said that Ice Hammer would be presenting awards to some of the soldiers. He wondered who those would be and what they had done to get such an award.

Sergeant Major Olafson called out for everyone to come to attention. The man was a giant who looked like something out of a comic book about Vikings. He also had a voice that sounded like thunder. The entire group snapped erect, the position of attention, heels smacking together in almost perfect unison. General John Charles strode to the podium on the tall wooden platform that had Ben had seen being set up in the common area earlier that day, silver stars glittering on his epaulets. Ben wondered if the general was related to his brother's now dead best friend Charlie Charles, a Yupik Eskimo who'd been killed during the Russian attack on their last camp.

"Warriors!" John spoke into the microphone on the podion, his voice booming over the speakers positioned around the common area. He had an accent not too different than Charlie's. "Two years ago, there were only a few dozen of us. Today, our militia stands at just about two thousand soldiers and our community nearly five thousand strong. We defend what is left of Alaska against the invaders. You are the two-edged sword of the American military. You are the last good hope for freedom. Today,

214

we are organized to recognize the myriad accomplishments of our military members in this public ceremony. Brad Stone, the Ice Hammer, is going to present these awards and recognitions to those who have been selected by their peers as valiant fighters, and other contributors to the struggle for our freedom."

A figure came out of the headquarters building at the edge of the common area just behind the stage. The man was average height, thin, with dark hair and a brown beard streaked with wisps of gray. In the distance, sunlight flashed against his eyes, reflecting a steely glare set in a strong-looking brow. He was accompanied by two others who walked just behind him. One of his companions had a huge ball of black hair around his head like a massive afro, except his skin was not as dark as a black man of African ancestry, more like a dark-skinned Middle-Eastern man. His appearance reminded Ben of the owner of the Goldmine Bake Shoppe, where they got donuts every Sunday after church back in the before. The Middle-Eastern-looking man did not walk like a soldier, stiff and martial. He looked more like some kind of animated cartoon character. The other man behind him did walk like a soldier, one with an obvious limp like he'd been badly wounded in his leg. Ben could not see Ice Hammer's face very clearly in the distance, but he did seem to be an impressive man. Broad shoulders, thin build, yet muscular. He moved like a natural predator, fluid motions brought to mind a jaguar on the prowl, projecting carnivorous intentions with every step. In spite of all that, something about the man seemed familiar. His mind raced to find the context, but the answer eluded him.

"Army of Chiknik," Gunnar's voice bellowed, echoing across the still morning air. "Prepare for inspection!"

The entire group of soldiers, already at attention, snapped their eyes to the newly arrived supreme commander with an almost audible click. The Ice Hammer strode to the first line of soldiers at the opposite end of the formation stopping briefly to speak directly with a soldier every so often, sometimes shaking hands or saluting.

Ian glanced over and whispered, "Is this the super guy we heard of?"

Ben gave him a look, then turned his eyes back to the front. Ian glanced back up toward the podium. Ben followed his gaze and noticed a woman standing at the row of chairs on the stage. She too seemed familiar to him, as if he had seen her before. She held a baby at her chest and looked over the formation as if she were a queen.

She must be Ice Hammer's wife.

He followed the young mother's eyes back to her husband and watched as Ice Hammer made his way across the formation, occasionally stopping in front of a soldier to say something. He spoke to several of the men and women as he moved from company to company. Ben's eyes scanned back to the woman on the stage.

Sammi, that's her name. She was one of our Sunday school teachers. What kind of chance is that?

He heard a rustle of movement and realized the Ice Hammer's entourage was at the head of his group of soldiers. They had stopped and were positioning themselves to face the main body of watchers. General John stepped in front of him at that point and called out to the assembled crowd.

"Ladies and gentlemen," the general's voice rose above every other noise in the commons, "we will now present awards to our soldiers for bravery in the face of the enemy, as well as non-combat deeds that led directly to the preservation of life and safety."

Ice Hammer stepped up to the first person in the formation of soldiers in Ian's group. The limping sergeant beside him handed him a paper and a small medal on a red ribbon. He read the citation; his voice amplified over the speaker system so the whole assembly could hear.

"Medical Sergeant Giacolone, for your actions combat in the ambush on the Old Glenn near Butte, please accept this recognition of the deeds you performed that saved the lives of numerous soldiers in that action."

He handed a similar paper and medal to the next people in the formation, one at a time, reciting their actions as well.

"Sergeant Phillip Staley, also for the ambush on the Old Glenn Highway near Butte, please accept this recognition for your actions that resulted in the destruction of numerous enemy vehicles and soldiers, as well as organizing the successful evacuation, in the face of overwhelming enemy forces, of the surviving members of the Ranger platoon involved in the initial attack."

"Corporal Martin Staley, for deeds of heroism saving the lives of several of your teammates and leading the recon element of numerous ambushes."

"Sergeant Amanda Phillips, for recognizing the need for and implementing the position of senior watch officer to oversee the patrols of the wall."

Sergeant Phillips' medal hung from a blue ribbon, signifying non-combatant contributions.

"Staff-Sergeant Hernandez, for heroic deeds in the assault against unknown enemy forces near Glennallen last fall."

Ben listened as the list went on. These people had seen a lot of action with the Rangers, and had done some pretty crazy stuff or had been highly organized and fast thinkers to do things that made like better for everyone. He did not know why he was in this line. The only thing he had done since joining the Rangers was let his brother get captured and then participate in his rescue at the cost of other men's lives.

As Ice Hammer came through the lines, Ben stole a few glances his way to try and catch his face. The man moved with a tempo and rhythm that was familiar enough to make him think of his father, who he hadn't seen in more than two years. But this man, bearded and deeply tanned, and with deep wrinkles around his eyes, was way too thin and did not limp as much his father had due to injuries he'd incurred in the military long before Ben was born. The man moved closer down the line. He was two soldiers away when Ian suddenly gasped, then choked up. Ben started to reach for his brother, then saw what he saw.

"Dad?" Ian gasped.

"Daddy?" Ben stuttered as he caught his breath, words rolling out of their own will. "Appa?" he switched to the Korean word for Daddy. He took a half step forward and fell to his knees. "Appa, how…?"

Ice Hammer looked at him, and seemed to swoon, nearly fainting, his eyes wide as if he'd seen a ghost.

"Ian?" he muttered, blinking with disbelief. "Ben?"

"Daddy?" Ben cried, emotion ripping into his voice.

"Boys!" Brad said, spreading his arms and receiving the sons he had assumed he would never lay eyes on again. "Oh God! You're alive!"

"Dad!"

"Appa!"

CHAPTER 32

Reunion

"How?" Ben started. "What happened? How are you Ice Hammer?"

"It is a very long story," Brad replied. "To be honest, I really don't know how I got this far myself. Me and Kharzai saw you boys running toward the Knik glacier when those helicopters came in. We held them back so you guys could cross."

"That was you?"

"Yes, son." Brad nodded. "That was me."

"Why didn't you follow us?" asked Ian. "You could've lived with us."

"I tried," said Brad, "but the helicopter that crashed onto the glacier's edge broke off the access. There was a two-hundred-foot gap from the shore to the ice."

A heavy silence came over the room for several moments as each of them went back to that day in their minds.

"So…how have you boys been?" Brad awkwardly switched it back to his son's storyline. "What have you been doing all this time?"

"Surviving," said Ian.

"Taking the fight back to the enemy," said Ben. "We spent the first winter training under Mike. He was one of the scout dads who led us out of Gorsuch on the first day."

"He's a retired Green Beret," added Ian. "Well…he was. He was killed when they hit our second base in the spring. Him and Tommie taught us a lot of useful things."

"Tommie?" Brad asked.

"He's a friend of Mike," Ben said. "An Irish mercenary he'd met in his army job."

"They taught us a lot," Ian repeated. "After a year of training, we started attacking the Russians."

"You guys have been doing live missions?" Brad was incredulous. He still pictured his sons as kids playing little league and learning to swim. The thought of them in actual combat was at first abhorrent, then in another glance he saw the men his boys had become, now nineteen and sixteen, looking like grown men. Ben was the same age as when Brad had earned his place in the Force Recon community in the Marines. But his eyes told of seeing more combat at his age than Brad had ever seen. Ian, his sweet and smiling youngest son, now had eye that looked like blazing coals and wore a hard-looking scar on his cheek.

"Yes," said Ben. "We've had more than twenty combat actions since this time last summer."

"And no losses until they attacked our last home base. More than half our people were killed in that fight," said Ian.

There was a long pause.

"Have you heard anything about Jay or Mom?" Ian asked.

"No, at least nothing about Jay." Brad choked a little, unsure of how to answer the second part of the question. He had seen their mother dead, but then almost two years later he saw, or thought he saw, her alive again, as he blew up the vehicle she was in. He took a deep breath then added, "I went back to rescue your mother, but…" His chest shuddered with emotion at the memory of the first days, "I saw her body in her car. She was killed in the initial attack."

The boys were silent. They stared down at the floor. One of them let out a barely audible exhalation. Their breathing grew heavy, weighted with long held back sorrow, the boys barely holding back sobs that threatened to flow over at the news.

"Are you sure?" Ian said, voice cracking as it penned in a potential storm burst of emotion. "Are you sure it was her you saw dead?"

"She had the 'Hollywood Style' shirt on," her favorite shirt, one they all knew, "and was in her new car."

"So you didn't see her face?" Ben said.

"There was no face to see, son," Brad said, instantly regretting the stark picture that painted for his boys.

Ian's body trembled visibly, hands gripping the arms of his chair. His emotions stretched to break free for the first time since it all started. He spoke with a quiver in his voice.

"I was so certain she was alive still. She still feels alive in my chest."

Ben drew shaky breaths, closed his eyes, and stretched his face toward the ceiling.

"Are you sure it was her?" Ben said, tears welling up over his eyelids, sliding down his cheeks and disappearing into the the legs of his dark green trousers. "Like Ian said, I've felt like you were both alive all this time."

It was Brad's turn for a shaky breath. He had seen her body. He had also seen her face in Zhang's vehicle seconds before it blew up.

"I only know what I saw that day, son," he said. "Things can be, and often are, very different from what we think we saw. Until now, I was convinced."

Another long pause. Each of them stared at the space near their feet, one occasionally glancing at the others before again focusing on the floor. After several seconds, Ben straightened, sucked in a deep breath, and wiped the moisture from his face with the back of his sleeves.

"So," he sniffed, "where do we go from here?"

"What do you mean?" asked Brad.

"What do we do, as father and sons, from this point?" Ian defined the question for his brother.

"Continue on," Brad answered. "Nothing has really changed. I am the leader of this village. You are my sons. You are also warriors. We keep bringing the fight to the enemies."

"But what about us," Ben asked, "as a family?"

"We saw Sammi. She's your new wife, isn't she?" Ian blurted. "And that baby, is our...sister."

There was another long silence, this one even less comfortable than the last.

"I..." Brad started. "Your mother is dead. Things happened and I..."

"I think we understand, Dad," said Ben. "Sammi is a good woman. She was my favorite Sunday school teacher when I was a little kid. I am sure she will be a good second wife."

"Look, boys," Brad said, the next words rolling out of him barely under control. "I am sorry for the loss of your mother. She was my wife for almost thirty years, much longer than either of you have been alive. I..." his eyes clouded, stinging from salty tears that rose and overflowed, "...there is nothing I can say or do to bring her back. Until I saw you guys out there this morning, I did not even know if either of you were alive, let alone Jay who I've heard nothing from."

Ian stared at his father, mourning seemingly already over, his expression one of observation, detached scientific inquiry. He tried to feel empathy for his father, tried to understand how he could have given up on their mother so quickly, while he himself was certain she was still alive. The answer would not come. Only anger filled the place that should have showed him that answer, anger and a sense a betrayal.

The door to the office creaked open. Sammi stepped inside, a little baby girl in her arms.

"Ben? Ian?" The smile that glowed on her face seemed genuine. A real sense of joy at seeing them alive. Ben rose to his feet and crossed the room, wrapping his arms around her in a hug.

"Hi, Sammi," he said, his voice choking with what Ian assumed to be a flood of memories. His brother was soft that way.

"It is so good to see you both!" Sammi said, wiping tears from her own eyes as they disengaged. "I am so happy that you guys are back with your dad."

"Who is this little one?" Ben said, smiling down at the baby.

"This is Victoria," Sammi said.

Ben touched her cheek, eliciting a happy gurgle from the infant. He smiled down at her.

"Would you like to hold her?" Sammi asked.

"Sure," Ben said. He had always been soft for babies and puppies. He took their half-sister in his arms, smiling and cooing at her.

Sammi crossed the room, arms wide to take Ian in a hug too. He rose to his feet, awkwardly accepting the embrace, his cheeks flushing. Ian wasn't sure why she would be so happy to see him. She was not his mother, and he'd be damned if he let her assume that place in his life.

"Ian," Sammi stared into his face, her hands grasping his muscular shoulders, "last time I saw you, you were maybe nine or ten, just a little boy. And now look at you, a full-grown man."

His face twisted in a semblance of a smile that failed to hide the discomfort he felt in the situation.

"It's nice to see you again too," he muttered, unable to look into her eyes.

She pulled him into another tight hug, planted a kiss on his cheek, then let him go. He sat back down and watched as she walked over and took a seat next to his dad. His father gave her a gentle smile and took her hand in his.

The scene looked like something out of someone else's life, like one of those stock pictures of smiling fake families in the frames at the store. His mind yearned to wake up from this slow-moving nightmare.

Ian longed for nothing but to hold his real mother one more time.

"So," said Todd as the brothers walked into the temporary housing they'd been assigned, "what's he like?"

"Who?" muttered Ben.

"Ice Hammer," said one of the other boys. "Your dad!"

"He's just a guy," Ian said.

"Just a guy?" said another scout. "Yeah, sure, he's just a guy who shot down a helicopter, then chopped up a bunch of Chinese special forces guys with an ice axe so that we could escape, and then had a bunch of refugees just automatically form around him, then fought against and escaped from an army ten times bigger when they came to capture him, then went on to become the leader of this whole city, and is the commander of the biggest militia in the state!"

"You make it sound like a lot, but he just did what any of us would have done," said Ian. "He is nothing special."

"Nothing special?" a voice spoke from the back of the crowd.

All twenty of the surviving boys and girls of Troop 104 filled the long room. Several were working on putting a large blue tarp up to divide the male and female sections of the space. The speaker could not be identified at first, until he stepped into the light from a window.

"You may not think that your dad is all that special," the boy who was not yet done with his puberty voice, "but he literally saved my life."

Ian squinted to see the source of the voice as it moved nearer, then his eyes grew wide.

"Aaron," he said, astonishment plain on his face as he recognized the boy who had abandoned them more than two years earlier. Aaron had joined with the group of parents and leaders that had doubted Mike and Tommie's leadership in the early days. They did not think it could possibly be a real war going on, so after two weeks of trudging over the mountains, they followed their doubts and turned back to hike along the highway to the city. The rest of the troop never learned what happened to them.

"You survived?"

"Yes," Aaron replied, "but only because of Ice Hammer."

"What happened to the others you left with?"

"They are all dead," Aaron replied, his eyes no longer holding that confused boy look of before. "We got attacked by a gang of biker guys, like the guys from Sons of Anarchy. I got knocked out and trapped under some dead bodies. The gang robbed us of all of our stuff and then left us there to rot. A couple days later, Ice Hammer's guys found me wandering around lost in the woods. They rescued me and let me stay with them. If they didn't let me join with them, I know for sure I would be dead too right now. We went through a lot of battles before we got here to Chiknik. We even had a house we were staying in that got attacked and burned to the ground by the Chinese, and the whole time your dad kept us together, organized us, and made us into fighting shape."

"I'm glad you are alive, Aaron," Ian said, reaching out to take the other boy's hand. "Really, I mean it. I am glad you are alive."

"If it weren't for your dad, I wouldn't be."

CHAPTER 33

Brad

Brad rubbed his eyes and tried to focus on the work in front of him. He'd had his sons and Ben's girlfriend Katarina, at their house for dinner the previous night. The evening had been as awkward as the first meeting in his office was. They managed to get some small talk, but in the end, the two women led most of the conversation, all three men too lost in their own thoughts and simply staring at each other to keep things going. They had invited the boys and Katarina to sleep there for the night, but they declined.

"As a squad leader, I need to be there to make sure everyone is up to PT tomorrow," said Ben.

"And for us lowly non-squad leaders," said Katarina, "we need to be up early because this guy is going to make us do PT in the morning. We'd hate to wake you and the baby when we leave at such an ungodly hour."

Ian had just nodded, not saying anything.

Family tensions or not, there was still a war on. Regardless of what was going on in each person's life, there really was only one primary focus for anyone who wanted to last very long. The next morning, he had to get up and come up with a plan to keep these people alive for another winter. That morning came early. Sammi had fallen asleep in his arms, Victoria sleeping in the basinet beside the bed. He laid there as long as his body could take it, until his joints became so stiff, he was afraid their creaking would awaken mother and daughter. He carefully slid Sammi off his arm, gently rolling her onto her side facing the baby, then pulled the blanket up to her shoulder and rolled himself off the other side. He dressed and made his way out of the house and the few blocks to his office. It was just before 4AM.

Brad glanced up from the sand table mock-up of downtown Palmer laid out on the conference table. It was a large-scale model of the area surrounding the former borough government headquarters, surrounding streets and structures set up in detail. The miniature version of the borough building, as well as the several acres of soccer and baseball fields around it, included the most recent updates brought back by recon teams that reported back. The area was fast being converted from a major FOB to a heavily fortified primary base.

Several colored flags stood atop pencil poles marking the various Chinese units that were known to be at the station already. Several other flags stood in a row along the side of the box indicating potential reinforcements their intelligence believed might be available to quickly add to their numbers.

"They're building the city into a straight-up primary military base," said Brad as he explained the situation to the west of Chiknik to Tommie and Steve. Prior to the war, Steve and he had spent many nights together camping in the mountains or on a river float trip with the original Troop 104. That was back when it was merely a Boy Scout Troop, and not a paramilitary guerilla force. They'd both been adult leaders of 104 for over ten years, their sons being nearly the same age. Tommie, he'd not met until that day.

"If they're able to get a fully fortified garrison there," he continued, "we may be done for. That will be a whole lot of men and armor coming our direction. We won't be able to hold them off for long once they're that close."

"What timeframe does it look like they'll be set up beyond our ability to damage them with our current resources?" asked Ken Caukins. His men, and their families, had moved to Chiknik to assist with training new troops that were coming in constantly.

"About late December," said John. "Christmas timeframe, give or take a week."

"That's not something you likely want in your stocking," said Tommie.

The group absorbed that knowledge, studying the sand table in front of them. Four months at most to train and move into place. All without being detected by the PLA or the Russians.

"How many men are at that base already?" Steve asked.

"About five hundred," John said. "A full-strength battalion, with some light armor and a couple of medium tanks. But our secret squirrel has informed us that they're supposed to be getting another entire regiment in there by year's end. That's another two-thousand soldiers. More than the entire Chiknik guard force, Rangers, and TPF combined."

"Why haven't they had more men there sooner?" Tommie asked. "Two years into the war and only five hundred men guarding the northern approaches?"

"They were focusing on the Kenai, Kodiak, and Southeast areas, and Bethel," Kharzai said. "All the big fisherfolk and Farmer Dans put up a pretty good fight. Mao's maniacs needed those areas to lock up the food resources. Remember, as Napoleon said, 'donnez-moi s'il vous plaît le bon vin, mon amour.'"

Tommie raised an eyebrow at the hairy madman. "Please give me the good wine, my love?"

"Preach it, baby." Kharzai waved a hand and nodded. "Wise, wise words. And not only that, but he also said another good one which is this, 'An army marches on its stomach.' Which always sounded very uncomfortable to me, I usually march on my feet, but you know, he was French."

"About a year and some months into the war, the Kenai surrendered," Brad said. The Kenai Peninsula as a whole was usually referred to as 'The Kenai,' as opposed to using simply 'Kenai' which indicated the city of six thousand for which the peninsula was named. The larger area is an Alaska borough, similar to a county in other states. While the concept of a borough is like a county, the physical size of the Kenai borough, at nearly twenty-five thousand square miles, is physically larger than ten American states. The Kenai includes the well-known Alaskan cities of Seward, Homer, and its namesake. The Kenai, as well as a few areas of the far southwestern tip of Alaska, provide the world with Alaskan red salmon, halibut, and king crab, staples for the local populations that were also delicacies sought for world wide.

"So, now that they've got the resistance pretty much subdued in that area, they're ready to really put a focus on us," said John. "Until now, the Russians have controlled the northern portions of the state and still control the oil pipeline, something I doubt they'd be willing to give their allies. But it looks like the Chinese want to grab a little more of a hold on the oil here, as well as the coal in the interior."

"We've been feeling their grip tighten already," Gunnar interjected. "Lots more recon patrols and anti-ambush teams than before. They've already got the added bodies available now to reach out and touch us a little harder."

"How soon are you planning to go in?" asked Tommie.

"We're making a preliminary plan for the attack," said Brad, "then have to let the other militia leaders know, the ones that have not already moved in with us. Once we've got assurance of who is with us, we'll set the exact date. I expect it will be by the end of October, maybe early to mid-November at the latest. Three months max."

"Ground is good and hard at that time, easy for transport," Tommie said. "Frozen, but not too much snow yet."

"Yup," Gunnar said. "Our SUSVEEs eat that stuff up fast."

"And harsher weather in the following months would prevent them from rebuilding for most of the rest of the year," Brad said.

"You guys got good night vision?" asked Steve. "'Cause that's when it is dark early."

"We've got plenty night vision tech," said Kharzai, "but we've also learned to do things the old-fashioned way."

"Oh?" said Tommie. "And what is that old-fashioned way?"

"We flash disco strobes at their night vision goggles then dance naked across the front line. Renders them defenseless every time. Brad usually leads with Gunnar repping the 'bigger' guys in the crowd."

Tommie and Steve both froze their stare onto Kharzai.

"Uh…" Brad muttered, "that didn't really…."

"That was a fun mission," Gunnar said, patting Kharzai on the shoulder and blowing him a kiss and a wink.

"What the…?" Brad blurted.

"What happens in Glennallen, stays in Glennallen," Kharzai muttered, showing a palm to Brad like some R&B diva.

"You guys are literally insane, right?" Tommie asked.

"How do you define…insane?" Kharzai said.

"Anyway," Brad said, pointing back at the sand table, "let's get back to some sort of reality."

He pointed down to the model. "Between our Rangers and the TPF, we have roughly two thousand fighters ready to deploy.

The other militias, as far as I can tell, can, combined, provide that many plus two to three hundred additional maybe."

"The Staley brothers pointed out an interesting feature of Palmer," Gunnar said. "Apparently, there are tunnels under the whole city, built back in the colony days in the 1930s. They connect most of the buildings built back then and up until the late forties and early fifties. The tunnels used to enable the residents to travel without going into the icy winds in the winter."

"I forgot about that," said Brad. "Are they still usable?"

"According to the Staleys, they were a few weeks before this crazy stuff started," Gunnar said. "They were running around in the tunnels deeper than most of the other teens in the town. According to them, most of the tunnels were clear and stable at that time."

"Can we bring the boys in here to get more details?" Brad asked.

"They are standing outside awaiting your invitation right now."

"Bring them in."

A moment later, Phil and Martin were led into the office. The space was nearly full so they remained standing near the door.

"Tell us about the tunnels under Palmer," Brad said.

"What do you want to know?" Phil asked. Then he walked over to a map of Palmer hanging on one wall. "Our favorite entrance was here, through the cellar doors of our neighbor's house. Their son Ted had discovered it in junior high, and we've been going in from there ever since, almost ten years now. There are a number of entry points around the city, mostly in the older housing areas that were built in my great-grandparent's times but most are still totally open, even though PPD tried to close them often due to the number of kids smoking dope down there."

"Sometimes kids were smoking so much that the fumes rose up into other people's houses and some apartment buildings," Martin added.

"We weren't part of that group," Phil clarified.

"No," said Martin, "we just knew they were there because we heard about the complaints. And because we could smell it when we went down."

"Anyhow," said Phil, "there were definitely fresh air gaps in the tunnel that could leak up into the above-ground buildings."

"How far do they go under the borough building and other structures the Chinese are using?"

"They go all the way under the borough building," Phil answered, "but the doors into that building are bolted shut pretty tightly." He picked up a pointer and traced the rest of the description over the model. "They cross under that building and go up to the Presbyterian Church and several older houses on the south side of town. One also goes over to the old CARRS grocery story there in the mall, although the old mall has been torn down now for some kind of new complex they were building on that space. The tunnels are still there, though, and are probably still accessible if you know where the entrance is."

"Do you know where the entrance is?" asked John.

"There were three under that mall," said Martin. "Originally, there were several houses there from the old days. Each of the entrances is covered by an iron plate and a massive lock."

"There are also gates under Pizza Delphi, Noisy Goose, and Potato Palace."

"Potato Palace?" Tommie asked.

"Yes," said Phil. "Best spuds you can imagine, like the best baked potatoes with every imaginable filling ever. Great place. And former site of a home that had enough money to build a tunnel all the way into downtown more than a half mile away.

Although it wasn't a single tunnel that far actually, it connects to the other tunnels in the area."

"This could be very useful," said Kharzai. "How wide are the tunnels? How many men can move down them?"

"Some," said Paul, "are barely wide enough for two thin men abreast, but others can hold four or five men side to side. Plenty of room to move a company or even a battalion element through fairly quickly."

After two years in the militia, Martin spoke as if he were a long-time military professional. He had picked it up naturally as he grew as an operator among the Rangers. He and his brother's innate knowledge of the Palmer/Wasilla/Butte areas had been, and still was, a valuable tool to getting into those and the surrounding areas.

"I've been thinking," said Phil, "we could always pack the tunnels full of explosives and collapse the building right under their feet."

"That is kind of exactly what I think we're thinking," said Kharzai.

"Well then," said Phil, "I think we think you'll think we are exactly who needs to go on this mission."

CHAPTER 34

Mai

After having had no satellite imagery for most of the year, and no drones in the air since a fuel delivery had been sunk several months earlier, a network of freshly built spacecraft had been placed in orbit and finally had come online. While the Americans had been unable to stop the ultimate destruction of their space and air superiority a previously unknown American-built space defense system had managed to partially survive the initial digital attack and deliver a retaliatory strike against several dozen enemy automated space craft. Adding to the expected amounts of defensive strength on the American part, was the truly frustrating fact an undetected security hole in their own systems had allowed the PLA's custor computer virus to get into many of their own satellites knocking an entire section of the observation grid, including parts Siberia, Alaska, and the Yukon, offline.

Adding to the difficulty, during the first two months of the war, a pair of American nuclear missile submarines had individually managed to evade Chinese and Russian forces long enough to launch a full-scale retaliatory attack that crippled China's capability to build new drones and satellites. Those factories were quickly rebuilt elsewhere, but the majority of existing new drones had been destroyed, not to mentioned tens of thousands of lives lost, including many of the brightest and best of China's engineers. After nearly two years the stockpiles had been rebuilt, PLA Alaska Command was back in business with a god's eye view of the rebel strongholds.

Mai's problem was that now that those satellites had been replaced, it was as if the spigot had been opened and her desk was flooded with more data than she could possibly sift through in a lifetime. Dual twenty-seven-inch computer monitors held similar aerial views of a cluster of buildings and a scattering of what looked like farm fields. On one screen was an image taken from a backed-up copy of Google Maps, dated ten years earlier. It was the latest version of the imagery database for the south-central Alaska region the Chinese government had copied down from the company's servers prior to full-on hostilities, prior to that company's satellites being turned into space bricks like almost every other man-made object floating around the earth. The second screen contained the latest new imagery from China's Ziyuan 6 northern hemisphere satellite system known as Běi yǎn, The Eye of the North.

Even with the use of the latest technology, the task was daunting, particularly in a place like Alaska where few places outside of the handful of modern cities were built with straight roads or a purposeful design. Unlike most modern places, where towns were built on grids and laid out in straight lines, Alaskan towns still had the haphazard design of places that had first been settled by a handful of people in isolated cabins, who eventually created meandering walking trails to each other's homes. Other homes were added over years or generations, until eventually, there was a town of a few hundred people scattered in the forest. Add to that the fact that Ice Hammer and his people, whom she had been tasked with finding the location of, were intentionally trying to hide their presence, and her task became even more difficult.

To that end, she was tasked with comparing the two sets of images for 'before and after' changes that may indicate a location for this, as Colonel Ping preferred to call it, 'mythical city' of Chiknik. While the city itself had existed prior to the war, it was little more than a village of scattered residences in the area of a very small footprint coal mining operation. The layout of steep mountain valleys, caves, and glaciers in the surrounding areas, combined with poor census data gathered from the traditionally anti-government population in the area, made it very difficult to pinpoint where the current settlement actually was to someone unfamiliar with the area.

To help with the search, complex algorithms had been created by the computer science nerds at central command, but those algorithms that work great in finding human-made patterns in urban and suburban areas kept pinging on random piles of glacially deposited rocks, icebergs, and natural mounds of vegetation. Twice, she'd investigated deeper only to find that the computer was concerned with a large pile of bear dung that a shadow had rendered into something like a small pyramid.

Mai closed her eyes, salty tears causing the dry surfaces to sting. She rubbed her eyelids with the tips of her fingers, blinked a few times, then leaned back into the desk. She swiped the touchpad beside her mouse, using the in-app command to move the images on both monitors the same distance and direction, and began playing 'spot the differences' on the next grid sector.

This sector had a dozen red boxes showing possible human structures, same as the last half dozen sectors. The only one that had turned out to be probably human-built was what looked like an abandoned cabin. The lack of any kind of worn trail leading to the structure indicated it had not been accessed by any significant group in ages.

She started in the top left corner of the screen and began slowly working her way down and to the right, zooming down to a one-square-kilometer area around each marked object, then pulling in closer until she could identify exactly what it was the computer thought was important. The first sector, a single red box in it, contained what turned out to be a pair of storm-fallen trees that landed perpendicular to each other, creating a right angle that the AI labeled as a dwelling.

She annotated her findings and moved to the next sector with a box. The next twenty square kilometers yielded a well-worn animal path, verified by an image of a dozen long ant-lered creatures, the kind Youngmi told her were locally called caribou, their young clearly visible walking with their mothers. She printed that hi-resolution close-up image and pinned it to her cubicle wall. Two hours later, she'd finished that sector with nothing that looked even remotely of human origin.

After a quick toilet break and refilling her tea from the urn at the end of the room, she sat down for yet another two-hour ses-sion of slowly going blind. She snapped over to the next sector in her assigned map only to find a large smear across the image cov-ering an area of several square kilometers. The anomalous section of the video was the same in both the old Google image and the new image, taken less than a month ago. The Glenn Highway and the Matanuska River were both clearly visible in the lower section of the sector image, but the middle of the image looked as though someone had smudged the lens after eating greasy food.

"Captain Shue," she called to the senior imaging technician in the room, "could you please come look at this, sir?"

The captain crossed the room and looked over her shoulder.

"What do you have, Lieutenant?"

"This, sir." She pointed to the smudged image. "I've never seen anything like it from a satellite image. Drone or aerial foot-age will sometimes do that due to moisture on the lens, but there is not moisture in space. And none of the other sectors have had anything like it. It is blurred in the infra-red and ultra-violet ranges too."

"Hrm," he said. "The fact that it shows up in those old images too proves it is not our equipment. Check and see the history of solar flares that contact the atmosphere over this area. Perhaps we are getting some sort of atmospheric resonance that is picking up over these mountains."

"Yes, sir." She pulled up a database of historical atmospheric and solar conditions. "You are right, sir, there does seem to be a pattern of very high auroral activity in a swathe over this section of the earth."

He pointed to the dates and times of the two images. "Since both of these shots were taken about the same time of year, and at an almost identical angle, that is likely your answer." He stood upright, speaking as he turned back to his own work. "Now that we have fuel, you can annotate to have a pass-run over that area for low altitude imagery to get a look."

"Will do, sir," she replied. "Any idea how far out they are scheduling flights?"

"Should be within the week," he said as he lowered himself into his chair. "Maybe within seventy-two hours."

She clicked send on the request and turned back to her screen.

CHAPTER 35

Archers

The small wiry man's accent was so thick, Ian imagined that he could build a wall with it. He strode purposefully across the front of the line of Rangers, making a fast-visual evaluation of each man and woman in the group. His current crop of trainees in the ancient arts of combat, comprised of the most recent groups of new Rangers, stood twenty yards away from the nearest row of hay bales, each five yards from the other. Another row stood thirty yards past that and another fifty yards further still, a hundred from the assembled group.

Each held in their hand a three-foot-long recurve bow. A quiver of a dozen arrows stood in a small wooden frame beside each of them. Rangers who actually wore the Archer tab would learn to make their own bows. Ian glanced at his brother who replied with a shrug, then looked back down at the targets.

"Each of you may wonder why, as part of your close-quarters combat curriculum, you are being trained on a medieval weapon," said the sergeant first class. His name was Ivan Czyrgiczlicz. He was from Romania. Prior to the being trapped in Alaska while on vacation at the outset of the war, he and his father had run a private military academy in Romania that had trained anti-Russian militias and even terrorists. "An arrow is a whisper compared to the bark of a suppressed firearm. It is also lightweight, and you can make them by hand from available natural materials if needed."

He plucked an arrow from the nearest quiver and held it up as if studying it. Using it as a pointer, he continued, "The psychological impact of seeing their buddies punctured full of arrows like in some old American Western cowboy movie, is absolute terror in the heart of the soldiers on the receiving end of a barrage of arrows, especially since our arrows are capable of penetrating body armor at two-hundred yards."

He stuck the arrow back into the quiver he'd taken it from and walked slowly down the length of the assembled Rangers, looking intently into each person's face as he strode past.

"You yourselves may not ever use one of these in actual combat, but all Rangers are required to be familiar with this weapon and be proficient enough to hit the target at least seventy-five percent of the time."

For the next several hours, Sergeant First Class Ivan Czyrgiczlicz and his team of combat archery instructors worked with them on body position and technique. Training started at eight in the morning, took a short break at noon to eat a cold lunch in place on the range, then continued until six in the evening, barely making it to the chow hall for dinner, last bodies through the doors before they closed the serving line.

"My shoulders are killing me," Todd said as he held up his tray for a serving of moose liver. The young lady behind the serving line smiled at him and dropped a generous portion of grilled onions on top of the slice of meat. Her smile brought a blush to his cheeks. He straightened his back, eliciting a pop as he squared his shoulders, grinning in spite of the pain.

Ben and Ian let out a snicker. Todd had been talking about the girl back in the barracks for weeks. Being raised a strict Mormon, he had never been on a date or been alone with a girl.

"I've never kissed a girl," he'd complained one night at their base near Klutina Lake. "I was sixteen when the war started, and none of the girls we rescued even give me half a glance. I have no hope of ever finding a wife."

Upon completion of Ranger School and being allowed to eat at the Rangers dining hall, Todd's hope was suddenly kindled. Anika was her name, and she was the same age as Todd and Ben, eighteen. Todd was utterly stunned by the girl and talked of nothing else for the majority of the time the boys were alone. The only problem was, every time he started to open his mouth around her, his courage utterly failed. He hoped his ruddy-faced silence was being translated by Anika as evidence of him being the strong silent type. In reality, he felt more like the mumbling idiot type.

"You should ask her to come to the fire pit tonight and hang out," Ian said in between wolfing down bites of lunch earlier in the day. "Second Company found an entire pallet of still mostly okay marshmallows on their last raid. The council let them keep two big cases to bring back. They invited us to share with them tonight."

"Don't worry, brother," Ben said, "we're here to back you up."

That evening, Ian nudged Todd forward as they moved up to get their food. Todd froze. Not a word from him.

"Hi, Anika." Ben slapped him on the back. "Todd has something to ask you."

Katarina convulsed with a snort. Purple splotches darkened Todd's face. He snapped a quick panicked glance at Ben and his companions, then back to Anika, his face twisted with an awkward-looking smile.

"Uh," his voice trembled, "Hi, Anika."

"Hi, Todd," she said, her own face brightening by a shade or two of pink.

"You know my name?" he stammered.

"Of course." She giggled, glancing over at the others as they silently cheered him on. She raised her eyebrows and cocked her head toward them. "Um, your friends' food is getting cold."

"Yeah, Todd," Ian said, "out with it. I'm starving."

"You want to come hang out at the Second Company fire pit tonight?" he blurted in rapid fire.

"Sure," Anika said without hesitation.

"Well, they've got a bunch of marshmallows from their last raid and they invited us to share and…"

"I said yes, silly," she said with a tiny laugh, her voice like the tinkling of a crystal wind chime.

"Oh, you did?" Todd stopped. "You did…wow."

"Pick me up at my house, number four, Third Avenue," she said.

Todd stared at her, a dim-looking smile on his face.

"Seven-thirty," Katarina said as she shoved her tray in front of him to get her serving of dinner. "He will be at your house by no later than seven-thirty."

She and Ben helped Todd make it to a table before he fell down. Ian joined right behind them, his plate mounded with more food than the rest.

"How'd you get portions like that?" Ben gave an incredulous stare at the mound of food on his brother's plate.

"I was the last in line and they only had like one or one and a half extra portions of each thing," Ian said as he stirred peas and carrots into a mountain of mashed potatoes and gravy. "If you go back, there might be some more of the blanched greens left. I didn't want extra of that one."

"No thanks," Ben said. "I'll just live vicariously through watching you eat."

★   ★   ★

On the last day of the course came the final exam, they would be graded as passing or failing. Anyone with less than 75 percent proficiency, as measured in hitting targets within a time limit, would cycle back through until they passed. Several of the instructors of the class had done just that, a couple recycling so many times they were experts before they were allowed to leave.

Fifty targets were arranged at distances starting at ten meters and going out to two hundred meters. Built of hay bales or wooden dummies, the center mass of each target was designed to simulate body armor. To get a point, the arrow had to pierce to a specific depth that varied with distance to the target. They could be shot in any order, from any position. The timer started the moment the shooter stepped across the starting line, the ending buzzer sounding three minutes later. A score of 75 percent meant that the shooter hit center mass of every target within fifty meters or less, and half the targets out to one hundred meters. One hundred percent meant hitting center mass on a target the size of a human torso every target including four at one hundred meters and two at two hundred meters, then crossing the finish line within that three minutes. A ten-point penalty was weighed against the score if a shooter failed to cross the finish line before time ran out, simulating that they died in the battle. Similarly, bonus points were awarded at a rate of one per second that a shooter finished under the three-minute mark with a perfect score. The current record was 121, held by Ivan himself.

Any person who passed the test with a 75 percent, earned the right to wear the 'Sagitta' patch, a circle dyed dark blue with red trim that had the Latin word for arrow arched across the top and a depiction of the stars that make up Orion the archer. All who passed with a 90 percent or higher had the same patch with a curved shoulder tab above it that read 'Archer.' The smaller group of 100 percenters added a black arrow beneath the patch and tab.

The first three had already finished, one veteran Ranger who was requalifying and two militiamen, one from Palmer and one from Wasilla, who volunteered and had just finished Ranger Indoc. Their scores were 91, 79, and 86 respectively. Katarina stepped up and raced through the course, managing to fire off her arrows in rapid-fire succession, grabbing four from the quiver each time she reached back, keeping them between her fingers as they'd been taught by Ivan.

Two seconds per shot.

Whack! Whack!

Whack! Whack!

One second to reload.

Whack! Whack!

Whack! Whack!

All while fast walking in a half-crouch from one end of the firing line to the other, turning before the finish line and moving back across. Her pace never slacked.

Just that fast, in under two minutes, every target in the first 100 yards, took an arrow within the center mass zone. Three targets remained at two hundred meters. Designed to look like a pair of six-foot-tall men standing up, painted in the colors of the PLA battle uniform, a hit at center mass on either man counted as a full point and would knock the pair down. The design of the targets was to teach that while not all the hits were bullseyes, each one counted as a disabling shot, which was often more important than killing the enemy, as that would take someone's attention off the battle to care for the fallen.

"It also seriously screws with their heads," Ivan had added in that lesson. He told of a time when he was assisting Ukrainian loyalist militias fighting Russian separatists. "We were near a castle that was reputed to be haunted, so I told them that we could be the ghosts of the ancient tsar of that castle. On several nights over the following month, every time the Russian forces passed through that area, we fired volleys of arrows at any exposed infantry, usually killing one of two before we escaped into the woods. By the third or fourth time a patrol came through our area, you could see the terror on their faces the moment they saw the 'haunted castle' and the deep dark d'yavol'skiy les; that's Russian for 'devil forest.' Eventually, the soldiers refused to patrol the area because our arrows scared the wheelies out of them."

The class had laughed at the phrase Ivan mangled. Kharzai had taught him the previous day the difference between 'the Whillies' and 'doing wheelies.' He still had them backwards. Although they laughed, the point went home. This was a different kind of war than what they'd watched in movies or read in books. This was less about massive armies facing off and more about common men and women coming up with ingenious tactics to keep their enemies from simply crushing them.

Katarina took a single arrow out of her quiver and turned, planted her feet, and aligned her body to the first target. She fired and missed. She repeated the shot and hit on the second try. With only ten seconds remaining, she hit a second two-hundred-meter target but was unable to cross the line before the buzzer sounded. Her 100-point score was docked to a 90, missing the black arrow by two seconds.

Ben ran through next. He hit every target with three seconds to spare and sprinted for the finish line. He tripped just as he approached and fast crawled the last five feet. The class roared with laughter as he barely earned the black arrow, literally earning it by the skin of his feet.

The rest of the class ran the course, all passing, most with scores in the 70s and low 80s. There were no other 100 percenters.

Ian came up last, having had to drop out of order next to his brother to repair a broken bowstring. He stepped up to the starting line, held his eyes shut for a second, and sucked in a deep breath. He slowly let it out and opened his eyes. Total focus. He saw only the line in the dirt in front of him, the targets to his right, the finish line at the end.

He burst onto the firing line, hand flashing to his quiver, coming back with four arrows at a time. He felt nothing, only sensed movement, targets sliding past him, arm pistoning back and forth, reaching down, coming parallel to the earth, pistoning a shot, repeating. Dark spots he knew to be targets, symbolic of men, men he wanted dead, appeared before him. Near. Far. Distant. Flashing. Move to the side. Move swiftly. Get out of range of their fire before they figure out what is happening.

A loud buzzer sounded near his head. He spun, reaching for more arrows. He suddenly realized he was past the finish line. Everyone was silent. Ivan's eyes were wide with shock. The chief instructor motioned and several of the others jogged through the course all the way to the two-hundred-meter targets. A minute later, they jogged back, the murmuring crowd falling silent.

"He hit every one, Sergeant," one of the instructors said breathlessly.

"Fully through all the plates and armor," said the other.

"Ladies and gentlemen," Ivan said, rubbing his stubbly chin, "we have just witnessed a once in a lifetime event."

He pointed to the time clock over Ian's head.

"Two minutes, four seconds with zero misses. That makes a score of 196." He slid off his cap and ran a hand over his stubbly scalp. "You have just set an unofficial world record, my young friend."

CHAPTER 36

Rangers

"**M**ind if we come in and join you for a bit of tea?" Staff-Sergeant Patrick Scott called up to the cave entrance with an attempt at a posh British accent that his native Alabaman mangled badly. His weapon pointed toward the mouth of a cave in the face of a short, scraggly cliff, just above the tips of the thick spruce forest.

"Scott," came a response from inside, "don't ever try to be a spy. You would be the absolute worst James Bond in the history of spies."

"Yeah, I love you too, little boy Leo," Scott called back.

"Get your asses up here so me and my crew can get trekking back home," Leo called back.

The sound of boots shuffling and things being moved echoed from inside the cave, amplified in the crisp September air as Scott and his four-man team clambered up the short distance to the shadowed chamber. Weapons at shoulders, they kept their muzzles pointed at their destination. He signaled with a short flick of his head and one of the men behind him fanned to the right, another to the left. The final man rotated toward the rear and scanned behind them through his rifle sight.

"Waffle," Scott called when they were just outside the entrance.

"Fried chicken," replied Leo.

"Coming in," Scott said.

"Enter," Leo replied.

They moved in, weapons still at the ready. A waist high wall of sandbags hiding the back half of the cave. First Sergeant Leo Weeks' four-man team greeted them with their own weapons as they came into view.

"Stand down," said Leo.

"Thanks for not being the bad guys yet again," Scott said as both sides lowered their weapons and rose, stepping forward to greet each other with handshakes.

"Alright, my boys," Leo addressed his team, "pack up for the quick hike home."

That *quick* hike home stretched across more than fifty miles of wild mountain and forest, traversed two icy rivers, and required crossing the mostly enemy-controlled Glenn Highway before getting back to the relative safety of Chiknik. Leo glanced across the Matanuska Valley, its namesake river an emerald green ribbon that snaked south and west for seventy-five miles. He turned to a small table made from branches on which sat a radio transceiver and picked up the handset. A wire ran from the set to the cave entrance, then out and up the stone cliff face, terminating in a small unidirectional antenna hidden beneath an outcrop of rock and tree roots that stays snow free all year. It pointed to an identical setup five miles across the valley.

Six weeks earlier, Ice Hammer had ordered these outposts to do more than just watch for any incoming enemy air or ground vehicles. They had been provided with four Stinger missiles in each cave specifically for the purpose of shooting down any helicopters coming up from Anchorage that followed a certain trajectory. Two other teams were in similar positions twenty miles to the east of Chiknik, watching for Russian aircraft. Aircraft that stayed directly over or to the south of the highway were allowed to pass unhindered. That had been all of the air traffic up to this point, as that was the most obvious route to travel between Russian and Chinese zones. The heading to arrive at Chiknik though was very specific, as the town was located halfway up a mountain valley with nothing but alpine wilderness to the north for nearly three hundred miles. If any troop-carrying craft or gunships veered north of the highway within twenty miles in either direction, it was to be shot down to keep the town from being attacked. The caves were roughly twenty-five miles out with clear sky visibility for another thirty miles past that before the curve of the earth sloped away at the horizon.

Leo clicked the transmit button twice then spoke.

"Rabbit, Rabbit, this is Beaver."

Ten seconds went by before the response came back.

"Beaver, this is Rabbit, go ahead."

"Status check," Leo said into the mic.

"Charlie bravo."

"Roger that, charlie bravo," Leo repeated back, acknowledging the report of 'clear blue,' indicating no enemy activity from their perspective.

He side-stepped as one of his men slung his rucksack onto his back in preparation for their return trip.

"Hey! Watch it!"

"Sorry, boss," replied the soldier. "Just ready to get on the road."

"Beaver nineteen, Fox thirty-seven," Leo said into the hand-set, giving the abbreviated police ten-code response indicating they were returning to base and that Fox team, Scott's men, were taking over for the next two-week shift.

"Roger that," Rabbit replied. "Beaver nineteen, Fox thirty-seven."

"Beaver out."

"Rabbit out."

"Charming conversationalist," Scott said. "Who's over there?"

"Carson," Leo replied as he shrugged into his own ruck, the weight of it bowing his legs slightly. In spite of the apparent wear and tear, after thirty years as an infantryman in the U.S. Army, and these last two bonus years in the Chiknik Rangers, he wore the accouterments of war like a second skin. "He was a military intelligence guy in DIA,"—Defense Intelligence Agency, the military's spies—"stickler for radio protocols and no chatter, even though this is a point-to-point line of sight laser connection. Not possible to be intercepted."

"Oh well," Scott said, "just means he won't get the invitation to my birthday party."

"It's your birthday?"

"Nah, but he ain't got to know that."

"See you next—" Leo was cut off as Rabbit's voice came over the radio.

"Beaver, Beaver, this is Rabbit." The voice had the same calm, recorded announcement tone as earlier. "Locust 14, locust 14. Trousers."

Leo and Scott both swung their attention to the cave mouth. Fourteen referred to the police code 10-14, multiple vehicles or a convoy. Locust told them it was helicopters. Trousers, as in a pair of, meaning two.

"I see them," said one of the men, pointing out the mouth of the cave.

The others followed his gesture and soon made out a pair of tiny dots the size of insects in the distance. Barely visible, the black shapes were moving fast at not much more than fifty feet above the treetops. The fact that they were so close before they were spotted meant they had been flying like that for probably fifty miles or more, as no one in either cave had reported seeing any objects in the bright and clear sky.

From the time Chiknik had become a base for so many refugees until just a few months earlier, there had been almost no air traffic this far up the valley from the Chinese headquarters in Anchorage. It had been surmised that Alaska was a less urgent theater of the war in the eyes of the high command back in Beijing, and General Zhang was provided only minimal air support capabilities shortly after the initial invasion. They had plenty of equipment but not enough jet fuel, and possibly not enough ammunition, to mount an air campaign against Chiknik.

Since the start of the war, only a single missile had been launched against the city of refugees. It resulted in the death of a six-year-old boy, who succumbed to infection after having initially survived his leg torn off above the knee. His loss was tragic, but the attack could have been a whole lot worse. Only two minutes earlier, over a hundred children and scores of parents had been standing in the courtyard where it had landed.

The bulk of the Chinese People's Army Air Force had been diverted further south to the population centers of the continental United States, and those military bases that had managed to survive the initial attack and hold out this long. The fight in the Kenai had probably required what limited air power Zhang had available. Now that the peninsula had capitulated, the general could focus all of his might northward, and start gaining control of the interior regions and the mineral resources locked in the earth. Ice Hammer and Chiknik were in their way.

"Stingers up," the team leaders shouted simultaneously, both hoisting binoculars to take a closer look.

"Z-11s," Scott said, referring to the PLA's recon and ground support combat helicopters.

"Yup," Leo replied, then he clicked the talk button on the radio handset. "Rabbit, we've got the front bird, you take the second."

"On it," came the response.

A man from each team grabbed up one of the pre-loaded handheld Stinger anti-aircraft missile launchers from their cases along one wall of the cave. They each hefted a battery coolant unit, BCU, and inserted them into the handles of the thirty-three-pound weapons, locking it into place with a quarter turn. A second Ranger followed each of them with a spare missile in its own launch tube and a two additional BCUs, each being a one-time use item. The BCU is used to energize the weapon's electrical circuits and to cool the IR detector in the missile's seeker prior to launch. Containing a thermal battery and pressurized argon gas coolant, the BCU is activated when the safety and actuator device on the gripstock is pressed forward, outward, and downward until a click is heard, and then released. Once activated, the BCU supplies electrical power and seeker coolant to the weapon for forty-five seconds or until missile launch. The BCU is not reusable after it is activated, that last being the reason the launch tubes and missiles each came with three of them.

The units they held had originally been found with IFF, Identify Friendly or Foe, antennae and interrogators, the latter being a computer that sends an encrypted signal to the targeted aircraft that attempts to verify whether it is an enemy or friendly aircraft. The Chiknik Rangers opted to not use the IFF system for two reasons. First, there was no *need* to use it. Almost all aircraft still in operation in Alaska were known enemy aircraft. Anything flying through this valley for the foreseeable future would be Chinese or Russian; no need to waste time that could be used killing the enemy. The second reason was that any kind of digital signal they ping off an enemy aircraft would automatically identify their own location to said enemy, something nobody wanted to have to happen.

They sighted the helicopters in their mounted scopes, placing their target in the appropriate reticle. Thumbs flicked the safety/actuator forward and down. Five seconds later, the whir of activating gyros signaled system startup was complete. Instantly, a weak tone sounded from a small speaker near each gunner's head. The tone grew stronger just as the rotor wash of the Chengze Z-11 reconnaissance gunships became audible to them. The tone rose to a distinct high pitch, indicating lock on the target. They squeezed the uncaging switches on and the signal increased.

"Acquired," said Hadley Walker from Leo's team. He'd been a veteran's service rep at the VA Hospital before the war and knew Brad Stone when he was just an IT guy, long before he became Ice Hammer. Another southerner, also from Alabama, his accent was still so thick, even after ten years in Alaska, that he made Scott sound like a Yankee.

"Acquired," repeated the gunner from Scott's team, Jeremy Price, a former Air Force Special Operations Weatherman. After more than three years of special forces training, followed by five years at a near constant stream of combat tours as an uncommonly lethal meteorologist, he decided to shift gears to a less stressful job and spent the rest of his Air Force career as an Explosive Ordinance Disposal technician, EOD. Apparently, being a weatherman was more stressful than defusing IEDs (Improvised Explosive Devices) made in some slum apartment by a nineteen-year-old terrorist with maybe a third-grade education.

"Firing," they called over each other, sucking in a huge breath and holding it as they squeezed their triggers.

Missiles leapt from the launch tubes, booster motors blasting them to a distance far enough that the rocket engines could safely ignite without burning the team members to death. Twin plumes of rocket fuel exhaust traced a bee-line directly for the lead helicopter, marking their paths with bright white contrails like chalk lines broadcasting not only their existence, but where they came from as well. An identical pair of chalk lines erupted from the other side of the valley, streaking toward the second helicopter.

When the toxic fumes had subsided, they let their breath out and watched as the enemy pilots fired flares to divert the infrared seekers from their turbo-jet engines. Once the flares lit up, they started evasive maneuvers. The pilot of the first shot skyward, door gunners holding on for dear life, straining against their harnesses in the multi g-force turn as evidenced by their legs flailing out the open doors, visible from nearly two miles away. Thirty seconds of struggle ended in a ball of flame that snapped helicopter two in half, the rotor spinning away on its own as the machine fell to the earth.

The missile teams snapped new missile tube assemblies onto their firing handles, the empty tubes of the first shots laying in the dirt a few yards away. They went through the drill to activate a second missile in case the pilot managed to escape.

"Acquired!" shouted Hadley.

"Same!" replied Jeremy.

"He's really buckin' that bitch," said Hadley, tracking it through his scope as the helicopter performed a high-speed banking maneuver.

"Damn," said Jeremy, "those poor gunners gotta be dying with all that flapping around."

"It's still tracking," said one of the spotters.

The helicopter suddenly juked left and up at an angle, then banked left again as if the pilot was doubling back to the get behind the stinger. The closest of the missiles zoomed past. The pilot must've been following it with his eyes because the craft suddenly seemed to become less chaotic, as if the men inside felt like it was over.

The second missile proved them wrong. It entered via the port-side gunner's torso, cutting him in half then detonating a few feet further in, directly between the pilot and co-pilot. The helicopter burst open like a popcorn kernel, the engine and rotor ejecting in opposite directions. Everything seemed to hang in the air for several moments like some real-life Wile E. Coyote cartoon before gravity took over and all the pieces of metal and men scattered to the earth below.

"Aw hell yeah!" Hadley called out, hell sounding like 'hayul.'

"Booyah!" Jeremy added.

The missile teams quickly hustled back into the cave and packed up the unused rockets and stuffed the BCUs back in their places in the carrying case. The others had already finished packing everything up. Leo and his team would still be heading back to Chiknik, but he offered to help Scott's team lug the remaining missiles and equipment to a new position five miles further out. The old cave would not be able to be used again for many months, in case it was observed by satellite or some other type of surveillance the Chinese had in place.

CHAPTER 37

Kharzai

"The big night has finally come," Kharzai said, firelight reflecting off his face, darkening the shadows of his pitch-black hair and beard. "I am so nervous, are you nervous? I am seriously like, enduring actual butterflies actually dancing in my actual belly."

The autumn evening was already growing dark at six o'clock. Tall oil torches lit the area, providing both light and warmth to the audience of several hundred. He gazed out at the faces of the gathering crowd sitting in the log benches that lined the amphitheater. Many were laying out blankets at the top of the earthen ring that encircled the grassy half acre in the center, a large wooden stage built into one side of the ring. He grasped Erika's hand in his right and Jung's in his left. Many people, even most perhaps, always assumed he was that kid in school with ADHD, Attention Deficit Hyperactive Disorder, who had to be medicated to sit still in school. In reality he had escaped part of that label, the attention deficit part, by demonstrating that while he was very hyperactive he was also capable of processing multiple conversations simultaneously, often in more than one language, and could repeat back details of what he saw and heard verbatim.

So a new label was created for him, one he felt rather proud of as a kid, Bilateral Rapid Uptake Hyper Attentive Hyper Active, or BRUHAHA. His behaviors had become a way of dealing with all of the things he could not unsee, could not forget, would not leave his waking thoughts. His craziness, was his coping mechanism, a way to stuff the bad memories and image deep inside where they were less likely to get his full attention.

"Don't worry, Kharzai." Erika squeezed his hand. "We've practiced so much that you've probably already forgotten more than most people will ever know about this song."

"That's what I thought too," Kharzai said. Leila's face flashed before his eyes. For only a second, a single heartbeat. He blinked and Erika was back. He was holding hands with her and Jung. The memory gone as fast as it had come. Nothing more than a blink.

He saw someone he knew in the audience and BRUHAHA took over. He suddenly let go of the girls' hands, jumped up, and waved at the guy. He turned and gave two thumbs up to someone else in the crowd and shouted, "Davey boy!" then sat back down.

Mission accomplished. Memory stowed. Focus on the now!

He took both of their hands back, sucked in a deep breath, and let it out with a hiss and continued. "Anyhow, I am just now coming to realize that nobody knows this rendition? What if my entire mind goes blank?"

"Honey," Jung said, "if your mind ever goes blank for even a second, we will have bigger problems than surviving a talent show, 'cause you'll probably be dying or something. By the way, did you pay the life insurance bill?"

"I love you too, Kimchi mama."

"Shush," said Erika, "they're starting."

Electric lights popped on, illuminating the stage and the podium on a high dais jutting from the back wall. A concession had been made to leave electricity up for an extra two hours to put the show on. Those who did not come to the festivities got to enjoy double the amount of power time to do whatever they did that needed electricity.

"Hello," the school principal called over the microphone on the podium. "Okay, class, it is time to get started!"

Amplified over the speakers, the headmistress's voice immediately grabbed everyone's attention.

"Today's lessons will now begin!"

She handed a clipboard to her husband, one of the council members. "So we will get right to it as Thomas introduces our first act."

He took the clipboard, looked at the first listed act, then stepped to the microphone.

"Howdy folks! Let me introduce our first act by asking, how do you make a tissue dance?"

Someone in the audience called out, "We don't know! How do you make a tissue dance?"

"First you have to put a little boogie in it," Thomas replied, and the audience let out a collective groan. He smiled wider, happy to strike home with the first Dad-joke of the night. He continued, laughter in his voice, "In this case, it's Irish Boogie by Keegan and Moire Boyle, who are actually from Ireland in real life. The lovely lasses will be dancing an Irish Treble Reel."

The high-school-age sisters ran out onto the wooden stage, dark hair in tight ringlets that quivered as they trotted out before the audience, long legs jutting from traditional style Irish dance costumes. The fast beat of traditional Irish drums, bodhran, sounded, fiddles and pipes joining in to accompany the girls as they performed an impeccably coordinated dance in four-four time. Feet a blur as they bounced up and down, their legs twisted at angles that looked like they should fly off at the knee on the next hard kick.

After their high-speed performance came the students of a Tae Kwon Do instructor who'd started a school shortly after joining Chiknik. As the night went on, singers sang in pairs, duets, and ensembles. A couple child musicians wowed the crowd with their talent alongside family-friendly comedians, musicians, acrobats, and jugglers of various skill levels and types of material. Thirty acts in all, they kept to a PG rating for the sake of the kids in the show and audience alike.

"And now presenting our next act," the principal said, as a thirteen-year-old boy in a wizard costume took the folding table on which he'd been doing card tricks and walked off stage. The principal turned to her husband.

"The final act of the night," the councilman said in turn.

"Oooh...that's us," Kharzai said, shaking with anticipation. "Has to be, since we're the only ones who haven't gone yet."

Erika snorted a laugh.

"The members of this performing duo," said the principal, "have been with Chiknik since the first spring."

"Many of you who know them well may often wonder about the sanity of one of the members of this team." Thomas looked directly at Kharzai, seated in the wing beside the stage. "And why such a nice girl would partner up with this guy! The guy I refer is most definitely not normal. I know that I have often wondered if he is fully human, or a cross between Scooby Doo and a giant mutant squirrel with Tourette's syndrome."

"Oooh!" Kharzai started to rise. "That *is* us! I recognize my description!"

"Ladies and gentlemen, we present to you the one," the principal said.

"The only," the councilman said.

They finished in unison, "Erika Baker and Kharzai Ghiassi performing as 'The Dashingly Dutiful, Daringly Beautiful, Not-So-Dreadful Dancing Duet of The Day—Part Un!'" They indicated the exclamation point with a slash and dot of their finger accompanied by mouth noises à la Victor Borge's Phonetic Punctuation.

Erika and Kharzai ran onto the stage, stopping dead center in front of a pair of microphones placed by the crew during their introduction. Kharzai signaled the sound engineer and a moment later, the sound of trumpets rolled across the cool night air, leading into a 1940s swing beat that quickly had the entire audience tapping their feet and clapping their hands. The duo took each other's hands and went straight into a high-energy song and dance medley of swing, jazz, and show tunes they had mixed together using an old iPhone whose transceiver chips had been removed in Franklin's lab so that it could act like a tiny tablet, or music player, without the threat of giving away their location in the event it pinged off an active cell tower.

The last song built to a crescendo, their voices rising with it. Kharzai leaned over as Erika rolled over his back, then came upright. He stood, and she vaulted from the floor to his hand and up in a back flip. She nailed the landing, jutted a hip at the audience, then took two mincing steps back toward him singing the final words of the song. He blinked and Leila's face smiled back at him. The music pulsed and Erika's face returned. He caught himself just in time to keep the next beat of the song and burst into the climactic ending together.

The music ended.

They froze briefly.

Silence descended for a beat, then the audience burst into applause. Erika and Kharzai bowed low, blowing kisses to the audience as they walked off stage. They returned to their seats to be met with backslapping and laughter as the principal and Thomas stepped back up to the microphone. In the end, after enduring an intolerable number of Dad-jokes, they managed to barely squeak into third place in the adult category, right behind the Irish girls and a comic ventriloquist/juggler. They barely beat out another comedian who sucked spaghetti noodles up his nostrils and made the dangling strands dance to the beat of the tequila song.

"Thanks for letting me borrow your man for the show," Erika said, leaning in and giving a playful squeeze around Jung's shoulders.

"Oh, better you than me," Jung replied. "There was no way I could ever have done that routine. Even in my twenties!"

"I don't know how you handle him," Erika said.

"Torture," Jung said. "Whips, chains, electric shock, all that."

"You'd best stop there, my love," Kharzai said, turning toward the fifty-something Korean lady. "You're getting me all hot and bothered."

Erika stuck her fingers in her ears. "Not listening! Old people talking kinky!"

"It's only kinky, Erika," Kharzai said, "if the consenting people involved think it is unusually weird."

"You are unusually weird," Jung said, "and it is kinky."

"This is really encroaching on the legal limits of TMI," Erika said.

"Don't worry," Kharzai said, "the scars on your imagination will heal in time."

"I don't really use whips on him," Jung said. "Cuffs sometimes when he's too fidgety."

"The padded kind, right?" Erika said. "Leave no physical marks?"

"You're getting it," Jung replied.

"Okay," Erika said, putting her hand over her eyes and turning away. "I'm going to go try and forget this whole conversation over drinks with my other friends, the ones who are not like my weird aunt and uncle," Erika said. She turned to leave, muttering, "I need some eye bleach."

"Have fun storming the castle," Kharzai said she walked off. She turned back, a smile on her face. She was Leila again, smiling at him. She looked away, then turned her head partially back toward them, and the profile was Erika's.

He shook his head and turned to Jung, wrapping her hand in his fingers. His eyes suddenly felt dull, energy vanishing, his mind washed with exhaustion.

"Hey beautiful, do you mind if we don't hang out here long?"

She looked into his eyes, her expression confirming that she saw what he felt.

"Are you okay, Kharzai?"

"Yeah," he said, a barely noticeable hitch in his voice. "I'm just really tired, and we have a lot of training to plan with the new guys, and...I...I just don't feel like talking with anybody right now."

"Okay," she said, concern in her eyes. "You want to go now?"

"Sure." He rose, still holding her hand. "Let's go to bed early."

CHAPTER 38

Sammi

The walk back from the talent show was quiet. Brad held Victoria in his arms, the infant wrapped in a blanket, keeping her warm against the cool evening. The temperatures had dipped into the mid-50s once the sun went down. The day itself had been beautiful. Clear sunny skies with little cotton ball puffs of cloud gave the day a storybook feeling.

Harvesting of most of the vegetables had already been done. Larders were full of cabbage, potatoes, beets, and carrots. Leafy vegetables and edible greens had been blanched and dried for winter use. Berries were mostly harvested, except for cranberries that needed to wait until after the first frost. Hunting parties were being sent out to gather in the caribou and moose that would keep them fed through the cold months, alongside fish and game birds.

The school was scheduled to reopen in two weeks, and Sammi intended to return to work as teacher and assistant principal, bringing Victoria with her whenever Brad could not watch her, which she assumed would be most of the time.

Something had changed in Brad since the mission last spring, the one where he had attempted to blow up the Chinese general but failed to kill him. He'd killed the driver and guard, and put the man's mistress in the hospital, but General Zhang had apparently walked away with only minor injuries. She could understand why her husband would not be happy with that result but could not see how that had caused such a gulf to open between them. The mission seemed to have—she struggled to find the right description—*damaged* him in some way. It was as if he had seen something in Anchorage that had flipped a switch in his head, illuminating a room in his thoughts only he could see, and he would not let her in.

She looked up at him, moonlight casting angular shadows across his cheek and jaw. He looked so different now. Different than he had two years ago when he'd rescued her and the others and led them to that first winter of plenty in the millionaire's playhouse, the dream that burnt to the ground and ended her mother's life. He looked different than he had nearly fifteen years earlier, when her young teen self first fell in love with him. Then he had a soft face, a gentle yet still masculine visage. He was the kind of man most women like to be around: kind, tender, yet not a wimp, not delicate.

But he had changed. The rough parts of his personality had become rougher, edges sharper. His face had angles and dark lines that were never there before, not all of them from weight loss.

"It was a fun show tonight," Sammi said, pushing her hand through the crook of his arm and leaning in close.

He adjusted the baby in his other arm and wrapped the free one around her shoulders.

"It was," he said, then leaned in and kissed her on the head.

"Thanks for taking us out on a date this evening."

"Thank you, ladies, for agreeing to accompany me."

She reached her arms around his middle and squeezed. They walked slowly as they approached their house, parting their hold as they stepped up onto the porch. Sammi reached for the door handle and pulled it open. They stepped in, kicked off their shoes. She flicked on a wind-up lantern that glowed dimly, needing a windup charge soon. She turned back and took the sleeping child from him. He stepped over to the woodstove. It was not cool enough yet at night to fire up big boiler that heated the floor, but a small fire in the cast iron woodstove would take the edge of the late season chill.

Sammi set the lantern on a shelf that jutted from a support post, laid Victoria in her bassinet and moved it near the couch, lowering herself into the cushions, watching him light the tinder, place the kindling, and once the flames took hold, some more substantial split wood. Once satisfied it would stay lit, he joined her on the couch, pulling her in close to him. She nestled in his embrace, resting her head on his chest, wrapping a blanket around them. They sat there, listening to the crackle of the wood and the pop of heating metal, their daughter snoring softly beside them. The flames grew steady, heat emanating from the open door. Old-fashioned country warmth.

"Brad," Sammi said, her voice a whisper.

"Yeah?"

"Can I ask you something?"

"Of course, ask me anything."

"Please don't be mad, but," she paused, then said quietly, "can you tell me what happened in Anchorage last spring?"

"What do you mean?" he asked, his voice low, instantly nervous sounding. "You already know what happened."

"No, I mean, what happened to you?"

Silence.

"You have changed, Brad," she continued. "You are not the same as you were before that mission. Something is wrong, but I can't help you because I don't know what it is."

Another long silence. She waited for him to speak, could sense the gears of his mind grinding at a response that did not want to come out on its own.

"I..."

He paused. Let out a breath. Sucked another in. He squeezed his eyes shut, breathed again, opened them.

"I told you back when we first met at the farm, that Youngmi was dead. That I had seen her body, in her car."

"Yes." Sammi straightened. Looking into his eyes. "You said that she was...um..."

"She was wearing her favorite T-shirt, in her new car." His voice caught in his throat. "But...her face was...it was...gone."

She stared at him, watching him closely. His obvious agony caused an ache in her soul. Wetness glistened in his eyes.

"I know what I saw that day," Brad said, wiping at his eyes. "But last spring, as I gave the order to fire a rocket at General Zhang's vehicle, there was a woman in the back seat with him."

Sammi waited for more. He was quiet for a long moment. The battery in the lantern ran down its charge, the light faded out. Only the flickering glow of the fire through the small square opening in the stove lit the room.

"It was her," he finally said. "Youngmi was in the car with Zhang."

"Maybe you just thought you saw her." Sammi leaned in, put her hand on his chest. "Maybe it was a Chinese woman that just looks like Youngmi and your mind just—"

"No," Brad said. He took her hand and held it, turned to meet her eyes, "No, I know it was her."

"But what if it's...?"

Brad shook his head, eyes closed.

"At first, I thought I had transposed her memory onto some other woman's body. I was sure I was going mad and that it would happen again. But I haven't been able to recreate the event since. Never have I seen her face on anyone else's or heard her voice calling me in the forest. I've never even accidentally called you by her name."

He stared into the stove. Silence lay between them for a time. Neither moved. The fire popped, a few small sparks flew from out of the fire, landing on the cinder blocks that acted as a hearth floor.

"Sammi." He took her hands in his, wrapping both of them, gently caressing her fingertips with his lips. He squeezed them, then kissed the back of her hand. "I am sorry I let this come between us like it has. I, just…I…I didn't know what to do about it."

"If she is alive still, what does this mean for us?"

"Until a couple months ago," he said, "I was certain she was dead. Now I just have to continue in that same belief, as if that is still the case. What is done is done, and things will never be the same as they were."

He put his arms around her, pulling her in close.

"I love you, Sammi. You are my wife now. You are Mrs. Stone."

CHAPTER 39

Mai

The door to the classroom was still open. Mai peaked inside.

"Hi, Ayi," she called as she stepped through, waving a greeting at Youngmi who was putting a laptop in her bag.

"Hi, Mai," she replied, hefting her bag, flipping the strap onto her shoulder. She continued in English, "You're not in uniform. Is this your day off?"

Mai was wearing sneakers, blue jeans. and an untucked white blouse that reached to just above her thighs. Her recent promotion from second to first lieutenant came with the added perk that she was not required to wear only her issued uniforms at all times. That freedom quickly found her at the nearest shop stocking up on the kind of clothes she had only been able to look at for more than six years, from her days as a sixteen-year-old cadet until three weeks ago.

"No, I had a very early shift, then went to the gym for a workout. Just changed and I'm getting ready to go out. What do you think of my outfit?"

"Very nice," Youngmi said. "You'd better be careful or you're going to start grabbing the attention of all the young men around here."

Mai blushed as she strolled slowly up the aisle between the tables.

"Done with class for the day?"

"Yes, the last class of the day finished twenty minutes ago. Junior officers and junior NCOs today, senior officers and senior NCOs tomorrow."

"It is like boys one day and old men the next." Mai laughed. "You should mix them up so they can learn from each other."

"I thought of that but Major Chi brought up a good observation." Youngmi stepped around the front desk and walked between the rows of tables and chairs. "He said that the older men would be less likely to participate if the younger men were to see them perform poorly. I thought that made sense, so, first and second lieutenants stay together, while captains and majors each get their own."

"I thought you had a class of colonels too."

"I did last session." Youngmi came up beside her, accepting the young woman's outstretched hand as they walked toward the door. "But the only colonel who signed up this session was 'you know who.'"

"Yu No Hoo?" Mai screwed up her face, confused. "Is that a new commander?"

"No." Youngmi pointed at her, then to her head, then out the door, and repeated the phrase slowly. "You...know...who."

"Oooh!" Mai said. "You mean that I already know who it is!"

"Yes." Youngmi nodded. "The only person that signed up for the colonel's class was 'you know who,' and there was no way I was going to do one-on-one sessions with that man."

"But which one do you...?" Mai's eyes suddenly stretched wide. "Oh! You mean my...uh...him?"

Youngmi matched Mai's expression and gave an exaggerated nod.

"No way." Mai pulled her face back in a mask of disgust. "I bet he said something to make the others not sign up in hopes of being alone with you."

"Probably," Youngmi said. "He apparently does not remember Seward at all."

Mai had been the only one other than her brother Po who knew the truth about what had happened to Ping's nose in Seward. People may think that she was a flighty young woman, but the top-secret clearance she carried was not awarded to her because her father was a two-star general. She earned and kept that clearance because she knew how to keep a secret. She felt especially honored that Youngmi not only thought of her as a daughter, but that she trusted her enough to confide in her. A trust that she had earned when she discovered that Youngmi had been the wife of Brad Stone, the Ice Hammer. Mai had tampered with state and municipal databases, changing Youngmi's official records, deleting any pictures of her. Mai had literally risked her life to protect this woman, this woman who had taken the place of the real mother she missed so much. A real mother to whom she could confide, could trust with a secret, just like she herself could be trusted. Someone she knew would not hurt her if she made herself vulnerable.

"So, you canceled the class?"

"Yes," Youngmi said. "He was not happy, but that's too bad."

Mai nodded. "Good for you."

There was a long pause as they stepped out the door into the hall and started toward the wing where their rooms were located.

"Ayi?"

Mai felt heat in her cheeks. Butterflies started to dance in her stomach.

"Yes, Mai?" Youngmi glanced sideways at her. "You are flushed, are you okay?"

"I am okay," Mai said. "Can we find a private place to talk? My room maybe?"

"Sure, but will your roommate walk in?"

"No," Mai said. "Fan Hua is on temporary assignment with General Fang's staff. I have the room to myself for right now, although I have heard there is another female lieutenant who will be here tomorrow on another temporary assignment and is being assigned her bed. So, I will only get to be alone for tonight."

"It should be peaceful for you then," Youngmi said.

"Hopefully."

They turned a corner into the hall where the junior officer's quarters were and went into her room. Mai closed the door behind them, hands shaking slightly as she twisted the lock.

"Mai?" Youngmi looked worried and switched to Mandarin. "Seriously, are you okay? You look like something is bothering you."

"Please, Ayi," Mai motioned to a chair, "I have something very heavy to ask you. Something very important."

Youngmi took the seat, concern written in her features.

"My goodness," she said, "what has got you so worked up?"

"I am…" Mai paused, unsure of how to say what was eating at her. She clenched her fists, then loosened them, repeating the gesture as she tried to get the thought into words. "I…I think…"

"Mai, why don't you sit down?" Youngmi motioned to the other chair.

She sat down, immediately rose back to her feet, took a step away, then came back and sat down again.

"I don't know how to say…" She blinked, feeling like tears were going to spill over. If the heat in her cheeks was as real as it felt, they would evaporate the instant they started down.

"Just come out with it," Youngmi said as she faltered again. "We can always backtrack if you lose me."

"I think I am in love with a boy…OH!…I mean, a man!" She put her hands on her face, the embarrassment too much to bear. She sucked in a breath, dropped her hands, squeezed her eyes shut, and let the words boil out unhindered. "I have been going out with father's assistant, Lieutenant Jin, for two months now, and I think I am in love. I mean, I have feelings for him like I've never had before for any boy…I mean…man…not that I have ever had any kind of relationship with a man before, because since I was old enough I was always working and studying and never had time, not that I wasn't interested in boys, I mean men, and I know they were looking at me too but I am not like Fan Hua, I don't like being looked at by men like that, and Jin doesn't look at me that way, he looks at me like he wants to talk to me and when we talk, he actually says things that make sense and we have conversations and he's not just trying to get into my pants like the guys that go after the other girls. He likes me even though I am the general's daughter and even though I am a nerd, and not the sexy fake nerd girls that look like Fan Hua, but don't have her brains, not that Fan Hua is fake, she really is a nerd, and she really is sexy too, I mean from a girl's perspective she looks incredible naked, but Jin likes it that way, and he likes me in that kind of way."

Mai stopped to take a breath, saw Youngmi's expression, and suddenly added, "Not that Jin's thinking of Fan Hua and me naked together in that kind of way! I don't like girls that way! Jin likes me and I like him, and I think I am in love with him but don't know how to find out if he feels the same way! I am so mixed up, Ayi!"

Youngmi's eyes were as wide as seemed possible. She blinked, long and slow, looked down at the table, blinked again. She faced up, blinked once more, then looked straight into Mai's eyes.

"Is he who you are going out with this evening?"

"Yes," Mai said, suddenly sheepish again. "Sorry I didn't tell you sooner."

"Well, your father…"

"Oh, don't tell Father." Mai seemed desperate. "He can't know. Please. He would punish Jin."

"He already knows," Youngmi said flatly. "We've both known since before your first date."

Mai stared at her, flabbergasted.

"Lieutenant Jin is not only really nice boy…er…man," Youngmi held back a smile, "he is also a very good soldier, and asked your father's permission before he asked you to dinner the first time. And your father told me that same night."

"You knew I was seeing him even before I knew I was seeing him?"

"Yes."

Youngmi's answer hung in the air for several seconds. Mai stared at her, then her eyes drifted off, as if she were following the words as they descended to the floor and vanished.

"Why didn't you…?"

"Because you are a grown woman, responsible for yourself, and capable of taking care of yourself if he turned out to not be so nice in private."

Mai's vision cleared, and she focused back on Youngmi. She opened her mouth to speak but Youngmi cut her off.

"But, you have an even bigger question that you need answered. One that even your father has no idea what to say about." She reached over and took Mai's hand. "You think you are in love and want to know if he feels the same way. This is a new thing for your father's generation, when he was your age most men were still working around arranged marriages, not love-based relationships. While your father definitely loved your mother, it was a love that grew out of getting to know each other over many years. It was not the same as the feeling you have in your belly when you see Jin. Not the same kind of fire. But that fire, I am familiar with."

"So, what is your advice?" Mai asked. "How can I tell if he loves me back? American girls in the movies always know what to do, and you're the only American girl I know that I can talk to."

"I cannot tell if he feels the same for you as you do for him," Youngmi said. "I do know that the only way to find out, is to take it slowly, over time. You two are young, so don't rush. In time, he will let his feelings known to you. The fact that he continues to go on dates with you is a very good sign. What is this, eight times now?"

"You even know how many times we've been together?"

"Not details, he is a gentleman about that. We only know the number of times you've been out with him; a couple were guesses on our part when Jin was off duty. Your father needs to be aware of where he is at all times, you know."

"No details?" Mai said. "So you don't know if we've…"

"No details," Youngmi said. "Like I said, Lieutenant Jin is a gentleman."

"Ayi," Mai flushed again, "can I confess something that I hope you don't already know?"

"Of course," Youngmi replied, giving her hand an assuring squeeze.

"I wish I was married to Jin," Mai said.

"If he is the man for you, then you will be in time. Don't rush it."

"Ayi, there is a war on."

"Yes, that is true."

"I am in the army, which means I could be in the fighting at some point. And Jin, he is a man. Even though he is my father's assistant, he came from an infantry unit and saw combat before I met him, and he will eventually have to go to a line unit again where he could get killed."

"We don't know what our fates will be," Youngmi started to stay something more, but Mai interrupted her.

"I want to be married to Jin and grow old with him." Mai stopped, tears overflowing this time, running down her cheeks. "I don't want to die a virgin, Ayi. I want to have a husband and I want to have children."

Youngmi felt her heart reach out to Mai. She wanted to tell her how fragile such a dream was. How even the reality of a happy marriage could be crushed and made nothing faster than one even knew what was happening. Instead, she rose from her seat, pulled Mai up by her hand, and wrapped her arms around her, embracing her as her own mother would have.

"Don't worry, Mai, you will have your time."

CHAPTER 40

Brad

Winter had come on time, at least as far as temperatures were concerned. It was plenty cold for the end of October, dipping to sub-zero temperatures on a couple of clear nights already, but there had yet to be any snow. Sounds echoed across the hard-frozen ground of the training range as the last shooters finished zeroing weapons. In just over two months' time, the disparate militia units that had joined them had been trained to a level that expanded the Chiknik forces by nearly a thousand bodies.

The fight they were about to take to the enemy would be the first coordinated, full-on assault against the enemy for most of these men and women. Most of them had been part of small unit actions against the Chinese forces, some against the Russians to the east as well. But those fights had revolved around sabotage of equipment or ambush and IED attacks. Few had ever taken part in an attack in force. Four thousand attackers performing a massive combined arms assault with sappers, archers, snipers, and artillery, all preparing the ground for an infantry assault against General Zhang's first major outpost encroaching into the north.

The Palmer outpost had been a small FOB for two years from which the PLA had run short range patrols to keep the resistance fighters in the Mat-Su Valley at bay. Those patrols seldom ventured far out of town and had not come near Chiknik, with one exception. The previous summer, a special unit patrol led by General Zhang's son, Major Po Zhang, had gotten much closer than what was comfortable. A covert agent inside the Chinese headquarters had passed information on that included the mission plan for the patrol. Kharzai and Gunnar grabbed some Rangers and met Po's team as they came through. A dozen dead men and Kharzai scaring the crap out of the survivors by calling their commander out by name, in Mandarin, sent that team back. Once the need for troops in the Kenai was reduced though, the resistance groups and small militias in Palmer, Wasilla, and the communities just beyond felt the squeeze.

Shortly after the meeting with the group leaders earlier in the summer, two men in Wasilla were arrested for suspicion of being black marketers who were illegally hoarding gasoline. While searching the house, a coded document had been found. The Chinese police tortured the men for hours to get the decryption key but they did not give in. The officer in charge of their interrogation brought in the wives of two of the men and switched to torturing them instead. They got their decryption key, then set the prisoners free. The key they got correctly decrypted less than half the document. But that was enough to lead within a few days of the discovery to two of the resistance leaders. The men were captured, tortured, and then since both were single with no other family alive in the area, the wives of their nearest neighbors were taken instead. The women were publicly humiliated, forced to stand naked on the back of a flatbed truck while being paraded through residential areas throughout town. The resistance leaders were bound to the metal frame at the front of the bed, forced to look at the women. The husbands were tied opposite them, hatred smoldering in their eyes for being drawn into it. Whether that hatred was for the two men who had condemned their wives to this degradation or for the Chinese soldiers who put them through it would never be known. After half a day being driven from neighborhood to neighborhood, the procession ended in the parking lot of Wasilla High School. The residents of the nearby neighborhoods were forced from their homes to hear the warning delivered by the commander of the military police. As they all watched, listening to the threats, the prisoners were shot, both the resistance leaders and their neighbors. The bodies were cut down and dumped from the bed of the trucks. They were ordered to be left exposed on the pavement of the school parking lot as an example to anyone who dared allow the resistance to operate near them.

The three men who'd initially been captured were given credit by name as having provided the information used to locate and apprehend the others. The bodies of those three men, and the two wives, were found a few days later by a police patrol. The bullet-riddled bodies had been propped up against trees at the end of the driveway of one of the men's homes, signs hung around their necks with the word 'traitor' painted on. Chinese authorities reported that other rebel fighters had murdered their own in revenge for the loss of their leader. The actual resistance members knew that it was the police that had executed them. Those that were able to made their escape with their families before more could be named and arrested. They started making their way toward Chiknik several weeks earlier than had originally been planned.

The new members who were of military age were quickly assimilated into the TPF and trained as regular infantry. Forty of the new arrivals also qualified as Rangers, in addition to retired Marine Lieutenant Colonel Ken Caukins and his entire twenty-man team. At 53, Caukins was the oldest Ranger in the unit. The real-world experience his team was able to contribute was of extreme value. Those men, most of whom had been in some type of door-kicker unit in America's previous wars, a few in special operations, were able to join the cadre of instructors to ensure as much coverage as possible in the short time they had to get the new guys ready.

"The special units are ready," John said, his breath billowing in white puffs on the frigid air. He pointed away from the rifle range toward a group of Rangers seated at a table under a tarp strung beneath a ring of tall, white, paper birch trees. "The sapper teams are going over their assigned plan."

"The Staleys better be right about all those tunnels being open," Brad said, voice uncharacteristically agitated.

"They scouted with a couple recon squads just last week," John replied. "The tunnels are open."

Brad crossed his arms over chest, let out a breath, steamy mist rising from the exhalation.

"What do you think of all this?"

John turned toward him, raised an eyebrow. "Kind of late for second thoughts."

"I know," Brad said, staring at the group of young warriors as they talked through their mission. "Too late for backing out. I just want to know your personal opinion after having watched these new guys train with ours for the last two months. Is it coming together as well as it could?"

"There's always room for improvement." John looked up as a group from Palmer walked past, throwing salutes their way. They responded in kind and he continued, "But they're sincere, and hard working. Most of them are pretty good learners; those that aren't are generally good followers."

"What do you think our chances of success are?"

"As long as we stick with the plan of attack and don't improvise too much, I think it will go as well as it can."

Brad gave him a sideways look. "Have you been taking dialogue lessons from Kharzai? That was about the most convincing non-answer I've ever heard."

"Look, Brad." John turned to face him directly. "I have no idea how it will end. Do I think it is a solid plan to cause expensive damage to Zhang's infrastructure? Yes, I do. Do I think it is going to stop the inevitable attacks against this city? No. It will slow them down a bit, and maybe put him off kilter for six months or a year, maybe more. But they will still come at us at some point."

He turned back to the men at the table.

"But then again, attacks just like this are how the North Vietnamese eventually beat us. The politicians didn't like seeing the losses for no apparent financial returns. The talking heads back at the politburo in Beijing may say, 'Hey, General Zhang, we have the seafood lanes and the oil fields, don't waste resources on the interior.' Then they just leave us alone and hope we starve out."

"When you say it like that, it really seems like a naïve plan."

"Well, Pollyanna, it is. But it is also all we've got," John said. "We are hitting them with a major force, but it is still just an oversized hit-and-run raid. They are going to think we've blown our whole wad and expect us to fade away, not knowing we've amassed more than three times the arms and ammunition we need to pull off an attack like this. First time they come after us, we hit them again just as hard, and they will have second thoughts before going for a another shot."

"I hope that is not necessary," Brad said. "We may have a lot of gear, but we only have a finite number of bodies. If we take heavy casualties on this, folks might not be willing to make that second stand."

"That is a concern, for certain." John squinted up at the glow of the early winter sun, barely above the treetops at four o'clock. "One good thing going for us is that the secret squirrel says that they won't have much if any air cover available for the next month or two thanks to another fuel ship being lost at sea a few weeks ago. I think this is our best window to hit them hard with fewer losses than we originally expected on our end. It may be our only chance to do major damage to them with minimal cost to us."

The two of them turned and started to walk back to their offices at the headquarters building. A squad of Ranger candidates fast-marched into the compound from a trail that led to the land navigation test course. At just a day or two past the halfway point of the Indoc, they looked exhausted.

"These young kids are all so gung-ho," Brad said.

He called them young kids, but in fact the group that passed them at that moment ranged in age from sixteen to thirty. The previous group had included two men who were over forty. Before that the trainee's included a thirty-something widow whose story had been like many who still trickled into the settlement. Her two children had died of exposure the previous autumn as they made their way to Chiknik from their ruined home in Palmer. Her husband had been killed defending their neighborhood against a raid taking people for forced labor collectives, a 'temporary detail' that few ever returned from. They had heard from someone who'd escaped the search in the next neighborhood that they were focusing taking children under age twelve, or no bigger than that age, their small bodies suited for specialized, and very dangerous, labor inside cargo ships. The fighters had broken out a cache of weapons hidden by the resistance and they were able to hold off the military policemen long enough for their wives and children to escape. As the fighters made their withdrawal, reinforcements arrived and the enemy got its act together. Of the several dozen that had stayed behind, only half of the men had survived and managed to catch up to the others.

"Yeah, well, unlike years past," John replied, "especially pre-9/11, these *kids*, as you call them, not only know that they might end up going to war when they volunteer, they can be certain they will be going to war. The vast majority of them have already experienced the beast full-on. They know exactly what they're getting into."

★　　★　　★

"Operation Colonial Dissent," John said. "That is what we've decided to call this mission."

"Let it be known," Kharzai rose from his chair in the front row and faced the audience, "that my choice of cool operation names was a close second place."

"Yes, Kharzai," John said with a smirk, "Operation Slippery Duck Waggle was indeed a close second, garnering ten percent of the vote among the senior officers. Which since it was one of only two options, means that Operation Colonial Dissent won ninety percent."

"Second place is still a silver medal," Kharzai replied.

Gunnar pulled him back down to his seat.

"Down, Fuzzball," the Swede growled.

"Anyhow," Kharzai flapped his hand dismissively, "carry on, sir-general John."

Snickers and soft laughter rumbled through the room, most having come to expect such antics any time the hairy Persian was present at an event. This time though, the laughter was subdued, nervous. This was no training brief, or business meeting. This was the real thing.

"Over the next twenty-four hours, we will be embarking on a major mission, the first of its kind here in Alaska, at least that we've heard about." John clicked a remote in his hand and the large screen behind him lit up with a PowerPoint slide with the name of the operation imposed over a pre-war satellite image of Palmer.

Google Maps had gone offline the first day of the war, but members of the area's local HAM radio operators/zombie apocalypse preppers/high-tech club had anticipated such an event and had built an array of heavily shielded servers that regularly downloaded the latest updates of both Google's and half a dozen other online mapping applications. The maps and satellite images included at least one source that Franklin recognized as possibly classified government material that they probably should not have had access to, not that he was going to turn them in to the feds now. Once he knew what they had, he requested the survivors of that nerd club be assigned to work in his shop.

John clicked the remote and the operation name shrunk to one corner, colored borders outlining sections of the satellite image of Palmer.

"In the morning, advanced teams will be leaving Chiknik to begin the journey to Palmer. They will be moving in with SUSVEEs along the mine roads and logging trails, part of that through raw forest and marsh." He pointed to the officer in charge of transportation. "As cold as it was these last couple weeks, the marshes should be solid frozen. Once those men have been dropped off, the SUSVEEs will return to pick up the next batch, the sappers. After them will be the archers and snipers. Each successive unit will already have been moved closer by way of trucks. The infantry will be right behind the special teams, leaving on foot at the same time as the first teams leave in vehicles. Once the trucks have dropped their passengers at the pickup point, they will return and ferry infantry forward until everyone has got into position. This should take not more than a thirty-six hours total to get everyone to the assembly point here." He put the green dot on a spot five miles northeast of Palmer. "If all goes well, it could be a few hours less. Each of you has been assigned your team color and can see on the map where you will be assembling the morning of the attack. You should each have a copy of this and the next map to take back to your units."

He clicked the remote again and the image zoomed in to the area around the borough building, headquarters of the increasingly built-up FOB. A computer graphics artist had drawn in fortifications and various facilities over the pre-war image.

"This shows roughly what the compound looked like as of our latest intel from ten days ago. There may be some changes to smaller structures, particularly HESCO—Himalayan Environmental Studies and Conservation Organization—unit configuration, but the major structures like this steel shelter here," he circled a large building on the display with his laser pointer, "being used as a motor pool cannot be easily moved, especially with the ground frozen like it is now. Everything should be pretty much like what you see here."

He clicked again and the map had a new overlay, with lines running in apparently random patterns that all culminated immediately beneath the borough building.

"Recon teams have scouted the length of these tunnels under the old city of Palmer, leftovers from the colony days almost a hundred years ago. Surprisingly, with all the earthquakes we get, these tunnels are still mostly sound structural speaking, and reasonably safe to use, at least for our purposes. As long as you don't make a ton of noise, you should be able to get into position without detection. To our knowledge, the Chinese are not aware of the existence of the tunnels yet. With one exception being this one." He circled a line that crossed the former baseball diamonds. "This is the only one that still has an obvious above-ground entrance, but the tunnel itself we're told was not disturbed. Once the teams come up to the surface, get away from those areas fast as the sappers will be setting short timers to collapse those tunnels. You do not want to be standing on one of these lines when those things go up."

He traced the lines with the laser.

"Archers and sniper teams will be hitting the guard posts and guns manning the wall. After a few rounds of psyops killing,"— the archers' mission was to freak the hell out of the enemy in the initial assault by, as Kharzai put it, 'going medieval on their hineys'—"the archers will join red and green teams assaulting the north gate, while the mortar teams will pummel walls to either side of the gate. Rangers coming up from the tunnels, do not move too close to the walls until after the mortars have stopped. We don't want you hit by friendly fire."

He moved the pointer to the side of the map indicated as east.

"Blue team, you will assault the east gate the moment you hear the first explosion. You must hold it and keep it clear for exfiltration. Most of our troops who are inside will be coming out that gate. From flag up to final exfil, the actual assault and escape should take no more than thirty minutes tops. Leave as much destruction and as many booby traps behind as you can. Kill everyone and destroy everything that is not one of us or something of ours. Do not take loot; there will be no time. We will need to hit them fast and be gone because there will be reinforcements on the way fast. Possibly by air."

He pointed to Lazy Mountain, across the Matanuska River and a couple miles east of Palmer.

"Our Humvee-mounted Stinger missiles will be stationed here on the mountain, and at this point," he moved the green dot to the northwest, illuminating an area just on the edge of town overlooking the approaches to the city, "we will also have two, man-portable Stinger teams a little closer in if needed."

John motioned to Brad where he sat in a chair at one side of the stage. Brad rose and crossed to the center of the platform, boots clomping heavily, ominously. He stopped and turned to address the collected officers and senior NCOs, silently scanning the two hundred or more uniformed men and women packed into the relatively small space.

"I wish I was good at making motivational speeches, but I am not. I wish I could do the whole Patton speech scene like George C. Scott, but any attempt to do so would only disappoint," he said. "What I may lack in oratory though, you make up for in courage. What I lack in 'Oorah-factor,' you have in actual skill. I will not mince my words. I do believe that we will prevail in this attack but am aware that some of us will not be coming back when this fight is over. Some of us will pour our lives onto the soil of the Greatland. No one can know when it is their time to die, but all of us know that we are not immortal. I choose to live my life with no fear. I will not back down. And when it is my time, I will go face first into that next world. But before that time comes, I intend to send a whole lot more of Zhang's men ahead of me."

The crowd erupted in loud cheering that morphed into a deep grunted chant.

"Oorah, oorah, oorah!"

Brad lifted his hand and the chant gradually subsided.

"Go home tonight to your families, your loved ones. Hug your children, make love to your spouse. Pray to God. Do whatever rituals prepare you for it, then be back here at this time tomorrow with only one thing on your mind: Kill the enemy."

A sound like a huge train barreling down the tracks rumbled in the distance, a low bass roar that picked up in intensity, rolling toward them from the southwest, from Anchorage and Palmer. The ground beneath their feet suddenly shook. Shocked yelps sounded from around the room as people dropped to their knees, curling into a fetal position, backs raised, heads under chairs. Mercury lamps on the ceiling swung to the rhythm of the quake, casting weird shadows whose movement amplified the sensation of motion. The microphone thumped against the podium, blasting screeching feedback from the speakers. The PowerPoint image bounced on the waving screen. The earth's motion moved on, continuing north in a diminishing wave. Less than thirty seconds and it was over, no damage visible in the gymnasium. Brad slowly rose from the hunched position he'd bent into in anticipation of falling things that never came.

"Hopefully that was a confirmation of the plan," he said.

CHAPTER 41

Youngmi

Snowflakes drifted in large clumps, like tiny angelic beings falling from the sky. The snow had finally come after weeks of frigid temperatures and had turned the ground hard as concrete. Clouds filtered out any bright light, bathing the world in a grey blanket through which light only came as a pale glow. The temperature was in the low 20s and was forecast to stay that way. The snow was the only thing that saved Youngmi from dropping into a depressed funk on days like this. The cold, colorless days of winter had weighed on her more and more since oming to Alaska with Brad after the Marines. Occasional vacations in December and January were the only thing that had kept her sane some winters. The clean white of fresh snow did at least cheer her up a little. The forecast said to expect another six to twelve inches in the following days. Winter was here to stay, yet again.

"How would you like to go on a long date? A tour of sorts?" General Zhang took hold of Youngmi's hand as he spoke, his tone inviting her to smile and accept whatever he was offering. "I need to go to Palmer to inspect the layout of the FOB and the progress to convert it into a major base. It is a relatively safe area, as safe as any place in Anchorage lately, and you look like you could get out away from town a little bit."

"Can I make the dinner recommendations?" she said, a smile in her eyes. "I know a perfect place. At least, it was a perfect place before the war."

"What is this perfect place you seek?" he asked, hoping it was still in business and with the same menu.

"Potato Palace," she said. "I know, sounds cheap, but it is actually a very, very good restaurant. Or, at least it was last time I was there. Not fancy French cuisine like the Crow's Nest, but good Alaskan comfort food."

Potato Palace had been a long-time staple, selling Palmer's prized giants: potatoes the size of Nerf footballs. The monster spuds were served with a wide array of toppings that ranged from the standard sour cream, chives, and bacon bits, to chili, broccoli, smoked steak, or salmon lox, with any number of other accoutrements.

"Let me inquire as to said establishment." Zhang lifted his mobile phone and called the staff duty officer via speakerphone. "Lieutenant Jin, please check into whether a restaurant in Palmer called The Potato Palace is still in operation, and if so, make a reservation for myself, Ms. Ma, and my daughter for dinner tomorrow evening."

The lieutenant's voice came across the speaker, tinny and distant even though he was just down the hall. "Shall I invite Colonel Gao and his senior staff as well?"

"Yes. Include yourself and a two-person staff. Make sure the security team gets a chance to eat if possible, as well." Zhang hung up and turned back to Youngmi. "I hope you don't mind the company of Colonel Gao and Mai."

"Not at all," Youngmi said, a sly grin crossing her lips. "As for Gao, I recall meeting him in Seward back in August. He seemed like a decent man. That said, while you know I love Mai's company anytime, I also know that you know that Lieutenant Jin and she have a bit of thing going on for each other."

"Are you saying I might have ulterior motives?" Zhang acted aghast.

She rose from her seat. "Can I get your nightly glass of wine, Papa Matchmaker?"

"Sure, make it a sherry tonight," he said. "I am in the mood for something sweet."

She turned and flicked her hip at him. "Are you saying I am not sweet enough?"

"No! Never! I would never want to diminish your sweetness!" Zhang replied. Setting his cellphone down on the coffee table, he continued, "As for Mai's love life, I don't want her to be like her brother. I want at least one of them to give me grandchildren, and not just be married to the army."

She walked back with two small glasses of the liqueur, his full to just below the brim, hers less than half. It was a brand from Australia that she'd recognized from before the war, silky smooth on the tongue and richly sweet with a distinct chocolatey after-taste. As she handed his drink down to him, his phone rang. He took the glass with one hand, picked the phone back up with the other, and answered on speaker with a flick of his thumb.

"Yes, Lieutenant?"

"The Potato Palace is indeed still open, sir. I have reserved the entire restaurant for tomorrow night. I offered Colonel Gao an invitation as well, but he was not available to confirm. His adjutant stated he expected the colonel would be there but will verify upon our arrival tomorrow."

"This is my third winter in Alaska and I still cannot get used to how dark it is in the morning," Mai grumbled lightly. It was just after eight and still completely dark, with no sign of dawn on the horizon. The sun would not show its light for at least another hour and would only be fully risen a little after ten o'clock. "Winter is only just beginning, yet I wish it was already spring."

"I don't mind the dark," said Lieutenant Jin as he opened the door for the women to get into the up-armored SUV. "It makes it easier to concentrate for me, to focus on the thing that is in front of me without distraction."

He put his hand out for Youngmi, helping her climb up into the vehicle. She got in, scooting across the seat.

"I need sunlight," Mai said, taking his hand and following Youngmi.

Youngmi glanced out at Jin, saw the expression on his face as he helped Mai in. He looked desperate to say something intelligent.

"I have said the same thing for more than twenty-five years," Youngmi said, "and yet, here I still am."

"You have lived here that long, Ms. Ma?" Jin asked. "I have not lived in one place for more than four years ever. My parents were both soldiers as well, and we moved a lot. Other than college, I have moved every two or three years."

"Same with me," said Mai, her eyes flashing to the young lieutenant as he stood at the door awaiting the general. Their eyes held for a moment then Jin quickly looked away. "Constant moves across China, Asia, and Africa, then I became a soldier and now I move on my own!"

General Zhang came out of the building, striding toward the vehicle. Jin snapped to attention and pulled a smart salute that practically clicked with the precision of the move. Zhang passed him and climbed into the seat across from Youngmi.

"Come in, Lieutenant," he said. "Sit back here with us so we can talk some business."

"Yes, sir." Jin stepped in, sitting directly across from Mai.

"So what were you all talking about while you were waiting?" Zhang asked as he buckled his seatbelt.

"Mai was commenting how she was thinking of getting married and settling down to have children," Youngmi blurted.

Jin and Mai both nearly choked.

"Really?" Zhang said. "Is that true, Mai?"

"Ayi!" Mai cried out. "That's not what I said, Father."

Jin's face grew red, leaning to purple.

"I..."

Before Zhang could form the sentence, a sound like a rolling artillery barrage echoed across the base grounds. The SUV lurched and bounced on its springs, giving the sensation like a boat on the ocean in choppy weather. Several loud thumps shook the air, then it stopped, small aftershocks rumbling in the distance as the subterranean storm moved north.

Zhang stepped out of the vehicle.

"Report," he called out to the driver and radio operator in the front seat.

"Standing by for damage assessments, sir," the radio man, a senior corporal, replied from the passenger seat.

"Are you ladies alright?" He poked his head in through the back door, took Youngmi by the hand, and looked into her eyes. She nodded and he glanced over at his daughter and the lieutenant. Jin had his hand on Mai's knee. Her eyes were wide with shock that slowly morphed into a smile, then turned into an embarrassed giggle.

"I am fine, Father," she said. "Jin protected me."

"Sir," the radio man called out from the front, "preliminary reports have it at a magnitude six, forty kilometers south of Anchorage, and about ninety kilometers underground. Damage assessments are coming in stating little if any structural damage to PLA assets so far. A building in downtown Anchorage seems to have fallen. No casualties reported yet, sir."

A tall officer jogged up to the general and jolted to a stop at full attention. He snapped a salute.

"Yes, Captain Moon," Zhang said, nodding at the man. "How is the column?"

"No damage, sir," Moon said as he lowered the salute. "And you and your family, sir?"

"Fine," Zhang said.

"I've sent a scouting party of combat engineers ahead to radio back on the highway and bridge conditions," Moon said.

"Good," Zhang said. "We will move out once they radio back with a good report."

An hour later, the engineer team radioed that the roads ahead, and all bridges, were undamaged. A final magnitude of 6.2 was given to the quake that had rolled through, only causing one unoccupied building to collapse, an already condemned structure that had been heavily damaged in the early fighting and was scheduled for demolition anyway. No military or civilian casualties were reported. A two-foot-high tsunami did roll up the Kink and Turnagain Arms of Cook Inlet, but since it was low tide, it had no effect even in the low lands.

At just after noon, the heavily armed caravan stopped in front of the headquarters building of the Palmer FOB, formerly the Matanuska-Susitna Borough Building. They climbed out of the vehicles to be greeted by Colonel Gao and a dozen guards at the front doors. Youngmi had been here many times in the past. Her husband Brad had worked at this building for a few years when they had first moved down from his hometown of Fairbanks. The three-story white structure bore the distinct shape of a 1930s government building: squat, square, painted stark white. While not intended to look so when it was stood up most of a century earlier, it fit the appearance of the military headquarters it now was.

Gao, commander of the eight-hundred-plus soldier brigade that manned the growing base, saluted as Jin held the door open for the general to exit the vehicle. The women followed.

"General Zhang," Gao said, "it is good to see you again. Welcome to Palmer FOB, sir. Please join us for tea inside. The troops will be ready for review in about thirty minutes."

They went in, going to the third-floor executive office meeting room where porcelain cups were laid out along with several steaming pots of tea. As they sat down, the door opened, and Colonel Ping stepped in.

"General," Ping said, his voice still notably more nasal since having his nose broken in Seward, "it is good to see you here."

"Colonel Ping," Zhang said. "I did not realize you were in Palmer. When did you get here?"

"I have been here since yesterday, sir," he replied. The black rings around his eyes had mostly faded now, but his nose had been poorly reset and was still, maybe permanently, flat. "I had to come out to guide an interrogation of a resistance member that had been captured recently. He had information that appears to corroborate other intelligence we'd received about activity north of here. Information that may lead us to Ice Hammer."

Youngmi glanced at him, raised an eyebrow.

"Are you close to catching him?" she asked.

"Catching him really is not the goal, Ms. Ma," Ping said, his lips curling in a sneer that nearly touched the tip of his flattened nose, "but we will find him and put an end to his violence."

"Yes, of course."

"At any rate," Ping said, "I must be returning to my duties with the prisoners."

"I thought it was only one that was captured," Youngmi said.

"It is only one of the rebel fighters," Ping replied, "but we brought in his family members too. Parents and teenage siblings. They are much more cooperative when we include everyone."

Zhang nodded as if agreeing with Ping's stated tactic, said, "Will you join us for tea?"

"Thank you, General, but the interrogation team is waiting for my orders," Ping said. "Perhaps later this evening. I plan to return to headquarters early in the morning."

Ping bowed out as Gao came back into the room. The latter briefed them with an in-depth map showing the status of the region as of that morning's patrols. Youngmi actually found the presentation fascinating as she gained firsthand knowledge that no civilians would typically be privy to. She imagined Brad sitting back in his fortified city with his young wife and child. He was living a new life, without her, but she could not fault him. As far as he knew, she had willingly come into this relationship with Zhang. Well, that didn't matter anymore. She was willingly staying with Zhang. Brad got a start over, and so did she. She did wonder where her sons were though. If they were with their father. If they were safe. One thing she did not wonder was if they were alive. That she knew in her heart. She could feel them out there, somewhere. She was certain.

After the presentation, Gao led the general out to the parade field where two companies of his troops, nearly half their current strength, stood in formation. Mai and Youngmi stayed inside where it was warm. They watched from the window as the general approached the formation. Six inches of new snow had been plowed to the edges of the parade field, the ground hard as concrete beneath their boots, the sound of heels grinding against the surface audible from where the women stood as the soldiers came to attention. Uniforms crisp, freshly cleaned weapons glistening with oil, they looked like rows and columns of toy soldiers, tiny robots in an animated movie. They ran through their inspection drills as if they were on a training ground back in China, rather than on the forward most operating base in Chinese-occupied Alaska.

After a quick inspection and review, the troops were dismissed to return to their duties. Youngmi and Mai rejoined them as Gao led them on a tour of the base. He introduced them to the junior officers, the captains, and lieutenants in charge of each unit, moving through each area in the general's SUV. They got out at each unit's billet. Zhang shook hands with officers and enlisted alike, the men bowing politely to Youngmi, casting glances at Mai as she stood just behind her father, Jin at her side.

Youngmi glanced at the lieutenant from time to time, gauging his reaction to the stares being directed at the girl. The young lieutenant's face grew tight when he noticed other men ogling her, but he did not otherwise betray jealousy. She thought he was keeping it well hidden.

They returned to the main building after the 'meet and greet.' It was five in the evening. The winter sun had gone down just before four o'clock, a total of six hours of sunlight for the day.

"Colonel, you seem to have things well in hand," Zhang said. "We are famished. Will you join us for dinner?"

"I had intended to when I received the invitation yesterday," Gao replied, "but I am afraid I have unexpected duties keeping me here, sir. This morning's earthquake damaged the motion-sensor grid, and the constant aftershocks have rendered it unusable. I'm afraid that I need to stay on the grounds here until I know we are fully secure."

"Good work, Colonel," Zhang said. "Lead from the front."

CHAPTER 42

Youngmi

After she'd first mentioned Potato Palace, Zhang had his people check it out ahead of time, both to ensure it was still there, and that they still served the good food Youngmi had talked about. He had no intention of crushing her memories by bringing her to a place that was only a shadow of its former glory. As it turned out, the restaurant had earned a reputation as a favorite of Chinese forces in the valley. Potatoes had become almost as popular as rice in China thanks to a government push a couple of decades earlier to encourage production of the tubers. Potatoes hold more nutrition than rice but take a lot less water for cultivation and can be grown in far more areas than rice can, a perfect combination for the cash-strapped China of the '90s.

"This is quite a selection they have," Zhang said, looking at the menu. "Even in these trying times."

"The menu looks as if it's not been altered from the original before the war," Youngmi said.

The place had even added new locally hunted items such as ptarmigan, and moose and caribou meat, which had been illegal for a restaurant to sell in times past. Youngmi got a basic potato with sour cream, chives, bacon, and broccoli. Zhang got one with the same toppings but added smoked moose and caribou, as well as a handful of locally made cheese, shredded to melt uniformly. Mai's spud had sour cream, bacon, and smoked salmon lox. Jin's was covered with a Chinese version of chili made with fermented black beans and fried noodles.

The potatoes were huge, as the area was known for, filling a medium-sized plate, the toppings spilling over. Every ingredient was locally made or wildly acquired. Cream from the Matanuska dairy, bacon from the two pig farms in the area, and vegetables from several local vendors.

"You were right, Youngmi," Zhang said, a third of the way into his pile of food, steam still rising from the potato flesh roiling out of his mouth as he spoke, "this is simply delicious. I had no idea that potatoes could taste this good."

"I could eat this every day, Ayi," Mai said. "Although I don't think any man would want to marry me after a few months. I'd be so fat I'd tip the bed over on its side."

"I don't think you have to worry about that, Mai," Youngmi said, the candlelight on the table reflecting a soft glow across her face. "You are so thin that I doubt these potatoes would put a single noticeable centimeter on you for a long, long time. You'd have to eat this kind of food every day for a decade to see a difference."

"Ayi," said the younger woman, "you don't know how chubby I was as a girl. I was not always thin and sexy like I am now." Mai immediately blushed after the words left her mouth.

"That is right," Zhang said. "I used to call her my panda when she was little; a cute little round-bottomed sleeping bear."

Mai blushed. Jin smiled, saw her blush, then blushed himself.

Youngmi let out a laugh. "That is funny. My nickname when I was Mai's age was 'sleeping bear' because I hated to wake up in the morning, and would hit the snooze button on my clock until I was almost late for classes."

Laughter erupted. The staff officers at the next table glanced over, then returned to their own meals. The food was good, the company even better.

At ten o'clock, after food and wine, Zhang turned to Jin and said, "I have concluded that driving an hour back to Anchorage would be too much. We should stay the night at the Palmer base if they have room."

"Of course, General Zhang," said Colonel Gao once they returned to the base. "We keep extra rooms ready at all times just in case a need like this arises."

The rooms, converted offices next to the executive space, proved as comfortable as any hotel. With only one room of senior officer-quality available in the borough building itself, Youngmi wondered if Colonel Gao had given up his own room for General Zhang and herself to share. Jin would sleep on a couch in what had once been the employee break room three doors down, a space shared with the nightshift watch officer, radio operator, and a bank of radios and glowing computer monitors.

Mai's room was a basic space, a tiny six-by-eight office space furnished with a simple bed and table where junior officers or NCOs who were required to do round the clock shifts could crash for short periods. This night, no one was using it, so she got to have it to herself. The younger woman practically glowed at the thought of having a room to herself.

She smiled, tired eyes sparkling, as she told Youngmi, "I have only slept in a room by myself maybe ten times in all of my life. I've always had to share a room with other women. My aunts or cousins when I was young, and after going to the military academy when I was sixteen I slept in rooms with women I barely knew. I have almost never been able to sleep in silence, alone. It is so restful when I get the chance."

Youngmi's life hadn't been all that different. Having a sister two years younger meant they always shared a room. In Korea, she'd gone to a private girl's school from the time she was five until their parents had split up when she was eight. At that school, she slept in a long room with fifty other young girls and two Catholic nuns keeping an eye on them. Later, she lived with her father, usually in a one-room house or apartment shared with her sister Youngji, as well as up to a dozen other relatives depending on where she was. At twelve, she finally got to have a room to herself for a short time; she fondly remembered that space. She had a desk she could use all to herself, the idea of being able to put her pencils and diary in her own drawer where no one else could even look inside was a treasured memory. Through high school though, Youngmi shared a room with both her sister and her youngest aunt, only a couple of years older than she was. When they moved to America, she eighteen and Youngji sixteen, they continued to share a room in their mother and stepfather's house. At twenty years old, she married Brad and not only shared a room every night, but also shared a bed for nearly thirty years. After more than two years of having a room of her own, albeit as a virtual prisoner of the Chinese People's Liberation Army, Youngmi again found herself sharing a room, as well as a bed, with someone.

This relationship, only the second bed partner of her entire life, was with the most powerful man in the Chinese Army Alaska Command. A man who ruled over half a million square miles of the northern territories of the U.S. and Canada.

"Sleep well, Mai," Youngmi said.

"And you sleep well, Ayi," replied the younger woman. She turned and entered her small space and shut the door behind her.

Youngmi entered her room. The general was already out of his uniform, dressed only in skivvies and a T-shirt. He grabbed his toiletries bag from the suitcase open on the bed. He always kept a full kit with him wherever he went, in the event he needed to unexpectedly stay where he was. Whenever Youngmi went with him, the same was provided for her. She followed his example and removed everything down to the thigh-length silk slip that covered her bra and panties.

"If you'd like to shower first, go ahead," Zhang said through a mouthful of toothpaste. "There is plenty of hot water here I am told."

She walked over to him and wrapped her arms around his waist, resting her head on his back between his shoulder blades, fingers intertwined over his well-maintained abdomen. She could feel the furrows of muscle that Brad had never had, not even when he was a Marine. Brad had been buff, but never defined, always with just enough body fat to hide the strong outlines under a smooth belly. Zhang, on the other hand, was built like a thoroughbred racehorse, thick, sinuous muscles visibly rippling beneath his skin when he moved.

"Or, we could scrub each other's backs," Youngmi purred.

Zhang's body stiffened. He glanced in the mirror but couldn't see her face. He spit, rinsed, then turned in place, her arms still locked around him. He put his hands on her hips, squeezed lightly.

"There is that possibility."

"If you don't mind," she purred. "I haven't had my back scrubbed in a long time."

"Nor I," he replied, his voice rumbling low in his chest.

Youngmi felt another slight stiffening from him, lower down, specific. She released her grip around him, took his hand, and led him toward the shower. Forty-five minutes later, they were very clean, and very tired. After toweling off, they slipped into the queen-sized bed and quickly fell asleep in each other's arms, still naked.

Loud thumps exploded against the quiet of the dark room, someone pounding on the door. Youngmi sprang upright in the bed, clutching the sheets over her bare breasts. The lights came on, forcing her to close her eyes. Confusion clouded her mind as she struggled to come fully awake.

"General Zhang!" the voice of Jin called through the door to their room. "I am sorry to wake you, but Colonel Gao requests an emergency meeting, sir."

"One minute," Zhang replied.

Youngmi followed Zhang with her eyes as he rushed to dress. He quickly pulled on his underclothes, reached into his bag, and grabbed his camouflage battle uniform. The significance was not lost on her. He always carried several different uniforms whenever he traveled, to meet whatever requirements he might find at any destination. All the previous day, he'd been wearing his dress uniform. To switch to his battle uniform meant only one thing.

"What's going on?" she said, panic in her voice.

"Don't worry," he said, his voice not reassuring. "I am sure it is nothing major. But get dressed in case you need to evacuate."

"Evacuate?"

"Just be ready," Zhang said. "If we do come under attack, I want you away from here."

He stepped out the door to the waiting men on the other side. Youngmi climbed out of the bed and dressed in a hurry. She fixed her hair in a simple bun and rushed through cleaning her teeth. She opened her makeup pouch, but the tone of the voices in the hall said that would be an unwise vanity. She glanced at the clock on the nightstand. They'd slept for a little less than three hours. Voices carried through the door.

"We just received actionable intelligence of rebel movement in the area," Gao's voice. "One of our patrols found signs of a large force about twenty miles north of the FOB, vehicle tracks and footprints that the new snow had only partially covered up. The tracks are from within the past twenty-four hours. Ice Hammer's men conducted small raids twice before, both prior to the FOB being built up. This is likely the same people, possibly with reinforcements."

Zhang's deep voice replied, "What kind of timeline are we looking at?"

"Intel group says there may be an attack coming soon, possibly in the next twenty-four to forty-eight hours," Gao replied. "With that in mind, General, I would like to evacuate you and your family with the small convoy that is preparing to leave now."

"I will send my daughter and Ms. Ma back to Anchorage, but I will not go with them," Zhang said. "If the rebels are coming, I am not going to run away."

"But, General, it could get very dangerous here," said another voice Youngmi did not recognize. "You should not risk yourself here."

"There are many qualified men who can take my place if something happens to me," Zhang said, his tone firm and resolute. "The enemy will not hear that I ran from them. This is non-negotiable."

"Yes, General," multiple voices replied.

"The intel and operations officers will be in the conference room in ten minutes," Gao said.

"I will be there," Zhang said. "Lieutenant Jin, go tell Mai to prepare to leave."

"Yes, sir," the young officer replied.

The opened the door and he stepped back into the room. He closed it and said, "Youngmi, you and Mai need to return to Anchorage without me, immediately."

"What is going on?" she asked, unable to erase the fear from her voice.

"They are concerned the base may come under attack and I want to be sure you are safely away from here if it does."

"But what about you?"

"I will stay," Zhang said, his voice still strong, but not as forceful as it had been with the men outside. She could hear the resolve in it nonetheless. He was not going to change his mind. "Nothing will happen to me, Youngmi. There is nothing these rebels can do to remove our army."

CHAPTER 43

Youngmi

"Youngmi Ayi," Mai held Youngmi's shaking hand, "do not worry."

Youngmi took a deep breath, closed her eyes, let the breath out, forcing calm into her body.

"I guess I don't do well being woke up in the middle of the night like this," she said.

"Come with me, ladies," Lieutenant Jin said. "There is a vehicle outside that is already heading back to headquarters. You will ride with them."

They hustled out of the building, the frigid air sending a shiver through Youngmi. A soldier opened the back-passenger door to a large SUV very similar to the generals. An armored Humvee sat in front of it, a big scary-looking gun in the turret manned by a stern-faced soldier. The Humvee would lead the way back down the Glenn Highway toward their home base. Like the vehicle they'd come in on, the big black Suburban was set up like a limousine with the pair of rear seats facing each other. The space was large enough to allow six passengers to hold a business meeting back there as they cruised to their destination. The women sat across from one another on the passenger side, leaning in and grasping hands. The rear driver's side door suddenly opened, shadows passed over the opening, a voice grumbling expletive-laced complaints.

"This is not a public transit vehicle." Colonel Ping's acid tones were unmistakable, even when masked by the newly flattened nasality. He started into the space, a sour expression on his face, then backed off as he saw who his travel companions actually were. "Please forgive the harshness of my words, Youngmishi,"—while he used the Korean honorific, his natural tone of voice turned the words into an insult—"and daughter of the general, Lieutenant Zhang. I do hope I did not sound unbecoming. It has been a very long day and I was not aware that you two were to be my passengers. I'd only been told that someone was sharing my vehicle back to headquarters."

"I am sorry if we are an inconvenience to you, Colonel Ping," Youngmi said. "We did not know we would be returning to Anchorage either until only moments ago."

"These are definitely trying times," Ping said. His aid, another lieutenant slightly older than Mai, smiled in an uncomfortable kind of false politeness, bowing toward the women. Youngmi had seen him in her English classes at the headquarters but had not gotten to know him very well. The aid always wore a creepy half grin on his face that made her uncomfortable, the kind of man mothers thought of when they warned their children not to get in a car with or take candy from. He made her skin crawl whenever he looked at her. Ping continued, "I am, of course, most willing to share my vehicle with such esteemed guests."

"If we are too much of an inconvenience to you," Youngmi said, "we can request another ride back, so as not to hinder your important mission."

"No, no, you are no hindrance to me or my mission, Ms. Ma," Ping said in a placating tone. He reached over and patted the back of her hand lightly.

She withdrew the hand with an involuntary jerk and quickly tried to cover her disgust with an apologetic grimace. He eyed her up and down with a leering stare, apparently not seeing her reaction, or not caring.

"You, yourselves are part of my mission. Ensuring the peace of mind of the commanding general is in itself the entirety of my mission."

She gave him a look that she hoped appeared politely grateful, even though her insides felt like tossing up on his lap. Youngmi considered getting out of the SUV with Mai in tow and begging General Zhang to let them ride back with anyone else. That, of course, would only cause more problems than were already at hand. She wanted to get this short journey over as fast, with as little conflict as possible.

A short squawk over the radio signaled the order to move and the lead vehicle started toward the south gate, the SUV rolling into motion right behind it. Their journey was set. No way out but to move ahead.

CHAPTER 44

Phil Staley

Phil's four-man team moved through the north side of Palmer through fresh, ankle-deep snow. More of the white stuff slowly descended in large clusters of snowflakes, gliding silently to the earth. The new snow was perfect, a Godsend, covering their tracks within minutes of their passing. He prayed it would continue all day. The shadowy shapes were like ghostly apparitions in the three-a.m. darkness, alert and attentive, drawing no attention to themselves and the hundred-pound load of TNT, detonating cord, and initiators.

Getting into town covertly had not been as difficult as they had expected. The secure area of the base extended from Gulkana Street on the east to Valley Street on the west, and Fireweed Avenue on the south to Cottonwood Avenue on the north. The area included the borough building, city police HQ and state trooper barracks, the jail and courthouse, the library and park on one side and on the other side, the huge field that had been home to several baseball diamonds and soccer fields. The entire area was surrounded by a perimeter of twelve-foot-high HESCO MIL units topped with concertina wire that draped over the exterior down to the surface.

Introduced during the first Gulf War in 1991, the HESCO multi-cellular barrier system is manufactured from welded zinc-aluminum-coated steel wire mesh and joined with vertical, helical-coil joints to ensure they stay connected even under intense artillery fire. The units are lined with a heavy-duty polypropylene fabric. When joined and filled with earth, the system creates a virtually impenetrable barrier.

While security around the immediate area was very tight, a couple blocks north of the compound, it was nearly non-existent. Few patrols went much further than a mile or two out, as if the Chinese were afraid to travel beyond that extent. Concrete and barbed wire barricades had been placed. blocking all vehicular traffic turning south a little over half a mile north of the compound at intersections along Arctic Avenue, funneling traffic to single entry points on the east side of the base.

Houses and business, as well as two churches, both on the grounds of the base and in the general area had been forcibly evacuated. The barricades they encountered were not manned, just sitting there trying to block off the streets. The scene reminded Phil of the story of Hadrian's Wall, where the Romans, unable to conquer the wild Celts and Picts of Scotland, decided to simply stop at one point and build a twelve-foot-high stone wall with ditches alongside it and forts at regular intervals to keep the crazy blue-painted naked warriors on their side of the border. In the end, the Romans left Britain, and the Scots are still there to this day. Of course, Roman rule in Britain took nearly three hundred years to bring to an end. Phil prayed evicting the Chinese and Russians would not take nearly so long.

As they approached the treed corner of the back lot of the Pizzeria Delphi restaurant, Phil pulled a large bolt-cutter from the side of his ruck. The 1930s-style cellar door had originally been attached to a house that had inhabited that spot years before the boys were born. A metal shed had covered the entrance for many years after the house came down, up until one of the Mat-Su Valley's infamous hurricane-force windstorms—one of the reasons the tunnels had been built back in the day—blew the shed apart, leaving nothing but twisted sheets of metal scattered in the neighbor's yards. He pulled back a tangle of dry vines, snow falling off like salt from a shaker. The boys and their friends had cultivated the vine that hid the door for years, until it completely covered their secret entrance.

One look at the cellar door and his heart thumped in his chest. A lock. A huge lock. It appeared old and rusty, as if it had been there a long time. The brothers had been coming here since they were in middle school. There had always been a lock on it in the past, and they had learned to pick locks because of it, but this was not the one he remembered from the last time they'd come here to recon the area a few weeks earlier. He motioned to his older brother. Martin knelt beside him.

"Where did that come from?" Martin said.

"That's not the lock that was there last time we were here," replied Phil. "Think we've been compromised?"

"Dunno, but we've carried this stuff an awful long way." Martin swiped at his eyebrows, wiping away a few snowflakes that had stuck there, threatening to drip into his eyes as they melted. "Sweep the area for signals with Franklin's Scan-O-Matic."

Phil pulled out the device. Franklin had worked hard over the last few months significantly modifying the scanners to read more than just RFID signals. His creation could now read the signal coming from motion detectors, as well as sniff out the presence of most types of explosives used by either side, even if it was only a minute residue on something. Phil ran the device over the seams in the door, and on the lock and hasp, watching the indicator for the lights that would tell him what he needed to know.

"Coming up clean," he said, "but I don't know how well this thing can read through the door to the other side."

"Well, there is only one way to make sure," said Paul.

Martin signaled for the two Rangers providing security to get down and prepare for a boom. Phil reached out with the bolt cutters, took a deep breath, and snapped the rusty steel with a quick squeeze of the two-foot-long handles.

No boom.

He opened the door and reached inside with the scanner.

"All clear," Phil whispered, wiping sweat from his forehead.

Martin signaled the others and they silently descended into the tunnel that had been his and his brother's secret teen hideout from parents and teachers. From Pizza Delphi, the tunnel ran in a straight line under several blocks to the Matanuska Susitna Borough building. At about the same time they were entering their tunnel, another four-man team led by Tommie was making their way in from the opposite direction, near the Matanuska Telecom Association, MTA, building more than a mile south of downtown. The teams would cross the distance to the perimeter of the base, then continue on until they were under the borough building itself, planting their explosives and scouting the way for the initial assault force that would emerge from other gate locations inside the compound. Two of those gates were actually inside the big building.

They were to prep the gates to blow outward, allowing the assault force to pop up inside the compound initiating the attack. In one hour, two dozen ten-man teams would be entering the tunnels, taking positions at their designated exits. A total of 240 Rangers would then rush out, the sapper teams joining them. Fifteen minutes later, hopefully when they were all clear of the building and areas directly above the tunnels, several very big booms would rock the morning. Booms that they hoped would give them an unfair advantage.

As they descended into the dark tunnel, stale air assaulted them, dank and old. After a couple years of breathing the fresh air of the forest, the odors of the ancient subterranean highway's dust, mold, and long-dead things was a motivator to keep moving and get back above ground as quick as possible. The nostalgia of their childhood no longer held any pleasure for the brothers. They were to destroy the playground of their youth. The soft patting of their footfalls echoed dully in their ears. The sound of an untraveled space that had forgotten what to do with trespassers.

The lack of constant human traffic for most of a century, other than occasional clusters of teenagers who, other than the Staley boys, seldom ventured far in, had left the space dead to the outside world. They pulled down their battery-powered infra-red night vision monocles, using only one eye so as to retain natural vision in the other in case a sudden flash blinded the first. In the green light of the monocles, the deeper parts of the tunnel system looked like a time capsule, discarded items still laying where they had been left decades ago.

A few bits of graffiti appeared here and there, but less than one might expect. Without lights, the tunnel was absolutely dark. No external light ever reached far into the underground passages. Life below was quiet, almost peaceful as if nothing existed above ground. The tunnels were unaware of the war and death that raged above on the surface, as well as what was soon to be their own fate.

Fifteen minutes into the journey, they passed the mark they'd made during their previous recon of the area, indicating the point where the tunnel crossed under the first perimeter around the base, a ten-foot-high wall of looping razor wire. Fifty feet after that, they passed the mark for the inner perimeter. Martin raised his hand.

"Small cave-in here, recent. Wasn't here when we came down a few weeks ago. Probably the earthquake the other day."

There was enough room for them to move through single file without disturbing the mound of dirt. When 120 more Rangers came through in a bit, it might be a different story.

They set to on placing bundles of TNT along structural supports. Tommie had recommended TNT rather than Semtex or C4 due to its slower detonation rate. Whereas the latter two explosives are very powerful and somewhat safer to handle, their blasts were more suited to blowing in doors or cracking large structures. TNT was better at moving earth with its relatively slow explosive rate that would shake the earth to pieces and throw it out, rather than merely cut a hole in it.

Within the prescribed hour, they set over one-hundred pounds of TNT along more than a mile of tunnels, both the main one under the building and several that branched off to areas that had once contained other now long-gone structures. They returned to their designated gate as the first team of Rangers drifted in behind them. The sound of over a hundred more shuffled quietly through to the next gates, getting into their positions for the assault.

CHAPTER 45

Youngmi

The first fifteen minutes of the hour-long ride back to headquarters was uneventful. The aid sat on the seat beside Mai, Ping on the side with Youngmi. The two men seemed glued to their tablets, the blue-white light of the devices illuminating their faces. Ping was reading messages in the PLA's secure instant messaging app. Youngmi could make out the borders and icons of the application, but she could not see the contents of the messages clear enough to read as the words scrolled quickly up the screen. While her Chinese speech had expanded immensely, her ability to surreptitiously read over someone's shoulder had not grown enough to make out what Ping was so focused on. The aid had his tablet turned at such an angle that she could see nothing.

Youngmi glanced at Ping's tablet again, but still could not make out what he was typing. She turned toward Mai. The younger woman made eye contact with her then looked toward the aid, her eyes widening as they focused on the reflection of the tablet screen against the mirror-like black-tinted window. Youngmi quickly put her eyes on the same spot and made out three very clear characters. Characters that had only one meaning. A very vulgar meaning. Ping saw Mai staring, followed her gaze to the reflection.

"Lieutenant," he grunted. "Now!"

Ping dropped his tablet and grabbed Youngmi's arms, forcing her hand onto his crotch. The aid took hold of Mai's shoulders and pulled her toward himself, crushing a sloppy kiss onto her lips. Youngmi managed to yank one hand free and gouge at Ping's eyes, polish hardened nails digging into the soft flesh. Ping screamed in a painful rage, drew back his hand, gathered it into a fist, and punched Youngmi in the gut, sending the wind out of her lungs. Her eyes bulged as she fell on her back against the door. She had never felt anything like it in her life. She tried to force her lungs to expand again, could feel the tension in her body as breath would not come. Vision zoomed down to two narrowing channels, shutting out the peripheral world like looking through a long dark tunnel, brain going numb as it was starved of oxygen. She could feel her heart pounding in her chest.

Two loud explosions rang against her eardrums, startling her. Her lungs reflexively sucked in air, remembering how to breathe again. The SUV lurched off the road, rushed down a steep embankment. The aid flopped onto the floor beside Mai, his face a shattered mess. A splash of blood fanned across the ceiling. Mai's gun was in her hand, eyes fixed on the dead man.

The SUV slammed against a huge rock at the base of the roadside ditch, coming to an immediate halt fifty feet or more beneath the road. Ping's head slammed against the half-open Plexiglass barrier between the back and front seats. He collapsed onto the seat, groaning. The driver slumped over the steering wheel, a dark hole at the base of his skull. He had probably died instantly. Heart, lungs, nerves, all shut off the instant the bullet passed through. Blood dripped from the windshield, a neat white starburst on the glass.

Mai reached up behind her and popped the door open, toppling the women onto the snowy ground outside the vehicle. The dead lieutenant's body flopped after them, getting hung up halfway out. A trickle of his blood drained out in a thin black river across the white snow. The women rolled out and down the gravel embankment, scrambled to their feet and hurried into the woods.

They had gone less than fifty yards when Ping's shout echoed through the trees. A shot rang out behind them. There followed a dozen more in rapid succession, a pause then a new magazine snapped into place followed by another thirteen rounds. Youngmi tripped over a tangle of brush letting out a yelp. Bullets whipped through her hair as she fell, landing hard. The sleeve of her coat snapped with an odd jerk as she slammed to the ground. She started to lift her arm and inspect the new hole when Mai hissed at her.

"Play dead," Mai whispered.

The pair lay still in the darkness, the younger woman grasping her pistol tight in her hand. She pointed to the sound of Ping's boots crunching on the frozen ground. The narrow sliver of a moon barely lit the women, vague shadowy images reflected dimly off the snow. As long as they didn't move, they were invisible. Ping stood at the edge of the trees, backlit by the crashed SUV's headlights.

The security Humvee had finally stopped, realizing something was wrong, and turned back around. The turret gunner called out as they approached, "Colonel Ping, sir! Are you okay?"

"We were ambushed," he called back. "The rebels killed my aid and driver and kidnapped the general's daughter and mistress!"

"Shall I put the spotlight on the area?"

"No, you idiot! That will draw the attention of their snipers."

"What are your orders, Colonel?"

Ping slowly backed up the embankment, keeping his eyes on the trees. He scanned for the women. Nothing moved.

Perhaps I killed them. That must have been the cry I heard.

"Take me back to the Palmer base. I must tell General Zhang."

Ping's boots crunched the snow as he went back up the embankment. The flat metallic sound of Humvee doors opening and closing, as well as the more solid notes of the SUV doors, echoed across the snowy ground. A moment later, the Humvee roared off, returning north toward Palmer, leaving the other vehicle behind. The women waited until the sound of the engine vanished, then waited several minutes more, listening for someone who may have been left behind to catch them. Confident they were alone, they rose from their hiding places. As soon as they rose, they started shivering, frigid air meeting the moisture that had seeped in from the melting snow they had lain in. They wiped snow from their clothes before more of it could soak them further and made their way back to the SUV to see if they could get it started.

The hulking black beast was not going anywhere soon. Steam rose from the smashed radiator and the rear passenger-side tire had come off its rim after it slammed a sawn-off tree stump on the way down the embankment.

"What are we going to do?" Youngmi muttered as she stared at the driver's mangled face. The bullet that had caught him in the back of his skull had exited through the center of his face, bursting his nose and eye sockets, whole white globes shining against the darkness of his ruptured sinus cavity. It was like looking into a forbidden place.

"We need to get back and tell my father what happened," Mai muttered.

"But Ping went that way," Youngmi said.

"Which is why we need to get there too." The young women snapped her attention away from the gruesome face. "If we tell father what happened, Ping will finally be finished."

The sound of vehicles rose from the south. The women ran up the embankment to the roadside. Dim headlights gradually materialized as a small convoy rolled toward them. Mai moved into the middle of the road, waving her arms and jumping up and down. Youngmi joined her.

Major Zhang scanned the infrared image of the road ahead on his tablet, the rooftop IR camera providing a relatively clear view of the area for two hundred meters in every direction.

"Slow down the convoy," he said abruptly. "Someone is in the road ahead."

Without needing to be prompted further, his radioman signaled the other vehicles. "Slow to ten, persons on road ahead. Prepare for possible ambush."

The eight-vehicle convoy immediately slowed to a ten-mile-per-hour crawl. Major Zhang zoomed the IR display in on the persons in the road, his eyebrows screwing up in confusion. What were his sister and Ms. Ma doing in the middle of the highway out here?

"Convoy stop," Zhang ordered. "Full security."

The radioman repeated the order. They came to a complete stop, all weapons pointing into the darkness, men leaping from vehicles forming a perimeter.

"Falcon Three," he pressed his mic button, calling the point vehicle commander, "get into the left lane; I will take the right. Approach slowly, eyes wide, three sixty."

The pair of Humvees proceeded toward the two women moving at barely more than walking speed. Turret gunners slowly scanned from front to their outside, while the soldiers in the back opened the rear gun ports, careful not to sweep their weapons over their comrades. They came to a stop twenty feet from the women. Zhang got out, rifle in hand. Mai started toward him.

"Stop!" he shouted, rifle coming up to his shoulder. "One more step and I will shoot you."

Mai froze in place. She recognized her brother's voice and knew he would shoot her even if he knew it was his sister.

"What are you doing out here?"

"We were attacked," she started.

"Rebels?"

"No," she said. "Let me come closer."

"Come forward," he replied, weapon still up, scanning for an attack. "Both of you."

The women quickly came to him.

"Get in the Humvee where it is warm."

They climbed into the back of his command vehicle with the radio operator. Zhang ordered the other soldiers to get into Falcon Three. He could trust his radioman and driver, but beyond that, he kept almost no one else in his confidence.

"Who attacked you if not the rebels?"

"Ping," Mai said. She fought to keep her emotions beneath the surface, barely managing it as moisture welled up in her eyes. "Father got word of a possible security risk and sent Youngmi Ayi and I back to Anchorage with Ping who was already on the way. We got halfway when he and his aid tried to rape us."

Youngmi kept her head down, still not comfortable around her lover's son. She already owed this man a double debt for having saved her from Ping twice; this was going to increase the debt yet again.

"What happened, and how long ago?"

318

"I shot his aid after he jumped on me. My second shot accidentally hit the driver. The car crashed, we fell out, and managed to escape into the woods. He left with the security team about 20 minutes ago, returning to Palmer Base. I think he believes he may have killed us when he shot as we ran away."

"Let's get back to base and get this information to General Zhang," he replied. "We will put an end to this once and for all."

Her brother's eyes glinted with a steely violence. Revenge would be had today.

CHAPTER 46

Brad

The archers moved into place first, setting up like snipers, but much closer and much quieter. The actual snipers set up nearly a mile further back on a series of high rooftops and a crumbling concrete tower at the edge of the city that had once been part of the old military communications network through the area. While the elevations were not the greatest—Palmer lay in a flat diluvial valley scraped out by a few thousand years of floods and glacial carving—they had more than 90 percent of the borough building and surrounding fields sighted in. The snipers watched through their scopes as the sapper teams moved silently through the early winter landscape, fresh snow and frozen soil barely crunching under their feet as they carried their loads of explosives into the underground network of tunnels that connected many parts of the city.

Palmer, Alaska was one of the last U.S. experiments in colonizing territory, and the last such experiment of any country on the North American continent. The government had purchased the Alaska Territory from Russia in 1867 for a little over seven million dollars, more than 110 million in the current pre-war dollar. A pretty good deal either way. After the gold rush of the

1890s, the population of Alaska surged, forming the origins of modern Anchorage and Fairbanks at the same time that entrepreneur George W. Palmer built a trading post on the Matanuska River. When the great depression hit, the U.S. government offered free land parcels to anyone who wanted to leave the hard-hit Midwest and move to Palmer, Alaska. The population of the town expanded exponentially with the influx of colonists to the farming project. In an effort to resist mother nature, those farmers, mostly Scandinavian immigrants who'd come from Minnesota, Wisconsin, and the Dakotas, unknowingly built the perfect weapon to use against the twenty-first-century invaders. Subterranean tunnels, meant to allow warm travel during the frigid winters, connected most of the old buildings erected prior to 1950.

Brad looked at his watch, waiting for the last few minutes to pass, marking the kickoff of the party. He had wanted to be in the first assault wave but was soundly talked down from that idea by the other leaders. He was the glue holding this whole operation together and could not be risked in the first volley. He settled for entering with the second wave coming after the gates were blown and breached. Teams from the various militia groups had staged in several locations, vehicles and men hidden, poised for the lightning strike needed to blast through with absolute shock and awe and then to vanish again, just as fast.

Several meetings over the summer and autumn with the various leaders left him certain he could trust most of them to carry out their assignments. Even if a couple of the leaders may flake out in the fight, Brad figured that most of their soldiers would pick up the banner and run with it. This was their homeland after all.

CHAPTER 47

Ben

en watched the men in his Ranger platoon move through the shadows, beasts of war, wolves on the prowl for man-flesh. Due to an injury to the previous platoon leader a month earlier, a fractured tibia during a rock-climbing exercise, Ben had been elevated to the position by unanimous approval of the men and the company leadership. That man's accident put Ben in charge of a team of twenty-one Rangers, at the razor point of the spear in the first wave of the Palmer assault. Three six-man rifle squads, a medic, and Staff-Sergeant Patrick Scott, a man who Ben had learned quickly to lean on for his years of experience. With Scott and all, it made twenty-one lives Ben had to account for. Twenty-one humans that would go to their deaths at his command. Katarina was the platoon medic. The girl he loved was one of those fated to his call. This was not what he had imagined life would be at nineteen.

Their task, after the sapper's bombs blew the west gate, was to rush in and murder everyone on the other side, blasting a pathway for the second wave to move in by the hundreds. Once that was secured, his team was to head to the motor pool and blow up as many vehicles as they could before continuing through the east gate and toward their escape vehicles across the river.

Ben had no illusions about what was to come. It sounded simple enough in training, but after two years of battle, he learned that it was never simple in execution.

CHAPTER 48

Ping

Colonel Ping's vehicle returned to the Palmer base, pulling straight to the front of the headquarters building. It was a quarter to four in the morning; they'd been gone a little more than an hour. He got out of the vehicle, slammed the door, and walked briskly into the building. The guards at the front entrance saluted smartly. He ignored them, catching a glimpse of his reflection in the mirrored window, a growing purple bruise coloring the left side of his face. His nose ached. He continued in and up the stairs to the upper floor commander's suite.

General Zhang was wearing a camouflage combat uniform, his sidearm in a hip holster, instead of the dress uniform he'd been wearing the previous day. The general leaned over the long table in Colonel Gao's conference room.

Gao's executive officer, a major named Ho, was briefing them on the stack of intelligence spread on the table. The seismic devices they used for motion sensing had been making noise all day long with a constant stream of small aftershocks from the previous morning's earthquake. But one of the technical analysts had found a segment of noise that was too repetitive to be an aftershock. Just a half hour ago, the sound of thirty or more boots was detected crossing through a section of field a few blocks beyond the camp perimeter.

"Has someone gone out to check the area?" Gao asked. Ping entered the room, flustered. Gao blurted, "What are you doing here?"

General Zhang turned as Ping stepped into the room. "Colonel Ping? You are supposed to be in Anchorage by now."

"I am sorry, General," he said. "I have bad news."

"What happened?" Zhang demanded. "Where is Youngmi? Where is my daughter?"

"Sir," Ping replied, "your daughter and mistress have been taken by rebels that ambushed us on the road. The vehicle I was in was directly targeted. My driver and aid are dead, and the two women missing."

"Why did you not search for them immediately?" Zhang said, his voice a deepening growl.

"Sir, I only had four men," Ping stammered. "The rebels were on us in force."

Zhang turned from the conference table toward his aid. "Major Zhang is coming this way with a half-strength special operations company. Radio him with the coordinates of the attack and order them to initiate a search of the area. They are to get back to me as soon as they find the trail of these rebels. If they locate them before they are fully out of the area, they are to rescue the women and execute all prisoners except their officers. The officers are to be brought before me immediately."

CHAPTER 49

Po Zhang

"**S**tand by for patch through," the radioman said into the microphone, as he reached up to tap his commander on the shoulder. "Urgent order from General Zhang, sir. Patching over to you."

Zhang pulled his microphone down. "Falcon One."

"Falcon One, urgent orders from Falcon Supreme."

He recognized Lieutenant Jin's voice.

"Go ahead."

"Mountain Falcon and Dragon Mother have been taken by rebel forces in an ambush." Jin used the code names assigned to Mai and Youngmi. "You are to proceed to these coordinates and begin a search for them. Eliminate all resistance except for their senior officers. Bring them in to Falcon Supreme."

"Understood," Zhang replied. "We will divert to," he repeated the coordinates and orders back to verify he understood.

"Acknowledged."

The call ended.

"Why did you not tell him you have us already?" Mai asked her brother.

"I want to catch Ping by surprise," Major Po Zhang said. "I want to see his expression as we walk in and step on his balls."

It took less than ten minutes to finish the journey to the base. As they closed on the last mile, Zhang's radio operator called the Palmer west gatehouse.

"Palmer Base, this is Falcon One."

"Go ahead, Falcon One," came the reply.

"Request immediate high-speed no-stop entry due to high-value casualties onboard."

"What is your security code, Falcon One?"

He passed the correct security codes and encrypted signature and two minutes later, they flashed through the gate at forty-miles-per-hour. They made a beeline straight to the headquarters building. Ping's Humvee stood parked in front, a heavy machine gun manned by a nervous-looking young soldier. The young man looked at them, then nearly choked as the women's faces became visible in the light of a street lamp.

"Lieutenant Zhang?"

"Who are you?" Mai said, the soldier's face darkened by shadow.

"Choo, Private Choo from the soccer league," he replied. "The colonel said you were taken by the rebels."

"Is Ping inside?" Major Zhang demanded, his tone full of icy blades. A strange snapping sound echoed across the compound from the north. Moments later, screams of terror erupted from the guard posts at the main gate and from the watchtowers. More snapping twangs and more screams. Then the night erupted with explosions. Gunfire rattled from the walls surrounding the base as well as from inside the headquarters building. Soldiers sprinted past, surprised expressions on their faces, weapons up as they ran toward the gunfire.

"Come with me!"

Po whisked the two women around the south side of the building, hiding them in deep shadows, the world around the base sparkling with muzzle flashes and exploding mortars.

CHAPTER 50

Kharzai

"You know," Kharzai said, a contemplative expression on his face, "I really do like my job."

He raised the longbow, pointing the steel tip of the arrow at a spot about a hundred yards away. He watched the shape of a man lean over the wall and look out over the small town, silhouetted by lights further back in the compound. The figure was lean and fit, probably young, young enough to be his son. The man jerked, his head snapping forward as if he had let out a sneeze. He turned to the man behind him.

Kharzai loosed the arrow. He watched with childlike wonder as it soared skyward. His eyes traced the arc of its descent. The young soldier turned back toward his post. A heartbeat later, Kharzai saw the young man jerk again, his face shining in the moonlight, mouth stretched open, trying to scream but prevented by the three-foot-long birch rod jutting from his throat. No cry came from that direction. The razor head of the arrow had severed his larynx and was probably embedded in his spine. A heartbeat after Kharzai's arrow hit home, more than a hundred others around the base met the same fate. A second round of arrows peppered the perimeter accompanied by the distant snap-twang of bowstrings, a sound not commonly recognized on battlefields for the past couple of hundred years.

Cries started to ring out from inside the base, some shouting the Chinese word for medic, many others the terrified screams of men surprised by death's sudden appearance within their personal space. A body hung over the edge of one of the guard towers, half a dozen arrows sticking out of his back like a porcupine. The base defenders started to get their act together and put down return fire, but it was random. The survivors on the wall had no idea where to return fire in the silent night.

Their intel source inside the Chinese headquarters had provided a copy of the most recent wall-to-wall inventory of the base. One of the items on the spreadsheet had caught Kharzai's eye. As of a month ago, they only had early third generation night vision capabilities that limited them to a little more than one hundred meters in visible range at night. They had no thermal imaging scopes. And there were only six of those devices for the entire base; a far cry from America's soldiers of the twenty-first century where nearly every infantryman and every sentry had night vision. Of course, a lot of that stuff had been made in China when the countries had played at being allies and ceased to work the day the invasion got underway. Thanks to a dearth of technology in the far reaches of conquest, the PLA was about to get slapped silly by a bunch of Alaska bushmen.

CHAPTER 51

Ian

Right on time, the first Ranger team showed up at the innermost tunnel gate, head-mounted night vision goggles strapped over their eyes. The team leader tapped Martin on the shoulder, letting him know they were there while maintaining silence. Martin drew close to him and spoke in a nearly silent whisper that Ian could barely make out from the first position behind him.

"When the gate charge goes up, count to ten to let the big chunks of debris settle then go. You are going to come up in the basement of the building. There might be people in there or not. Years ago, our dad was a maintenance guy here and I remember the IT office was in the basement. Exit stairs are fifty feet to the left, short flight 'cause it is only a half basement. We heard armor moving around up there about twenty minutes ago, and it sounds like a bunch of vehicles are idling out front. You might be jumping right into a hornet's nest so be ready." He glanced at the luminous dial of his old-fashioned wind-up watch. "Thirty seconds."

The team leader nodded and gave the hand signal for his men to prepare for the blast. Those with night vision goggles removed them. They all turned, closing their eyes and huddling twenty feet away. Hands clasped tightly over their ears, they opened their mouths wide against the coming blast to keep the pressure from scrambling their brains.

"Five, four, three, two…"

Phil skipped one then hit the button on zero. The tunnel instantly filled with bright white light. The concussion was focused up and outward but it still slammed their bodies in the split second before the gate burst open. Chunks of concrete and steel burst into the room on the other side, smashing anything in their path. The Rangers poured through the opening. Two dozen other explosions erupted at several points around the base, some straight up through vertical hatches in the grounds others through normal doors in small utility buildings that had been welded shut years earlier.

Sheetrock dust and smoke filled the air in the space they entered. It was indeed some type of IT shop. Ian remembered his dad often saying IT shops were typically in the least desirable spots in offices, most often in basements, attics, or out-buildings. Several bodies lay scattered on the floor among overturned desks. A foot stuck out from beneath a large piece of concrete jammed against the wall. Random computer parts were strewn about. A couple of the occupants were still living, a condition quickly remedied as Rangers put a round into their foreheads as they passed through. They did not take prisoners.

Within seconds, the team was out of the room. Ian sprinted forward, taking the lead as they rushed to the exit stairs. An explosion of adrenaline raced through him as his foot touched the top stair. A Chinese officer rounded the corner at the same instant, pistol raised. In the nanosecond reaction time of his hyped-up senses, Ian instantly recognized the rank on the other man's shoulder board that identified him as a colonel. In the next nanosecond, he stitched the colonel's chest with a burst from his short-barreled AK-12 carbine. The man collapsed in a heap, dead in his tracks. The shadow of another figure suddenly loomed. A second burst from his weapon and the shadow vanished. He waved his arm for the rest of the team to pass while he covered them. Ian loosed another burst of gunfire blindly up the stairs to keep anyone up there out of the way as they rushed through the main entrance. A golf-ball-sized grenade bounced around the corner. Ian kicked it down the next lower flight of stairs then dove out the door after his team. He felt the jolt of the blast, its sound muffled by the below-ground space. A Humvee stood in the road directly in front of the doors, a terrified-looking young soldier standing in the turret, trying desperately to unjam his weapon. Ian ended his striving with two shots to the torso, and the soldier slumped sideways onto the roof the vehicle. They moved off into the darkness, toward the most beautiful chaos Ian had ever seen: a real battlefield.

The defender's weapons had been set to repel an attack on the outside, not an attack by hundreds of fighters on the inside. Bedlam reigned as the pre-dawn darkness was lit up with muzzle flashes, tracer rounds, and explosions. The Chinese seemed to hit each other as much as the Rangers in their midst.

Ian dropped men with quickly aimed double shots as they jogged through the compound on their way to their next target. Magazines dropped from his weapon as they emptied, fresh ones inserted with practiced motions. Within minutes, he had put over ninety rounds, three magazines, into the defenders. Forty or more dead by his hand. This was violence in its purest form.

Rage.

Bloodlust.

No thought.

Action and reaction.

Muscle memory and practiced reactions that had been instilled in him by both the long experience with Troop 104, and the past six months of intense training and drills with the Rangers. Purity of thought. No confusion or fear. Bright. Crystal clear. Austere. Combat was the perfect narcotic, the most ancient addiction.

Ian Stone was in his natural element.

CHAPTER 52

General Zhang

Several explosions sounded all at once, the floor beneath them reverberating with what had to be at least two bombs at a fairly shallow depth almost directly beneath them. Seconds later, muffled gunshots sounded from the lower floors of the building, followed by grenade blasts. General Zhang got a look out the window. Flashes of explosions sent geysers of earth and concrete skyward at points across the compound. Men emerged from holes in the ground like so many demons escaping hell.

"The base has been undermined," someone shouted.

Colonel Gao rushed out the door and sprinted downstairs, sidearm in his hand, bodyguard just behind. Zhang and his team rushed after him, weapons drawn. Gao turned the corner of the bottom flight of steps, in time to catch a burst of gunfire in the chest. He dropped to the ground like a sack of cement. The close shots ripped through his torso, splashing a red liquid mess from wall to wall. One of Zhang's guards bodily yanked the general back as the other rushed forward and turned to fire a burst from his carbine around the wall. The act earned him the same reward as Gao.

The second bodyguard tossed a tiny, golf-ball-sized grenade around the corner. It bounced against a couple of surfaces and clattered across the tile floor, then exploded. For such a small device, it had a lot of punch. He counted a fast three seconds after the blast then reached around and sprayed the stairwell with an entire thirty round magazine of 5.8x42 ammunition, dropped the empty, and reloaded. He peeked around the corner, listened intently, then motioned for the general to follow. Zhang turned the corner onto a scene of utter carnage. The general glanced back toward Colonel Ping, who grimaced at the sight. The small space of the stairwell and ground floor lobby was a charnel house, from wall to wall. They quickly picked their way through, trying not to slip on the blood-soaked floor, making for the front door.

The attackers who'd come from below had quickly moved on. Wild fights raged in pockets all over the base, explosions large and small coming from every direction.

"Colonel Ping," Zhang directed. "You take some men and go check what is going on at the main gate; we need to make sure it is secure. I am going to get in radio contact with the company commanders and get a status report. You," he pointed to Colonel Gao's XO, "get those commanders on the air."

The XO ran to the nearby Humvee Ping had returned in and started fiddling with the radio to get it onto the right net for his men. Voices started crackling over the radio as Ping and half a dozen soldiers ran around the south side of the building toward the gate. A heartbeat after the last man disappeared around the corner, the earth seemed to inhale a deep breath, expanding beneath them, the building rising several feet off its foundation. The sound of the massive explosion rolled out of the ground, knocking them off their feet. The century-old building fell back to the surface with a resounding crash.

CHAPTER 53

Ben

At 4:30 a.m. on the dot, the north and east gates went up in balls of fire. When the explosions settled, the first frontal assault wave rushed through in vehicles and on foot, roaring a battle cry that could wither a man's soul. Before the defenders could bring their guns back around to the external attack, large sections of the defensive perimeter had been decimated. The Rangers poured through the gate, rushing to the slaughter.

While Ben had been in many fights, and had killed more men than he could remember, this was his first pitched battle in the traditional sense. This was no raid, and certainly no ambush. This was thousands of soldiers in two armies, intent on slaughtering each other. As he scanned the area for targets, it seemed that the element of surprise had worked. What looked like hundreds of Chinese lay dead or dying within moments of the initial assault. Screams of the wounded reverberated almost as loud as the gunfire in the early morning darkness. His platoon moved through the destruction, putting rounds into any enemy that moved.

No mercy, no quarter.

He glanced over toward the company commander and the old man, First Sergeant Leo Weeks, an animal glare in old NCOs eyes, visible energy rippling through his body. A spray of something dark colored his face as he charged into the fight. An old warrior on his home turf.

The occupiers seemed totally shocked by the swiftly moving events. Ben was suddenly not as impressed with these enemies he'd heard so much about. Whistle blasts screeched the rhythmic tweets of the Chinese recall signal, a communication method used since Mao's old-style People's Army of the Cold War era. The enemy pulled back, regrouping, forming a smaller perimeter, only to come up against the sapper teams rushing up like goblins from beneath the ground.

CHAPTER 54

Kharzai

The archers fired their final volleys of arrows just as the Rangers hit the north gate of the FOB. The mortar teams continued to rain explosives down inside the compound until the breach was successful then focused the remainder of their ammunition on the east gate, where the militia troops would exfiltrate after inflicting maximum damage.

A heavily armored D11 bulldozer rolled out of cover and across the hundred yards of open land, rounds pinging off the thick steel in showers of sparks. One of the Palmer-based teams had worked it over in an underground shop, welding half-inch steel plates around the cab of the beast that left the driver looking through a slit to see where he was going. The cage behind the driver had been converted to mount a .50 caliber machine gun that was operated by a soldier inside another armored box. The gun started blazing, three-foot-long flames leaping from the muzzle, the chunk-chunk-chunk of the gun thundering over the rattle and whine of the 850 horsepower engine as it crawled at an agonizingly slow seven miles per hour toward the HESCO wall.

Bullets pinged uselessly off the hundred-ton behemoth. Rocket-propelled grenades streaked toward it, exploding in great yellow gouts that left nothing more than scorch marks to show for the effort. It took four minutes to reach the wall. The .50-gunner, the archers, and the mortars kept the rate of fire up, and Chinese heads down. It reached the perimeter and kept going, as if nothing blocked its way. The driver raised the massive dozer blade, continuing forward until it connected with the top of the twelve-foot-high wall. Recon patrols had discovered the Palmer FOB had received two different shipments of HESCO units. Some had steel wire mesh, but a large segment of the wall was made of units with a cheaper plastic mesh. The barrier of sand, dirt, and gravel was plenty strong enough to stop pretty much any ordnance from bombs to bullets. But when the D11's blade put its considerable force to bear at the top, the units fell into the compound, taking more units on either side until the pressure snapped the plastic mesh. A more than fifty-foot-wide section collapsed, reducing the wall to a four-foot-high obstacle the men could easily clamber over. The D11 abruptly dropped its blade, slicing through the tangles of razor wire, then backed up, pulling the mass aside to leave an opening for the men to cross in through.

"Up and at 'em, big guy." Kharzai slapped Gunnar on the back as he rose from behind the cover of a large bush. "Time to go play stormtrooper! The WWII kind, not the Star Wars kind. We need to actually hit our targets the majority of the time."

"Right behind you, fuzzy man," Gunnar said as he stepped from behind a tree.

He slung his bow across his back, switching to the M4 hanging from his chest rig, a grenade launcher beneath the gun barrel. He signaled with a wave of his arm and the rest of the archer teams did the same down the line. They rushed across the field toward the gap as the monster machine backed out of the hole it had created. Within seconds, another couple hundred Alaskan fighters were inside the base, guns blazing.

The unmistakable rip of a machine gun sounded to their left, dropping men in the gap instantly, both the attackers and defenders. Gunnar spun, dropped to a knee, and fired a 40mm grenade toward the muzzle flash, arching the round through the air to land directly on the gun crew. The explosion silenced that threat with crump barely heard over the din around them.

"Good job!" Kharzai called out, putting rounds into two soldiers attempting to set up an RPG for a shot. "You just earned an extra cookie for lunch tomorrow."

"I love cookies!" Gunnar shouted back.

The sound of incoming rounds snapped past his head. There was a meaty thwack behind him, a man falling with a grunt. They pressed the attack with constant forward movement, squads leap-frogging each other, providing cover fire in turns as they charged the opponent, the sounds of battle a non-stop, deafening roar. Men fell everywhere, dropped by bullets and shrapnel. Screams of the wounded echoed across the FOB. Kharzai stepped over a man whose guts were strung out in front of him, his face a mask of terror and pain.

Ten minutes into the attack, it was moving along as smoothly as a battle can. He glanced left and right, making sure he was not ahead of the rest of the teams. He emptied his weapon into a cluster of figures setting up a machine gun, the last round locking back the bolt of his weapon. He pressed the magazine release, let the empty drop to the ground, and slid a fresh thirty rounds in with the smooth motion of someone who had done this maneuver thousands of times. The bolt snapped back into place and he resumed the killing without a break in stride.

Gunnar walked alongside, ten feet to his left, pouring destruction into everything in front of him. Weapon pressed into his meaty shoulder, he moved like a machine, a deadly automaton mowing down whatever was in his path.

A line of Humvees poured through the ruined gate, roof-mounted guns sending lead ahead of them, while hundreds of dismounted infantry followed through both the gate and the gap in the wall. Pockets of fierce fighting erupted into hand-to-hand battles, men driving bayonets into each other, beating each other with rifle butts, fists and feet, anything that could be a weapon.

Then came the new sound, unmistakable over the battle space. A pair of WZ-10 helicopter gunships roared into the fight. Streaks of flame erupted beneath the pinions of the first, making a beeline straight for the D11. The anti-tank rockets flipped the massive dozer onto its side with a deafening explosion. The second chopper followed, its 25mm cannon chewing up the ground, and a bunch of men, as it zipped over their heads.

A pair of bright flashes erupted from the treeline where the archers had been, Stinger missiles sending the gunships on the defensive. The first chopper evaded one of the missiles, only to be hit by the second, the Stinger ramming straight up the exhaust, blowing the tail clean off. The two halves of the dead craft crashed in a corner of the FOB, taking out their own men. The pilot of the surviving helicopter shot straight skyward, the second Stinger zipping past, losing its target and self-detonating seconds later. Two more helicopters roared past, banked, turned, and lined up for another run.

Another pair of Stinger missiles hissed from the men in the trees, accompanied by half a dozen more launched from the Humvee-mounted Avenger systems hidden on the hillsides east and west of the base. Within seconds, two more birds were burning wrecks inside the compound. The final WZ-10, damaged by a near miss, turned tail and limped back toward base.

"I really hope our friend was right about them not having fuel to put more birds in the air," Gunnar shouted.

A Chinese sergeant leaped out from behind a barrier right in front of the giant Swede. The look of surprise on his face as he realized he had misjudged both the distance and size of the man in front of him was instantly erased as Gunnar smashed it in with the butt of his M4.

"Turn right," Kharzai shouted, giving the signal for the men to follow. "Group up with the main element!"

The company of archers-turned-infantry wheeled right, following the two leaders into the fight.

CHAPTER 55

Ben

en's team peeled off from the main assault to follow their secondary objective. They ran perpendicular to the advancing Rangers and militiamen, pushing their way to the motor pool. They were to destroy as many enemy vehicles as they could by slapping thermite charges over cowlings of the engine blocks. Each team member had ten of the pre-set charges. Manufactured in Chiknik with equipment found in welding shops, the grapefruit-sized devices could generate over four thousand degrees of heat. When placed on an armored engine hood, the firebombs would melt through the armored plates and enough of the engine block to make it irreparable.

A series of massive explosions rocked the earth, much larger than the ones that opened the entry points for the sapper teams. A number of cavernous trenches opened under the base, nearly splitting it in two halves, tendrils of collapsing earth trailing out like crazy vines. Men and vehicles tumbled into the gaping crevasses. Two forty-ton Type-96B main battle tanks flopped sideways with a thunderous crunch, nearly vanishing into the twenty-foot-deep pit that erupted beneath them. In another area, the underground explosions threw men and equipment skyward. A bright orange mushroom of flame blossomed skyward near the north corner of the compound, a fuel supply dump, lighting the dark pre-dawn sky like sunrise in Hell.

Ben signaled and his team made for the covered motor pool area, skirting the bulk of the fighting as they crossed behind the advancing Rangers. They hooked around the remains of the borough building and sprinted toward a large, hastily built structure made of earth-filled HESCO units covered over with a roof of corrugated metal sheets. They slowed as they drew near, keeping on a 360-degree swivel as they rounded a corner heading toward the east-facing entrance of the structure. Three enemy soldiers ran out from the structure, passing only a few feet in front of the team. A quick burst from two of his team's rifles took them down, their blood on the fresh snow standing out black in the light of fires.

The team stopped at the edge of the structure. Ben peered around a corner. Three sand-bagged emplacements stood ten yards or so in front of the building. Machine guns focused eastward across the former soccer field, toward the main gate from which the four-man gun crews, gunner, loader, and two riflemen, assumed an assault would come. A fight was indeed raging over there, but not the one these guys would be part of.

Ben made hand signs indicating the number of enemies and that there were three positions. Six of his team leaped out from the wall long enough to pick their target and toss hand grenades, two per machine gun, directly into the emplacements. They ducked back as the bombs went off. A second later, the zing of shrapnel had stopped and they charged around the corner into a chorus of screaming wounded. They fired a single round into each man living or already dead, quieting their cries and guaranteeing no one would get them from behind.

The walled area contained rows of various types of vehicles parked ten across and as many deep. Several large transport vehicles and a few tankers sat to one side. Two of the tanker trucks were labeled with the international symbols indicating hazardous materials, HAZMAT. Beside that, a red diamond with a bursting flame in the center indicated flammable liquid inside, most likely diesel fuel. While diesel fuel in the open will burn hot, it is not explosive in the air like gasoline. But if the diesel is contained inside a sealed steel tank, according to the explosives training they'd received at Ranger School, that much fuel could produce a bomb ten times more powerful than what knocked down the Oklahoma City Federal Building in the '90s.

"Save those tankers for last!" Ben shouted over the growing din of the overall battle. His men spread out, each three-man fireteam, two per squad, six teams in all, taking a row of vehicles. Running down their rows, they slapped thermite charges on the hood of each vehicle they passed, snapped off the safety tab that set the ninety-second timer, then moved on to the next.

Ben and Scott took the first row, Katarina following and listening to the other teams in case they called for a medic. Two Chinese soldiers popped out from behind a Humvee and fired a spray of bullets their direction. Ben's weapon snapped their direction and fired a burst without thinking, a totally mechanical process. The pair of Chinese soldiers crumpled like ragdolls, their blood spattering the vehicle behind them. He turned to see Katarina running her hands over Scott's torso and legs, looking for wounds, then she cut open his left sleeve revealing an ugly hole, shiny red muscle tissue puffing out the back of his arm. The hole went clean through his bicep. Katarina speedily stuffed an entire roll of gauze into it, eliciting a string of curses. Once the gauze poked out the other side, she wrapped it tightly with a length of self-adherent bandage. Soon as she was done, Sergeant Scott forced himself back to his feet and they kept moving.

"Let's go," shouted Ben. "We've got thirty seconds before these things start going off. I want to be far away by then."

They sprinted down the rest of the column, Katarina with her rifle and Scott holding his QBZ one-handed with his right while Ben planted their bombs on each vehicle they passed. They stopped at the tankers at the end of the row. Ben climbed up the ladder on the back of his tanker. He peered over the top, then reached up and placed his last two charges on top of the fuel tank. Bullets slapped at the steel around him, showering him with sparks. A ricochet zipped past his head with a loud snap, sending him ducking back down the ladder. Scott and Katarina fired at the machine gunner. Ben lurched back up to set the timer, only to be showered with another raking of machine gun fire that sent him back down.

The man on the tanker behind his toppled off his ladder, the top of his head sheared off in a clean line above his eyebrows. One of the dead man's teammates took his place, instantly jumping into position with two more bombs. He snapped off the safeties, setting the timers while under cover, then climbed the ladder, slapped them onto the surface, and leaped down.

Ben saw what he'd done and called down to Scott, "Hey, gimme two bombs!"

The staff sergeant dropped his weapon to its sling and tossed them to him one at a time, then snatched his rifle back to firing position and resumed defending one-handed. Ben snapped the timers off, yanked himself up, slapped them onto the fuel tank, then scrambled back down to the ground just as a loud hiss drew his attention. Bright white flames burst from the first vehicles at the other end of the row. An explosion of small arms fire in the area of the machine gun that was harassing them drew all of their attention. One of the other teams had moved in and taken them out.

"Let's get out of here!" he shouted to the remainder of the team.

They sprinted out and around the HESCO wall, three fewer than when they'd entered, rushing to regroup with the rest of his company and make their escape out the east gate once the place went up. As they ran, something drew his eye in the direction of the partially collapsed borough building, a shape moving. A woman, in civilian clothes. Long, wavy black hair, a memory of something familiar.

Then she turned, glancing his way, then disappearing into the shadows.

"Take them to the rendezvous," he shouted. "I'll catch up."

"But..."

"Go!"

CHAPTER 56

Youngmi

Po Zhang shoved the women around the corner just before the group of rebels burst from inside the building. The amount of gunfire and screams that erupted told them the insurgents had killed everything in their path then kept moving, a specific target apparently on their mind. Moments after they were gone, Po Zhang rose, poking his head around the corner, back where they had come from. He instantly snapped back.

"We need to find a safe space for you two," he said in as close to a whisper as he could affect in the environment.

Mai jutted past her brother and saw their father and several other men charge out of the building, eyes wide with battle rage. Ping was next behind the general. She spun back toward her brother, opened her mouth to say something angry. The entire white-painted, wooden, three-story building suddenly leaped into the air, defied gravity for several seconds, then slammed back on to its foundations, the upper floors collapsing onto themselves, internal framework collapsing inward. Po instinctively wrapped his arms around both women. A large piece of the building helicoptered toward them from the blast. Po spread his back at the pulsing sound coming at them. Youngmi felt a hard thud punch through his body and into her own, throwing them to the hard ground, the young officer rolled off the women, out cold, his body slumped sideways. As soon as she could suck air into her lungs, Youngmi let out a shriek. She grabbed Mai, panic in her eyes. The younger woman was little better. Mai desperately scanned the area, looking for where to run, where to turn for aid.

Fast moving footsteps came around the corner of the building. They both leaned up for a better look, praying it was not the rebels who would likely kill them where they sat. Men jogged around the corner, drawing fast on the women. Youngmi's heart sank in her chest. The fires and few working street lights lit the faces of the men coming their way, Ping's glowing in a spotlight.

"We'd be better off with the rebels," she whispered to Mai.

Ping took several more steps then stopped, his men jolting to a halt behind him. He stared at Youngmi in shock.

"You...why won't you just die?" he spat in rage. "Why do you keep haunting me?"

He closed the distance between them in two quick strides, reached down, and yanked Youngmi to her feet so hard she thought he'd wrenched the shoulder out of joint. She let out a yelp, steeled herself, then sucked in a lungful of air, forcing calm into her panicking body.

Deep breaths, slow breathing, water, ocean, children, Brad.

"Stand still, witch!" He shook her arm, sending lightning bolts of pain through her damaged shoulder. "Stand still!"

Youngmi sucked in another deep breath, rising to her full height. Her eyes bored into Ping's. Mai forced herself up beside her, defiance blazing in her aura. Ping raised his pistol, ordering his men to raise their weapons in suit. Youngmi felt a sudden, overwhelming calm wash over her.

This is not the end.

This is only the end of the beginning.

A child's prayer floated across her lips in a whispered catechism.

If I should die, before I wake, I pray the Lord my soul to take.

"Weapons down!" Ping shouted. "Sergeant Kong, you stay with me here. The rest of you, recon the gate and report back to General Zhang."

The soldiers reacted to their orders. Youngmi's eyes widened with the realization of what Ping seemed to be intending. Surely he would not attempt to…a blinding white light filled her vision. Her ears instantly blasted a high-pitched screech that seemed like it could sear her brain. The same sound as when Brad had tried to blow her up.

I forgive him.

The thought came unbidden.

The wind was again knocked out of her and she slammed onto the frozen earth, rocks hammering in new bruises, icy blades of frozen grass stabbing into her face and eyes. This time, she knew to suck the air back into her lungs quickly, by force of will. She forced herself to a sitting position, then rocked onto her knees, feeling her body for injuries shock was hiding from her. As her vision refocused, she wished she had stayed down without witnessing what lay around them.

None but her was upright. Several of Ping's men lay in jumbles of bone and flesh. Another looked normal, seemingly asleep, until she realized there was a large gap between the man's hips and the top of his thighs. A pair of boots marked the place of a sixth man who'd been standing when the mortar bomb landed between his feet. A direct hit.

Youngmi reached to her right to take Mai's hand. She caught only air. She turned to see where her surrogate daughter was. The young woman lay flat on her back, long black hair splayed like the rays of an ebony halo around her head. Mai's eyes were open, staring from a pale, cherubic face. A tiny stream of blood trickled across her forehead from a whole the size of a pencil eraser just above her left eyebrow. Youngmi shifted her eyes to Mai's chest, looking for breaths, any sign of life. With the winter coat and flickering light, she could not tell. She pivoted toward Mai, but was unexpectedly launched backward, off her feet.

"DIE, WITCH!"

Ping grabbed her by the arm, attempting to haul her to her feet again, but slipped in the steaming remains of one of his men. He fell, a sickeningly wet crunch as he landed hard onto the corpse. His grip slipped off her arm.

Youngmi leaped to her feet and sprinted for the brightly lit area in front of the remains of the borough building, the place she was certain her general would be. As she broke around the first corner of the building, a line of machine gun fire stitched the ground in front of her. She dove back toward the shadow and straight up against Ping. Both of them surprised, she bounced off his chest then sprang back across the space where the machine gun had ripped at a full sprint. They fired another burst, icy chunks of frozen soil stinging her legs and back. They had missed her. Ping held back for long enough that she put some distance between them. She took cover behind a disabled truck to catch her breath.

How do I get out of this place?

Peering around the truck, utter murderous chaos ruled. Crouching in the middle of the battlefield, she came to the disheartening realization that she had jumped out a frying pan and into a fire. From a scenario where Ping was attempting to rape and probably kill her, into one where certain death rained down all around her, on every side.

Pressing herself flat into the cold earth, she glanced around the rear tires of the vehicle, in the direction of the main entrance to the now demolished borough building. The general stood beside the open door of a Humvee a hundred yards away, talking into a radio handset. Youngmi turned back to scan for what had happened to Ping. He was nowhere she could see.

Maybe the rebels got him.

She glanced around more, looking for any open avenues through which she could run to Zhang, and safety. From one angle, it looked like there was a possible blind spot for the machine gunner that she could take advantage of. She was beginning to get the concept of this war stuff.

Do everything you can to survive longer than those who want to kill you.

That was something Brad used to teach their three sons. She'd always thought of it as nothing more than brash, big man bravado. Big bad dad teaches sons to be big bad dads. But now she realized, after all this time, he was getting them ready for this day.

They are out there, I can feel them. My sons. My husband.

Youngmi glanced back at the general and felt a sudden twinge of guilt for thinking of her husband, as she was about to run to his mortal enemy for rescue. She poised her body to leap into a full sprint, took a deep breath, closed her eyes for a moment, then something like a brick smashed the side of her head.

The hard ground rushed up, tearing her skin on jagged mounds of uneven earth made by frozen tire tracks made when the ground was still muddy. Blood oozed from several lacerations as she bounced from the surface. She felt herself being dragged over the rough ground, sensing herself pass into a deep shadow. Rough fingers tried to rip her pants off.

What is wrong with this man? We're in the middle of a battle and this is what he wants?

Youngmi let out a scream, but it was drowned by sounds around them. She slapped at his face and tried to struggle but that only seemed to brighten his evil smile. She thrashed about with her arms, her hand landed on a twisted piece of metal pipe. She wrapped her fingers around it and swung with all her might. There was a loud crack and something gave way inside Ping's face. He let out a roar of pain, his arms flying up to protect himself. She cranked the pipe again, this time to the ribs, and was rewarded with a satisfying crunch, his lungs releasing a whoosh of air as he toppled off her.

Youngmi jumped back to her feet and made like a rabbit from behind the truck. She had crossed two-thirds of the distance, almost there. Boots crunched behind her. Her head snapped back as her pursuer grabbed her hair and yanked her against his chest, wrapping around her chest in a crushing one-armed grip. She let out another scream. The cold metal of a gun barrel against her head told her in no uncertain terms that Ping's rape fantasy was over now.

This would be the end.

No more of his monstrous advances, but also no more of the love of General Zhang Ko Bai, and never a chance to know what happened to her sons. Tears stung her eyes, welled up, and dropped across her cheeks.

CHAPTER 57

Brad

John stayed back in the command center coordinating the various sections of the attack while Brad led the main body of the Rangers in the final above-ground assault wave. Once the infiltration and sapper teams came in via the tunnels, the breaching teams blew open the gates and made a way for the mounted units to burst in with armored vehicles and big guns. More than four thousand soldiers from a dozen militias had joined the attack against the base that currently housed less than one thousand Chinese military personnel and a few hundred civilian workers.

The militias had come together almost seamlessly, with the majority of the groups willing to follow the leadership of the Chiknik army, who made up the vast majority of the fighters on scene. Brad was making a very hard gamble. He'd left only a couple hundred fighters to defend the entire city of Chiknik, with three thousand elderly, women, and children to back them up. Everything hinged on this attack, and the hopeful disabling of the invader's army for an extended period. But there were no guarantees. In war, the only constant was chaos.

As his armored Humvee charged through the blown west gate, .50 caliber machine gun pounding away atop the turret, he scanned the carnage of war around him. Destruction lay everywhere. The Humvee crunched over the bodies of men who had met their end on the road inside the gate. Brad stared ahead, blood lust rising.

Just as his vehicle passed into the gated area, the major explosions inside the tunnels went off. The large white building that housed the borough headquarters since the mid-1930s rose off the ground then slammed back to the earth, the top two floors collapsing onto the first as the near-century-old structure buckled on landing. The early morning darkness was lit with thousands of twinkling lights accompanied by the crack of gunfire and the snap of bullets in the air.

An explosion in front of them blinded him for a moment. The driver suddenly lurched the Humvee to the right, rolling around the vehicle that had been in front of them. It was on its side, the front passenger door caved in as if a huge fist had punched it, the vehicle out of commission. Three men clambered out of the back and joined the fight on foot. Brad noted that the other three that had been in there did not clamber out.

Brad's radio headset crackled with status reports from unit commanders, calm voices mechanically relaying that they'd met their goals and were proceeding. Brad remembered that U.S. Marine General James "Mad Dog" Mattis had the call sign "Chaos" when he was supreme commander of the U.S. Marine forces, then later of all of the U.S. and NATO forces in both the Iraq and Afghanistan wars. Chaos was Mattis' nom de guerre, and he was one of the most feared leaders of American forces in both wars.

Chaos.

Destruction.

Destroying in order to restore.

Killing in order to live.

That was what Brad's life had become. A cycle of violence that maybe forged a pathway for eventual peace. He only hoped that he could come even close to peace in his lifetime.

A sudden rattle against his door jolted him. Two bright starbursts appeared in the side window, rounds making their mark on the bulletproof glass. More bullets impacted against the thick armor plating, rattling his arm like hits from a BB gun. Without the armor and thick bulletproof glass, he would have been shredded. For the first time in his life, he thanked the lowest bidder on a government contract for the quality of his work. He almost felt invincible in this vehicle, except for the fact that where those last two rounds hit, the glass was now opaque. To be immortal yet blind was not a great exchange. To survive some small arms fire only to be blasted by an unseen rocket was no better.

The Chinese forces were trying to organize, but it was pretty clear they were having issues. The three-pronged attack had thrown them off their guard, and they were struggling to catch up. When the earth erupted under them, slicing the base into almost neat sections, that cut off a lot of the response. Twenty-foot valleys appeared where there had been solid ground moments earlier, halting tanks and assault vehicles in their tracks.

A snap of gunfire across the windshield snatched his attention forward. The .50 caliber in the turret roared like a Midwest thunderstorm, but exponentially more hateful. The column fanned out, stopped, and disgorged their riders in a wave of a thousand Rangers and militiamen, rounding the blown tunnels and running sidelong against the enemy. The Chinese could not get their weapons to bear without hitting their own men. The battle had ratcheted up tenfold with the addition of that many rifles and machine guns as the infantry broke free of the vehicles and rushed into the melee.

Brad leaped from his own vehicle to join the fight, eyes wide, teeth bared in a death grimace. Rage rose inside him, a sensation he'd only experienced a handful of times since the war had come to his homeland. It was like the greatest high, better than any drug or alcohol. The feeling that life and death combat gave was unlike any of those substances. A surge of energy, a blood-borne rage that pushed his senses outside normal time and space. Every bullet that snapped past his head clicked his pissed-off-meter up another notch. Each miss making him feel more invincible.

Then something in the corner of his eye grabbed his attention. Youngmi.

Standing alone.

No. She was being held by a Chinese officer. He had a gun to her head. Other Chinese officers approached them.

Brad looked at her, then back to the battle in front of him. His heart pounded in his chest. His men could take the battle. His twice undead wife needed him. He snapped a command to his second, broke away from the team, and sprinted toward Youngmi. He passed a flaming barricade, face lit by the firelight.

"Youngmi!" Brad heard another man's voice. A moment later, he saw the man who had called her name running toward her, half a dozen soldiers behind him, that many more joining when they saw the leader moving, the man's face visible as he passed into a circle of light from a lone functional street lamp.

General Zhang.

Youngmi replied in Mandarin, words Brad could not understand.

Brad kept moving, slowing to a cautious pace as he drew closer. Zhang saw him, instant recognition in his eyes. Both immediately moved their gaze and pointed their weapons toward the man holding Youngmi with a gun to her head. Their aim moved from Ping to each other, then back again.

"Youngmi!" Brad called to his wife.

"Brad!" Youngmi gasped, seeing him for the first time.

CHAPTER 58

Zhang

A woman's scream drew Zhang's attention over the din of the battle. Recognizing Youngmi's voice, he snapped his head in the direction it came from, spotted her struggling less than thirty yards away, being held by a man with a gun.

"Youngmi!" he called out.

"My general!" She thrashed violently only to have the pistol shoved up against her head. Zhang's eyes widened as he recognized Youngmi's assailant.

"Youngmi!" another voice called her name from off to his left.

Youngmi's eyes shone with a new kind of terror, as if seeing a ghost.

"Brad?"

The man moved carefully toward them, weapon up, two rebel soldiers keeping up, one on either side of him.

Zhang pointed his weapon at the other man, then back toward Ping.

"What have you done to my wife, you bastard?" Brad growled.

"Your wife?" Zhang felt an instant flash of confusion, shock.

"Enough of this!" Ping shouted, drawing all eyes back to himself. He stepped into the edge of a pool of light from the single street lamp that somehow still functioned, its glow enhanced by the flames of burning structures. His face and hands were covered in dried blood. A smudge of dark red on Youngmi's coat traced the path of his arm across her chest.

"Colonel Ping!" Zhang said in Mandarin. "What are you doing?"

"I am sorry, General Zhang, but I cannot let this witch live!"

"What are you talking about?" the general demanded. "What has she done?"

"Your whore is a spy for the resistance, General. Can't you see? Didn't you just hear? That man is her husband! She's been spying for him the whole time!"

"No, my general," Youngmi pleaded, her voice shrill, desperate, "it is not true."

"Shut up, Xiu Ying!"

Zhang's face twisted in deeper confusion. "Xiu Ying?"

"Xiu Ying came back to avenge herself against me!" Ping's voice was that of a mad man. His eyes darted from one person to another as the other men slowly advanced on him. He jerked Youngmi up higher, her body covering his like a shield, his raspy voice tainted with madness. "You should have stayed in the grave, witch!"

Zhang froze in his place. Images of his wife dying of intestinal cancer burst into his mind. Another image of Ping's unconvincing, sad expression beside her coffin overlaid the image. Everything suddenly came together.

"You," Zhang said, his voice a growl barely audible over the sound of battle. "You killed Xiu Ying. You killed my wife."

"And her ghost came back to possess this Korean bitch to haunt me!"

"Why, Ping," Zhang said. "Why would you do this to me, your friend?"

"Friend? You stole everything from me!" Ping screamed the words. "My woman, my career, my life."

"What are you talking about?" Zhang said. "You are the most decorated intelligence officer in the PLA. You have a great…"

"Yet you are the general!" Ping shouted in response. "You stole Xiu Ying from me. Your children should have been my children. Your general's stars should have been mine! I am always your subordinate, following your orders! While you, the great general, strut around forcing your will on those you call friends."

"Umma?" Half a dozen weapons turned to the sound as a young man's voice called with the Korean word for mommy. Several rifles spun toward the new threat.

"Hold your fire! Everyone!" Zhang shouted to his men, not wanting Youngmi to be hit in a crossfire. He instantly repeated the command in English.

A shadowy figure stalked steadily toward the tense crowd, weapon at his shoulder, darkly smudged face belying the youthful voice.

"Umma? What's going on? What is this?"

"Ben?" Youngmi cried out. "Benny?"

The battle surged to a frantic pitch, drowning all external sound. The sky erupted in what seemed like a way-too-fast sunrise as twenty-thousand gallons of diesel fuel exploded, slamming a silencing pre-dawn fist over the conflagration for several heartbeats. The shockwave washed over the battlefield, knocking people off their feet. A massive orange mushroom cloud rose over the city, lighting the battle space for a long moment. The bright flash illuminated pieces of men and broken equipment scattered about in every direction. As the world-breaking wall of sound subsided, gunfire and hand grenades almost instantly rose to their former levels.

Zhang righted himself, weapon still trained on Ping. The colonel yanked his captive up higher to cover his own body, pressing the end of his pistol into Youngmi's head, forcing her to twist at a painful angle.

CHAPTER 59

Ben

Moving carefully, rifle up, butt pressed hard into his shoulder, he scanned the area around his mother. A pair of Chinese soldiers swung their weapons toward him, a dozen more kept their aim solidly on almost an equal number of Chiknik men that materialized around him, Weeks and Scott among them.

"Umma?" Half a dozen weapons on both sides turned to the sound as a young man's voice called with the Korean word for mommy. Several rifles spun toward the new threat.

Zhang shouted a command in Chinese, then repeated what he assumed was the same in English. "Hold your fire! Everyone!"

"Umma? What's going on? What is this?"

"Ben?" Youngmi cried out. "Benny?"

A blast like the end of the world ripped the morning, the shockwave nearly knocking him to the ground. Hot chunks of steel whistled through the air, a horizontal rain of destruction. The fuel tankers had finally passed critical mass. A sheet of metal roofing four feet wide and eight feet long flew with a warbling sound as it careened into the edge of the assembly around his mother, cutting two enemy soldiers in half at the waist where they stood at the periphery of the group. He glanced the direction of the motor pool. Flames several stories high rose into the air, roiling pillars of smoke rose in sinsiter black clouds against the morning darkness.

He shook his head, cleared the concussion cobwebs, and righted himself. The interspersed enemies immediately snapped weapons back on to their potential targets.

The phrase 'Mexican standoff' flashed through his mind.

If one person twitches, everyone here could be dead very fast.

Shadowy figures moved to his right, the movement barely visible in his peripheral vision. Several shapes, but two very distinct. A thin man with a ball of black hair and beard surrounding his head, and a fast-moving giant of a man. Kharzai and Gunnar, with what looked like a squad of archers, crossed from one deep shadow to another, moving to get at the unwatched flank of the general's men.

CHAPTER 60

Kharzai

"Ruh-roh! Looks like Mr. Brad is having a get-together." Kharzai pointed to the cluster of Chinese and Chiknik troops facing off to each other, Brad and Zhang at the center. The enemy general's mistress, Brad's wife, the focus of both men's attention.

"Looks like a damsel in distress too," Gunnar replied, seeing the same scene.

"Well, let's see if we can save the day then," Kharzai said. He took off at a jog.

Gunnar turned to the men with him. "Second squad with us, everyone else continue to the east gate."

A dozen of the archers jogged after the Persian and the giant. The rest charged into the raging battle, destroying as much stuff and as many people as possible as they moved toward the exfiltration point.

Just past halfway to Brad and the gang, the FOB exploded in a blaze of light. They instinctively dropped low, shrapnel and chunks of metal and wood zinged through the air above them. A Humvee careened skyward, the three-ton vehicle landing on a group of men scrambling for cover. He could not see whose men they were.

Kharzai curled his nose at a new stink, an uncomfortable sensation on his scalp. He reached up and touched the side of his head, hand coming away covered with curly little bits of black ash. He smelled his hand, singed hair stinging his nostrils, and twisted his face in rage.

"Oh! Oh! Oh, that does it!"

A bunch of Chinese fighters burst from behind a vehicle, running parallel to his men. He opened fire with consecutive three-round bursts, dropping them like a switch had been turned off. "Burn the hair, meet your maker!"

He turned back toward Brad's situation, saw Ben Stone bounce back to his feet like only the young can do, weapon instantly back on track. Kharzai put up his hand, motioning Gunnar and the squad to halt in a dark shadow.

"What have we here?" He assessed the gathering. Ben was just visible at the edge of the pool of light, two Chinese soldiers pointing their weapons at him. Leo Weeks and Scott stood just behind Brad, their weapons trained on soldiers across from them, who were returning the gesture.

"Crap," Gunnar's deep voice muttered over his shoulder. "Looks like that woman is being held hostage by that Chinese colonel."

"That woman," Kharzai replied, "is Youngmi Stone, Brad's first wife."

"Huh? I thought he said she was killed at the start of the war."

"He did say that, and he was certain it was true too, until she showed up in Zhang's car the day we failed to blow the bastard up."

"Oh, man," Gunnar's voice dropped to a deep mumble. "It's like a love story written by a sadist."

"Well said." Kharzai motioned with his hand in a curving gesture. "Let's get around their flank and kill all of these guys so we can let those two figure out the future."

They led the squad around the right. Staying to the darkest shadows, deepened by the blazing columns of the inferno of the wrecked motor pool, they skirted the standoff, eyes scanning in all directions. Further on, he saw an individual shadow stalking toward the collected figures locked in stalemate beneath the incongruously lit street lamp, gait recognizable.

"Ruh-roh, ruh-roh," Kharzai muttered. "Young wolf is on the prowl. Things are about to get a bit more murdery around here."

CHAPTER 61

Ian

A squad of Chinese burst from around the corner of a burning building just as Ian's team rushed from the opposite direction. Too close to stop, the men dove into the melee, shooting, clubbing, and stabbing like gladiators in an arena death pit. Moments later, eight out of ten Rangers remained standing. The same was not true of a dozen Chinese soldiers, broken bodies draining their lives onto the snow. Flames danced all around them, illuminating the battle space in a surreal glow. A pair of massive explosions flashed like lightning, thunderous concussions shaking the earth. The concussion slammed him to his back on the hard ground, knocking the wind out of him like a gut punch from a giant.

The pillar of fire lit the area in an eerie glow, hellish shadow warrior locked in mortal combat. Men shielded their eyes as the flash temporarily blinded many. Like a scene from hell, shadows stretched and deepened in the pulsating glare. Struggling to catch his breath, he rose unsteadily back to his feet, his team nowhere in sight. A body few feet in front of him caught his eye, one of his own, a face he could not soon forget.

Tommie lay on his back, arms splayed out, eyes wide open, mouth agape. A hole the size of a bowling ball had been drilled through his torso. Whatever had done it must have been white hot, searing the wound as it passed through bone and flesh, leaving surprisingly little blood. The Irishman had probably died instantly, his heart completely ripped away from his body in a flash.

Movement to his right snatched his attention, Alaskans and Chinese in a standoff of some sort. His father was at one edge of a pool of light. Then he made out one of the other faces. There was no mistaking the beauty of it, and the terror. His heart pounded against his ribs, stomach nearly flipping inside his gut.

"Momma," the word stuck in his throat.

His father stood ten yards from her, eyes and rifle barrel moving quickly from her attacker to the tallest Chinese officer. Ian now could see the rank on his uniform: General Zhang. Two other Chinese officers and a hard-faced sergeant aimed at his dad, the act copied by Weeks and Scott behind Ice Hammer. Scanning the area just outside the light, he realized another dozen Chinese soldiers stood in similar array against a similar number of Chiknik fighters.

Behind his mother a face appeared, eyes glowing with the fire of a madman. Ian raised his rifle to his shoulder, red dot site centering between her captor's eyes.

Movement in the periphery of his vision made him instinctively drop. A gunman fired a three-round burst, gouts of fire strobing from the muzzle. Something burned across his back. He rolled over the jagged ground, skin blazing with fiery pain where a bullet had scored a line between his shoulder blades. He came out of the roll and squeezed his own trigger.

Nothing happened.

He yanked the charging handle of the weapon, but it was stuck fast, jammed. Ian continued into another roll, another burst sending gouts of frozen earth erupting just beyond him. He dropped the rifle and slid his hand down to the pommel of the tomahawk that hung from his belt. He emerged from the roll, arm cocked like a spring, and let fly the weapon. The razor-sharp blade spun through the air, a blur of rotations as it crossed the space toward his assailant.

CHAPTER 62

Po Zhang

Po Zhang had forced his mind and body back to consciousness, the back of his head throbbed. His brain swam with concussion as he rose to his feet, trying to regain his sense of direction. A scream sounded behind him: Youngmi. He turned to run toward it. A swirl of pain, like an invisible blade trying to cleave the top of his skull off, nearly knocked him back to the ground. He paused, put his hands on his knees, and vomited onto the hard-frozen ground. The pain inside his head flashed like bolts of lightning with every heave. He mastered himself, forced the dizziness aside, wiped a sleeve across his face, and rose to his full height. He sucked in a lungful of cold air tinged with the smell of burning fuel and gunpowder. He willed his brain to get his body where it needed to be. Then he saw her.

Flat on her back, on the dirty snow. A small, round hole just above her left eyebrow, a trickle of blood running down her forehead. His sister stared unseeing into the dark morning sky. Snowflakes drifted down, settled on her pale, bloodless face, frozen in a serene, restful expression. The rest of the dead.

Rage built in his chest. Adrenaline surged, all the pain and confusion instantly evaporated. He snatched up his weapon and started in the direction he'd heard Youngmi's scream.

As he turned the corner of the destroyed headquarters building, he saw another figure heading the same direction. A small axe hung from his belt, short-barreled AK-12 carbine in his hand. As the man passed through a corridor of light, he caught a glimpse of the face. One of the most wanted rebels in Alaska, the one the Russians called Dracovacz, The Harvester. He raised his weapon. The man dropped and rolled just as Po squeezed the trigger. The way the man lurched he was sure he'd hit him, but the figure kept rolling over the snowy surface, his rifle falling away from his hands. Po adjusted and fired another burst, sending spurts of hard earth and snow into the air just beyond the target.

As the enemy fighter emerged from his second rotation, an object tumbled through the air toward Po. His arm flew up to deflect it, the shape rolling around and over his raised forearm. Icy cold air blasted his senses, rushing from between his eyes to the center of his brain. His vision split in two impossible directions, neither able to focus to his front. Confusion mounted as Po's limbs jerked uncontrollably. His legs buckled beneath him. Hands and arms spasmed, his rifle involuntarily flung aside. The ground rushed up at him. His body tingled with waves of erratic electricity that quickly subsided to a thrumming pulse that grew weaker with every heartbeat, like a train vanishing in the distance. He lay in the snow but felt no cold. No pain. No anything. A voice rang like a bell at the back of his thoughts, indiscernible, fading to silence before he could make it out.

Darkness enveloped him.

CHAPTER 63

Stone

Ian leaped to his feet, sprinted across the space, and retrieved his tomahawk. He stomped his boot onto the mess of the man's face, yanking it from where it had embedded between his eyes, wedged into the thick bones of the man's forehead halfway up to his scalp. The rank patch on his camouflage parka showed he was, had been, a major. He was dead major now, the top half of his face cloven in two, dull eyes looking in opposite directions.

The tomahawk came out with a sickening wet crunch, bone against steel, the music of Ian's chosen profession. He wiped the blade across the man's coat, leaving behind a dark smear blood and bits of brain matter. He slid the bladed weapon back into its sheath then squatted down and released the dead man's rifle from its chest rig, attaching it to his own, and snatching two spare magazines from the man's harness. It was a QBZ-95 carbine model, typically carried only by special operations troops.

He rotated in place, scanned for new attackers. Seeing none, he moved toward the growing crowd near his mother. He stalked to the edge of the shadows, assessing as he moved, counting enemies and allies. None seemed to detect him as he drew near. He visually measured the distance to his target, the man holding his mother.

Fifty yards.

He scanned the body language of those he could see. Nerves were way beyond their frayed edges. Scenarios flicked through his mind, sliding multiple iterations through the steps of the OODA loop in fractions of a second. Observe. Orient. Decide. Act.

One of the psalms of King David he had memorized with his father long ago floated to his mind.

Who is God besides the Lord? Who is the Rock except our God?

He balanced the carbine in his right hand, the short-barreled bull-pup weapon easily lending itself to one-handed firing.

It is God who arms me with strength and keeps my way secure.

Ian reached across his body with the left, drew the tomahawk.

He makes my feet like the feet of a deer; he causes me to stand on the heights.

He lowered the visor of his cap, shading his eyes from the towers of flame that danced all over the greater field of view.

He trains my hands for battle; my arms can bend a bow of bronze.

Vision focused, narrowed in on a single point, the world around him pulsed in shades of red.

I pursued my enemies and overtook them.

His mother slid down a little in the man's grip.

I did not turn back 'til they were destroyed.

Ben caught shadowy glimpses of Kharzai and Gunnar's squad moving into position behind the enemy soldiers that had a bead on him and his father. His own weapon was trained on a Chinese lieutenant positioned between himself and the general. The other man had him zeroed in too. Their eyes locked. Each seeming to will the other man to lower his weapon. Neither wanting to die, both unable to back down.

Time stretched. Minutes between each heartbeat. The words of Psalm 144 came to him in bits and pieces, remnants of Sunday school.

Praise be to the Lord my Rock.

A bead of sweat rolled down his back, cold against his skin.

He trains my hands for war,

The other man's eyes flicked toward the general, and beyond that to Ben's mother.

And my fingers for battle.

The general shouted something at the man holding her. He jerked her head to the side, screaming something back in response.

Reach down your hand from on high,

A figure moved from the darkness behind the lieutenant, measuring, timing his movements. The glint of blood-stained steel reflected in the fiery light.

And rescue us from the hands of foreigners.

Brad kept his weapon trained on the colonel holding Youngmi. He had seen Ben come from the shadows on his right, knew he and whoever was with him had him covered from Zhang's men. The general himself seemed equally as concerned for Youngmi as he was.

Zhang shouted something in Chinese. The man screamed something back then jerked Youngmi's head violently, pressing his gun hard into her cheek. She let out a terrified yelp, her eyes wild with terror.

The lieutenant beside Zhang kept his weapon trained past Brad, likely on Ben a few yards away. A mean-looking sergeant moved his weapon between father and son, ready to take either.

"Brad Stone," Zhang called to him in his own language. Brad was surprised; the man sounded as if he'd grown up in California. "You are the Ice Hammer I have been hunting for two years, and now we meet."

373

"Again," Brad replied.

"Right," Zhang said. "Again. It appears we both have the same concern here. We don't want Youngmi hurt."

"Yup."

"Who does she go home with?"

Brad kept his eyes on the man holding her.

"Her choice," Brad answered. "I've seen her dead twice, already. First by your hand, then by mine. I can't bear to see it again."

"No English!" the hostage taker screamed. Then he switched to Chinese, pouring out a rapid-fire stream of words like a man who'd lost his mind.

A shadowy figure slowly emerged behind the general's aid, something shiny, medieval looking in his left hand. Torso splashed with streaks of blood.

Kharzai motioned to the archers in the deep shadows around him. They pulled the bows off their backs, silently slid four arrows each from their quivers, one nocked to the string, the others gripped between fingers, ready for rapid-fire. He pointed to the lone figure of Ian as he crept from the darkness behind the general and his men, gave a signal to wait. The team saw; they would act on Dracovacz, The Harvester's, cue.

The boy seemed to think about something for a very brief moment, slid his tomahawk into his left hand, holding the short rifle in just his right. He moved closer, weapon pointed at the man holding Brad's wife. Kharzai watched as the boy's lips moved, what looked like a prayer.

Youngmi's heart pounded in her chest. Her breath raspy, white mist encircling her head, Ping's sour odor filling her nostrils. Tears clouded her vision. This had to be a dream, a very bad dream. She must have been knocked unconscious when she fell in the woods after Ping's attack. All of this was a very vivid nightmare. Her husband and her lover both trying to save her from this madman, neither able to take a step closer.

To add to the nightmare, the ghostly image of Benjamin appeared to float into the scene behind Brad. She had heard him call her Umma. It was his voice, but it was not the face of Ben as she remembered; this was a terrifying man, black smudges hiding his features. A man whose eyes were made dark from years of violence and war.

Ping yanked her head back, ripping at her hair, twisting her neck so that she had to struggle to stay upright. He pressed the frigid steel of the gun muzzle into her cheek, her skin tearing from the force, a trickle of warm blood mingling with the tears that rolled from her eyes. Her head forced to the left, she opened her eyes and yet more proof that this was a nightmare materialized from the shadows beyond General Zhang.

The flash of an explosion exposed the movement of a ghostly apparition that floated through the morning darkness toward her. For the brief instance, her youngest son Ian was lit as if by a flashbulb. Her mind recognized the shape of his face only the way a mother could, telling her consciousness that it was him. This vision of her boy was not merely a grown version of the gentle youth from her memory. This was her baby child turned into a monster, a demonic aberration of the boy she had raised.

CHAPTER 64

A strange silence fell over the space around them. The sounds of pitched battle raged beyond, the intensity gradually moving east toward the gate on that side of the FOB. It was as if the area just beyond the circle of light from the street lamp was separated from them by an invisible force field that muffled the gunfire and explosions, allowing only the flickering strobes of muzzle flashes and bomb bursts through. It felt like a surreal silent movie.

Then all possible points of action and reaction resolved into a chaos of destructive precision. Ian squeezed off a shot one-handed, and the side of Ping's head fountained a jet of blood, black in the mercury glow from the lamp above. He fell, still gripping Youngmi tight to his chest. She landed hard, her head bouncing off the frozen ground, losing consciousness.

Arrows shafts suddenly jutted from the bodies of half a dozen Chinese soldiers. Fingers closed around triggers. Lieutenant Jin and Ben fired at the same time, Jin's a full-auto sweep that knocked down Scott and caught Ben, spinning him, as tracers painted a deadly green arc that tore through his shoulder. Ben's rounds threw Jin to the ground as well, arms grasping at the red froth bubbling from a ruined throat, legs flailing as his life flowed out.

Ian swung his tomahawk into the big sergeant's neck, slicing through muscle and tendon, and into the man's spine, dropping him instantly. The boy fired his rifle into the other officer's head, the bodies falling parallel to Jin's.

Zhang and Brad rushed forward to grab Youngmi both lowering their weapons, no threat to each other.

"You are really her husband?" Zhang said.

"Yes," Brad grunted, kneeling beside her.

"Has she been spying for you?"

"No," Brad said. "I didn't even know she was alive until I tried to kill you last spring."

"Who does she go home with?"

"Let her choose."

"She's unconscious and cannot choose," Zhang said. "I know that you've remarried. What can she have with you now? If she comes back with me, at least I can keep her safe."

"Like you did here?"

"You are the one who attacked this base, not me."

"You are the one who inva—"

The air around them erupted with the rattle of a machine gun, bullets snapping past. Zhang dove over Youngmi, protecting her body with his own. Brad did likewise, wrapping himself around them both. There was a sound like someone speed punching a side of beef.

Ian emptied his magazine in the direction of the muzzle flashes, dropping the empty carbine. Two shadows collapsed; no more fire came their way. He could not tell if it was a pair of enemy soldiers who saw the rebels and opened up, or rebels who saw Zhang and did the same. Either way, his mother was in the line of fire. They would not make such a mistake anymore, whoever they were.

He snatched up the dead sergeant's weapon and ran to where his parents lay. His father lay on his side, unmoving, steam rising from his back. Ian yanked the unconscious general from the heap, the man's face spattered with blood. He placed his hand on her chest, could feel her heartbeat, chest rising and falling with unsteady breaths. He slung the rifle across his back, sheathed the tomahawk, and quickly hefted Youngmi into a fireman's carry, ran her to a nearby idling Humvee, opened the back door, and gently lay her into the seat.

Leo Weeks followed, Brad hanging limp over his shoulder. He put him in the front seat, strapped him in with the seatbelt, body slumping against the radio console between the seats. Two of Kharzai's men helped Ben into the backseat, beside his mother, his arm hanging loose, blood running down his arm, dripping from his fingertips. Katarina jumped in the back, started assessing them, Weeks acting as her assistant.

"Stuff this into Ben's shoulder wound," she said, handing him a pack of gauze.

The sergeant did so, the big man's finger shoving the dressing in with nothing resembling tenderness. The hole had gone in the front and come out in his armpit. Ben's face screwed up in agony.

"Done," Weeks grunted.

"I am okay," Ben said. "It didn't hit any bones, I can fight still."

"No," ordered the sergeant. "Your mother needs you."

"But…"

"Don't be an ass!" Ian shouted across the seat. "Umma is alive. Dad's not going to make it. She needs you."

Ian suddenly jumped away from the vehicle, firing several shots at something. He leaned back in, tenderly kissed his mother on the cheek, pressed his hand against her head, felt the soft brown hair, put his lips next to her ear and whispered, "I love you, Umma." He quickly backed out again and turned to one of the archers. "Get them out of here, now!"

Ian leaned back in.

"If you get out of this vehicle, brother, I will kill you myself."

The look in his youngest sibling's eyes said he was not using a figure of speech. He would do it. Weeks slammed Ben's door shut, making him wince. When he opened his eyes again, Ian was gone, the other door closed. Katarina leaned toward the front, felt Brad's neck, said nothing. She turned back to attending his mother. The archer jumped into the driver's seat, gunned the engine, and set a course for the exfil.

"They are away," Ian shouted toward Kharzai and his men.

He started back to the battle, to finish the mission, to kill more Chinese. He passed Zhang, still lying on the ground unconscious, and raised his weapon to put a bullet into the man. No mercy. No quarter.

Gunnar started to turn his way and took in a breath as if to shout an order. An explosion knocked them both sideways, ripping the big man's weapon from his grip. The giant seemed to lose his balance, falling sideways with a ground-shaking thump. He attempted to right himself, to get back up, but could not. He wavered. Ian heard the all too familiar sound of bullet impacts, and blood erupted from Gunnar's chest. He flopped back to the crimson ice.

Ian spun on the ground, put his weapon across Zhang's body, and fired at a group that had charged in, probably to rescue their general. Between his and Kharzai's rounds, the threat was eliminated. The hairy man lunged toward his friend.

"No! Not you, Gunnar," Kharzai cried. "No! No! No!"

The giant Swede gasped for breath, a rattling sound as if dice were being rolled in his chest. Blood soaked through the bright white of the snow smock he wore over his uniform, his torso shattered beyond repair. The stain spread, bright red droplets spraying from his lips with every breath. His left hand grasped at something beneath his collar, Mjölnir, the hammer pendant. His right hand thrashed about, grasping at the ground, desperately searching for something.

Kharzai leaped over to him, snapped up his friend's rifle where it had fallen, and put it in his hand. He wrapped Gunnar's fingers around the pistol grip, held them in place, and leaned in close to his friend's face. The Viking's eyes rolled, lids shutting, then reopening. His gaze fixed on Kharzai's, blue eyes like an icy fire. He tried to speak, but only blood came out. His body convulsed, legs shaking, quivering in final agony. He seemed to calm, rattled a few more shallow breaths, then slowly rested his head on the ground. New snow drifted down, mingled with ash as it settled on his already cooling face.

"Go with God my friend," Kharzai whispered. "Save a seat for me in Valhalla."

CHAPTER 65

Out of the thousands of Alaskans that had taken part in the assault on the Palmer FOB, nearly one-fifth had lost their lives either during the battle or shortly after as a result of injuries. Almost a thousand fighters. The majority of the dead were never recovered from the battlefield, ending in a mass grave in Palmer somewhere.

The battle had been the most intense action since the opening weeks of the war. Damage to the Palmer FOB had been severe enough that the Chinese had nothing left to give chase to the rebels. The reported fuel shortages prevented any more air power being deployed to cut their victory short. Shoulder swathed in bandages, Ben had held his mother against his body the whole way back, wrapping her in a blanket that had been found under the seat. Katarina was on her other side.

"What about my dad?" Ben said once they were away from the sounds of the battle.

Katarina looked across the seat at him, eyes red with exhaustion and sorrow. She tried to speak, opened her mouth, then shut it again, lips tightening as tears rolled down her cheeks. She shook her head. No need to speak the obvious.

Unable to bury the dead in the frozen earth, those last few who had succumbed to their injuries after returning to Chiknik were to be cremated. Since a column of smoke would be visible for very long distances, the cremations only took place at night, fires put out and buried in snow before the morning sun rose. Rangers had stood vigil over the bodies of the fallen for a day and a night as pyres were erected. Birch and spruce logs interspersed to form the final resting places.

Unable to stand from the injuries she'd incurred, Youngmi sat wrapped in blankets on a fur-lined chair attached to a sled that had been anchored to the ground in front of the place they would lay her husband for the flames.

Ben and Ian, with John and Kharzai, carried Brad's body up on a stretcher made of birch poles and laid it upon one of the platforms. The four men carefully lowered the stretcher, rose to stand at attention facing each other, took a step back, and saluted in unison, slow and deliberate, paying homage to their fallen leader. They held the position for several seconds, then slowly lowered their arms, about-faced, and descended.

Sammi followed the procession, baby Victoria on her arm. Katarina came as well. The younger women moved up on either side of Youngmi. Sammi put a hand on her shoulder as the men stepped back from the pyre. Once the rest of the bodies for this night's ceremony had been laid in place, the boys and eight others lifted torches soaked in pitch made from spruce sap, lit them from a small fire pit, then stepped up to the stack. Without a word, they touched the bottom rung of logs, also covered in pitch, backed up, and watched as the flames took, then gradually rose, until the pyre was fully ablaze.

In the flickering golden glow, Youngmi reached up and took hold of Sammi's hand, pressed it to her face. Warm tears flowed down her cheeks, sparkling in the firelight, dripped onto the fingers of her husband's other wife. She drew in a shaky breath, closed her eyes, let it out. Ben and Ian moved to join them. Katarina stepped aside to let Ben stand beside his mother. She tried to reach up and touch his face, but cringed from the pain in her damaged shoulder. He knelt down beside her, wrapped his good arm around her shoulders, turned, and kissed her tenderly on her forehead.

Ian leaned in from the other side, Sammi making room for him. He put his lips against their mother's ear and whispered something only she could hear. A gentle sob came from her lips, and she caressed Ian's face with her hand, then reached across and caressed Ben's as well.

Ben glanced up at his younger brother. Ian pressed a delicate kiss on Youngmi's head and rose to his full height, facing the pyre. The smoke disappeared in the darkness as it rose into the night sky. The flames grew higher as the bodies caught, whipping the blaze into swirling tendrils of fire like ascending spirits. The flames danced in Ian's eyes, as if reflecting from their very source, a place where the fire is never quenched.

EPILOGUE

Work Camp Six
Russian Territory
North Coast of Alaska

"Hey," the man at the table called across to the cook who was cleaning up the serving line in preparation for the dinner meal to be served to the last guard shift for the night. "Isn't your last name Stone?"

"Yeah," Jay replied wearily. "You've known me for almost five years, Pete, and you've forgotten my name?"

"Spelled S T O N E, right?"

"Of course." He stopped what he was doing. "Why are you asking?"

"The Worker's Journal has an article about one of your relatives," Pete replied. "Some guy named Bradley Stone, AKA Ice Hammer. Apparently, he was some kind of resistance leader that got killed a few months ago down south somewhere." He paused scanning the page. "Here it is, Palmer. He got killed in, '*a foolish, and failed, attempt to assassinate General Zhang and sabotage the Chinese People's Liberation Army's new fortified base in Palmer.*' You're from Fairbanks, though, right?"

Jay stepped around the serving line, tightening the worn-out belt around his waist as he moved. He'd had to cut several new holes into it, having lost more than a hundred pounds since the Russians had taken over the North Slope oil fields. The barely adequate rations the Russians allowed the laborers, including himself, was just enough to keep them alive to do the work they were forced to continue, for a while at least. Jay and Pete were the last two survivors of the original hundred-plus workers trapped at what had been the oil company town of Deadhorse on the coast of the Arctic Ocean eight hundred some odd miles north of Anchorage. Replacements had been brought in, forced into slave labor, drawing more oil from the ground. Most who worked out on the rigs themselves did not last more than a few months in the brutal weather, before succumbing to poor nutrition, the mind-numbing cold and long months of darkness. They fared little better in the short, mosquito-filled summer.

"Yeah." He walked over to where Pete had laid out the newspaper on the table. "But we moved to Anchorage when I was in middle school."

"This guy an actual relative then?"

"My father's name was Bradley."

"There's a picture."

Jay leaned over the paper.

"That's my dad." Jay nodded.

"Oh God," Pete said, "I'm sorry, man. I shouldn't've…"

Jay stared at the black and white image. He glanced out the window of the dining facility. The electric light above the door outside shone in a circle that caught the edge of the row of bodies. Those men, the dead, left out for the polar bears. He looked across the room to the stack of clothes those men would never need again.

The day-shift guards, relieved for the night, shuffled through the blowing snow toward the dining facility. Time to get their evening meal. One he had made from a special recipe that had been popular for before the war. This variation though was laced with homemade botulinum toxin he'd processed from leftover meat and his own feces. Tasteless and odorless, the deadly cocktail had been well mixed into the meals all of the Russian guards had eaten that day, the laborer's weak gruel and stale bread the only food left clean. Early symptoms were probably already starting to show in some of the soldiers who'd been first in line for breakfast that morning. By the end of the next three days, all of the Russian soldiers in the camp should be dead, either by his homemade poison, or murdered by the prisoners once they were too weak to resist.

Chef Jay Stone would probably never get south again. He regretted that he would not be able to tell his mother and brothers what had happened, that he would never see any of them again. Not in this life at least.

"I will see you soon, Dad," he muttered as he moved back behind the serving line.

ABOUT THE AUTHOR

Authoring action packed novels and short stories, Basil has built an audience of tens of thousands to his eBooks and audiobooks.

The tapestry on which his tales began started at birth in rural interior Alaska and his school years among the Ohio cornfields, where he wished to be anywhere else as long as it was exciting. He has lived in Alaska, San Diego, DC, Baltimore, and Ohio. He tried a career in the Marines, but injuries sent him home after only six months. He worked as dining manager at NSA, owned a computer shop, was a carpenter, farmer, actor, lumberjack, voice actor, EMT, network admin, helpdesk supervisor, Boy Scout leader, IT trainer, radio talk host, youth minister, and after 9/11, a sergeant in the Alaska Defense Force Coastal Scouts.

Until a ski injury slowed him down, he had been an avid weight lifter and could bench press 420 lbs. Now he's limited to a bit on the elliptical machine each day and curling the occasional pint of Guinness.

He lives in Anchorage, Alaska, with his wife and sons.

PERMUTED PRESS
needs *you* to help

SPREAD (THE) INFECTION

FOLLOW US!

f | Facebook.com/PermutedPress
🐦 | Twitter.com/PermutedPress

REVIEW US!

Wherever you buy our book, they can be reviewed! We want to know what you like!

GET INFECTED!

Sign up for our mailing list at PermutedPress.com

PERMUTED
PRESS

THE ULTIMATE PREPPER'S ADVENTURE.
THE JOURNEY BEGINS HERE!

The long-predicted Coronal Mass Ejection has finally hit the Earth, virtually destroying civilization. Nathan Owens has been prepping for a disaster like this for years, but now he's a thousand miles away from his family and his refuge. He'll have to employ all his hard-won survivalist skills to save his current community, before he begins his long journey through doomsday to get back home.

PERMUTED
PRESS

THE MORNINGSTAR STRAIN HAS BEEN LET LOOSE—IS THERE ANY WAY TO STOP IT?

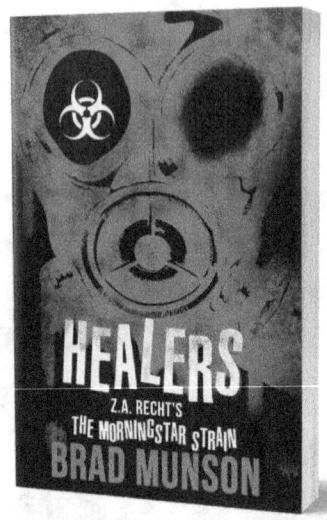

An industrial accident unleashes some of the Morningstar Strain. The

EAN 9781618686497 $16.00

doctor who discovered the strain and her assistant will have to fight their way through Sprinters and Shamblers to save themselves, the vaccine, and the base. Then they discover that it wasn't an accident at all—somebody inside the facility did it on purpose. The war with the RSA and the infected is far from over.

This is the fourth book in Z.A. Recht's The Morningstar Strain series, written by Brad Munson.

PERMUTED
PRESS

GATHERED TOGETHER AT LAST, THREE TALES OF FANTASY CENTERING AROUND THE MYSTERIOUS CITY OF SHADOWS...ALSO KNOWN AS CHICAGO.

EAN 9781682612286 $9.99   **EAN** 9781618684639 $5.99   **EAN** 9781618684899 $5.99

From *The New York Times* and *USA Today* bestselling author Richard A. Knaak comes three tales from Chicago, the City of Shadows. Enter the world of the Grey—the creatures that live at the edge of our imagination and seek to be real. Follow the quest of a wizard seeking escape from the centuries-long haunting of a gargoyle. Behold the coming of the end of the world as the Dutchman arrives.

Enter the City of Shadows.

PERMUTED
PRESS

WE CAN'T GUARANTEE
THIS GUIDE WILL SAVE
YOUR LIFE. BUT WE CAN
GUARANTEE IT WILL
KEEP YOU SMILING
WHILE THE LIVING
DEAD ARE CHOWING
DOWN ON YOU.

EAN 9781618686695 $9.99

This is the only tool you
need to survive the zombie apocalypse.

OK, that's not really true. But when the SHTF, you're
going to want a survival guide that's not just geared
toward day-to-day survival. You'll need one that
addresses the essential skills for true nourishment of
the human spirit. Living through the end of the
world isn't worth a damn unless you can enjoy
yourself in any way you want. (Except, of course, for
anything having to do with abuse. We could never
condone such things. At least the publisher's
lawyers say we can't.)

www.ingramcontent.com/pod-product-compliance
Lightning Source LLC
Chambersburg PA
CBHW051440260626
47162CB00001B/183